"MacLEAN HAS A HUGE TALENT"
—The New York Times

ALISTAIR MacLEAN's reputation as an outstanding writer of suspense was established with the success of his first novel, *H.M.S. Ulysses*. That story grew out of his background in the Royal Navy, where he spent five years as a torpedo man during World War II.

Several of his highly successful and critically acclaimed works have been made into motion pictures, including *The Guns of Navarone, Ice Station Zebra,* and *Where Eagles Dare.*

"A PROVEN WRITER OF ADVENTURE YARNS"
—Cincinnati Enquirer

Fawcett Crest and Gold Medal Books
by Alistair MacLean:

H.M.S. ULYSSES
THE GUNS OF NAVARONE
SOUTH BY JAVA HEAD
THE SECRET WAYS
NIGHT WITHOUT END
FEAR IS THE KEY
THE BLACK SHRIKE
THE GOLDEN RENDEZVOUS
THE SATAN BUG
ICE STATION ZEBRA
WHEN EIGHT BELLS TOLL
WHERE EAGLES DARE
FORCE 10 FROM NAVARONE
PUPPET ON A CHAIN
CARAVAN TO VACCARES
BEAR ISLAND
THE WAY TO DUSTY DEATH
BREAKHEART PASS
CIRCUS
THE GOLDEN GATE
SEAWITCH

The
BLACK
SHRIKE

by Alistair MacLean

[This book was originally published
under the pseudonym IAN STUART.]

FAWCETT GOLD MEDAL • NEW YORK

To Douglas and Violet

Published by Fawcett Gold Medal Books, a unit of CBS
Publications, the Consumer Publishing Division of CBS Inc.,
by arrangement with Charles Scribner's Sons

THIS BOOK CONTAINS THE COMPLETE TEXT
OF THE ORIGINAL HARDCOVER EDITION.

ISBN: 0-449-13903-4

Printed in the United States of America

29 28 27 26 25 24 23 22 21 20

Prologue

A SMALL dusty man in a small dusty room. That's how I always thought of him, just a small dusty man in a small dusty room.

No cleaning woman was ever allowed to enter that office with its soot-stained heavily curtained windows overlooking Birdcage Walk: and no person, cleaner or not, was ever allowed inside unless Colonel Raine himself were there.

And no one could ever have accused the colonel of being allergic to dust.

It lay everywhere. It lay on the oak-stained polished floor surrounds that flanked the threadbare carpet. It filmed the tops of bookcases, filing cabinets, radiators, chair-arms and telephones: it lay smeared streakily across the top of the scuffed knee-hole desk, the dust-free patches marking where papers or books had recently been pushed to one side: motes danced busily in a sunbeam that slanted through an uncurtained crack in the middle of a window: and, trick of the light or not, it needed no imagination at all to see a patina of dust on the thin brushed-back hair of the man behind the desk, to see it embedded in the deeply trenched lines on the grey sunken cheeks, the high receding forehead.

And then you saw the eyes below the heavy wrinkled lids and you forgot all about the dust; eyes with the hard jewelled glitter of a peridot stone, eyes of the clear washed-out aquamarine of a Greenland glacier, but not so warm.

He rose to greet me as I crossed the room, offered me a cold hard bony hand like a gardening tool, waved me to a chair directly opposite the light-coloured veneered panel so incongruously let into the front of his mahogany desk, and seated himself, sitting very straight, hands clasped lightly on the dusty desk before him.

"Welcome home, Bentall." The voice matched the eyes, you could almost hear the far-off crackling of dried ice. "You made fast time. Pleasant trip?"

"No, sir. Some Midlands textile tycoon put off the plane to make room for me at Ankara wasn't happy. I'm to hear from his lawyers and as a sideline he's going to drive the B.E.A. off the European airways. Other passengers sent me

5

to Coventry, the stewardesses ignored me completely and it was as bumpy as hell. Apart from that, it was a fine trip."

"Such things happen," he said precisely. An almost imperceptible tic at the left-hand corner of the thin mouth might have been interpreted as a smile, all you needed was a strong imagination, but it was hard to say, twenty-five years of minding other people's business in the Far East seemed to have atrophied the colonel's cheek muscles. "Sleep?"

I shook my head. "Not a wink."

"Pity." He hid his distress well and cleared his throat delicately. "Well, I'm afraid you're off on your travels again, Bentall. Tonight. 11 p.m., London Airport."

I let a few seconds pass to let him know I wasn't saying all the things I felt like saying, then shrugged in resignation. "Back to Iran?"

"If I were transferring you from Turkey to Iran I wouldn't have risked the wrath of the Midlands textile industry by summoning you all the way back to London to tell you so." Again the faint suggestion of a tic at the corner of the mouth. "Considerably further away, Bentall. Sydney, Australia. Fresh territory for you, I believe?"

"Australia?" I was on my feet without realising I had risen. "Australia! Look, sir, didn't you get my cable last week? Eight months' work, everything tied up except the last button, all I needed was another week, two at the most—"

"Sit down!" A tone of voice to match the eyes, it was like having a bucket of ice-water poured over me. He looked at me consideringly and his voice warmed up a little to just under freezing point. "Your concern is appreciated, but needless. Let us hope for your own sake that you do not underestimate our—ah—antagonists as much as you appear to underestimate those who employ you. You have done an excellent job, Bentall. I am quite certain that in any other government department less forthcoming than ours you would have been in line for at least an O.B.E., or some such trinket, but your part in the job is over. I do not choose that my personal investigators shall also double in the role of executioners."

"I'm sorry, sir," I said lamely. "I don't have the overall—"

"To continue in your own metaphor, the last button is about to be tied." It was exactly as if he hadn't heard me. "This leak—this near disastrous leak, I should say—from our Hepworth Ordnance and Fuel Research Establishment is about to be sealed. Completely and permanently sealed." He glanced at the electric clock on the wall. "In about four hours' time, I should say. We may consider it as being in the past. There are those in the cabinet who will sleep well tonight."

He paused, unclasped his hands, leaned his elbows on the desk and looked at me over steepled fingers.

"That is to say, they should have been sleeping well tonight." He sighed, a faint dry sound. "But in these security-ridden days the sources of ministerial insomnia are almost infinite. Hence your recall. Other men, I admit, were available: but, apart from the fact that there is no one with your precise and, in this case, very necessary qualifications, I have a faint—a very faint—and uneasy feeling that this may not be entirely unconnected with your last assignment." He unsteepled his fingers, reached for a pink polythene folder and slid it across the desk to me. "Take a look at these, will you?"

I quelled the impulse to wave away the approaching tidal wave of dust, picked up the folder and took out the half-dozen stapled slips of paper inside.

They were cuttings from the overseas vacancy columns of the "Daily Telegraph". Each column had the date heavily pencilled in red at the top, the earliest not more than eight months ago: and each of the columns had an advertisement ringed in the same heavy red except for the first column which had three advertisements so marked.

The advertisers were all technical, engineering, chemical or research firms in Australia and New Zealand. The types of people for whom they were advertising were as would have been expected, specialists in the more advanced fields of modern technology. I had seen such adverts before, from countries all over the world. Experts in aero-dynamics, micro-miniaturization, hypersonics, electronics, physics, radar and advanced fuel technologies were at a premium those days. But what made these advertisements different, apart from their common source, was the fact that all the jobs were being offered in top administrative and directorial capacity, carrying with them what I could only regard as astronomical salaries. I whistled softly and glanced at Colonel Raine, but those ice-green eyes were contemplating some spot in the ceiling about a thousand miles away, so I looked through the columns again, put them back in the folder and slid them across the desk. Compared to the colonel I made a hardly noticeable ripple across the dust-pond of the table-top.

"Eight advertisements," the colonel said in his dry quiet voice. "Each over a hundred words in length, but you could reproduce them all word for word if need be. Right, Bentall?"

"I think I might, sir."

"An extraordinary gift," he murmured. "I envy you. Your comments, Bentall?"

"That rather delicately worded advertisement for a thrust and propellant specialist to work on aero engines designed for speeds in excess of Mach. 10. Properly speaking, there are no such aero engines. Only rocket engines, on which the metallurgical problems have already been solved. They're after a top-flight fuel boffin, and apart from a handful at some of the major aircraft firms and at a couple of universities every worthwhile fuel specialist in the country works at the Hepworth Research Establishment."

"And there may lie the tie-in with your last job," he nodded. "Just a guess and it could be far more easily wrong than right. Probably a straw from another haystack altogether." He doodled in the dust with the tip of his forefinger. "What else?"

"All advertisements from a more or less common source," I went on. "New Zealand or the eastern Australian seaboard. All jobs to be filled in a hurry. All offering free and furnished accommodation, house to become the property of the successful applicant, together with salaries at least three times higher than the best of them could expect in this country. They're obviously after the best brains we have. All specify that the applicants be married but say they're unable to accommodate children."

"Doesn't that strike you as a trifle unusual?" Colonel Raine asked idly.

"No, sir. Quite common for foreign firms to prefer married men. People are often unsettled at first in strange countries and there's less chance of their packing up and taking the next boat home if they have their families to consider. Those advertisers are paying single fare only. With the money a man could save in the first weeks or months it would be quite impossible to transport his family home."

"But there are no families," the colonel persisted. "Only wives."

"Perhaps they're afraid the patter of tiny feet may distract the highly-paid minds." I shrugged. "Or limited accommodation. Or the kids to follow later. All it says is 'No accommodation for children'."

"Nothing in all of this strikes you as being in any way sinister?"

"Superficially, no. With all respects, I question whether it would strike you either, sir. Scores of our best men have been lured overseas in the past years. But if you were to provide me with the information you're obviously withholding, I might very well begin to see it your way."

Another momentary tic at the left-hand corner of the mouth, he was really letting himself go today, then he fished out a small dark pipe and started scraping the bowl with a penknife. Without looking up he said: "There was a further coincidence that I should have mentioned. All the scientists who accepted those jobs—and their wives—have disappeared. Completely."

With the last word he gave me a quick up-from-under glance with those arctic eyes, to see how I was taking it. I don't much like being played cat-and-mouse with, so I gave him back his wooden Indian stare and asked: "In this country, en route or after arrival?"

"I think maybe you *are* the right man for the job, Bentall," he said inconsequently. "All of them left this country. Four seem to have disappeared en route for Australia. From the immigration authorities in New Zealand and Australia we have learned that one landed in Wellington and three others in Sydney. And that's all they know about them. That's all any of the authorities in those countries know. They arrived. They vanished. Finish."

"Any idea why?"

"None. Could be several alternatives. I never waste my time guessing, Bentall. All we know—hence, of course, the very great official anxiety—is that though all the men concerned were engaged in industrial research, their unique knowledge could all too easily be put to military uses."

"How thorough a search has been made for them, sir?"

"You can imagine. And I'm led to believe that the police forces in the—ah—Antipodes are as efficient as any in the world. But it's hardly a job for a policeman, eh?"

He leaned back in his chair, puffing dark clouds of foul-smelling smoke into the already over-weighted air and looked at me expectantly. I felt tired, irritable, and I didn't like the turn the conversation was taking. He was waiting for me to be a bright boy. I supposed I'd better oblige.

"What am I going out as? A nuclear physicist?"

He patted the arm of his chair. "I'll keep this seat warm for you, my boy. It may be yours some day." It's not easy for an iceberg to sound jovial, but he almost made it. "No false colours for you, Bentall. You're going out as precisely what you were in the days you worked at Hepworth and we discovered your unique gifts in another and slightly less academic field. You're going out as a specialist in fuel research." He extracted a slip of paper from another folder and tossed it across to me. "Read all about it. The ninth advertisement. Appeared in the 'Telegraph' a fortnight ago."

I let the paper lie where it had fallen. I didn't even look at it.

"The second application for a fuel specialist," I said. "Who answered the first? I should know him."

"Does that matter, Bentall?" His voice had dropped a few degrees.

"Certainly it matters." My tone matched his. "Perhaps they—whoever 'they' may be—picked on a dud. Perhaps he didn't know enough. But if it was one of the top boys—well, sir, the implication is pretty clear. Something's happened to make them need a replacement."

"It was Dr. Charles Fairfield."

"Fairfield? My old chief? The second-in-command at Hepworth?"

"Who else?"

I didn't answer immediately. I knew Fairfield well, a brilliant scientist and a highly-gifted amateur archaeologist. I liked this less and less and my expression should have told Colonel Raine so. But he was examining the ceiling with the minute scrutiny of a man who expected to see it fall down any second.

"And you're asking me to—" I began.

"That's what I'm doing," he interrupted. He sounded suddenly tired, it was impossible not to feel a quick sympathy for the man, for the heavy burden he had to carry. "I'm not ordering, my boy. I'm only asking." His eyes were still on the ceiling.

I pulled the paper towards me and looked at the red-ringed advertisement. It was almost but not quite the duplicate of one I'd read a few minutes earlier.

"Our friends required an immediate cable answer," I said slowly. "I suppose they must be getting pushed for time. You answered by cable?"

"In your name and from your home address. I trust you will pardon the liberty," he murmured drily.

"The Allison and Holden Engineering Company, Sydney," I went on. "A genuine and respected firm, of course?"

"Of course. We checked. And the name is that of their personnel manager and an airmail letter that arrived four days ago confirming the appointment was on the genuine letterhead of the firm. Signed in the name of the personnel manager. Only it wasn't his signature."

"What else do you know, sir?"

"Nothing. I'm sorry. Absolutely nothing. I wish to God I could help more."

There was a brief silence. Then I pushed the paper back to him and said: "Haven't you rather overlooked the fact that this advert is like the rest—it calls for a married man?"

"I never overlook the obvious," he said flatly.

I stared at him. "You never—" I broke off, then continued:

"I suppose you've got the banns already called and the bride waiting at the church."

"I've done better than that." Again the faint tic in the cheek. He reached into a drawer, pulled out a nine by four buff envelope and tossed it across to me. "Take care of that, Bentall. Your marriage certificate. Caxton Hall, ten weeks ago. You may examine it if you wish but I think you'll find everything perfectly in order."

"I'm sure I will," I muttered mechanically. "I should hate to be a party to anything illegal."

"And now," he said briskly, "you would, of course, like to meet your wife." He lifted a phone and said: "Ask Mrs. Bentall to come here, please."

His pipe had gone out and he'd resumed the excavations with the pen-knife, examining the bowl with great care. There was nothing for me to examine so I let my eye wander until I saw again the light-coloured panel in the wood facing me. I knew the story behind that. Less than nine months ago, shortly after Colonel Raine's predecessor had been killed in an air crash, another man had sat in the chair I was sitting in now. It had been one of Raine's own men, but what Raine had not known was that that man had been subverted in Central Europe and persuaded to act as a double agent. His first task—which would also probably have been his last— was simple and staggering in its audacity: nothing less than the murder of Raine himself. Had it been successful, the removal of Colonel Raine—I never knew his real name— chief of security and the receptacle of a thousand secrets, would have been an irreparable loss. The colonel had suspected nothing of this until the agent had pulled out his gun. But what the agent did not know—what nobody had known before then—was that Colonel Raine kept a silenced Luger with the safety catch permanently off fastened to the underside of his chair by a spring clip. I did think he might have had a better job made of repairing that splintered panel in the front of his desk.

Colonel Raine had had no option, of course. But even had

he had the chance of disarming or just wounding the man, he would probably still have killed him. He was, without exception, the most utterly ruthless man I had ever met. Not cruel, just ruthless. The end justified the means and if the end were important enough there were no sacrifices he would not make to achieve it. That was why he was sitting in that chair. But when ruthlessness became inhumanity, I felt it was time to protest.

I said: "Are you seriously considering sending this woman out with me, sir?"

"I'm not considering it." He peered into the bowl of his pipe with all the absorbed concentration of a geologist scanning the depths of an extinct volcano. "The decision is made."

My blood pressure went up a couple of points.

"Even though you must know that whatever happened to Dr. Fairfield probably happened to his wife, too?"

He laid pipe and knife on the desk and gave me what he probably imagined was a quizzical look: with those eyes of his it felt more as if a couple of stilettos were coming my way.

"You question the wisdom of my decisions, Bentall?"

"I question the justification for sending a woman on a job where the odds on chances are that she'll get herself killed." There was anger in my voice now and I wasn't bothering very much about concealing it. "And I do question the wisdom of sending her with me. You know I'm a loner, Colonel Raine. I could go by myself, explain that my wife had taken ill. I don't want any female hanging round my neck, sir."

"With this particular female," Raine said drily, "most men would consider that a privilege. I advise you to forget your concern. I consider it essential that she go. This young lady has volunteered for this assignment. She's shrewd, very, very able and most experienced in this business—much more so than you are, Bentall. It may not be a case of you looking after her, but vice versa. She can take care of herself admirably. She has a gun and she never moves without it. I think you'll find—"

He broke off as a side door opened and a girl walked into the room. I say 'walked' because it is the usual word to describe human locomotion, but this girl didn't locomote, she seemed to glide with all the grace and more than the suggestion of something else of a Balinese dancing girl. She wore a light grey ribbed wool dress that clung to every inch of her hour-and-a-half-glass figure as if it fully appreciated its privilege, and round her waist she wore a narrow belt of darker grey to match her court shoes and lizard handbag. That would be where the gun was, in the bag, she couldn't have concealed a pea-shooter under that dress. She had smooth fair gleaming hair parted far over on the left and brushed almost straight back, dark eyebrows and lashes, clear hazel eyes and a delicately tanned fair skin.

I knew where the tan came from, I knew who she was. She'd worked on the same assignment as I had for the past six months but had been in Greece all the time and I'd only seen her twice, in Athens: in all, this was only the fourth time I'd ever met her. I knew her, but knew nothing of her, except for the fact that her name was Marie Hopeman, that she had been born in Belgium but hadn't lived there since her father, a technician in the Fairey Aviation factory in that country, had brought her and her Belgian mother out of the continent at the time of the fall of France. Both her parents had been lost in the 'Lancastria'. An orphan child brought up in what was to her a foreign country, she must have learned fast how to look after herself. Or so I supposed.

I pushed back my chair and rose. Colonel Raine waved a vaguely introductory hand and said: "Mr. and—ah—Mrs. Bentall. You have met before, have you not?"

"Yes, sir." He knew damned well we'd met before. Marie Hopeman gave me a cool firm hand and a cool level look, maybe this chance to work so closely with me was the realisation of a life's ambition for her but she was holding her enthusiasm pretty well in check. I'd noticed this in Athens, this remote and rather aloof self-sufficiency which I found vaguely irritating, but that wasn't going to stop me from saying what I was going to say.

"Nice to see you again, Miss Hopeman. Or it should be. But not here and not now. Don't you know what you're letting yourself in for?"

She looked at me with big hazel eyes wide open under her raised dark brows, then the mouth curved slowly into an amused smile as she turned away.

"Has Mr. Bentall been coming all over chivalrous and noble on my account, Colonel Raine?" she asked sweetly.

"Well, yes, I'm afraid he has, rather," the colonel admitted. "And, please, we must have none of this Mr. Bentall-Miss Hopeman talk. Among young married couples, I mean." He poked a pipe-cleaner through the stem of his pipe, nodded in satisfaction as it emerged from the bowl black as a chimney sweep's brush, and went on almost dreamily. "John and Marie Bentall. I think the names go rather well together."

"Do you feel that, too?" the girl said with interest. She turned to me again and smiled brightly. "I do so appreciate your concern. It's really most kind of you." A pause, then she added: "John."

I didn't hit her because I hold the view that that sort of thing went out with the cavemen, but I could appreciate how the old boys felt. I gave her what I hoped was a cool and enigmatic smile and turned away.

"Clothes, sir," I said to Raine. "I'll need to buy some. It's high summer out there now."

"You'll find two new suitcases in your flat, Bentall, packed with everything you need."

"Tickets?"

"Here." He slid a packet across. "They were mailed to you four days ago by Wagons/Lits Cook. Paid by cheque. Man called Tobias Smith. No one has ever heard of him, but his bank account is healthy enough. You don't fly east, as you might expect, but west, via New York, San Francisco, Hawaii and Fiji. I suppose the man who pays the piper calls the tune."

"Passports?"

"Both in your cases in your flat." The little tic touched the side of his face. "Yours, for a change, is in your own name. Had to be. They'd check on you, university, subsequent career and so forth. We fixed it so that no enquirer would know you left Hepworth a year ago. Also in your case you'll find a thousand dollars in American Express cheques."

"I hope I live to spend it," I said. "Who's travelling with us, sir?"

There was a small silence, a brittle silence, and two pairs of eyes were on me, the narrow cold ice-green ones and the large warm hazel eyes. Marie Hopeman spoke first.

"Perhaps you would explain—"

"Hah!" I interrupted. "Perhaps I would explain. And you're the person—well, never mind. Sixteen people leave from here for Australia or New Zealand. Eight never arrive. Fifty percent. Which means that there's a fifty percent chance that we don't arrive. So there will be an observer in the plane so that Colonel Raine can erect a tombstone over the spot where we're buried. Or more likely just a wreath flung on the Pacific."

"The possibility of a little trouble en route had occurred to me," the colonel said carefully. "There will be an observer with you—not the same one all the way, naturally. It is better that you do not know who those observers are." He rose to his feet and walked round the table. The briefing was over.

"I am sincerely sorry," he finished. "I do not like any of this, but I am a blind man in a dark room and there is no other course open to me. I hope things go well." He offered his hand briefly to both of us, shook his head, murmured: "I'm sorry. Goodbye," and walked back to his desk.

I opened the door for Marie Hopeman and glanced back over my shoulder to see how sorry he was. But he wasn't looking sorry, he was just looking earnestly into the bowl of his pipe, so I closed the door with a quiet hand and left him sitting there, a small dusty man in a small dusty room.

CHAPTER ONE

FELLOW-PASSENGERS on the plane, the old hands on the America-Australia run, had spoken of the Grand Pacific Hotel in Viti Levu as the finest in the Western Pacific, and a very brief acquaintance with it had persuaded me that they were probably right. Old-fashioned but magnificent and shining like a newly-minted silver coin, it was run with a quiet and courteous efficiency that would have horrified the average English hotelier. The bedrooms were luxurious, the food superb—the memory of the seven-course dinner we'd had that night would linger for years—and the view from the verandah of the haze-softened mountains across the moonlit bay belonged to another world.

But there's no perfection in a very imperfect world: the locks on the bedroom doors of the Grand Pacific Hotel were just no good at all.

My first intimation of this came when I woke up in the middle of the night in response to someone prodding my shoulder. But my first thought was not of the door-locks but of the finger prodding me. It was the hardest finger I'd ever felt. It felt like a piece of steel. I struggled to open my eyes against weariness and the glare of the overhead light and finally managed to focus them on my left shoulder. It was a piece of steel. It was a dully-gleaming .38 Colt automatic and, just in case I should have made any mistake in identification, whoever was holding it shifted the gun as soon as he saw me stir so that my right eye could stare down the centre of the barrel. It was a gun all right. My gaze travelled up past the gun, the hairy brown wrist, the white-coated arm to the brown cold still face with the battered yachting cap above, then back to the automatic again.

"O.K., friend," I said. I meant it to sound cool and casual but it came out more like the raven—the hoarse one—croaking on the battlements of Macbeth's castle. "I can see it's a gun. Cleaned and oiled and everything. But take it away, please. Guns are dangerous things."

"A wise guy, eh?" he said coldly. "Showing the little wife what a hero he is. But you wouldn't really like to be a hero,

17

would you, Bentall? You wouldn't really like to start something?"

I would have loved to start something. I would have loved to take his gun away and beat him over the head with it. Having guns pointed at my eye gives me a nasty dry mouth, makes my heart work overtime and uses up a great deal of adrenalin. I was just starting out to think what else I would like to do to him when he nodded across the bed.

"Because if you are, you might have a look there first."

I turned slowly, so as not to excite anyone. Except only for the yellow of his eyes, the man on the other side of the bed was a symphony in black. Black suit, black sailor's jersey under it, black hat and one of the blackest faces I had ever seen: a thin, taut, pinch-nosed face, the face of a pure Indian. He was very narrow and very short but he didn't have to be big on account of what he held in his hands, a twelve-bore shotgun which had had almost two-thirds of its original length sawn off at stock and barrels. It was like looking down a couple of unlit railway tunnels. I turned away slowly and looked at the white man.

"I see what you mean. Can I sit up?"

He nodded and stepped back a couple of feet. I swung my leg over the bed and looked across to the other side of the room where Marie Hopeman, with a third man, also black, standing beside her, was sitting in a rattan chair by her bed. She was dressed in a blue and white sleeveless silk dress and because it was sleeveless I could see the four bright marks on the upper arm where someone had grabbed her, not too gently.

I was more or less dressed myself, all except for shoes, coat and tie, although we had arrived there several hours earlier after a long and bumpy road trip forced on us by a lack of accommodation at the airfield at the other end of the island. With the unexpected influx of stranded aircraft passengers into the Grand Pacific Hotel the question of separate rooms for Mr. and Mrs. John Bentall had not ever arisen, but the fact that we were almost completely dressed had nothing to do with modesty, false or otherwise: it had to do with survival. The unexpected influx was due to an unscheduled stopover at the Suva airfield: and what the unscheduled stopover was due to was something that exercised my mind very much indeed. Primarily, it was due to a medium-scale electrical fire that had broken out in our DC-7 immediately after the fuelling hoses had been disconnected, and although it had been extinguished inside a minute the plane captain had quite properly refused to continue until airline technicians had flown down from Hawaii to assess the extent of the damage: but what I would have dearly loved to know was what had caused the fire.

I am a great believer in coincidences, but belief stops short just this side of idiocy. Four scientists and their wives had already disappeared en route to Australia: the chances were even that the fifth couple, ourselves, would do likewise, and the fuelling halt at the Suva airfield in Fiji was the last chance to make us vanish. So we'd left our clothes on, locked the doors and taken watches: I'd taken the first, sitting quietly in the darkness until three o'clock in the morning, when I'd given Marie Hopeman a shake and lain down on my own bed. I'd gone to sleep almost immediately and she must have done exactly the same for when I now glanced surreptitiously at my watch I saw it was only twenty minutes past three. Either I hadn't shaken her hard enough or she still hadn't recovered from the effects of the previous sleepless night, a San Francisco-Hawaii hop so violent that even the stewards had been sick. Not that the reasons mattered now.

I pulled on my shoes and looked across at her. For the moment she no longer looked serene and remote and aloof, she just looked tired and pale and there were faint blue shadows under her eyes: she was a poor traveller and had suffered badly the previous night. She saw me looking at her and began to speak.

"—I'm afraid I—"

"Be quiet!" I said savagely.

She blinked as if she had been struck across the face, then tightened her lips and stared down at her stockinged feet. The man with the yachting cap laughed with the musical sound of water escaping down a wastepipe.

"Pay no attention, Mrs. Bentall. He doesn't mean a thing. The world's full of Bentalls, tough crusts and jelly inside, and when they're nervous and scared they've just got to lash out at someone. Makes them feel better. But, of course, they only lash out in a safe direction." He looked at me consideringly and without much admiration. "Isn't that so, Bentall?"

"What do you want?" I asked stiffly. "What is the meaning of this—of this intrusion? You're wasting your time. I have only a very few dollars in currency, about forty. There are traveller's cheques. Those are no good to you. My wife's jewellery—"

"Why are you both dressed?" he interrupted suddenly.

I frowned and stared at him. "I fail to see—"

Something pressed hard and cold and rough against the
19

back of my neck, whoever had hacksawed off the barrels of that twelve-bore hadn't been too particular about filing down the outside edges.

"My wife and I are priority passengers," I said quickly. It is difficult to sound pompous and scared at the same time. "My business is of the greatest urgency. I—I have impressed that on the airport authorities. I understand that planes make overnight refuelling stops in Suva and have asked that I should be notified immediately of any vacancies on a westbound plane. The hotel staff has also been told, and we're on a minute's notice." It wasn't true, but the hotel day staff were off duty and there would be no quick way of checking. But I could see he believed me.

"That's very interesting," he murmured. "And very convenient. Mrs. Bentall, you can come and sit by your husband here and hold his hand—it doesn't look any too steady to me." He waited till she had crossed the room and sat down on the bed, a good two feet from me and staring straight ahead, then said: "Krishna?"

"Yes, captain?" This from the Indian who had been watching Marie.

"Go outside. Put a call through to the desk. Say you're speaking from the airport and that there's an urgent call for Mr. and Mrs. Bentall, that there's a K.L.M. plane with two vacant seats just stopped over for refuelling. They've to go at once. Got it?"

"Yes, captain." A gleam of white teeth and he started for the door.

"Not that way, fool!" The white man nodded to the French doors leading to the outside verandah. "Want everyone to see you? When you've put the call through pick up your friend's taxi, come to the main door, say you've been phoned for by the airport and come upstairs to help carry the bags down."

The Indian nodded, unlocked the French doors and disappeared. The man with the yachting cap dragged out a cheroot, puffed black smoke into the air and grinned at us. "Neat, eh?"

"Just what is it that you intend to do with us?" I asked tightly.

"Taking you for a little trip." He grinned, showing irregular and tobacco-stained teeth. "And there'll be no questions—everyone will think you have gone on to Sydney by plane. Ain't it sad? Now stand up, clasp your hands behind your head and turn round."

With three gun barrels pointing at me and the furthest not

more than eighteen inches away, it seemed a good idea to do what he said. He waited till I had a bird's eye view of the two unlit railway tunnels, jabbed his gun into my back and went over me with an experienced hand that wouldn't have missed even a book of matches. Finally, the pressure of the gun in my spine eased and I heard him taking a step back.

"O.K., Bentall. sit. Bit surprising, maybe—tough-talking pansies like you often fancy themselves enough to pack a gun. Maybe it's in your grips. We'll check later." He transferred a speculative glance to Marie Hopeman. "How about you, lady?"

"Don't you dare touch me, you—you horrible man!" She'd jumped to her feet and was standing there erect as a guardsman, arms stretched stiffly at her sides, fists clenched; breathing quickly and deeply. She couldn't have been more than five feet four in her stockinged soles but outraged indignation made her seem inches taller. It was quite a performance. "What do you think I am? Of course I'm not carrying a gun on me."

Slowly, thoughtfully, but not insolently, his eyes followed every curve of the more than adequately filled silk sheath dress. Then he sighed.

"It would be a miracle if you were," he admitted, regretfully. "Maybe in your *grip*. But later—neither of you will be opening those bags till we get where we're going." He paused for a thoughtful moment. "But you do carry a handbag, don't you, lady?"

"Don't you touch my handbag with your dirty hands!" she said stormily.

"They're not dirty," he said mildly. He held one up for his own inspection. "At least, not really. The bag, Mrs. Bentall?"

"In the bedside cabinet," she said contemptuously.

He moved to the other side of the room, never quite taking his eye off us. I had an idea that he didn't have too much faith in the lad with the blunderbuss. He took the grey lizard handbag from the cabinet, slipped the catch and held the bag upside down over the bed. A shower of stuff fell out, money, comb, handkerchief, vanity case and all the usual camouflage kit and warpaint. But no gun. Quite definitely no gun.

"You don't really look the type," he said apologetically. "But that's how you live to be fifty, lady, by not even trusting your own mother and—" He broke off and hefted the empty bag in his hand. "Does seem a mite heavy, though, don't it?"

He peered inside, fumbled around with his hand, withdrew it and felt the outside of the bag, low down. There was a

21

barely perceptible click and the false bottom fell open, swinging on its hinges. Something fell on the carpet with a thud. He bent and picked up a small flat snub-nosed automatic.

"One of those trick cigarette lighters," he said easily. "Or it might be for perfume or sand-blasting on the old face powder. Whatever will they think of next?"

"My husband is a scientist and a very important person in his own line," Marie Hopeman said stonily. "He has had two threats on his life. I—I have a police permit for that gun."

"And I'll give you a receipt for it so everything will be nice and legal," he said comfortably. The speculative eyes belied the tone. "All right, get ready to go out. Rabat"—this to the man with the sawn-off gun—"over the verandah and see that no one tries anything stupid between the main door and the taxi."

He'd everything smoothly organised. I couldn't have tried anything even if I'd wanted to and I didn't, not now: obviously he'd no intention of disposing of us on the spot and I wasn't going to find any answers by just running away.

When the knock came to the door he vanished behind the curtains covering the open French windows. The bell-boy came in and picked up three bags: he was followed by Krishna, who had in the meantime acquired a peaked cap: Krishna had a raincoat over his arm—he had every excuse, it was raining heavily outside—and I could guess he had more than his hand under it. He waited courteously until we had preceded him through the door, picked up the fourth bag and followed: at the end of the long corridor I saw the man in the yachting cap come out from our room and stroll along after us, far enough away so as not to seem one of the party but near enough to move in quick if I got any funny ideas. I couldn't help thinking that he'd done this sort of thing before.

The night-clerk, a thin dark man with the world-weary expression of night clerks the world over, had our bill ready. As I was paying, the man with the yachting cap, cheroot sticking up at a jaunty angle, sauntered up to the desk and nodded affably to the clerk.

"Good morning, Captain Fleck," the clerk said respectfully. "You found your friend?"

"I did indeed." The cold hard expression had gone from Captain Fleck's face to be replaced with one that was positively jovial. "And he tells me the man I really want to see is out at the airport. Call me a taxi, will you?"

"Certainly, sir." Fleck appeared to be a man of some

consequence in those parts. He hesitated. "Is it urgent, Captain Fleck?"

"All my business is urgent," Fleck boomed.

"Of course, of course." The clerk seemed nervous, anxious to ingratiate himself with Fleck. "It just so happens that Mr. and Mrs. Bentall here are going out there, too, and they have a taxi—"

"Delighted to meet you, Mr.—ah—Bentall," Fleck said heartily. With his right hand he crushed mine in a bluff honest sailorman's grip while with his left he brought the complete ruin of the shapeless jacket he was wearing another long stage nearer by thrusting his concealed gun so far forward against the off-white material that I thought he was going to sunder the pocket from its moorings. "Fleck's my name. I must get out to the airport at once and if you would be so kind—share the costs of course—I'd be more than grateful . . ."

No doubt about it, he was the complete professional, we were wafted out of that hotel and into the waiting taxi with all the smooth and suave dexterity of a head-waiter ushering you to the worst table in an overcrowded restaurant: and had I had any doubts left about Fleck's experienced competence they would have been removed the moment I sat down in the back seat between him and Rabat and felt something like a giant and none too gentle pincers closing round my waist. To my left, Rabat's twelve-bore: to my right, Fleck's automatic, both digging in just above the hip-bones, the one position where it was impossible to knock them aside. I sat still and quiet and hoped that the combination of ancient taxi springs and bumpy road didn't jerk either of the forefingers curved round those triggers.

Marie Hopeman sat in front, beside Krishna, very erect, very still, very aloof. I wondered if there was anything left of the careless amusement, the quiet self-confidence she had shown in Colonel Raine's office two days ago. It was impossible to say. We'd flown together, side by side, for 10,000 miles, and I still didn't even begin to know her. She had seen to that.

I knew nothing at all about the town of Suva, but even if I had I doubt whether I would have known where we were being taken. With two people sitting in front of me, one on either side, and what little I could see of the side-screens blurred and obscured by heavy rain, the chances of seeing anything were remote. I caught a glimpse of a dark silent cinema, a bank, a canal with scattered faint lights reflecting from its opaque surface and, after turning down some narrow unlighted streets and bumping over railway tracks, a long row of small railway wagons with C.S.R. stamped on their sides. All of those, especially the freight train, clashed with my preconceptions of what a south Pacific island should look like, but I had no time to wonder about it. The taxi pulled up with a sudden jerk that seemed to drive the twelve-bore about halfway through me, and Captain Fleck jumped out, ordering me to follow.

I climbed down and stood there rubbing my aching sides while I looked around me. It was as dark as a tomb, the rain was still sluicing down and at first I could see nothing except the vague suggestion of one or two angular structures that looked like gantry cranes. But I didn't need my eyes to tell me where I was, my nose was all that was required. I could smell smoke and diesel and rust, the tang of tar and hempen ropes and wet cordage, and pervading everything the harsh flat smell of the sea.

What with the lack of sleep and the bewildering turn of events my mind wasn't working any too well that night, but it did seem pretty obvious that Captain Fleck hadn't brought us down to the Suva docks to set us up aboard a K.L.M. plane for Australia. I made to speak, but he cut me off at once, flicked a pencil torch at two cases that Krishna had carefully placed in a deep puddle of dirty and oily water, picked up the other two cases himself and told me softly to do the same and follow him. There was nothing soft about the confirmatory jab in the ribs from Rabat's twelve-bore. I was getting tired of Rabat and his ideas as to what constituted gentle prods, Fleck probably fed him on a straight diet of American gangster magazines.

Fleck had either better night eyes than I had or he had a complete mental picture of the whereabouts of every rope, hawser, bollard and loose cobble on that dockside, but we didn't have far to go and I hadn't tripped and fallen more than four or five times when he slowed down, turned to his right and began to descend a flight of stone stairs. He took his time about it and risked using his flash and I didn't blame him: the steps were green-scummed and greasy and there was no handrail at all on the seaward side. The temptation to drop one of my cases on top of him and then watch gravity taking charge was strong but only momentary; not only were there still two guns at my back but my eyes were now just sufficiently accustomed to the dark to let me make out the vague shape of some vessel lying alongside the low stone jetty at the foot of the steps. If he fell now, all Fleck would suffer would be considerable bruising and even greater damage to
24

his pride which might well make him pass up his desire for silence and secrecy in favour of immediate revenge. He didn't look like the kind of man who would miss so I tightened my grip on the cases and went down those steps with all the care and delicate precision of a Daniel picking his way through a den of sleeping lions. And there wasn't all that difference here, just that the lions were wide awake. A few seconds later Marie Hopeman and the two Indians were on the jetty behind me.

We were now only about eight feet above water level and I peered at the vessel to try to get a better idea of her shape and size, but the backdrop of that rain-filled sky was scarcely less dark than that of the land and sea. Broad-beamed, maybe seventy feet long—although I could have been twenty feet out either way—a fairly bulky midships superstructure and masts, whether two or three I couldn't be sure. That was all I had time to see when a door in the superstructure opened and a sudden flood of white light completely destroyed what little night sight I'd been able to acquire. Someone, tall and lean, I thought, passed quickly through the bright rectangle of light and closed the door quickly behind him.

"Everything O.K., boss?" I'd never been to Australia but I'd met plenty of Australians: this one's accent was unmistakable.

"O.K. Got 'em. And watch that damned light. We're coming aboard."

Boarding the ship was no trick at all. The top of the gunwale, amidships where we were, was riding just level with the jetty and all we had to do was jump down the thirty inches to the deck below. A wooden deck, I noticed, not steel. When we were all safely down Captain Fleck said: "We are ready to receive guests, Henry?" He sounded relaxed now, relieved to be back where he was.

"Stateroom's all ready, boss," Henry announced. His voice was a hoarse and lugubrious drawl. "Shall I show them to their quarters?"

"Do that. I'll be in my cabin. All right, Bentall, leave your grips here. I'll see you later."

Henry led the way aft along the deck, with the two Indians close behind. Once clear of the superstructure, he turned right, flicked on a torch and stopped before a small square raised hatch. He bent down, slipped a bolt, heaved the hatch-cover up and back and pointed down with his torch.

"Get down there, the two of you."

I went first, ten rungs on a wet, clammy and vertical steel

ladder, Marie Hopeman close behind. Her head had hardly cleared the level of the hatch when the cover slammed down and we heard the scraping thud of a bolt sliding home. She climbed down the last two or three steps and we stood and looked round our stateroom.

It was a dark and noisome dungeon. Well, not quite dark, there was a dim yellow glowworm of a lamp behind a steel-meshed glass on the deckhead, enough so that you didn't have to paw your way around, but it was certainly noisome enough. It smelled like the aftermath of the bubonic plague, stinking to high heaven of some disgusting odour that I couldn't identify. And it was all that could have been asked for in the way of a dungeon. The only way out was the way we had come in. Aft, there was a wooden bulkhead clear across the width of the vessel. I located a crack between two planks and though I couldn't see anything I could sniff diesel oil: the engine-room, without a doubt. In the for'ard bulkhead were two doors, both unlocked: one led to a primitive toilet and a rust-stained wash-basin supplied by a tap that gave a good flow of brown and brackish water, not sea-water: the other opened on to a tiny six by four cabin where nearly all the floor space was occupied by a low made-up bunk without sheets but with what seemed, in the sputtering light of a match, to be fairly clean blankets. Near the two for'ard corners of the hold were six-inch diameter holes in the deckhead: I peered up those, but could see nothing. Ventilators, probably, and they could hardly have been called a superfluous installation: but on that windless night and with the ship not under way they were quite useless.

Heavy spaced wooden battens, held in place by wooden slots in deck and deckhead, ran the whole fore-and-aft length of the hold. There were four rows of those battens, and behind the two rows nearest the port and starboard sides wooden boxes and open-sided crates were piled to the very top, except where a space had been left free for the air from the ventilators to find its way in. Between the outer and inner rows of battens other boxes and sacks were piled half the height of the hold: between the two inner rows, extending from the engine-room bulkhead to the two small doors in the for'ard bulkhead, was a passage perhaps four feet wide. The wooden floor of this alleyway looked as if it had been scrubbed about the time of the Coronation.

I was still looking slowly around, feeling my heart making for my boots and hoping that it was not too dark for Marie Hopeman to see my carefully balanced expression of insouciance and intrepidity, when the overhead light dimmed to a

26

dull red glow and a high-pitched whine came from aft: a second later an unmistakable diesel engine came to life, the vessel began to vibrate as it revved up, then as it slowed again I could just hear the patter of sandalled feet on the deck above—casting off, no doubt—just before the engine note deepened as gear was engaged. It didn't require the slight list to starboard as the vessel sheered off from the jetty wall to tell us that we were under way.

I turned away from the after bulkhead, bumped into Marie Hopeman in the near darkness and caught her arm to steady her. The arm was goose-fleshed, wet and far too cold. I fumbled a match from a box, scratched it alight and peered at her as she screwed her eyes almost shut against the sudden flare. Her fair bedraggled hair was plastered over her forehead and one cheek, the saturated thin silk of her dress was a clammy cocoon that clung to every inch and she was shivering constantly. Not until then did I realise just how cold and dank it was in that airless hole. I waved the match to extinction, removed a shoe, started hammering the after bulkhead and, when that had no effect, climbed a few steps up the ladder and started beating the hatch.

"What on earth do you imagine you're doing?" Marie Hopeman asked.

"Room service. If we don't get our clothes soon I'm going to have a pneumonia case on my hands."

"Wouldn't it suit you better to look round for some kind of weapon?" she said quietly. "Has it never occurred to you to ask *why* they've brought us out here?"

"To do us in? Nonsense." I tried out my carefree laugh to see how it went, but it didn't, it sounded so hollow and unconvincing that it lowered even my morale. "Of course they're not going to knock us off, not yet, at least. They didn't bring me all the way out here to do that—it could have as easily been done in England. Nor was it necessary to bring *you* that I should be knocked off. Thirdly, they didn't have to bring us out on this boat to do it—for instance that dirty canal we passed and a couple of heavy stones would have been all that was needed. And, fourthly, Captain Fleck strikes me as a ruffian and a rogue, but no killer." This was a better line altogether, if I repeated it about a hundred times I might even start believing it myself. Marie Hopeman remained silent, so maybe she was thinking about it, maybe there was something in it after all.

After a couple of minutes I gave the hatch up as a bad job, went for'ard into the tiny cabin and hammered against the bulkhead there. Crew quarters must have been on the other side for I got reaction within half a minute. Someone heaved open the hatch-cover and a powerful torch shone down into the hold.

"Will you kindly quit that flamin' row?" Henry didn't sound any too pleased. "Can't you sleep, or somethin'?"

"Where are our cases?" I demanded. "We must have dry clothes. My wife is soaked to the skin."

"Comin', comin'," he grumbled. "Move right for'ard, both of you."

We moved, he dropped down into the hold, took four cases from someone invisible to us then stepped aside to make room for another man to come down the ladder. It was Captain Fleck, equipped with a torch and gun, and enveloped in an aroma of whisky. It made a pleasant change from the fearful stink in that hold.

"Sorry to keep you waiting," he boomed cheerfully. "Locks on those cases were a mite tricky. So you weren't carrying a gun after all, eh, Bentall?"

"Of course not," I said stiffly. I had been, but it was still under the mattress of my bed back in the Grand Pacific Hotel. "What's the damnable smell down here?"

"Damnable? Damnable?" Fleck sniffed the foul atmosphere with the keen appreciation of a connoisseur bent over a brandy glass of Napoleon. "Copra and shark's fins. Mainly copra. Very health-giving, they say."

"I dare say," I said bitterly. "How long are we to stay in this hell-hole?"

"There's not a finer schooner—" Fleck began irritably, then broke off. "We'll see. Few more hours, I don't know. You'll get breakfast at eight." He shone his torch around the hold and went on apologetically: "We don't often have ladies aboard, ma'am, especially not ones like you. We might have cleaned it up more. But there's a bunk there, quite clean. Don't either of you sleep with your shoes off."

"Why?" I demanded.

"Cockroaches," he explained briefly. "Very partial to the soles of the feet." He flicked the torch beam suddenly to one side and picked up a couple of brown monstrous beetle-like insects at least a couple of inches in length that scuttled out of sight almost immediately.

"As—as big as that?" Marie Hopeman whispered.

"It's the copra and diesel oil," Henry explained lugubriously. "Their favourite food, except for D.D.T. We give them gallons of that. And them were only the small ones, their parents know better than to come out when there are people around."

28

"That's enough," Fleck said abruptly. He thrust the torch into my hand. "Take this. You'll need it. See you in the morning."

Henry waited till Fleck's head was clear of the hatch, then pushed back some of the sliding battens that bordered the central aisle. He nodded at the four foot high platform of cases exposed by this.

"Sleep here," he said shortly. "There's more than cockroaches down this hold. And keep that light on."

"Why? What is there here that—"

"I don't know," he interrupted. "I've never spent the night here. There's not enough money to pay me to." With that he was gone and moments later the hatch shut to behind him.

"Spreads sweetness and light wherever he goes, doesn't he?" I asked. "I wonder what he *does* mean? But I'd take any money they're not hired assassins. Murderers don't—"

"Do you mind?" she interrupted. "My suitcase. I'd like to change."

"Sorry." I passed it to her, along with the torch. "Did you pack any slacks?"

She nodded.

"Then wear them." I rummaged in one of my own cases, brought out a couple of pairs of socks. "Pull these over them. Anti-cockroach. You can change up in the cabin there."

"You didn't think I was going to do it here," she said coldly. No gratitude. I grinned at her, but no answering smile. She closed the cabin door behind her, not gently.

I'd finished changing by the faint glow of the overhead light and was tapping a cigarette out of its packet when a sudden scream of pure terror from the cabin froze me immobile for a second. But only for a second: four steps and I was at the cabin door just as it was torn violently open and Marie Hopeman came stumbling frantically out, struck her head a glancing blow against the low overhead doorway and literally fell into my arms. She grabbed me and clung on desperately, a young koala bear stranded on its first eucalyptus tree had nothing on Marie Hopeman at that moment. At any other time it would have been very pleasant but just then it wasn't getting us anywhere.

"What happened?" I demanded quickly. "What on earth is it?"

"Take me away from here!" she sobbed. She twisted in my arms and looked over her shoulder with wide horror-filled eyes. "Please. At once! Away." Her eyes widened still further, she took that deep breath that is so often prelude to a scream, so I picked her up hurriedly, walked the ten feet to where Henry had pushed the battens aside and sat her there, her back propped up against the inner battens.

"What was it?" I asked urgently. "Quickly."

"It was horrible, horrible!" She didn't know what I was saying, her breath was coming in long quivering gasps and she was trembling violently. She felt me straightening and sunk her fingers deep into my arms. "Don't leave me. Don't!"

"I'll only be a moment," I said soothingly. I pointed to where a beam of light lay angled across the floor of the cabin. "I want that torch."

I broke away from her desperate grip and almost literally flung myself through the small cabin door. This wasn't courage, it was the lack of it, I didn't know what the fauna of the South Pacific was but it might have ranged from nests of cobras to colonies of black widow spiders and if I'd stopped to think of all the unpleasant possibilities it might have taken me a very long time indeed to cross that threshold.

I picked the blazing torch off the floor and swung it round in a complete circle, all in one movement. Nothing. Another, a much slower and more thorough inspection. Still nothing, nothing except a pile of damp clothes and a couple of my socks on the bed. I went out, taking the socks with me, and pulled the door tight shut behind me.

Her breathing had quietened but she was still trembling badly when I got back. The change from the cool, self-sufficient and rather aloof young lady who had flown out to Fiji with me to this panic-stricken defenceless girl was just within the limits of credibility and it gave me no pleasure at all. Her fair hair was in wild disorder. She was wearing a matched jumper and cardigan and a pair of light blue slacks. On her left foot she wore two of my socks: the right foot was bare.

I turned the torch on this bare foot, leaned forward suddenly and swore. On the outside of the foot, just behind the little toe, were two narrow deep punctures from which blood was slowly welling.

"Rat!" I said. "You've been bitten by a rat."

"Yes," she said shakily. Her eyes darkened in remembered terror. "It was horrible, horrible, horrible! A black rat, huge, as big as a cat. I tried to shake it off but it hung on and on and on—"

"It's all over now," I said sharply. The hysteria had been climbing back into her voice. "Just a moment."

"Where—where are you going?" she asked fearfully.

"First aid kit in my case." I fetched it, squeezed out the wounds and soaked up all the blood with cotton-wool, used iodine liberally, applied a plaster dressing and pulled on the socks. "You won't come to any harm from that."

I lit and gave her a cigarette, ripped a spar off one of the wooden crates, used it as a lever to rip off a larger spar from another crate and finally used that to wrench off a three-foot long three by one from the biggest crate I could see: with three three-inch nails sticking out from the far end it made quite a weapon, more than a match for the fangs of any rat. As big as a cat, Marie Hopeman had said, but I took that with a pinch of salt—they might be as long as a cat but never as big—but for all that black ships' rats could be vicious, especially in numbers. I went into the cabin again, peered around cautiously for the enemy, found none, picked up the two pillows and blankets from the bunk, went out again, shook the blankets ostentatiously to demonstrate that there were no rats concealed in the folds, wrapped them tightly round her, put the pillows behind her back, dug out a spare jacket from one of my cases, made her put it on and stepped back to admire my handiwork.

"Not bad at all," I admitted. "I have the touch. Mirror and comb, perhaps? They tell me it does wonders for a woman's morale."

"No." She smiled shakily at me. "As long as I can't see it, I don't worry. You know, I don't really think you're tough at all."

I smiled back at her, very enigmatic I thought, then used my tie to hang the torch from a batten, close by the deckhead. I pulled back some battens across the aisle from her and hoisted myself up on a platform of wooden boxes, the three by one ready to hand.

"You can't sleep there," she protested. "It's too hard and—and you'll fall off." This was something new, Marie Hopeman showing any concern for me.

"I've no intention of going to sleep," I said. "That's for you. Rat-catcher Bentall, that's me. Goodnight."

We must have been well clear of the land by this time, for the schooner was beginning to roll, not much, but enough to be perceptible. The timbers creaked, the torch swung to and fro throwing huge black moving shadows and, all the time, now that our movements and voices had ceased, I could hear a constant sibilant rustle, either our rodent pals on safari or a cockroach battalion on the march. The combination of the creaking, the rustling and the black ominous shifting shadows was hardly calculated to induce a mood of soporific tranquillity, and I was hardly surprised when, after ten minutes, Marie Hopeman spoke.

"Are—are you asleep? Are you all right?"

"Sure I'm all right," I said comfortably. "Goodnight."

Another five minutes then:

"John!" It was the first time she'd ever called me that except when company had made it necessary to keep up the fiction of our marriage.

"Hullo?"

"Oh, damn it!" There was vexation in her voice, a small reluctant anger at herself, but there was nervousness, too, and the nervousness had the upper hand. "Come and sit beside me."

"Right," I said agreeably. I jumped down to the deck, swung myself up on the other side and seated myself as comfortably as I could with my feet propped against the outboard battens. She made no move or stir to acknowledge my arrival, she didn't even look at me. But I looked at her, I looked and I thought of the change a couple of short hours could make. On the four-stage hop from London airport to Suva she'd hardly acknowledged my existence as a human being, except in airport terminals and conspicuous seats in a plane, where she'd smiled at me, taken my arm and sweet-talked me as any bride of ten weeks ought to have done. But the moment we had been alone or secure from observation her normal cool aloof remote personality had dropped between us like a portcullis with a broken hoist-rope. The previous afternoon, waking out of a short sleep on the Hawaii-Suva hop and drowsily forgetting that we weren't being watched, I'd incautiously taken her hand: she'd taken my right wrist in her right hand, slowly—far too slowly—withdrawn her left hand, at the same time giving me the kind of look that stays with you for a long time to come: if I could have hidden under the seat I'd have done just that and with the size I'd felt it would have been no trick at all. I didn't make the same mistake again, I'd sworn to myself that I wouldn't make the same mistake again, so now, sitting beside her in the dank and chilly hold of that gently rolling schooner, I reached down and took her hand in mine.

Her hand was ice-cold and stiffened immediately at my touch: next second it was clamped round mine and doing its best to give an imitation of a small but powerful vise. I hadn't taken all that of a chance, she wasn't scared, she was terrified, and that was all out of character with Marie Hope-man: I could feel her shiver from time to time and it wasn't all that cold down in the hold.

"Why did you bawl me out back in the hotel room?" she said reproachfully. "It wasn't nice."

"I seldom am," I agreed. "But that was different. You were about to start apologising to me for falling asleep."

"It was the least I could do. I—I'm sorry."

"Didn't it strike you that our friend Fleck might have found it rather curious?" I asked. "Innocent people with nothing to hide don't strive to keep awake all night along. My one thought at the moment was that the less reason Fleck had to suspect us of being anything other than we claimed the greater would be our later freedom of movement."

"I'm sorry," she repeated.

"It doesn't matter. No harm done." A pause. "Did you ever read George Orwell's '1984'?"

" '1984'?" Her voice was surprised and wary at the same time. "Yes, I have?"

"Remember how the authorities finally broke the resistance of the central character?"

"Don't!" She jerked her hand from mine and covered her face with her hands. "It's—it's too horrible."

"All sorts of different people have all sorts of different phobias," I said gently. I took one of her hands away from her face. "Yours just happens to be rats."

"It—it's not a phobia," she said defensively. "Not liking things is not a phobia. All sorts of people, especially women, hate rats."

"And mice," I agreed. "They yell and they scream and they dance about and they make for the highest piece of furniture they can reach. But they don't have the pink fits, not even if bitten. They're not still shaking like a broken bed-spring half an hour after it happens. What started all this off?"

She was silent for half a minute, then abruptly pushed up the tousled blonde hair at the side of her neck. Even in the dim half-light I had no difficulty in seeing the scar behind the right ear.

"It must have been a mess at the time," I nodded. "Rat, I take it. How?"

"After my parents were drowned on the way to England I was brought up by my uncle and aunt. On a farm." Her voice was not that of a person discussing the faraway green fields of treasured memories. "There was a daughter three or four years older than I was. She was nice. So was her mother, my aunt."

"And he was the wicked uncle?"

"Don't laugh. It's not funny. He was all right at first, until my aunt died about eight years after I came to them. Then

33

he started drinking, lost the farm and had to move to a smaller place where the only room for me was an attic above the barn."

"Okay, that's enough," I interrupted. "I can guess the rest."

"I used to lie awake at night with a torch in my hand," she whispered. "A ring of eyes round the room, red and pink and white. Watching me, just watching me. Then I'd light a candle before going to sleep. One night the candle went out and when I woke up this—this—it was caught in my hair and biting and it was dark and I screamed and screamed—"

"I told you, that's enough," I said harshly. "Do you like hurting yourself?" Not nice, but necessary.

"I'm sorry," she said in a low voice. "That's all. I was three weeks in hospital, not with my neck but because I was a bit out of my mind and then they let me out again." All this in a very matter-of-fact voice. I wondered what it cost her to say it. I tried not to feel sorry for her, not to feel pity: involvement with any person was the one thing I couldn't afford. But I couldn't help myself from saying: "Your unpleasant experiences weren't just confined to the rats, were they?"

She twisted to look at me, then said slowly: "You are more shrewd than I had thought."

"Not really. When you find women behaving in the hands-off down the nose snooty superciliousness affected by some, it's because they think it's an interesting attitude or a mark of superiority, or provocative, or simply because it's a cover-up for the fact that they haven't sufficient intelligence or common sense to behave and converse like a human being. We include you out. How about the wicked uncle?"

"He was wicked all right," she said, unsmiling. "By and by my cousin ran away because she couldn't stand him any longer. A week later I did the same, but for different reasons, some neighbours found me crying in the woods in the dark. I was taken to some institution, then put in care of a guardian." She didn't like any of this and neither did I. "He had a sick wife and a full-grown son and—and they fought over me. Then another institution and another and another. I had no family, I was young, a foreigner and had no money: some people think the combination entitles them to—"

"All right," I said. "You don't like rats. And you don't like men."

"I've never had any reason to change my mind about either."

It was hardly the time to point out that with her face and

34

her figure she had as much chance of escaping attention as a magnet would have of moving untouched through a heap of iron filings. Instead, I cleared my throat and said: "I'm a man, too."

"So you are. I'd quite forgotten." The words meant nothing but the little smile that went with them made me feel ten feet tall. "I'll bet you're just as bad as the rest."

"Worse," I assured her. "'Ravening' would be a weak word to describe me."

"That's nice," she murmured. "Put your arm around me."

I stared at her. "Come the dawn," I said, "you'll regret this weakness."

"Let the dawn look after itself," she said comfortably. "You'll stay here all night?"

"What's left of it."

"You won't leave me?" This with a child-like persistence. "Not even for a moment?"

"Nary a minute." I rattled my club against the battens. "I'll sit here and I'll keep awake and I'll fight off every rat in the South Pacific. Every man in the South Pacific, too, if it comes to that."

"I'm quite sure you would," she said peacefully. She was asleep inside a minute.

CHAPTER TWO

Tuesday 8:30 A.M.-7 P.M.

SHE slept serenely, like one dead, for over three hours, her breathing so quiet that I could hardly hear it. As the time slipped by, the rolling of the schooner became increasingly more pronounced until after one particularly violent lurch she woke up with a start and stared at me, her eyes reflecting confusion and perhaps a touch of fear. Then understanding came back and she sat up, taking the weight off my arm for the first time in hours.

"Hullo, knight-errant," she said.

"Morning. Feel better?"

"Mmm." She grabbed a batten as another violent lurch sent some loose boxes banging about the hold. "But I won't be for long, not if this sort of thing keeps up. Nuisance, I know, but I can't help it. What's the time?"

I made to look at the watch on my left wrist, but the arm was quite dead. I reached it across with my right hand, trying not to wince as the pins and needles of returning circulation shot through it. She frowned and said: "What's wrong?"

"You told me not to stir all night," I pointed out patiently. "So I didn't. You are no light weight, young lady."

"I'm sorry," she said quickly. She looked at me quizzically, colour in her cheeks, but smiled without embarrassment. "It's come the dawn and I still don't regret my weakness. . . . Half-past eight, your watch says. Must be broad daylight. I wonder where we're heading?"

"North or south. We're neither quartering nor corkscrewing, which means that we have this swell right on the beam. I don't remember much of my geography but enough to be pretty sure that at this time of the year the steady easterly trades push up an east-west swell. So, north or south." I lowered myself stiffly to my feet, walked for'ard along the central aisle to where the two narrow spaces, one on each side, had been left clear of cargo to give access to the ventilator intakes. I moved into those in turn and touched both the port and starboard sides of the schooner, high up. The port side was definitely warmer than the starboard. That meant we were moving more or less due south. The nearest land in that direction was New Zealand, about a thousand miles away. I filed away this helpful information and was about to move when I heard voices from above, faint but unmistakable. I pulled a box down from behind its retaining batten and stood on it, the side of my face against the foot of the ventilator.

The ventilator must have been just outside the radio office and its trumpet-shaped opening made a perfect earphone for collecting and amplifying soundwaves. I could hear the steady chatter of morse and, over and above that, the sound of two men talking as clearly as if they had been no more than three feet away from me. What they were speaking about I'd no idea, it was in a language I'd never heard before: after a couple of minutes I jumped down, replaced the box and went back to Marie.

"What took you so long?" she asked accusingly. She knew the rats were still around and a phobia doesn't die away in a night.

"Sorry. But you may be grateful yet for the delay. I've found out that we're travelling south but, much more important, I've found out that we can hear what the people on the upper deck are talking about." I told her how I'd discovered this, and she nodded.

"It could be very useful."

"It could be more than useful." I watched her as she

swung her legs over the side of the boxes, then touched the side of the right foot, gently. "How does it feel?"

"Stiff. Not very sore."

I pulled off the socks and one side of the plaster bandage. The wound was clean, slightly swollen and slightly blue, but no more than it had any right to be.

"It'll be O.K.," I said. "Hungry?"

"Well." She made a face and rubbed a hand across her stomach. "It's not just that I'm a bad sailor, it's the fearful smell down here."

"Those ventilators appear to be no damned help in the world," I agreed. "But perhaps some tea might be." I moved into the tiny cabin, striking an apprehensive match or two to make sure that there were no rats lurking around and called for attention as I'd done a few hours earlier by hammering on the bulkhead. I moved aft and within a minute the hatch was opened.

I blinked in the blinding glare of light that flooded down into the hold, then moved back as someone came down the ladder. A man with a lantern-jawed face, lean and lined and mournful.

"What's all the racket about?" Henry demanded wearily.

"You promised us some breakfast," I reminded him.

"So we did." He looked at me curiously. "Had a good night?"

"You might have told us about the rats."

"I might have. Hopin' they didn't show themselves. Trouble?"

"My wife was badly bitten on the foot." I dropped my voice so that Marie couldn't hear it. "Rats carry plague, don't they?"

He shook his head. "Rats carry fleas. The fleas carry plague. But not here. Place is awash in D.D.T. Breakfast in ten minutes." With that he was gone, shutting the hatch behind him.

Less than the promised time later the hatch opened again and a stocky brown-haired youngster with dark frizzy golliwog hair came nimbly down the ladder carrying a battered wooden tray in one hand. He grinned at me cheerfully, moved up the aisle and set the tray down on the boxes beside Marie, whipping a dented tin cover off a dish with the air of Escoffier unveiling his latest creation. I looked at the brown sticky mass. I thought I could see rice and shredded coconut.

"What's this?" I asked. "Last week's garbage?"

"Dalo pudding. Very good, sir." He pointed to a chipped enamel pot. "Here is coffee. Also very good." He ducked his head at Marie and left as nimbly as he had come. It went without saying that he shut the hatch behind him.

The pudding was an indigestible and gelatinous mess that tasted and felt like cooked cowhide glue. It was quite inedible but no match for the fearful coffee, lukewarm bilge-water strained through old cement sacks.

"Do you think they're trying to poison us?" Marie asked.

"Impossible. No one could ever eat this stuff in the first place. At least, no European could. By Polynesian standards it probably ranks with caviar. Well, there goes breakfast." I broke off and looked closely at the crate behind the tray. "Well, I'll be damned. Don't miss very much, do I? I've only been sitting with my back against it for about four hours."

"Well, you haven't eyes in the back of your head," she said reasonably. I didn't reply, I'd already unhitched the torch and was peering through the inch cracks between the spars of the crate. "Looks like lemonade bottles or some such to me."

"And to me. Are you developing scruples about managing Captain Fleck's property?" she asked delicately.

I grinned, latched on to my anti-rat club, pried off the top spar, pulled out a bottle and handed it to Marie. "Watch it. Probably neat bootleg gin for sale to the natives."

But it wasn't, it was lemon juice, and excellent stuff at that. Excellent for thirst, but hardly a substitute for breakfast: I took off my jacket and began to investigate the contents of the schooner's hold.

Captain Fleck appeared to be engaged in the perfectly innocuous business of provision carrier. The half-filled spaces between the two sets of battens on either side were taken up by crates of food and drink: meat, fruit and soft drinks. Probably stuff he loaded up on one of the larger islands before setting off to pick up copra. It seemed a reasonable guess. But then, Fleck didn't seem like an innocuous man.

I finished off a breakfast of corned beef and pears—Marie passed it up with a shudder—then began to investigate the contents of the boxes and crates packed ceiling high between the two outer rows of battens and the sides of the schooner. But I didn't get very far. The battens in those rows weren't of the free-sliding type in the inboard rows but were hinged at the top and were designed to lift upwards and inwards: with their lower halfs jammed by the boxes in the inner rows, this was quite impossible. But two of the battens, the two directly behind the lemonade crate, were loose: I examined their tops with the torch and could see that there were no hinges attaching them to the deckhead: from the freshness of the wood where the screws had been, the hinges appeared to have been recently removed. I pushed the battens as far apart as possible, wrestled the top box out of position without breaking my neck, not so easy as it sounds for the boxes were heavy and the rolling of the schooner pretty violent by this time—and placed it on the platform where we'd spent the night.

The box was about two feet long by eighteen inches wide and a foot deep, made of oiled yellow pine. On each of the four corners of the lid was the broad arrow property mark of the Royal Navy. At the top, a stencil semi-obliterated by a thick black line said 'Fleet Air Arm.' Below that were the words 'Alcohol Compasses' and beneath that again 'Redundant. Authorised for disposal', followed by a stencilled crown, very official looking. I pried the top off with some difficulty and the stencils didn't lie: six unmarked alcohol compasses, packed in straw and white paper.

"Looks O.K. to me," I said. "I've seen those stencils before. 'Redundant' is a nice naval term for 'Obsolete'. Gets a better price from civilian buyers. Maybe Captain Fleck is in the legitimate ex-Government surplus stock disposal trade."

"Maybe Captain Fleck had his own private stock of stencils," Marie said skeptically. "How about the next one?"

I got the next one down. This was stencilled 'Binoculars' and binoculars it contained. The third box had again the Fleet Air Arm marking, semi-obliterated, and the stencil 'Inflatable Life-belts (Aircraft)', and again the stencil didn't lie: bright red life-belts with CO_2 charges and yellow cylinders marked 'Shark repellent'.

"We're wasting our time," I said. Having to brace one's self against the heavy rolling of the schooner made the lifting and prying open of the boxes heavy work, the heat in the hold was building up as the sun climbed in the sky and the sweat was pouring down my face and back. "Just a common-or-garden second-hand dealer."

"Second-hand dealers don't kidnap people," she said tartly. "Just one more, please. I have a feeling."

I checked the impulse to say that it was easy enough to have a feeling when you didn't have to do the sweating, lugged a fourth and very heavy box off the steadily diminishing pile and lowered it beside the others. The same disposal stencils as before, contents marked 'Champion Spark Plugs, 2 gross'."

It took me five minutes and a two-inch strip of skin from the back of my right hand to get the lid off. Marie carefully avoided looking at me, maybe she was a mind-reader, maybe she was just getting good and seasick. But she turned as the lid came clear, peered inside then glanced up at me.

"Maybe Captain Fleck *does* have his own stencils," she murmured.

"Maybe he does at that," I acknowledged. The case was full of drums, but the drums weren't full of spark plugs: there was enough machine-gun belt ammunition inside the case to start off a fair-sized revolution. "This interests me strangely."

"Is—is it safe? If Captain Fleck—"

"What's Captain Fleck ever done for me? Let him come if he wants to." I lugged out a fifth case, sneered at the 'Spark plug' stencil, wrenched off the lid with a combination of leverage and a few well-chosen kicks, stared down at the writing on the heavy blue paper wrapped round the contents, then replaced the lid with all the gentle tenderness and reverent care of a Chicago gangster placing a wreath on the grave of his latest victim.

"Ammonal, 25% aluminium powder?" Marie, too, had glimpsed the writing. "What on earth is that?"

"A very powerful blasting explosive, just about enough to send the schooner and everybody aboard it into orbit." I lifted it gingerly back into position and fresh sweat came to my face when I thought of the elan with which I had hammered it open. "Damn tricky stuff, too. Wrong temperature, wrong handling, excessive humidity—well, it makes quite a bang. I don't like this hold so much any more." I caught up the ammunition crate and returned that also: thistledown never fell so light as that box did on top of the ammonal.

"Are you putting them all back?" There was a tiny frown between her eyes.

"What does it look like to you?"

"Scared?"

"No. Terrified. The next box might have had nitro-glycerine or some such. That really would be something." I replaced all the boxes and battens, took the torch and went aft to see what else there was. But there wasn't much. On the port side, six diesel oil drums, all full, kerosene, D.D.T. and some five-gallon water drums shaped and strapped for carrying over the shoulders—Fleck, I supposed, would need these when he topped up water supplies in the more remote islands where there were no other loading facilities. On the starboard side there were a couple of square metal boxes half-full of assorted and rusted ship's ironmongery—nuts, bolts, eyebolts, blocks, tackles, bottle screws, even a couple of marlin spikes.

I eyed the spikes longingly but left them where they were: it didn't seem likely that Captain Fleck would have overlooked the possibility, but, even if he had, a marlin-spike was a good deal slower than a bullet. And very difficult to conceal.

I walked back to Marie Hopeman. She was very pale.

"Nothing there at all. Any ideas about what to do now?"

"You can do what you like," she said calmly. "I'm going to be sick."

"Oh, Lord." I ran for the cabin, hammered on the bulkhead and was standing below the hatch when it opened. It was Captain Fleck himself, clear-eyed, rested, freshly-shaved and clad in white ducks. He courteously removed his cheroot before speaking.

"A splendid morning, Bentall. I trust you—"

"My wife's sick," I interrupted. "She needs fresh air. Can she come up on deck?"

"Sick? Fever?" His tone changed. "I heard a rat had—"

"Sea-sick," I yelled at him.

"On a day like this?" Fleck half-straightened and looked around what he probably regarded as an expanse of flat calm. "One minute."

He snapped his fingers, said something I couldn't catch and waited till the boy who'd brought us breakfast came running up with a pair of binoculars. Fleck made a slow careful 360° sweep of the horizon, then lowered the glasses. "She can come up. You, too, if you like."

I called Marie and let her precede me up the ladder. Fleck gave her a helping hand over the edge of the hatch and said solicitously: "I'm so sorry to hear that you are not too well, Mrs. Bentall. You don't look too good, and that's a fact."

"You are most kind, Captain Fleck." Her tone and look would have shrivelled me, but it bounced right off Fleck. He snapped his fingers again and the boy appeared with a couple of sun-shaded deck-chairs. "You are welcome to remain as long as you wish, both of you. If you are told to go below you must do so immediately. That is understood?"

I nodded silently.

"Good. You will not, of course, be so foolish as to try anything foolish. Our friend Rabat is no Annie Oakley, but he could hardly miss at this range." I turned my head and saw the little Indian, still in black but without his jacket now, sitting on the other side of the hatch with his sawn-off shotgun across his knees. It was pointed straight at my head and he was looking at me in a longing fashion I didn't care for. "I must leave you now," Fleck went on. He smiled, showing his brown crooked teeth. "We shipmasters have our business to attend to. I will see you later."

He left us to fix up the deck-chairs and went for'ard into the wheelhouse beyond the wireless cabin. Marie stretched herself out with a sigh, closed her eyes and in five minutes had the colour back in her cheeks. In ten minutes she had fallen asleep. I should have liked to do the same myself, but Colonel Raine wouldn't have liked it. 'Eternal vigilance, my boy' was his repeated watchword, so I looked round me as vigilantly as I could. But there was nothing much to be vigilant about.

Above, a hot white sun in a washed-out blue-white sky. To the west, a green-blue sea, to the east, the sunward side, deep green sparkling waters pushed into a long low swell by the warm 20-knot trade wind. Off to the south-east, some vague and purplish blurs on the horizon that might have been islands or might equally well have been my imagination. And in the whole expanse of sea not a ship or boat in sight. Not even a flying fish. I transferred my vigilance to the schooner.

Perhaps it wasn't the filthiest vessel in all the seven seas, I'd never seen them all, but it would have taken a good ship to beat it. It was bigger, much bigger, than I had thought, close on a hundred feet in length, and everyone of them greasy, cluttered with refuse, unwashed and unpainted. Or there had been paint, but most of it had sun-blistered off. Two masts, sparred and rigged to carry sails, but no sails in sight, and between the mast-heads a wireless aerial that trailed down to the radio cabin, about twenty feet for'ard from where I sat. I could see the rusted ventilator beyond its open door and beyond that a place that might have been Fleck's charthouse or cabin or both and still further for'ard, but on a higher elevation, the closed-in bridge. Beyond that again, I supposed, below deck level, would be the crew quarters. I spent almost five minutes gazing thoughtfully at the superstructure and fore part of the ship with the odd vague feeling that there was something wrong, that there was something as it shouldn't have been. Maybe Colonel Raine would have got it, but I couldn't. I felt I had done my duty to the Colonel, and keeping my eyes open any longer wouldn't help anyone, asleep or awake they could toss us over the side whenever they wished. I'd had three hours' sleep in the past forty-eight. I closed my eyes. I went to sleep.

When I awoke it was just on noon. The sun was almost directly overhead, but the chair shades were wide and the trade winds cool. Captain Fleck had just seated himself on the side of the hatchway. Apparently, whatever business he had had to attend to was over, and guessing the nature of that business was no trick at all, he'd just finished a long and difficult interview with a bottle of whisky. His eyes were slightly glazed and even at three feet to windward I'd no difficulty at all in smelling the Scotch. But conscience or maybe something else had got into him for he was carrying a tray with glasses, a bottle of sherry and a small stone jar.

"We'll send you a bit of food by-and-by." He sounded almost apologetic. "Thought you might like a snifter, first?"

"Uh-huh." I looked at the stone jar. "What's in it? Cyanide?"

"Scotch," he said shortly. He poured out two drinks, drained his own at a gulp and nodded at Marie who was lying facing us, her face almost completely hidden under her wind-blown hair. "How about Mrs. Bentall?"

"Let her sleep. She needs it. Who's giving you the orders for all of this, Fleck?"

"Eh?" He was off-balance, but only for a second, his tolerance to alcohol seemed pretty high. "Orders? What orders? Whose orders?"

"What are you going to do with us?"

"Impatient to find out, aren't you, Bentall?"

"I just love it here. Not very communicative, are you?"

"Have another drink."

"I haven't even started this one. How much longer do you intend keeping us here?"

He thought it over for a bit, then said slowly: "I don't know. Your guess isn't so far out, I'm not the principal in this. There was somebody very anxious indeed to see you." He gulped down some more whisky. "But he isn't so sure now."

"He might have told you that before you took us from the hotel."

"He didn't know then. Radio, not five minutes ago. He's coming through again at 1900 hours—seven o'clock sharp. You'll have your answer then. I hope you like it." There was something sombre in his voice that I didn't find very encouraging. He switched his glance to Marie, looked at her for a long time in silence, then stirred. "Kind of a nice girl you got there, Bentall."

"Sure. That's my wife, Fleck. Look the other way."

He turned slowly and looked at me, his face hard and cold. But there was something else in it too, I just couldn't put my finger on it.

"If I were ten years younger or maybe even a half a bottle soberer," he said without animosity, "I'd have your front

43

teeth for that, Bentall." He looked away across the green dazzle of the ocean, the glass of whisky forgotten in his hand. "I got a daughter just a year or two younger than her. Right now she's in the University of California. Liberal Arts. Thinks her old man's a captain in the Australian Navy." He swirled the drink around in his glass. "Maybe it's better she keeps on thinking just that, maybe it's better that she never sees me again. But if I *knew* I would never *see* her again ..."

I got it. I'm no Einstein but I don't have to be beaten over the head more than a few times to make me see the obvious. The sun was hotter than ever, but I didn't feel warm any more. I didn't want him to realise that he had been talking to me, too, not just to himself, so I said: "You're no Australian, are you, Fleck?"

"No?"

"No. You talk like one, but it's an overlaid accent."

"I'm as English as you are," he growled. "But my home's in Australia."

"Who's paying you for all this, Fleck?"

He rose abruptly to his feet, gathered up the empty glasses and bottles and went away without another word.

It wasn't until about half-past five in the evening that Fleck came to tell us to get below. Maybe he'd spotted a vessel on the horizon and didn't want to take the chance of anyone seeing us if they approached too closely, maybe he just thought we'd been on deck long enough, or maybe it had something to do with that dark brown smudge I could vaguely make out on the southern horizon, just off the starboard bow. It could have been cloud, of course, but even through that heat haze it looked too solid—and too solitary—for cloud. It was difficult to estimate its distance—fifteen, maybe twenty miles away. The prospect of returning to that stinking and rat-infested hole was no pleasure, but apart from the fact that both of us had slept nearly all day and felt rested again, we weren't too reluctant to go: black cumulus thunderheads had swept up out of the east in the late afternoon, an obscured sun had turned the air cool and the rain wasn't far away. It looked as if it were going to be a black and dirty night. The sort of night that would suit Captain Fleck very well indeed: the sort of night, I hoped, that would suit us even better.

The hatch-cover dropped in place behind us and the bolt slid home. Marie gave a little shiver and hugged herself tightly.

"Well, another night in the Ritz coming up. You should

have asked for fresh batteries—that torch isn't going to last us all night."

"It won't have to. One way or another we've spent our last night on this floating garbage can. Just as we came down I thought I saw an island way ahead. I could be wrong and if I've made a mistake about it, well, it's my last mistake. But it's also our last chance. We're leaving this evening, just as soon as it's good and dark. If Fleck had his way we'll be leaving with a couple of iron bars tied to our feet: if I have mine, we'll leave without them. If I were a betting man, I'd put my money on Fleck."

"What do you mean?" she whispered. "You—you were sure that nothing was going to happen to us. Remember all the reasons you gave me when we arrived on board last night. You said Fleck was no killer."

"I still don't think he is. Not by nature, anyway. He's been drinking all day, trying to drown his conscience. But there are many things that can make a man do what he doesn't want to do, even kill: threats, blackmail, a desperate need for money. I was speaking to him while you slept. It seems that whoever wanted me out here no longer needs me. What it was for I don't know, but whatever it was the end appears to have been achieved without me."

"He told you that we—that we—"

"He told me nothing, directly. He merely said that the person who had arranged the kidnap thought that he no longer wanted me—or us. The definite word is to come through at seven, but from the way Fleck spoke there wasn't much doubt about what the word is going to be. I think old Fleck's got a soft spot for you and he spoke of you, by inference, as if you already belonged to the past. Very touching, very wistful."

She touched my arm, looked up at me with a strange expression I'd never seen before and said simply: "I'm scared. It's funny, all of a sudden I look into the future and I don't see it and I'm scared. Are you?"

"Of course I'm scared," I said irritably. "What do you think?"

"I don't think you are, it's just something you say. I know you're not afraid—not of death, anyway. It's not that you're any braver than the rest of us, it's just that if death came your way you'd be so busy figuring, planning, calculating, scheming, working out a way to beat it that you'd never even see it coming except in an academic sort of way. You're working out a way to beat it now, you're sure you will beat it; death for you, death that even one chance in a million
45

might avoid, would be the supreme insult." She smiled at me, rather self-consciously, then went on:

"Colonel Raine told me a good deal about you. He said that when things are completely desperate and there's no hope left, it's in the nature of man to accept the inevitable, but he said you wouldn't, not because it was any positive thing, but just because you wouldn't even know how to set about giving up. He said he thought you were the one man he could ever be afraid of, for if you were strapped to an electric chair and the executioner was pulling the switch, you'd still be figuring a way to beat it." She'd been abstractedly twisting one of my shirt buttons until it was just about off, but I said nothing, if that blur I'd seen on the southern horizon really had been cloud one shirt button more or less wasn't going to matter very much that night, and now she looked up and smiled again to rob her next words of offence. "I think you're a very arrogant man. I think you're a man with a complete belief in himself. But one of these days you're going to meet up with a situation where your self-belief is going to be of just no help at all."

"Mark my words," I said nastily. "You forgot to say, 'Mark my words'."

The smile faded and she turned away as the hatch opened. It was the brown-skinned Fijian boy, with soup, some sort of stew and coffee. He came and left without a word.

I looked at Marie. "Ominous, eh?"

"What do you mean?" she said coldly.

"Our Fijian friend. This morning a grin from ear to ear: tonight the look of a surgeon who's just come out to tell you that his scalpel slipped."

"So?"

"It's not the custom," I said patiently, "to crack gags and do a song-and-dance act when you're bringing the last meal to the condemned man. The better penitentiaries frown on it."

"Oh," she said flatly. "I see."

"Do you want to sample this stuff?" I went on. "Or will I just throw it away?"

"I don't know," she said doubtfully. "I haven't eaten for twenty-four hours. I'll try."

It was worth the try. The soup was good, the stew better, the coffee excellent. The cook had made a miraculous recovery from the depths he'd plumbed that morning: or maybe they'd shot the old one. I'd more to think of. I drained my coffee and looked at Marie.

"You can swim, I take it?"

46

"Not very well," she said hesitantly. "I can float."

"Provided there are no iron bars tied to your feet." I nodded. "That'll be enough. Would you like to do a little listening while I do a little work?"

"Of course." She was getting round to forgiving me. We went for'ard and I pulled down a couple of boxes for her to stand on, just below the opening to the port ventilator.

"You won't miss much of what they say up top," I said. "Especially, you'll hear everything that's said in or by the radio room. Probably nothing much before seven, but you never know. I'm afraid you're going to get a bit of a crick in the neck but I'll relieve you as soon as I'm through."

I left her there, went back to the after end of the hold, climbed three steps up the iron ladder and made a rough estimate of the distance between the top rung and the bottom of the hatch-cover above. Then I came down and started rummaging around in the metal boxes in the starboard corner until I found a bottle-screw that suited me, picked up a couple of hardwood battens and stowed them away, together with the bottle-screw, behind some boxes.

Back at the platform of wooden boxes where we'd spent the night I pushed aside the two loose battens in the outboard row, cautiously lifted down the boxes with the compasses and binoculars, shoved them to one side, took down the box with the aircraft-type life belts and emptied out the contents. There were twelve of the belts altogether, rubber and reinforced canvas covers with leather harness instead of the more usual tapes. In addition to the CO_2 bottle and shark-repellent cylinder, each belt had another water-proof cylinder with a wire leading up to a small red lamp fixed on the left shoulder strap. There would be a battery inside that cylinder. I pressed the little switch on one of them and the lamp at once glowed a deep bright red, indication that the equipment, though obsolete, was not old and good augury for the operating efficiency of the gas and water-tightness of the inflated belts. But it wasn't a thing to be left to chance: I picked out four belts at random and struck the release knob on the first of them.

The immediate hiss of compressed gas wasn't so terribly loud, I supposed, but inside that confined space it seemed as if everybody aboard the schooner must hear it. Certainly Marie heard it, for she jumped off her box and came quickly back into the pool of light cast by the suspended torch.

"What's that?" she asked quickly. "What made the noise?"

"No rats, no snakes, no fresh enemies," I assured her. The hissing had now stopped and I held up a round, stiff, fully-inflated lifebelt for her inspection. "Just testing. Seems O.K. I'll test one or two more, but I'll try to keep it quiet. Heard anything yet?"

"Nothing. Plenty of talk, that is, Fleck and that Australian man. But it's mostly about charts, courses, islands, cargoes, things like that. And their girl friends in Suva."

"That must be interesting."

"Not the way they tell it," she snapped.

"Dreadful," I agreed. "Just what you were saying last night. Men are all the same. Better get back before you miss anything."

She gave me a long considering look but I was busy testing the other lifebelts, muffling the noise under the two blankets and the pillows. All four worked perfectly and when, after ten minutes, none showed any sign of deflation, the chances seemed high that all the others were at least as good. I picked out another four, hid them behind some boxes, deflated the four I'd tested and replaced them in the box with the others. A minute later I'd all the battens and boxes back in place.

I looked at my watch. It lacked fifteen minutes to seven. There was little enough time left. I went aft again, inspected the water drums with my torch: heavy canvas carrying straps, the shell concave to fit the back, five-inch diameter spring-loaded lid at top, a spigot with tap at the bottom. They looked sound enough. I dragged two of them out of the corner, snapped open the lids and saw that they were nearly full. I closed the lids again and shook the drums as vigorously as possible. No water escaped, they were completely tight. I turned both the taps on full, let the water come gushing out on the deck—it wasn't my schooner—then, when they were as empty as I could get them, mopped their interiors dry with a shirt from my case and made my way for'ard to Marie.

"Anything yet?" I whispered.

"Nothing."

"I'll take over for a bit. Here's the torch. I don't know what things there are that go bump in the night in the Pacific Ocean, but it is possible that those lifebelts may get torn or just turn out to be perished through age. So I think we'll take along a couple of empty water drums. They have a very high degree of buoyancy, far more than we require, so I thought we might as well use them to take along some clothes inside, whatever you think you'll need. Don't spend all night deciding what to take. Incidentally, I believe many women carry cellophane bags in their cases for wrapping up this and that. Got any?"

"One or two."

"Leave one out, please."

"Right." She hesitated. "I don't know much about boats but I think this one has changed course once or twice in the past hour."

"How do you figure that out?" Old sea-dog Bentall, very tolerant to the landlubbers.

"We're not rolling any more, are we? The waves are passing under us from the stern. And it's the second or third change I've noticed."

She was right, the swell had died down considerably but what little was left was from aft. But I paid small attention to this, I knew the trades died away at night and local currents could set up all kinds of cross-motions in the water. It didn't seem worth worrying about. She went away and I pressed close to the deckhead.

All I could hear at first was a violently loud tinny rattling against the ventilator, a rattling that grew more violent and persistent with every second that passed. Rain, and very heavy rain at that: it sounded like rain that meant to keep going on for a long time. Both Fleck and I would be happy about that.

And then I heard Fleck's voice. First the patter of hurrying footsteps, then his voice. I guessed that he was standing just inside the doorway of the wireless cabin.

"Time you got your earphones on, Henry." The voice had a reverberating and queerly metallic timbre from its passage down the funnel-shaped ventilator, but was perfectly plain. "Just on schedule."

"Six minutes yet, boss." Henry, seated at the radio table, must have been five feet away from Fleck, yet his voice was hardly less distinct: the ventilator's amplifying effects were as good as that.

"Doesn't matter. Tune in."

I strained my ear against that ventilator until it seemed to me that I was about halfway up it, but I heard nothing further. After a couple of minutes I felt a tug at my sleeve.

"All done," she said in a low voice. "Here's the torch."

"Right." I jumped down, helped her up and murmured: "For heaven's sake don't move from there. Our friend Henry's listening in for the final word right now."

I had little enough left to do and three or four minutes saw me all through. I stuffed a blanket inside the cellophane bag and tied the neck securely: that made me the complete optimist. There were an awful lot of 'ifs' attached to that blanket. If we managed to break open the hatch, if we managed to get off the shcooner without too many bullet holes in us, if we didn't subsequently drown, if we weren't eaten alive by sharks or barracuda or whatever else took a fancy to us during the hours of darkness, if that island were far away from our jumping-off point or, worse, didn't exist at all, then it seemed like a good idea to have a water-soaked blanket to ward off sunstroke. But I didn't want to have to cope with its water-logged dead weight during the night: hence the cellophane bag. I tied the bag on to one of the drums and had just finished stowing some clothes and cigarettes inside the same drum when Marie came aft and stood beside me.

She said without preamble and in a quiet still voice, not scared: "They don't need us any more."

"Well, at least all my preparations haven't been wasted. They discussed it?"

"Yes. They might have been discussing the weather: I think you're wrong about Fleck, he's not worried about doing away with anyone. From the way he talked it was just an interesting problem. Henry asked him how they were going to get rid of us and Fleck said: 'Let's do it nice and quiet and civilized. We'll tell them that the boss has changed his mind. We'll tell them they're to be delivered to him as soon as possible. We'll forget and forgive, we'll take them up to the cabin for a drink, slip them the knockout drops then ease them soft and gently over the side.' "

"A charming fellow. We drown peacefully and even if we do wash up somewhere there'll be no bullet holes to start people asking questions."

"But a post-mortem can always show the presence of poison or narcotics—"

"Any post-mortem carried out on us," I interrupted heavily, "could be made without the doctor taking his hands from his pockets. If there are no broken bones you can't determine anything about the cause of death from a couple of nice clean shiny skeletons which would be all that was left after the denizens of the deep had finished with us. Or maybe the sharks eat bones, too: I wouldn't know."

"Do you have to talk like that?" she asked coldly.

"I'm only trying to cheer myself up." I handed her a couple of lifebelts. "Adjust the shoulder straps so that you can wear them both round your waist, one above the other. Be careful that you don't strike the CO_2 release accidentally. Wait till you are in the water before you inflate." I was already shrugging into my own harness. She appeared to be taking her time about adjusting the straps so I said: "Please hurry."

"There is no hurry," she said. "Henry said 'I suppose we'll have to wait a couple of hours before we do anything' and Fleck said, 'Yes, that at least.' Maybe they're going to wait until it gets really dark."

"Or maybe they don't want the crew to see anything. The reasons don't matter. What does matter is that the two-hour delay refers to the time when they intend ditching us. Maybe there *is* an island and they want to get well past it in case we should be washed up there before the sharks get to us. They could come for us any time. And you're overlooking the fact that when they do discover we're missing the first thing they'll do is to back-track and search. I don't much fancy being run down by a schooner or chopped to pieces by a propeller blade or just used for a little target practice. The sooner we're gone the less chance we have of being picked up when they do discover we're missing."

"I hadn't thought of that," she admitted.

"It's like the colonel told you," I said. "Bentall thinks of everything."

She didn't think that worth any comment so we finished fixing the lifebelts in silence. I gave her the torch and asked her to hold it in position while I climbed up the ladder with the bottle-screw and two hardwood battens and set about opening the hatch. I placed one of the hardwood battens on the top rung, set one end of the bottle-screw on the wood directly above the rung and unscrewed the upper eyebolt until it was firmly against the other batten which I'd placed under the hatch, to spread the load. I could hear the rain drumming furiously on the hatch and shivered involuntarily at the prospect of the imminent soaking, which was pretty silly when I came to consider just how much wetter I would be a few seconds later.

Forcing that hatch-cover was easy. Either the wood of the cover was old and dry or the screws holding the bolt in position were rusted for I'd only given the central shank of the bottle-screw half-a-dozen turns, the counter-threaded eyebolts steadily forcing themselves further apart, when I heard the first creak of the wood beginning to give way and splinter. Another half-dozen turns and suddenly all resistance to my turning had ceased. The bolt had come clear of its moorings and the way out was clear—if, that was to say, Fleck and his friends weren't standing there patiently waiting to blow my head off as soon as it appeared above the level of the hatch. There was only one way to find that out, it didn't appeal much but at least it was logical. I would stick my head out and see what happened to it.

I handed down the battens and bottle-screw, checked that the two water drums were conveniently to hand, softly told Marie to switch off the torch, eased the hatch-cover open a few inches and cautiously felt for the bolt. It was just where it ought to have been, lying loose on top of the hatch-cover. I lowered it gently to the deck, bent my back as I took another two steps up the ladder, hooked my fingers over the edge of the hatch-cover and straightened both back and arm in one movement so that the hinged cover swung vertically open and my head was suddenly two feet above deck level. A jack-in-the-box couldn't have done any better. Nobody shot me.

Nobody shot me because there was nobody there to shoot me, and there was nobody there to shoot me because no one but a very special type of moron would have ventured out on that deck without an absolutely compelling reason. Even then he would have required a suit of armour. If you were willing to stand at the bottom of Niagara Falls and say to yourself that it was only raining, then you could have said it was raining that night. If anyone ever gets around to inventing a machine gun that fires water instead of bullets I'll know exactly what it will be like at the receiving end. Enormous cold drops of water, so close together as to be almost a solid wall, lashed the schooner with a ferocity and intensity I would not have believed possible. The decks were a welter of white seething foam as those cannonball giant drops disintegrated on impact and rebounded high into the air, while the sheer physical weight, the pitiless savagery of that torrential rain drumming on your bent back was nothing short of terrifying. Within five seconds I was literally soaked to the skin. I had to fight the almost overwhelming impulse to pull that cover shut over my head and retreat to the haven of that suddenly warm and dry and infinitely desirable hold. But then I thought of Fleck and his knock-out drops and of a couple of nice new shiny skeletons on the floor of the sea, and I had the hatch-cover fully back and was on deck, calling softly for the water drums, before I was properly aware of what I was doing.

Fifteen seconds later Marie and the two drums were on deck and I was lowering the hatch-cover back into position and placing the bolt in approximately the original position in case someone did venture out later on a tour of inspection.

With the darkness and blinding rain visibility didn't exceed a few feet and we felt rather than saw our way to the stern of the schooner. I leaned far over the rail on the port counter to try to establish the position of the screw, for although the schooner was making hardly any more than three knots now—I supposed the lack of visibility must have forced Fleck to reduce speed—even so, that screw could still chop us up pretty badly. At least that.

At first I could see nothing, just a sea surface that was no longer that but a churned and hissing expanse of milky white froth, but my eyes were gradually becoming more adjusted to the darkness and after a minute or so I could clearly make out the smooth black water in the rain-free shelter under the long overhang of the schooner's stern. Not quite black—it was black flecked with the sparkling iridescence of phosphorus, and it wasn't long before I traced the area of maximum turbulence that gave rise to the phosphorescence. That was where the screw was—and it was far enough forward to let us drop off over the stern-post without any fear of being sucked into the vortex of the screw.

Marie went first. She held a water drum in one hand while I lowered her by the other until she was half-submerged in the water. Then I let go. Five seconds later I was in the water myself.

No one heard us go, no one saw us go. And we didn't see Fleck and his schooner go. He wasn't using his steaming lights that night. With the line of business he was in, he'd probably forgotten where the switch was.

CHAPTER THREE

Tuesday 7 P.M.-Wednesday 9 A.M.

AFTER the numbing stinging cold of that torrential rain the water in the sea was almost blissfully warm. There were no waves, any that dared show their heads were beaten flat by that deluge, and what little swell there was was long enough to be no more than a gentle undulation on the surface of the sea. The wind still seemed to be from the east: that was if my assumption that the schooner had still been travelling south had been correct.

For the first thirty seconds or so I couldn't see Marie. I knew she could be only yards away but the rain bouncing off the water raised so dense and impenetrable a curtain that nothing at sea level could be seen through its milky opacity. I shouted, twice, but there was no reply. I took half-a-dozen strokes, towing the can behind me, and literally bumped into her. She was coughing and spluttering as if she had swallowed some water, but she still retained hold of her water drum and seemed otherwise unharmed. She was high in the water so she must at least have remembered to operate the CO_2 release switch on her lifebelt.

I put my head close to hers and said: "All right?"

"Yes." She coughed some more and said: "My face and neck. That rain—they feel cut."

It was too dark to see whether her face was, in fact, cut. But I could believe it, my own face felt as if it had blundered into a wasp's nest. Black mark for Bentall. The first and most obvious thing that I should have done after opening that hatch and feeling the lash of that cannonading rain should have been to dig some of the left-over clothes out of our suitcases and wrap them round our heads, bandanna-fashion. But too late for tears now. I reached for the plastic bag attached to my drum, ripped it open and spread the blanket over our heads. We could still feel the impact of that rain like a shower of huge hailstones but at least our skins were no longer exposed. It was better than nothing.

When I'd finished arranging it Marie said: "What do we do now? Stay here in our tent or start swimming?"

I passed up all the obvious remarks about wondering whether we should swim for Australia or South America, they didn't even begin to seem funny in the circumstances, and said: "I think we should try to move away from here. If this rain keeps up Fleck will never find us. But there's no guarantee that it will last. We might as well swim west, that's the way the wind and the swell are running, it's roughly the direction in which the island would lie if Fleck hasn't altered course too much, and it's easiest for us."

"Isn't that the way Fleck would think, and move to the west looking for us?"

"If he thinks we're only half as twisted as he is himself, he'll probably figure we've gone in the other direction. Heads you win, tails you lose. Come on."

We made poor speed. As she'd said, she was no shakes as a swimmer, and those two drums and the soggy heavy blanket didn't help us much, but we did cover a fair bit of ground in the first hour, swimming for ten minutes, resting for five. If it hadn't been for the thought that we could do this sort of thing for the next month and still not arrive anywhere, it would have been quite pleasant: the sea was still warm, the rain was beginning to ease and the sharks stayed to home.

After an hour and a half or what I guessed to be approximately that, during which Marie became very quiet, rarely speaking, not even answering when I spoke to her, I said: "Enough. This'll do us. Any energy we have left we'll use for survival. If Fleck swings this far off course it's just bad luck and not much that we can do about it."

I let my legs sink down into the sea, then let out an involuntary exclamation as if I had been bitten or stung. Something large and solid had brushed by my leg, and although there are a lot of large and solid things in the sea all I could think of was of something about fifteen feet long with a triangular fin and a mouth like an unsprung bear-trap. And then it came to me that I'd felt no swirl or disturbance in the water and I cautiously lowered my legs again just as Marie said: "What is it? What's the matter?"

"I wish old Fleck *would* bring his schooner by here," I said yearningly. "That would be the end of both of them." It wasn't that something large and solid had brushed by my leg, it had been my leg brushing by something large and solid, which was a different thing altogether. "I'm standing in about four feet of water."

There was a momentary pause, then she said: "Me, too." It was the slow dazed answer of one who cannot believe something: more accurately, of one who can't understand something, and I found it vaguely puzzling. "What do you think—"

"Land, dear girl," I said expansively. I felt a bit light-headed with relief, I hadn't given tuppence for our chances of survival. "Must be that island we thought we saw. The way the sea-bed is sloping up it can be nothing else. Now's our chance to see those dazzling sands and waving palms and the brown-skinned beauties we've heard so much about. Give me your hand."

There was no answering levity or even gladness from her, she just took my hand in silence as I transferred the blanket to my other hand and started feeling my cautious way up the rapidly shelving sea-floor. In less than a minute we were standing on rock, and on any other night we would have been high and dry. In that rain, we were high and wet. But we were high. Nothing else mattered.

We lifted both water drums on to the shore and I draped the blanket over Marie's head: the rain had slackened, but slackening on that night was a comparative thing only, it was still fierce enough to be hurtful. I said: "I'm just going to take a brief look round. Back in five minutes."

"All right," she said dully. It didn't seem to matter whether I came or went.

I was back in two minutes, not five. I'd taken eight steps

and fallen into the sea on the other side and it didn't take me long to discover that our tiny island was only about four times as long as it was broad and consisted of nothing but rock. I would have liked to see Robinson Crusoe making out on that little lot. Marie hadn't moved from where I had left her.

"It's just a little rock in the middle of the sea," I reported. "But at least we're safe. For the present anyway."

"Yes." She rubbed the rock with the toe of her sandal. "It's coral, isn't it?"

"I suppose so." As with many others, the sun-drenched coral islands of the Pacific had formed a staple part of my earlier reading diet, but when I incautiously sat down to take the weight off my feet and stock of the situation my youthful enthusiasms vanished pretty rapidly. If this was coral it felt like the sort of thing an Indian fakir might graduate to after he'd mastered the easier stuff, like sleeping on a bed of red-hot nails. The rock was hard, broken, jagged and with frequent spiny razor-sharp edges. I pushed myself quickly to my feet, careful not to cut my hand on the coral, picked up the two drums and set them down on the highest part of the reef. I went back for Marie, took her arm and we sat down side by side on the drums with our backs to the wind and the rain. She offered me part of the blanket as protection, and I wasn't too proud to take it. It at least gave the illusion of shelter.

I talked to her for some time, but she had only monosyllables to offer in return. Then I dug a couple of cigarettes out from the packet I'd stowed in my water drum and offered her one, which she took, but that wasn't very successful either for the blanket leaked like a sieve and inside a minute both cigarettes were completely sodden. After ten minutes or so I said: "What's the matter, Marie? I agree that this is not the Grand Pacific Hotel, but at least we're alive."

"Yes." A pause, then matter of factly: "I thought I was going to die out there tonight. I expected to die. I was so sure I would that this—well, it's a sort of anti-climax. It's not real. Not yet. You understand?"

"No. What made you sure you were going to—" I broke off for a moment. "Don't tell me that you're still thinking along the same daft lines as you were last night?"

She nodded in the darkness. I felt the movement of the blanket rather than saw that of her head.

"I'm sorry, I really am. I can't help it. Maybe I'm not well, it's never been like this before," she said helplessly. "You look into the future but almost all the time there isn't any but if you do catch glimpses of it you're not there yourself. It's a kind of curtain drawn between you and tomorrow, and because you can't see past it you feel that there is none. No tomorrow, I mean."

"Superstitious rubbish," I said shortly. "Just because you're tired and out of sorts and soaked and shivering, you start having recourse to those morbid fancies. You're no help to me, just no help at all. Half the time I think Colonel Raine was right and that you would make a first-class partner in this godforsaken racket of ours: and half the time I'm convinced that you're going to be a deadweight round my neck and drag me under." It was cruel, but I meant to be kind. "God knows how you've managed to survive in this business until now."

"I told you it's new, something completely new for me. It *is* superstitious nonsense and I'll not mention it again." She reached out and touched my hand. "It's so terribly unfair to you. I'm sorry."

I didn't feel proud of myself at all. I let the subject go and returned to the consideration of the South Pacific. I was coming to the conclusion that I didn't much care for the South Pacific. The rain was the worst I'd ever known: coral was nasty sharp dangerous stuff: it was inhabited by a bunch of homicidally-minded characters: and, another shattered illusion, the nights could be very cold indeed. I felt clammy and chilled under the clinging wetness of that blanket and both of us were shaken by uncontrollable bouts of shivering which grew more frequent as the night wore on. At one stage it seemed to me that the sensible and logical thing for us to do would be to lie down in the very much warmer sea water and spend the night like that, but when I went, briefly, to test this theory, I changed my mind. The water was warm enough, what changed my mind was a tentacle that appeared from a cleft in the coral and wrapped itself round my left ankle: the octopus to which it belonged couldn't have weighed more than a few pounds but it still took most of my sock with it as I wrenched my leg away, which gave me some idea of what to expect if its big brother happened by.

It was the longest, the most miserable night I have ever known. It must have been about midnight when the rain eased off, but it continued in a steady drizzle until shortly before dawn. Sometimes I dozed off, sometimes Marie did, but when she did it was a restless troubled sleep, her breathing too shallow and quick, her hands too cold, her forehead too warm. Sometimes we both rose and stumbled around precariously on the rough slippery rock to get our circulation moving again, but mostly we just sat in silence.

I stared out into the rain and the darkness and I thought of just three things during the interminable hours of that night: the island we were on, Captain Fleck and Marie Hopeman.

I knew little enough about Polynesian islands, but I did recall that those coral islets were of two types: atolls, and barrier reefs for larger islands. If we were on the former, a broken, circular and probably uninhabited ring of coral islets, the future looked bleak indeed: but if it were part of a reef enclosing the lagoon round a large and possibly inhabited island, then we might still be lucky.

I thought of Captain Fleck. I thought of how much I would give for the chance of meeting him again, and what would happen then, and I wondered why he had done what he had done and who was the man behind the kidnap and attempted murder. One thing seemed certain and that was that the missing scientists and their wives were going to stay missing: I had been classified as redundant and would never now find out where they were or what had happened to them. Right then I wasn't so worried about them, the longing to meet up with Fleck was the predominant emotion in my mind. A strange man. A hard callous ruthless man but a man I would have sworn was not all bad. But I knew nothing of him. All I did know now with certainty was his reason for deciding to wait till nine o'clock before getting rid of us: he must have known that the schooner had been passing a coral reef and if they'd thrown us overboard at seven o'clock we might well have been washed up before morning. If we had been found, identified and traced back to the Grand Pacific Hotel, Fleck would have had a great deal of explaining to do.

And I thought of Marie Hopeman, not as a person but as a problem. Whatever dark forebodings had possessed her had had no validity in themselves, they were just symptomatic of something else, and I no longer had any doubts about what that something else was. She was sick, not mentally but physically: the succession of bad flights from England to Suva and then the night on the boat and now this all added up to far too little sleep and too little food, and the lack of those coupled with physical exhaustion had lowered her resistance till she was pretty open to anything that came along and what was coming along was fever or chill or just plain old-fashioned flu: there had certainly been plenty of that around when we had left London. I didn't like to think what the outcome was going to be if she had to spend another twenty-four hours in sea-soaked clothes on this bare and exposed islet. Or even twelve.

Sometime during the night my eyes became so tired from staring into the rain and the darkness that I began to have some mild forms of hallucination. I thought I could see lights moving in the rain-blurred distance, and that was bad enough: but when I began to imagine I could hear voices, I resolutely shut my eyes and tried to force myself into sleep. Sitting hunched forward on a water-can with only a soaking blanket for cover, falling off to sleep is quite a feat. But I finally made it, about an hour before the dawn.

I awoke with the sun hot on my back. I awoke to the sound of voices, real voices, this time. I awoke to the most beautiful sight I had ever seen.

I flung back the overhanging blanket as Marie stirred and rubbed the sleep from her eyes. It was a gleaming glorious dazzling world, a peaceful sun-warmed panorama of beauty that made the long night just gone a dark nightmare that could never have been.

A string of coral isles and reefs, reefs painted in the most impossible greens and yellows and violets and browns and whites, stretched away on both sides from us in two huge curving horns that all but encircled and enclosed a huge lagoon of burnished aquamarine, and, beyond the lagoon, the most remarkably-shaped island I'd ever laid eyes on. It was as if some giant hand had cut a giant Stetson down the middle, and thrown one half away. The island reached its highest point in the extreme north, where it plunged vertically down into the sea: from this peak, it sloped down steeply to the east and south—I could only guess that it would be the same on the west—and where the wide brim of the Stetson would have been was a flat plain running down to beaches of dazzling white sand which, even at that hour of the morning and at a distance of three miles, was positively hurtful to the eyes. The mountain itself, a rich bluish-purple in that early sunlight, was bald and bare of any vegetation: the plain below was bare, too, only scrub bushes and grass, with scattered palms down near the water's edge.

But I didn't spend much time on the scenery: I'd like to think I'd be right in there with the next man when it came to appreciating the beauties of nature, but not after a rain-soaked and chilly night on an exposed reef: I was far more interested in the out-rigger canoe that was coming arrowing in towards us through the mirror-calm waters of that green lagoon.

There were two men in it, big sturdy brown-skinned men with huge mops of crinkly black hair, and their paddles were driving in perfect unison into and through the gleaming glass of those waters faster than I would have believed possible, moving so quickly that the flying spray from the paddles was a continuously iridescent rainbow glitter in the rays of the rising sun. Less than twenty yards away from the reef they dug their paddles deep, slowed down their outrigger canoe and brought it slewing round to a standstill less than ten feet away. One of the men jumped out into the thigh deep water, waded towards us then climbed nimbly up the coral. His feet were bare but the sharp rock didn't worry him any that I could see. His face was a comical mixture of astonishment and good humour, astonishment at finding two white people on a reef at that hour in the morning, good humour because the world was a wonderful place and always would be. You don't see that kind of face often, but when you do you can never mistake it. Good humour won. He gave us a huge white grin and said something that meant just nothing at all to me.

He could see that it meant nothing at all and he wasn't the kind of man to waste time. He looked at Marie, shook his head and clucked his tongue as his eyes took in the pale face, the two unnaturally red patches on her cheeks and the purplish shadows under her eyes, then grinned again, ducked his head as in greeting, picked her up and waded out to the canoe. I made it under my own steam, lugging the two water drums along.

The canoe was fitted with a mast, but there was no wind yet, so we had to paddle across the lagoon to the island. At least the two brown men did and I was glad to leave it to them. What they did with that canoe would have had me gasping and wheezing in five minutes and in a hospital bed in ten. They'd have been a sensation at Henley. They kept it up non-stop for the twenty minutes it took us to cross the lagoon, churning up the water as if the Loch Ness monster was after them, but still finding time and energy to chatter and laugh with each other all the way. If they were representative of the rest of the island's population, we had fallen into good hands.

And that there were others on the island was obvious. As we came close to the shore, I could count at least half a dozen houses, stilted affairs with the floor about three feet off the ground and enormously deep-eaved thatched roofs that swept down steeply from high ridge-poles to within four or five feet of the ground. The houses had neither doors nor windows, understandably enough, for they had no walls either, except for one, the largest, in a clearing near the shore, close in to a stand of coconut palms: the other houses were set further back and to the south. Still further south was a metal and corrugated iron eyesore, grey in colour, like an old-fashioned crushing plant and hopper in a quarry. Beyond this again was a long low shed, with a slightly sloping corrugated iron roof: it must have been a real pleasure to work under that when the sun was high in the sky.

We were heading in just to the right of a small pier—not a real landing-stage with anchored piles but a thirty foot long floating platform of bound logs, secured on the shore end by ropes tied round a couple of tree stumps—when I saw a man lying on the shore. A white man, sunbathing. He was a lean wiry old bird with a lot of white hair all over his face, dark spectacles on his eyes and a grubby towel strategically placed across his midriff. He appeared to be asleep, but he wasn't, for when the bow of the canoe crunched into the sand he sat up with a jerk, whipped off his dark glasses, peered myopically in our direction, pawed around the sand till he located a pair of slightly-tinted spectacles, stuck them across the bridge of his nose, said "God bless my soul" in an agitated voice, jumped to his feet with remarkable speed for such an old duffer and hurried into a nearby palm-thatched hut, clutching his towel round him.

"Quite a tribute to you, my dear," I murmured. "You looking like something the tide washed up and the old boy about ninety-nine, but you can still knock him for six."

"He didn't seem any too pleased to see us, I thought," she said doubtfully. She smiled at the big man who'd just lifted her from the canoe and set her on her feet on the sand and went on: "Maybe he's a recluse. Maybe he's one of those remittance man beach-combers and other white people are the last he wants to see."

"He's just gone for his best bib and tucker," I said confidently. "He'll be back in a minute to give us the big hand."

And he was. We'd hardly reached the top of the beach when he reappeared from the hut, dressed in a white shirt and white ducks, with a panama on his head. He'd a white beard, flowing white moustache and plentiful thick white hair. If Buffalo Bill had ever worn tropical whites and a straw hat, he'd have been a dead ringer for Buffalo Bill.

He came puffing down to meet us, his hand outstretched in greeting. I'd made no mistake about the warmth of welcome, but I had about the age: he wasn't a day over sixty, perhaps only fifty-five, and a pretty fit fifty-five at that.

"God bless my soul, God bless my soul!" He wrung our hands as if we'd brought him the first prize in the Irish Sweepstake. "What a surprise! What a surprise! Morning dip, you know—just drying off—couldn't believe my eyes—where in all the world have you two come from? No, no, don't answer now. Straight up to my house. Delightful surprise. Delightful." He scurried off in front of us, god-blessing himself with every other step. Marie smiled at me and we walked after him.

He led us along a short path, across a white-shingled front, up a wide flight of six wooden steps into his house: like the others, the floor was well clear of the ground. But once inside I could see why, unlike the other houses, it had walls: it had to have to support the large bookcases and glass-covered show-cases that lined three quarters of the wall area of the room: the rest of the walls were given over to doors and window spaces, no glass in the windows, just screens of plaited leaves that could be raised or lowered as wished. There was a peculiar smell that I couldn't place at first. The floor seemed to be made of the mid-ribs of some type of leaf, coconut palm, probably, laid across close-set joists, and there was no ceiling as such, just steep-angled rafters with thatch above. I looked at this thatch for a long and very interested moment. There was a big old-fashioned roll-top desk in one corner and a large safe against the inside wall. There were some brightly coloured straw mats on the floor, most of which was given over to low-slung comfortable looking rattan chairs and settees, each with a low table beside it. A man could be comfortable in that room—especially with a drink in his hand.

The old boy—with that beard and moustache. I couldn't think of him as anything else—was a mind-reader.

"Sit down, sit down. Make yourselves comfortable. A drink? Yes, yes, of course, first of all a drink. You need it, you need it." He picked up a little bell, rang it furiously as if he were trying to see how much punishment it could stand before it came apart in his hands, replaced it and looked at me. "Too early in the morning for whisky, eh?"

"Not this morning."

"And you, young lady. Some brandy, perhaps? Eh? Brandy?"

"Thank you." She let him have the smile she never bothered letting me have and I could just about see the old boy's toes curling. "You are very kind."

I was just coming to the resigned conclusion that his staccato and repetitive way of talking was habitual and was going to be a little wearing if we had to stay with him for any length of time—and I had the thought, even then, that the voice was vaguely familiar to me—when a rear door opened and a Chinese youth came in. He was very short, very thin, dresed in khaki drill, and the only use he had for his facial muscles was to keep his expressions buttoned up for he didn't even bat an eyelid when he saw us.

"Ah, Tommy, there you are. We have guests, Tommy. Drinks. Brandy for the lady, a large whisky for the gentleman and—let me see now, yes, yes, perhaps I rather think I will—a small whisky for me. Then run a bath. For the lady." I could get by with a shave. "Then breakfast. You haven't breakfasted yet?"

I assured him we hadn't.

"Excellent. Excellent!" He caught sight of the two men who had rescued us standing outside on the white shingles with the water drums, raised a bushy white eyebrow in my direction and said: "What's in those?"

"Our clothes."

"Indeed? Yes, yes, I see. Clothes." Any opinion he held as to our eccentricities in the choice of suitcases he kept to himself. He went to the doorway. "Just leave them there, James. You've done a splendid job, both of you. Splendid. I'll speak to you later."

I watched the two men smile broadly, then turn away. I said: "They speak English?"

"Certainly. Of course they do."

"They didn't speak any to us."

"Um. They didn't, eh?" He tugged his beard, Buffalo Bill to the life. "You speak any to them?"

I thought, then grinned: "No."

"There you are, then. You might have been any of a score of nationalities." He turned as the Chinese boy came in, took the drinks from the tray and handed them to us. "Your excellent health."

I grunted something appropriate and as short as it could decently be and went for that drink like a thirst-stricken camel for the nearest oasis. I insulted a perfectly good Scotch by swallowing half of it at one gulp, but even so it tasted wonderful and I was about to start on the remainder when the old boy said: "Well, preliminaries over, decencies observed. Your story, sir. Let's have it."

It brought me up short and I looked at him cautiously. I could be wrong about him being a hoppity old fusspot. I was wrong. The bright blue eyes were shrewd, and what little of his face was available for expression seemed to indicate a certain carefulness, if not actual wariness. Being a little odd in your behaviour doesn't necessarily mean that you're a little odd in the head.

I gave it to him, short and straight. I said: "My wife and I were en route to Australia, by plane. During an overnight stop at Suva we were taken from our hotel room at three in the morning by a Captain Fleck and two Indians, forced to board his schooner and locked up. Last night we heard them planning to murder us, so we broke out from the hold where they'd put us—it was a bad night and they didn't see us go—jumped over the side and after some time washed up on a coral reef. Your men found us there this morning."

"God bless my soul! What an extraordinary tale. Extraordinary!" He kept on blessing himself and shaking his head for a bit, then looked up at me from under bushy white eyebrows. "If we could have it with a little more detail, perhaps?"

So I gave it to him again, telling him everything that had happened since we had arrived in Suva. He peered at me through those tinted glasses all the time I was speaking and when I finished he sighed, did some more headshaking and said: "Incredible. The whole thing's quite incredible!"

"Do you mean that literally?"

"What? What? That I don't believe you? God bless——"

"This might convince you," Marie interrupted. She slipped off her shoe and peeled back the plaster to show the two deep fang marks on her foot. "The rat caused that."

"But I *do* believe it, young lady! It's just that everything is so bizarre, so—so fantastic. Of course it's true, how else would you be here? But—but why should this villainous fellow, this Captain Fleck kidnap you and talk of killing you? It all seems so purposeless, so mad."

"I've no idea," I said. "The only thing I can think of—and even that is ridiculous—is that I'm a scientist, a specialist in fuel technology and maybe someone wanted to extract some information from me. Why on earth they should want to do that I just can't imagine. And how the skipper of an obscure schooner knew that we should be flying out to Australia via Fiji—well, it doesn't make any kind of sense at all."

"As you say, it makes no sense at all, Mr.—ah—Bless my soul, you must forgive me! I haven't even asked your names yet!"

"Bentall. John Bentall. And this is my wife, Marie." I smiled at him. "And you don't need to tell me who you are. It's just come back to me. Dr. Harold Witherspoon—

64

Professor Witherspoon, I should say. The doyen of British archaeologists."

"You know me then? You recognized me?" The old boy seemed quite bucked about it.

"Well, you do get a good deal of newspaper space," I said tactfully. Professor Witherspoon's love of the public limelight was a byword. "And I saw your series of lectures on television, about a year ago."

He didn't look so pleased any longer. He suddenly looked downright suspicious, and his eyes narrowed as he said: "You interested in archaeology, Mr. Bentall? Know anything about it, I mean?"

"I'm like a million others, professor. I know about this Egyptian tomb and this lad Tutenkhamon who was in it. But I couldn't begin to spell his name, I doubt if I'm even pronouncing it properly."

"So. Good. Forgive my asking, I'll explain later. I am being most remiss, most remiss. This young lady here is far from well. Fortunately, I'm a bit of a doctor. Have to be, you know. Living your life at the back of beyond." He bustled out of the room, returned with a medical case, took out a thermometer and asked Marie to put it in her mouth while he took her wrist.

I said: "I don't want to appear ungrateful or unappreciative of your hospitality, Professor, but my business is rather urgent. How soon will we be able to leave here and get back to Suva?"

"Not long." He shrugged. "There's a ketch from Kandavu—that's about a hundred miles or so north of here—calls in about every six weeks. It was last here, let me see—yes, about three weeks ago. So, another three weeks."

That was handy. Three weeks. Not long, he said, but they probably had a different time scale on those islands and looking out over that shimmering lagoon with the coral reefs beyond I found it easy to understand why. But I didn't think Colonel Raine would be so happy if I just sat back and admired the lagoon for three weeks, so I said: "Any planes ever pass this way?"

"No ships, no planes, nothing." He shook his head and kept on shaking it as he examined the thermometer. "Bless my soul. A hundred and three and a pulse of 120. Dear, dear! You're a sick young lady, Mrs. Bentall, probably taken it from London with you. Bath, bed and breakfast in that order." He held up his hand as Marie murmured a token protest. "I insist. I insist. You can have Carstairs' room. Red Carstairs, my assistant," he explained. "In Suva at present, recuperating from malaria. Rife in those parts. Expect him back on the next ship. And you, Mr. Bentall—I expect you'd like a sleep, too." He gave a deprecating little laugh. "I daresay you didn't sleep too soundly out on that reef last night."

"A clean-up, shave and a couple of hours on one of those very inviting chairs on your verandah will do me," I said. "No planes either, eh? Any boats on the island I could hire?"

"The only boat on the island is the one belonging to James and John. Not their right names, those natives from Kandavu have unpronounceable names. They're here on contract to supply fresh fish and whatever food and fruit they can gather. They wouldn't take you anyway—even if they would, I'd absolutely forbid it. Absolutely."

"Too dangerous?" If it was, I was right with him.

"Of course. And illegal. The Fijian Government forbids inter-island proa travel in the cyclone season. Heavy penalties. Very heavy penalties. For breaking the law."

"No radio we could use to send a message?"

"No radio. Not even a radio receiver." The professor smiled. "When I'm investigating something that happened many thousands of years ago I find contact with the outside world disturbing in the extreme. All I have is an old-fashioned hand-wound gramophone."

He seemed a harmless old duffer, so I didn't tell him what he could do with his gramophone. Instead, while Marie bathed, I had another drink, then after a shave, change and first-class breakfast, stretched out on a low rattan armchair in the shade of the verandah.

I meant to do some heavy thinking for it seemed to me that the situation was such that it was long past time that I showed some rudimentary signs of intelligence, but I'd reckoned without my weariness, the warmth of the sun, the effects of a couple of double Scotches on an empty stomach and the soporific sound of the trade-wind whispering its sibilant clicking way through the nodding plams. I thought of the island and how anxious I'd been to leave it and what Professor Witherspoon would say if he knew that the only way to get me off now would be by sheer force. I thought of Captain Fleck and I thought of the Professor, and I thought of them both with admiration, Fleck for the fact that he was twice as smart as I'd thought—which made him at least twice as smart as me—and the Professor for the fact that he was as polished and accomplished a liar as I'd ever met. And then I fell asleep.

CHAPTER FOUR

THERE was a war on and I was right in the middle of it. I couldn't see who or what was to the right or the left of me and I wasn't even sure whether it was day or night. But there was a war on, I was sure of that. Heavy artillery, laying down a barrage before an attack. The low ominous rumble of explosions, the very earth shaking. I was no hero. Let me get out of the way. I wasn't going to be cannonfodder for anyone. I moved, seemed to stumble and felt the sharp pain in my right arm. Shrapnel, perhaps, or a bullet. Maybe they'd invalid me out, it would be a change from the front line. Then I opened my eyes and found that I wasn't in the front line: I'd achieved the near impossible feat of falling out of an armchair and had landed on the wooden floor of Professor Witherspoon's verandah. I seemed to have made a neat one point landing. On my right elbow. My elbow hurt.

I'd been dreaming, but I hadn't been dreaming about the rumble of the explosions and the earth-shaking. As I got to my feet, clutching my arm and trying not to hop around too much, I heard another couple of distant muffled thuds and the floor of the verandah shook both times, quite violently. I hadn't even had time to try to guess at the source of those disturbances when I caught sight of Professor Witherspoon standing in the doorway leading in off the verandah, his face filled with concern. At least, his voice was, so I assumed that what lay behind the foliage would reflect his voice.

"My dear fellow, my dear fellow!" He came hurrying forward, hands outstretched as if he thought I was going to collapse at any moment. "I heard the sound of the fall. By jove, it was loud! You must have hurt yourself. What happened?"

"I fell out of my chair," I said patiently. "I thought it was the Second Front. It's my nerves."

"Dear me, dear me, dear me!" He fussed and fluttered around without achieving anything. "Have you—have you damaged anything?"

"Only my pride." I felt my elbow with cautious fingers. "Nothing broken. Just numbed. What's making all that damned racket?"

"Ha!" He smiled, relieved. "I thought you'd want to know that. I'm just about to show you—thought you'd like to have a look over the place anyway." He regarded me with quizzical eyes. "Enjoy your two hour snooze?"

"Except for the waking-up bit, yes."

"You've been asleep for six hours, Mr. Bentall."

I looked at my watch and looked at the sun, already far past the meridian, and realised that he was right, but it didn't seem worth making a fuss over so I merely said, politely: "I hope that didn't cause you any trouble? Having to stay behind and look after me when you may have wished to be working."

"Not at all, not at all. No time clock here, young man. I work when I want to. Hungry?"

"Thank you, no."

"Thirsty? Some Hong-Kong beer before we go. Excellent stuff. Chilled. Eh?"

"Sounds fine, Professor."

So we went and drank his beer and it was as good as he had promised. We had it in the living-room where he'd first taken us and I looked at the various exhibits in the glass-fronted cases. To me they were only a mouldy collection of bones and fossils and shells, of stone pestles and mortars, of charred timber and clay utensils and curiously shaped stones. It was no difficulty at all not to show any interest and I didn't show any interest because the Professor had shown signs of being wary of any person interested in archaeology. But it seemed he'd given up being wary for when he caught my roving eye, he said enthusiastically: "Magnificent collection of specimens, eh? Magnificent!"

"I'm afraid it's hardly in my line," I began apologetically. "I don't know—"

"Of course not, of course not! Wouldn't expect you to." He went across to his roll-top desk, pulled out a handful of papers and magazines from the central drawer and gave them to me. "Those may help you understand better."

I leafed quickly through the magazines and papers. Nearly all of them were dated six months previously and of eight papers, five London national dailies and three major U.S. papers, no less than seven had given the professor page one headlines. It must have been a field day for the old boy. Most of the headlines were of the 'Archaeological Discovery of the Century' variety, far outranking in importance Tutenkhamon, Troy or the Dead Sea Scrolls. Every latest archaeological discovery, of course, was usually acclaimed in the same way, but there did appear to be some basis for this latest claim: Oceania, it seemed, had long been the dark continent of archeological research, but now Professor Witherspoon claimed to have discovered on the island of Vardu, south of the Fijis, complete proof of the migration of the Polynesians from the south-east of Asia and of there being some form of primitive civilization in those islands as far back as 5,000 B.C., some 5,000 years before the previous earliest estimate. Three magazines carried coloured spreads of the story, and one had a very fine picture of the professor and Dr. 'Red' Carstairs standing by what looked to me like a cracked paving stone but which the caption said was part of a stepped tomb. Dr. Carstairs was a remarkable looking character, six and a half feet tall if he was an inch, with a flaming red handle-bar moustache of heroic proportions.

"I missed it all, I'm afraid," I said. "I was in the Middle East at the time and pretty cut off from everything. This must have caused a terrific stir."

"It was the crowning moment of my life," he said simply.

"It must have been. Why haven't I read anything about this recently?"

"There's been nothing about it in the papers since and there won't be till I'm through here," he said darkly. "I foolishly granted news agencies, papers and magazines facilities to come here after my first announcement had caused some stir. They hired a special ship from Suva. Descended on me like locusts—like locusts, I tell you, sir. All over the shop, interfering, poking, ruining weeks of intensive work. Helpless, I was completely helpless." The anger deepened. "And there were spies among them."

"Spies? You must forgive me—"

"Rival archaeologists. Trying to steal my thunder." That would be just about the ultimate crime as far as the old boy was concerned. "Trying to steal other things, too, some of the most valuable finds ever made in the Pacific. Never trust a fellow archaeologist, my boy," he said bitterly. "Never trust 'em."

I said I wouldn't and he went on: "One of them actually had the effrontery to arrive here in a yacht a couple of months ago. American millionaire who does archaeology as a hobby. Just wanted credit. Damned impertinence to say he'd lost his way. Never trust an archaeologist. Threw him off. That's why I was suspicious of you. How was I to know you weren't a reporter, eh? At first, that is?"

"I quite understand, professor," I said soothingly.

"Got the government behind me now, though," he went on triumphantly. "British territory this, of course. All access to the island forbidden till I'm through." He drained his glass.

"Well, well, shouldn't be bothering you with my troubles. Shall we go for this look round?"

"Pleasure. Mind if I see my wife first?"

"Certainly, certainly. You know the way."

Marie Hopeman stirred, turned and looked up at me sleepily as I opened the creaking door. The bed was a pretty primitive affair, a wooden frame with criss-cross stringing, but she seemed comfortable enough. I said: "Sorry if I wakened you. How's it going?"

"You didn't waken me. Ten times better now." She looked it, the blueness had gone from beneath her eyes and the harsh red spots from her cheeks. She stretched luxuriously. "I don't intend moving for hours and hours. He's very kind, isn't he?"

"Couldn't have fallen into better hands," I agreed. I didn't bother to keep my voice down. "Best thing would be for you to go to sleep again, my dear."

She blinked a bit at the 'my dear', but let it go. "It won't be too difficult. And you?"

"Professor Witherspoon is going to show me around. Apparently he's made some very important archaeological discoveries here. Should be very interesting." I added a few more banalities, bade her what I hoped old Witherspoon would consider a suitable tender farewell and left.

He was waiting for me on the verandah, pith helmet on head, malacca cane in hand. The British archaeologist abroad, he was perfect.

"This is where Hewell lives." He waved his stick in the direction of the thatched house nearest his own. "My overseer. American. Rough diamond, of course"—the tone of his voice lumped 180,000,000 citizens of the United States into the same category—"but able. Yes indeed. Very able. This next house is my guest house. Unused, but having it done up. Looks a bit airy, I admit"—he wasn't exaggerating, all it consisted of was a roof, floor and four supporting cornerposts—"but very comfortable. Adapted for the climate. Reed curtain divides it in half and all the walls—screens of plaited coconut leaves—can be lowered to the floor. Kitchen and bathroom behind—can't have them inside a house of this type. And that next long house belongs to the workers—the diggers."

"And this eyesore?" I nodded at the corrugated iron building "Quarry hopper or crusher?"

"Not a bad guess at all, my boy. It *is* ghastly, isn't it? Property—or ex-property—of the British Phosphate Commissioners. You can see the name on the side if you look closely. Their crushing mill. That flat-topped shed behind was the drying plant." He waved his malacca around in a sweeping half-circle. "Almost a year since they left, but still the place is covered in this damnable grey dust. Killed off most of the vegetation on this side of the island. Damnable!"

"It's not very nice," I agreed. "What's a British firm doing out in this forsaken part of the world?"

"Not purely British. International, but run mostly by New Zealand. Digging out the rock, of course. Phosphate of lime. They were taking out a thousand tons a day a year ago. Valuable stuff." He peered at me shrewdly. "Know anything of geology, hey?"

The professor seemed suspicious of anyone who knew anything about anything, so I said I didn't.

"Ah well, who does, these days?" he said cryptically. "But to put you in the picture, my boy. You must understand that this island once probably lay on the bottom of the sea—and as the bottom of the sea is about three miles down here, that was a fair depth. Then one day—geologically speaking you understand, it probably took a million years—the bottom came up to near the top. Upthrust or volcanic activity associated with the continuous outpouring of lava. Who knows?" He coughed deprecatingly. "When one knows a little of those things"—from the tone of his voice I gathered that if he knew only a little anybody who claimed to know a lot was a liar—"you are unwilling to be dogmatic about it. Anyway, the net result was that after a few aeons you had this massive underwater mountain with the peak not yet above water but less than 120 feet below the surface."

He peered at me, waiting for the obvious remark, so I obliged.

"How can you be so certain about something that happened millions of years ago?"

"Because this is a coral island," he said triumphantly, "and the polyps that build the coral reefs must live in water but die below 120 feet. Well, some time later—"

"Another million years?"

"Give or take a million. This must have been a big low-lying coral reef when it was upthrust below. This upthrust probably coincided with the beginning of the age of birds. This became a sanctuary for untold numbers of birds—there are many such in the Pacific—who stayed here for countless years. Eventually you had a layer of guano, up to perhaps fifty feet thick. Millions of tons of it, millions of tons—and then island, coral and guano subsided and sank to the floor of the sea."

It seemed to me that this island had had a pretty chequered history.

"Some time later," he went on, "up it comes again. By this time the actions of sea deposits and salt water had changed the guano into a very rich phosphate of lime. Then came the slow laborious process of soil forming, of growing grass, shrubs, trees, a veritable tropical paradise. Then, probably in the last ice age, along came the wandering sea-rovers from south-east Asia and settled in this idyllic spot."

"If it was all that idyllic, why did they leave it?"

"But they never left it! They never left it for the same reason that those fabulous deposits of lime phosphate weren't discovered until recently, though most other deposits in the Pacific had been worked out by the end of the last century. This, Mr. Bentall, is a highly volcanic region—there are still active volcanoes on the neighboring Tonga Islands, you know. In the space of a few hours a gigantic volcano erupted out of the sea, drowning half of this coral island and covering the other half—coral, phosphate, vegetation and the unfortunate people who lived here in a tremendous layer of basaltic lava. The 79 A.D. eruption that destroyed Pompeii," Professor Witherspoon finished disparagingly, "was a bagatelle compared to this."

I nodded at the mountain sloping up sharply behind us. "That's the volcano that was formed?"

"Yes, indeed."

"What happened to the other half of it?"

"Must have been some ground fault formed at the same time as the volcano. One night it just broke in half and vanished into the sea. It took the seabed with it and the coral reefs built out to the north: you can see that the lagoon is open there."

He marched on at a brisk pace apparently undisturbed by the thought that he lived in a very dicey spot where cataclysmic upheavals of a very final nature were of the order of the day. He was angling his way slightly uphill, and less than three hundred yards from the crushing mill we came to a sudden cleft in the side of the mountain. It was about seventy feet high and thirty wide, vertical at the sides and back and with a flat floor leading in to a circular hole in the mountainside. There were railway tracks of very narrow gauge coming out from the hole, running along the horizontal floor of the fissure then turning to the south where they dipped from view. There were two or three small sheds just outside the entrance, and from one of these came the humming sound I'd been hearing more and more clearly on the way up.

Petrol-driven generators. It had never occurred to me until then but of course if the professor and his assistants were prospecting about inside the mountain they would have to have electric power for light and probably also for ventilation.

"Well, here we are," the professor announced. "This is the spot where some curious intelligent prospector for the phosphate company noticed this peculiar fault in the mountainside, started digging through the top-soil and struck phosphate before he'd gone three feet. Heaven knows how many million tons of rock they took out—the mountain is a perfect honeycomb. Just as they were finishing up here somebody found a few pieces of pottery and curiously-shaped stones. An archaeologist in Wellington was shown them and immediately sent them to me." The professor coughed modestly. "The rest, of course, is history."

I followed the history-maker through the entrance and along a winding horizontal passage-way until we came to a huge circular excavation in the rock. It was a gigantic cavern, forty feet high, twenty by the encircling walls, supported by concrete columns and about two hundred feet in diameter. Half a dozen tiny electric lights, suspended from some of the pillars at about a height of ten feet, gave the dingy grey rock an eerie and forbidding appearance and were but token illumination at best. Spaced evenly round the perimeter of this cavern were five more tunnels, each with its own railway track.

"Well, what do you think of this, Mr. Bentall?"

"It looks like the catacombs in Rome," I said. "But not so cheery."

"It's a remarkable mining feat," the professor said severely. He didn't care for any flippancy about his nearest and dearest, and his nearest and dearest would always be those dank and gloomy holes in the ground. "Very difficult stuff to work with, this limestone, and when you have to support a thick layer of basaltic lava and half the weight of a volcano above it it becomes very tricky indeed. This mountainside is honeycombed with similar caverns, all joined by tunnels. Hexagonal system. Those domed roofs give the greatest structural strength, but there's a limit to their size. The mining company only managed to get out about a third of the available limestone before the cost of supporting pillars to hold the roof in place became prohibitive."

"Doesn't that make this blasting rather dangerous, then?" I thought an interested question might put me back in his good books.

"Well, yes, it is, rather," he said thoughtfuly. "Chance we have to take. Chance we must take. Interests of science. Come and see where our first discoveries were made."

He led the way straight across the cavern to the tunnel opposite to the one by which we'd entered and went down this, hopping briskly along the sleepers of the railway tracks. After about twenty yards we entered another cavern, in height, width and number of exit tunnels the duplicate of the one we had just left. There was no illumination here other than one single lamp suspended from the electric light cable that traversed the width of the cavern and vanished down the faraway tunnel, but it was enough to let me see that the two tunnels to the left had been blocked off by heavy vertical baulks of timber.

"What happened there, professor? Cave-in?"

"Afraid so." He shook his head. "Two tunnels and parts of the caverns to which they led collapsed at the same time. Had to shore up the tunnel entrances in case the collapse spread to this chamber. Before my time, of course. I believe three men perished in the right-hand cavern in there—they'd just started to excavate it. A bad business, a bad business." He paused for a few moments to let me see how bad he thought it had been, then said brightly: "Well, this is the historic spot."

It was a five-foot niche in the wall just to the right of the tunnel by which we'd entered the cavern. To me it was just a five-foot niche. But to Witherspoon it was a temple and he himself the officiating priest.

"This," he said reverently, "is where the mystery of Polynesia and the Polynesians was solved. It was here that were found the first adze-heads, stone mortars and pestles. It was this that triggered off the biggest archaeological discovery of our generation. Doesn't it make you think, Mr. Bentall?"

"It certainly does." I refrained from specifying the nature of my thoughts. Instead I reached out for a spur of rock, damp and slimy to the touch, and pulled it off with little effort. I said in surprise: "Pretty soft stuff, this. You'd think picks or pneumatic drills would be almost as effective as blasting for removing this stuff."

"And so they are, my boy, and so they are. But how would you like to tackle basalt with a pick and shovel?" he asked jovially. "A different proposition altogether."

"I'd forgotten about that," I confessed. "Of course, when the lava poured down it covered everything. What kind of stuff do you find in the basalt—pottery, stone utensils, axe handles, things like that?"

"To name only a very few," he nodded. He hesitated, then said: "To speak frankly, unlike the average merchant, I put only my worst goods in the shop window. The things you saw in my room I regard only as trinkets, as the merest trifles. I have one or two hidden caches in here—I wouldn't dream of even hinting to you where they are—that contain a fantastic collection of neolithic Polynesian relics that will astound the scientific world. Astound them."

He moved off again, but instead of crossing the chamber and following the electric cable and far-spaced lights down the opposite tunnel, he switched on a torch and turned into the first tunnel on his right, pointing out the various places from which those Polynesian relics had been recovered. He stopped in front of a particularly large excavation in the limestone and said: "And here we excavated the joists and timbers of what must be the oldest wooden house in the world. In an almost perfect state of preservation."

"And how old was that?"

"Seven thousand years, near enough," he said promptly. "Van Duprez, of Amsterdam, who was out here with all the newspaper people, says it's only four thousand. But the man's a fool, of course."

"What basis do you use for assessing the age of those things?" I asked curiously.

"Experience and knowledge," he said flatly. "Van Duprez, despite his inflated reputation, hasn't got a great deal of either. Man's a fool."

"Um," I said non-committally. I looked apprehensively at the third chamber now opening out before us. "How deep are we here?"

"About a hundred feet, I should say. Perhaps a hundred and twenty. Moving into the side of the mountain, you know. Nervous, Mr. Bentall?"

"Sure, I'm nervous. I never realized you archaeologists went so deep or that you could find any trace of early life so deep. This must be about a record, eh?"

"Close to it, close to it," he said complacently. "Thought they went pretty deep in the Nile valley and Troy, you know." He led the way across the third chamber into a tunnel sparsely illuminated with battery lamps. "We should find Hewell and his crew down here." He glanced at his watch. "They must be about due to pack up shortly. Been at it here all day."

They were still working when we arrived at the spot where the tunnel began to open out into a rudimentary fourth chamber. There were nine men there altogether, some prising out lumps of limestone with pickaxes and crowbars to add to the heap of rubble at their feet, others loading the rubble on to rubber-tyred wheel-barrows while a gigantic man clad only in denim trousers and singlet closely examined each lump with a powerful torch.

Both the workers and the man with the torch were worth looking at. The workers were all Chinese, unusually tall and heavily-built for members of their race, and looked about the toughest and hardest-bitten characters I'd ever seen. But it could have been pure illusion: that feeble light shining on sweat- and dust-coated faces would have made anyone seem unnatural.

But there was no illusion about the foreman who straightened from his examination of the rock and came to meet us. He *was* the toughest and hardest-bitten character I'd ever seen. He was about six feet three inches tall, but stunted for his breadth, with a couple of massive arms ending in five-fingered shovels that almost brushed his knees. His face looked as if it had been carved from solid rock by a sculptor whose only ambition was to get the job done in a hurry: there wasn't a curve worth calling a curve in his entire face, just a granitic mass of crudely intersecting planes that would have had the old cubist boys jumping for joy. He had a chin like a power-shovel, a gash for a mouth, a huge beak of a nose and black cold eyes set so far back under the beetling overhang of tufted brows that you had the illusion of some wild animal peering out from the dark depths of a cave. The sides of his face—you couldn't have called them cheeks—and forehead were deeply trenched by a criss-cross of sun-weathered lines, like some ancient parchment. He would have had a terrible time making the romantic lead in a musical comedy.

Professor Witherspoon introduced us and Hewell stretched out his hand and said: "Glad to meet you, Bentall." His voice, deep and cavernous, matched both his vast frame and his occupation, and he was glad to see me with the same sort of gladness that you would have found in those same islands a hundred years previously when the cannibal chief hailed the arrival of the latest of a long line of toothsome missionaries. I braced myself as the giant hand closed over mine, but he was surprisingly gentle: it felt as if I was being pulled through a power wringer, but when he gave me back my hand all the fingers were still there, bent and mangled a bit, but still there.

"Heard about you this morning," he boomed. Canada or the American north-west, I couldn't be sure. "Heard your wife wasn't so well, neither. The islands: anything can happen in the islands. Must have had a terrible time."

We talked for a bit about the terrible time I had, then I said curiously: "You've had to go a fair way to recruit labour for this job?"

"Had to, my boy, had to." It was Witherspoon who answered. "Indians no damn good—sullen, uncooperative, suspicious, haven't the physique. Fijians have, but they'd have a heart attack if you suggested they do any work. Same with any white man you could pick up—loafers and wasters to a man. But the Chinese are different."

"Best workers I've ever had," Hewell confirmed. He had a curious trick of speaking without appearing to move his mouth. "When it comes to building railroads and driving tunnels you can't beat 'em. Never have built the western railroads of America without them."

I made some suitable remark and peered around me. Witherspoon said sharply: "What are you looking for, Bentall?"

"Relics, of course." The right note of surprise. "Be interesting to see one being excavated from the rock."

"Won't see none today, I'm afraid," Hewell boomed. "Lucky to find anything once a week. Ain't that so, professor?"

"If we're very lucky," Witherspoon agreed. "Well, well, mustn't hold you back, Hewell, mustn't hold you back. Just brought Bentall along to show him what all the bangs were about. We'll see you at suppertime."

Witherspoon led the way back through the mine, out into the brilliant sunshine and down to his house, chattering away all the time, but I wasn't listening any more, I'd heard and seen all I wanted to hear and see. When we got back he excused himself on the ground that he had some work to catch up on and I went to see Marie. She was sitting up in bed with a book in her hands and there wasn't anything much the matter with her that I could see. I said: "I thought you said you were going to sleep?"

"I said I wasn't going to move. Different thing altogether." She lay back luxuriously on her pillow. "Warm day, cool breeze, sound of the wind in the palms, the sea on the surf and all the blue waters of the lagoon and white sand out there. Wonderful, isn't it?"

"Sure. What's that you're reading there?"

"Book on Fiji. Very interesting." She gestured at the books piled on the table beside her. "Some more on Fiji, some on archaeology. Tommy—the Chinese boy—brought them to me. You should read them."

"Later. How are you feeling?"

"Took your time in getting round to ask me, didn't you?"

I frowned at her, at the same time jerking my head backwards. She caught on fast.

"I'm sorry, dear." The impulsive cry, very well done. "Shouldn't have said that. Much better, I'm feeling much better. Right as rain tomorrow. Had a nice walk round?" The banal touch, like the cry, perfectly done.

I was in the middle of telling her about the nice walk I'd had when there came a diffident tap on the door, a clearing of the throat, and Witherspoon came in. By my reckoning he'd been outside that door for about three minutes. Behind him I could see the brown-skinned forms of John and James, the two Fijian boys.

"Good evening, Mrs. Bentall, good evening. How are you? Better, yes, better? You certainly look better." His eyes fell on the books by the bedside and he checked and frowned. "Where did these come from, Mrs. Bentall?"

"I do hope that I haven't done anything wrong, Professor Witherspoon," she said anxiously. "I asked Tommy for something to read and he brought me these. I'd just started the first one and—"

"Those are rare and valuable editions," he said testily. "Very rare, very rare. Personal library and all that, we archaeologists never lend them out. Tommy had no right— well, never mind. I have an excellent selection of novels, detective fiction, you can have what you like." He smiled, the incident magnanimously forgotten. "I've come to bring you some good news. You and your husband are to have the guest house for yourselves during the remainder of your stay here. I've had John and James here at work most of the day clearing it up."

"Why, Professor!" Marie stretched out her hand and took his. "How very, very nice. It's so kind of you—it's really far too kind of you."

"Nothing at all, my dear, nothing at all!" He patted her hand and held on to it longer than was necessary, about ten times longer than was necessary. "I just thought you might appreciate the privacy. I dare say"—this with a crinkling of half-closed eyes which I took to be a dyspeptic twinge, but it wasn't dyspepsia, it was meant as a roguish twinkle—"that you haven't been married very long. Now, tell me, Mrs. Bentall, will you be fit enough to join us for supper tonight?"

She could be as quick as a cat. She caught the all but

imperceptible shake of my head and she wasn't even looking in my direction.

"I'm so sorry, Professor Witherspoon." It takes some doing to combine a dazzling smile with a tone of deep regret but she managed it. "There's nothing I'd like better, but I really do feel so weak yet. If I could be excused until the morning I—"

"Of course. But of course. Mustn't overdo the convalescence, must we?" He seemed to be on the point of grabbing her hand again, but thought better of it. "We'll send a tray along. And we'll also send *you* along. No need to stir."

At a signal from him the two Fijians caught an end of the bed apiece and lifted, not such a feat, as the bed itself probably didn't weigh even thirty pounds. The Chinese boy came in to carry all the clothes we had, the professor led the way and there was nothing for me to do but to take her hand as we walked between the two houses, bend over her solicitously and murmur: "Ask him for a torch."

I didn't suggest a reason why she should ask for one, for the excellent reason that none occurred to me, but she handled it beautifully. When the professor had dismissed the bearers and was expatiating at length on how the guest house was built entirely from the products of two trees, the pandanus and coconut palm, she interrupted diffidently to ask: "Is there—is there a bathroom here, Professor Witherspoon?"

"But of course, my dear. How remiss of me. Down the steps, to the left and it's the first small hut you come to. The next is the kitchen. For obvious reasons you can't have fire and water in houses like these."

"Of course not. But—but doesn't it get rather dark at night here? I mean—"

"God bless my soul! What must you think of me? A torch—of course you shall have a torch. You shall have it after our evening meal." He glanced at his watch. "Expect you in about half an hour, Bentall?" A few more platitudes, a smirk at Marie and he bustled briskly away.

The westering sun had already dipped behind the shoulder of the mountain but the heat of the day still lingered in the air. For all that Marie shivered and pulled the coverlet high about her shoulders. She said: "Would you care to let the side-screens down? Those trade winds aren't what they're cracked up to be. Not when the darkness comes."

"Let the screen down? And have a dozen listening ears pressed against them in a couple of minutes?"

"You—you think so?" she said slowly. "You feel there's something wrong here? With Professor Witherspoon?"

"I've long passed the feeling stage. I know damn well there's something wrong. I've known it ever since we arrived here." I pulled a chair up to her bed and took her hand: a hundred to one that we had a keen and interested audience and I didn't want to disappoint them. "What are *you* going on? Feeling fey again or womanly intuition or hard facts?"

"Don't be unpleasant," she said quietly. "I've already apologised for my foolish behaviour—just the fever, as you said. This is intuition, or a hunch—quite different. This ideal spot, those smiling Fijian boys, the marvellous Chinese servant, that Hollywood dream of what an English archaeologist should look like and behave—it's all too idyllic, too perfect. You get the impression of—of a carefully maintained facade. It's too dreamlike, if you know what I mean."

"You mean you'd feel better if you saw the professor roaring and cursing round the place or saw someone lying under a stoop and drinking from the neck of a whisky bottle?"

"Well, something like that."

"I've heard the South Pacific often affects people like that at first. The sense of unreality, I mean. Don't forget I've seen the professor several times on the screen. He's just as large as life. And if you want perfection marred, just wait until the boyfriend, Hewell, happens by."

"Why, what's he like?"

"Couldn't describe him. You're too young to have seen the King Kong films. You won't mistake him though. And while you're watching out for him I want you to check the number of people who come and go into the workers' hut. That's why I didn't want you to come across for supper."

"That shouldn't be hard."

"Nor so easy. They're all Chinese—the ones I've seen so far anyway—and they'll probably all look alike to you. Check what they're doing, how many stay in, whether the ones that come out are carrying anything or not. Don't let anyone guess you're checking. Let down the screens when it's dark enough and if there are no window cut-outs you can peek through—"

"Why don't you write it all down for me?" she said sweetly.

"O.K., so you've been at this longer than I have. Just a cowardly concern for my own neck. I'm going to take a walk around during the middle of the night and I'd like to know what the score is."

She didn't put her hand to her mouth or gasp or try to dissuade me, I couldn't even have sworn to it that the pressure of her hand had increased. She said, matter-of-factly: "Do you want me to come with you?"

"No. I just want to look around and there's nothing wrong with my own eyes. And while I don't expect trouble I can't see you'd be much help, if any did come along. No offence, of course."

"Well," she said doubtfully, "Fleck's got my gun, there wouldn't be much point in calling the cops and I don't suppose I could do very much if someone jumped me. But if someone jumped *you*, then I—"

"You have the wrong idea entirely," I said patiently. "You're not built for speed. I am. You never saw anyone who could run away from a fight as fast as Bentall." I crossed the coconut floor and pulled over a made-up string bed, placing it close to hers. "Do you mind?"

"Suit yourself," she said agreeably. She looked at me lazily under half-closed eyelids and an amused smile curved across her mouth, but it wasn't at all the same amused smile as she'd given me in Colonel Raine's office in London. "I'll hold your hand. I think you're just a sheep in wolf's clothing."

"Wait till I get off duty," I threatened. "You and me and the lights of London. You'll see."

She looked at me for a long moment and then turned to gaze out over the darkening lagoon. She said: "I don't see it."

"Ah, well. Wrong type. Lucky I'm not the sensitive kind. About this bed: I know this is going to be a big disappointment to you, but it occurred to me that when I took a walk tonight it might be a good thing to shove some sort of dummy in here and it's not likely they'll investigate its genuineness when the bed is so near yours." I heard the sound of voices, looked up and saw Hewell and his Chinese come into sight round a corner of the crushing mill: Hewell was a walking mountain, there was something almost frighteningly simian about the bowed form, the perceptibly rolling gait, the slow swing of the hands that all but brushed his knees as he walked. I said to Marie: "If you want to have the screaming heebie-jeebies during the night, turn round and have an eyeful. The boy-friend's here."

If it hadn't been for the boy-friend's face, the professor's incessant chatter and the bottle of wine he'd produced to mark, he said, the occasion, it would have been quite a pleasant meal: the Chinese boy certainly knew how to cook and there was none of this nonsense of birds' nests and sharks' fins, either. But I couldn't keep my eyes off that gaunt

81

and ravaged face opposite me—the immaculate white drills into which he'd changed only emphasised the Neanderthalic hideousness of it: I could shut my ears to Witherspoon's banalities: the wine, an Australian burgundy, was quite excellent if your tastes ran to sweetened vinegar, but I was thirsty and managed to force some down.

But it was Hewell, curiously enough, who made the meal tolerable. Behind that primitive broken face lay a keen mind—at least he was smart enough to stay away from the burgundy and drink Hong-Kong beer by the quart—and his stories of life as a hard-rock mining engineer in what seemed to have been half the countries in the world made good listening. Or they would have made good listening if he hadn't stared unwinkingly at me all the time he was speaking, the black eyes so far back in their sockets that the illusion of a bear peering out from his cave was stronger than ever. He'd the Ancient Mariner whacked to the wide. I might have been sitting there transfixed all night if Witherspoon hadn't finally pushed back his chair, rubbed his hands together in satisfaction and asked me how I'd enjoyed the meal.

"It was excellent," I told him. "Don't let that cook go. Very many thanks indeed. And now, if you will, I think I'll be getting back to my wife."

"Nonsense, nonsense!" The affronted host to the life. "Coffee and brandy to come yet, my boy. When ever do we archaeologists get an opportunity to celebrate? We're delighted to see a strange face here, aren't we, Hewell?"

Hewell didn't contradict him, but he didn't agree with him either. It didn't matter to Witherspoon. He brought forward a rattan armchair, set it in position for me and fussed around like an old hen until he was certain I was comfortably seated. Then Tommy brought in the coffee and brandy.

From that moment on, the evening went well. After the Chinese boy had brought in drinks for the second time the professor told him to bring the bottle and leave it there. The level in the bottle sank as if there was a hole in the bottom of it. The professor was in tremendous form. The level sank some more. Hewell smiled twice. It was a great night. The calf was being fatted for the kill. They weren't wasting all that excellent brandy for nothing. The bottle was emptied and another brought in. The professor told some mildly risque jokes and convulsed himself with laughter. Hewell smiled again. I wiped away some tears of mirth and caught the quick flicker of interchanged glances. The axe was starting on its back swing. I congratulated the professor on his wit in a slurred and stumbling voice. I never felt more sober in my life.

They'd obviously rehearsed the whole thing meticulously. Witherspoon, the dedicated scientist to the life, started to bring me some of the exhibits from the show-cases lining the walls, but after a few minutes he said: "Come, Hewell, we are insulting our friend here. Let us show him our real treasures."

Hewell hesitated doubtfully and Witherspoon actually stamped his foot on the floor. "I insist. Damn it, man, what harm in it?"

"Very well." Hewell crossed to the big safe on my left hand side and after a minute's fruitless twiddling of the knob, said: "Combination's stuck again, professor."

"Well, open it from the back combination," Witherspoon said testily. He was standing to my right, a piece of broken pottery in his hand. "Now look at this, Mr. Bentall. I want you to pay particular attention to . . ."

But I wasn't paying any attention, particular or otherwise, to what he was saying. I wasn't even looking at the pottery. I was looking at the window behind him, a window which the kerosene lamp inside and the darkness outside transformed into an almost perfect mirror. I was looking at Hewell and the safe that he was tilting away from the wall. That safe weighed three hundredweights if it weighed an ounce. And the way I was sitting, leaning to the right in the arm-chair and left leg crossed over the right, my right foot was sticking out directly in its path, if it toppled. And it was going to topple. The safe was now a good foot away from the wall at the top and I could see Hewell actually sighting along its side to see if my foot was in the line of fall. And then he gave it a push.

"My God!" Professor Witherspoon shouted. "Look out!"

The cry of horror was as perfectly done as it was calculatedly late, but he needn't have bothered himself, I was already looking out for myself. I was already starting to fall out of my chair as the safe fell on my leg, twisting my foot so that the side lay flush along the floor: the sole was more than half an inch of solid leather, but even so it was a chance. A long chance, but I had to take it.

There was nothing faked about my shout of pain. That stout leather sole felt as if it were being bent in half and so did my foot: but the safe didn't touch any other part of my foot or leg.

I lay there, gasping, trapped by the weight of the safe, until Hewell rushed round to the front to heave it up while

Witherspoon dragged me clear. I struggled painfully to my feet, shook off the professor's arm, took one step on my injured foot and collapsed heavily to the floor. What with the safe and myself, the floor was certainly taking a beating that night.

"Are you—are you badly hurt?" The professor was aghast with anxiety.

"Hurt? No, I'm not hurt. I just felt tired and lay down for a rest." I glared up at him savagely, both hands cradling my right foot. "How far do you think you could walk with a broken ankle?"

CHAPTER FIVE

Wednesday 10 P.M.-Thursday 5 A.M.

ABJECT apologies, restoring the patient with what few drops of brandy still remained, splinting and taping my ankle in a surgical dressing took about ten minutes. After that they half-helped, half-carried me back to the guest hut. The side-screens were down but I could see the chinks of light through them. The professor rapped on the door and waited. The door opened.

"Who—who is there?" Marie had thrown some kind of wrap over her shoulders and the light of the kerosene lamp behind her made a shining halo round the soft fair hair.

"Nothing to worry about, Mrs. Bentall," Witherspoon said soothingly. "Your husband's just had a slight accident. Hurt his foot rather, I'm afraid."

"Slight accident!" I yelped. "Hurt his foot. I've broken my bloody ankle." I pushed off the restraining hands, tried to lurch through the door, stumbled, cried out and measured my length on the floor of the guest house. I was getting good at measuring my length on floors, it was far quicker than using a tape. Marie, her voice high-pitched in anxiety, said something I couldn't catch above my own moans and dropped to her knees beside me, but the professor lifted her gently to her feet while Hewell picked me up and placed me on my bed. I weigh close on two hundred, but he lifted and set me down with as little effort as a girl her doll, except perhaps not quite so gently. But those string beds were stronger than they looked and I didn't go through to the floor. I moaned some more and then propped myself up on one elbow, letting them see how a stiff-lipped Englishman suffers in silent agony, wincing and screwing my eyes shut from time to time just in case they didn't get it.

Professor Witherspoon explained, rather haltingly, what had happened—at least, his version of what had happened, a convincing amalgam of jammed combinations, top-heavy safes and sagging floors which made safes unstable—and Marie listened to him in stormy silence. If she was acting, she'd missed out on her profession: the quick breathing, the compressed lips, the slightly flared nostrils, the tightly clenched fists, those I could understand: but to get your face as pale as she did hers you really have to put your heart into it. When he'd finished I really thought she was going to start in on him, she didn't seem the slightest scared or awed by Hewell's towering bulk, but she seemed to control herself and said in an icy voice: "Thank you both very much for bringing my husband home. It was most kind of you. I'm sure it was all an accident. Good-night."

That hardly left the door open for any further conversational gambits and they took themselves off hoping aloud that I would be better the next day. What they were really hoping they kept to themselves and they forgot to say how they expected a broken bone to set overnight. For about ten seconds more Marie stood staring through the door by which they'd left, then whispered: "He's—he's terrifying, isn't he? He's like something left over from the dark ages."

"He's no beauty. Scared?"

"Of course I am." She stood still for some seconds longer, sighed, turned round and came and sat on the edge of my bed. For a long moment she looked down at me, like a person hesitating or making up her mind, then she touched me lightly on the forehead with both cool hands, smoothed her fingertips past my hair and looked down at me, propped up by a hand on either side of my head. She was smiling but there was no amusement in the smile and her hazel eyes were dark with worry.

"I'm sorry for all this," she murmured. "It—it's pretty bad, isn't it, Johnny?" She'd never called me that before.

"Terribly." I reached my hands up, put them round her neck and pulled her down till her face was buried in the pillow. She didn't resist any, recovering from the shock of a first-time close-up of Hewell would always take time or maybe she was just humouring a sick man. She had a cheek like a flower petal and she smelled of the sun and the sea. I put my lips close to her ear and whispered: "Go and check if they've really gone."

She stiffened as if she'd touched a live wire, then pushed

herself upright and rose. She went to the door, peered through some interstices in the side screens, then said in a quiet voice: "They're both back in the professor's living room. I can see them lifting the safe into position."

"Put the lights out."

She crossed to the table, turned down the wick, cupped her hands above the top of the glass funnel and blew. The room was plunged into darkness. I swung off the bed, unwound the couple of yards of medical plaster they'd wrapped round splints and ankle, cursing softly as it stuck to the flesh, put the splints to one side, stood up and gave two or three experimental hops on my right foot. I was hopping almost as good as ever, the only pain was on the outside of my big toe which had taken the brunt of the weight of the safe when the sole had bent. I tried it again and it was still O.K. I sat down and began to pull on sock and shoe.

"What on earth are you doing?" Marie asked. The soft concern, I noticed with regret, had gone from her voice.

"Just testing," I said softly. "I think the old foot will carry me around a bit yet."

"But the bone—I thought the bone was broken."

"Just a natural fast healer." I tried the foot inside the shoe and hardly felt a thing. Then I told her what had happened. At the end she said: "I suppose you thought it was clever to fool me?"

I'd become used to a lot of feminine injustice in my life so I let it pass. She was too smart not to see how unfair she was, not, at least, when she'd cooled down. Why she had to cool down I didn't know, but when her temperature dropped she would realise the immense advantage I'd gained by having created the impression that I was completely incapacitated. I heard her moving across the room back to the bed and as she passed me she said quietly: "You told me to count the Chinese going in and out of the long hut."

"Well?"

"There were eighteen."

"Eighteen!" All I'd counted in the mine was eight.

"Eighteen."

"Notice what any of them was carrying when he came out?"

"I didn't see any come out. Not before it was dark."

"Uh-huh. Where's the torch?"

"Under my pillow. Here."

She turned in and shortly I could hear her slow even breathing, but I knew she wasn't asleep. I tore up strips of the plaster and stretched them across the face of the torch until there was only a quarter inch diameter hole left in the middle. Then I took up position by a crack in the side-screens where I could watch the professor's house. Hewell left shortly after eleven o'clock, went to his own house. I saw a light come on, then go out after about ten minutes.

I crossed to the cupboard where the Chinese boy had put our clothes, hunted around with the tiny spotlight of light until I'd found a pair of dark grey flannels and a blue shirt and quickly changed in the darkness. Taking a midnight walk in white shirt and white ducks was something that Colonel Raine wouldn't have approved of at all. Then I went back to Marie's bed and said softly: "You're not sleeping, are you?"

"What do you want?" No warmth in the voice, just none at all.

"Look, Marie, don't be silly. To fool them I had to fool you too when they were there. Don't you see the advantage of being mobile when they think I'm completely immobilised. What did you expect me to do? Stand there at the door supported by Hewell and the prof and sing out cheerily: 'Don't worry about this, dear. I'm only kidding'?"

"I suppose not," she said after a minute. "What did you want? Just to tell me that?"

"As a matter of fact it wasn't that, it was your eyebrows."

"My *what?*"

"Eyebrows. Your hair is so blonde, the eyebrows so black. Are they real? The colour, I mean?"

"Are you all right?"

"I want to blacken my face. Mascara. I thought you might have—"

"Why didn't you say that in the first place instead of trying to be clever?" Whatever her intelligence said about 'forgive' some other part of her mind was against it. "No mascara. All I have is black shoe polish. Top drawer, right side."

I shuddered at the thought but said thanks and left her. An hour later I left her altogether. I'd made up a rough dummy in my bed, checked every side of the house for interested spectators and left by the back, lifting a corner of the side-screens just sufficiently to squirm under. There were no cries or shouts or shots, Bentall abroad unobserved and mighty glad of it. Against a dark background you couldn't have seen me from five yards although you could have smelled me at ten times the distance down wind. Certain makes of boot polish are like that.

On the first part of my trip, between our house and the professor's, it wouldn't really have mattered whether my foot had been in commission or not. To anyone looking out from

Hewell's house or the workers' hut, I would have been silhouetted against the lightness of the sea and the white glimmer of the sands, so I made it on my hands and elbows and knees, heading for the rear of the house, out of sight of all the others.

I passed the corner of the house and rose slowly and soundlessly to my feet, pressing close in against the wall. Three long quiet steps and I was at the back door.

Defeat had come almost before I'd started. Because there had been a hinged wooden door at front I had assumed that there would be the same at the rear: but it was a plaited bamboo screen and as soon as I'd touched it it rustled and clicked with the sound of a hundred distant castanets. I flattened myself against the door, hand clenched round the base of my torch. Five minutes passed, nothing happened, nobody came, and when finally a passing catspaw of wind brushed my face the reeds rustled again, just as they had done before. It took me two minutes to gather up twenty reeds in one hand without making too much racket about it, two seconds to pass through into the house and another two minutes to let those reeds fall one by one into place. The night wasn't all that warm, but I could feel the sweat dripping down my forehead and into my eyes. I wiped it away, hooded my hand over the already tiny hole in the centre of the torch face, slid on the switch with a cautious thumb and started going over the kitchen.

I didn't expect to find anything there that I wouldn't have found in any other kitchen, and I didn't. But I found what I was after, the cutlery drawer. Tommy had a fine selection of carving knives, all of them honed to a razor's edge. I picked a beauty, a 10-inch triangular job, serrated on one side and straight on the other, that tapered from two inches below the hilt to just nothing at all. It had the point of a surgeon's lancet. It was better than nothing. It was a lot better than nothing: if I could find the gap between the ribs not even Hewell would think I was tickling him. I wrapped it carefully in a kitchen cloth and stuck it under my belt.

The inside kitchen door, the one giving on the central passage, was made of wood, to keep the cooking smells from percolating throughout the house, I supposed. It opened inwards on oiled leather hinges. I eased myself through into the passage and stood there listening. I didn't have to listen very hard. The professor was something less than a silent sleeper and the source of the snoring, a room with an opened door about ten feet up the passage on the right, was easy to locate. I had no idea where the Chinese boy slept, I hadn't seen him leaving the house so I assumed that he must be in one of the other rooms and I didn't intend to find out which. He seemed to me like a boy who would sleep very lightly indeed. I hoped the professor's adenoidal orchestration would blanket any noise I might make, but for all that I went up the passage towards the living-room door with all the rush and clatter of a cat stalking a bird across a sunlit lawn.

I made it in safety and closed the door behind me without even a whisper of sound. I didn't waste any time looking around the room, I knew where to look and went straight for the big kneehole desk. If the direction of the burnished copper wire not quite buried in the thatch that had caught my eye when first I'd sat in the rattan chair that morning hadn't been guide enough, my nose would have led me straight there: the pungent smell, however faint, of sulphuric acid is unmistakeable.

Most kneehole desks are lined on either side with a row of drawers, but Professor Witherspoon's was an exception. There was a cupboard on either side and neither of them was locked. There was no reason why they should have been. I opened the left-hand door first and shone the pencil beam of light inside.

The compartment was big, thirty inches high by eighteen wide and perhaps two feet in depth. It was packed with lead acid accumulators and dry batteries. There were ten of the accumulators on an upper shelf, big glass-sided 2.5 volt cells, wired together in series: below were eight Exide 120 volt dry-cell batteries, wired up in parallel. Enough power there to send a signal to the moon, if a man had a radio transmitter.

And the man had a radio transmitter. It was in the locker on the other side. It took up the entire space of the locker. I know a little of transmitter-receivers, but this metallic grey mass with its score or more of calibrated dials, wave-bands and tuning knobs was quite unknown to me. I peered closely at the maker's name and it read: 'Kuraby-Sankowa Radio Corporation, Osaka and Shanghai'. It didn't mean a thing to me, any more than the jumble of Chinese characters engraved beneath it. The wave-lengths and receiving stations on the transmitting waveband were marked in both Chinese and English and the needle was locked on Foochow. Perhaps Professor Witherspoon was the kind-hearted sort of employer who allowed his homesick workers to speak to their relatives in China. But perhaps he wasn't.

I closed the door softly and turned my attention to the upper part of the desk. The professor might have known I was coming, he hadn't even bothered to pull down the roll-top. After five minutes' methodical search I was beginning to understand why he hadn't bothered, there was nothing in the desk-top drawers and pigeon-holes worth concealing. I was about to give it up and fold my tent when I looked again at the most obvious thing on that desk—the blotting pad with its four-cornered leather holder. I took the blotters out of the holder and looked down at the piece of thin parchment paper that had been concealed between the lowest blotter and the pad.

It was a type-written list of six lines, each line consisting of a double-barrelled name followed by figures, eight figures every time. The first line read: 'Pelican-Takishmaru 20007815', the second: 'Linkiang-Hawetta 10346925' and so on with the other four lines containing equally meaningless names and combinations of figures. Then there was a space of an inch, then another line which read: 'Every hour 46 Tombola'.

I could make nothing of it. It seemed to be about the most useless information—if that's what it was—that anyone could ever want. Or I could be looking at the most important code I'd ever seen. Either way, it didn't seem much help to me. But it might help later. Colonel Raine reckoned I'd a photographic memory, but not for this kind of junk. I took pencil and paper from the professor's desk, copied the writing, put the parchment back where I'd found it, took off my shoe, folded the paper and placed it, wrapped in some waterproof cellophane, between the sole of my foot and my sock. I didn't fancy making that traverse through the passage to the kitchen again, so I left through a window remote from Hewell's and the workers' houses.

Twenty minutes later I was well clear of all the houses and rose painfully to my feet. I hadn't travelled so far on my hands, elbows and knees since my nursery days and I'd lost the hang of the thing: moreover, years of not moving around on them had made mine quite unsuitable for this kind of locomotion and they ached fiercely: but they weren't in any worse condition than the clothes that covered them.

The sky was almost completely overcast, but not quite, and every now and then a sudden unveiling of the almost full moon made me drop quickly into the shelter of some scrub or bush and wait until the sky darkened over again. I was following the line of the railway tracks which led from the crushing mills and drying shed round to the south and then, presumably, west of the island. I was very interested in this line and its destination. Professor Witherspoon had carefully refrained from making any mention of what lay on the other side of the island, but for all his care Professor Witherspoon talked too much. He'd told me that the phosphate company used to take 1,000 tons a day out of the hillside, and as it wasn't there any more they must have taken it away. That meant a ship, a big ship, and no big ship would ever have used that tiny floating pier of logs below the professor's house, even if it could have approached it closely enough in the shallow lagoon water, which it couldn't. Something bigger was needed, something much bigger: a stone or concrete pier, maybe one made from coral blocks, and either a crane or a raised hopper with a canted loading chute. Maybe Professor Witherspoon hadn't wished me to walk in this direction.

A few seconds later I was wishing the same thing myself. I'd just passed over a tiny culvert where a small stream, almost covered in with bushes and thickets, ran down from the mountain to the sea, and had taken no more than ten paces beyond when there came the quick stealthy rush of padding feet behind me, something heavy crashed into my back and shoulder and then, before I'd time to start reacting, something else closed over my upper left arm, just above the elbow, with all the power and brutal savagery of a sprung bear-trap. The immediate pain was agonizing.

Hewell. That was my first and instinctive reaction as I staggered and lurched and all but fell. Hewell, it must be Hewell, no one else I'd ever known could have a grip like that, it felt as if my arm was being crushed in half. I swung round in a vicious half-circle hooking with all the strength of my right arm for where his stomach ought to have been and all I did was make a hole in the night. I almost dislocated my right shoulder but I'd more to think about than that as I lurched sideways again, fighting for my balance. Fighting for my balance and fighting for my life. It wasn't Hewell who had me, but a dog about the size and power of a wolf.

I tried to tear him off with my right hand but all I did was to sink those huge teeth still deeper into my arm. I tried crashing my right fist again and again against that powerful body but he was so far to my left and back that I could barely reach him. I tried kicking, but I couldn't get anywhere near him. I couldn't get at him, I couldn't shake him off, there was no solid object I could crush him against and I knew that if I tried falling on top of him he'd have loosened his grip and had my throat before I knew what he was about.

He must have weighed between eighty and ninety pounds.

He had fangs like steel hooks and when you have steel hooks embedded in your arm and a weight of ninety pounds suspended from them only one thing can happen—the skin and flesh start to tear, and I haven't any different skin or flesh from anyone else. I could feel myself getting weak, I could feel the waves of pain and nausea washing over me when, in a moment of clarity, my mind or what passes for it started working again. I'd no trouble in getting the knife clear of my belt, but it took almost ten interminable and pain-filled seconds before I could free it one-handed from its cloth wrapping. After that it was easy, the stiletto point entered just below the breastbone and angled inwards and upwards for the heart, meeting almost no resistance. The bear-trap grip on my arm loosened in a fraction of a second and the dog was dead before it reached the ground.

I didn't know what kind of dog it was and I didn't care. I hauled him by his heavy studded collar till I came to the culvert I'd so recently crossed, dragged him down the short bank to the stream and pulled him into the water where the bushes were thickest. I thought he would be pretty well screened from sight above but I didn't dare use my torch to see. I jammed him in place with some heavy stones so that no freshet after heavy rain could wash him into view, then lay face down by the stream for almost five minutes till the sharpest of the pain, the shock and nausea had worn off and my racing pulse and pounding heart returned to something like normal. It had been a bad couple of minutes.

Getting my shirt and singlet off was no pleasure at all, the arm was already stiffening up, but I managed it and washed my arm thoroughly in the running water. I was glad it was fresh water and not salt. Washing my arm, I thought, was going to do me a great deal of good if that dog had been suffering from hydrophobia, about the same effect as if I washed my arm after a king cobra had struck. But there didn't seem to be much point in worrying about it, so I bandaged up my arm as well as I could with strips torn from my singlet, pulled on my shirt, climbed out of the culvert and continued on my way, still following the metal tracks. I carried the knife in my right hand now and I hadn't any cloth wrapped round it either. I felt chilled, cold with the ice-cold of a vicious anger. I wasn't kindly disposed towards anyone.

I was almost round to the south of the island now. There were no trees, just bushes and scattered low shrub that was no good for concealment at all unless you lay prone on the ground, and I wasn't in the mood for lying prone on the ground. But I hadn't altogether taken leave of my senses and when the moon suddenly broke through into a large patch quite free from cloud I dropped flat and peered out from the shelter of some bushes that wouldn't have given decent cover to a rabbit.

In the brilliant wash of the moonlight I could see now that my first impression of the island from the reef that morning hadn't been entirely accurate, the early morning mists had obscured the true features to the south of the island. True, the narrow plain at the foot of the mountain did, from where I lay, seem to go all the way round the island, but it was much narrower here than in the east. Moreover, it didn't slope steadily towards the sea but seemed even to slope from the sea to the base of the mountain: which meant only one thing, that the island to the south must end in a very steep drop to the lagoon, perhaps even a sheer cliff-face. And I hadn't been right about the mountain either, although this new feature I couldn't have seen from the reef: instead of having the continuously smooth steeply-sloping surface of a cone, the mountain seemed to be almost completely bisected down its southerly face by a gigantic cleft or ravine, no doubt a relic of that catastrophic day when the northern half of the mountain had vanished into the sea. What this entire physical configuration amounted to was that the only way from east to west on this island appeared to lie across the narrow connecting belt of plain to the south: it couldn't have been more than a hundred and twenty yards wide.

Fifteen minutes later that patch in the clouds was twice as large and the moon still in the middle of it, so I decided to move. In that bright moonlight a move backwards would have been just as conspicuous as a move forwards, so I decided I might as well keep going on. I cursed that moon pretty steadily. I said things about that moon that the poets and the Tin Pan Alley merchants wouldn't have approved of at all. But they would have approved of the unreserved apology I made to the moon only a couple of minutes later.

I had been inching forward on what was left of my elbows and knees, with my head about nine inches above the ground, when suddenly I saw something else about nine inches above the ground and less than a couple of feet from my eyes. It was a wire, strung above the ground on little steel pins with looped heads, and I hadn't seen it further away because it was painted black. The paint, its low height above the ground, the presence of a dog wandering around and the fact that the wire wasn't strung on insulators made it pretty clear that it wasn't an electric circuit carrying some kind of lethal current. It was an old-fashioned trip wire. It would be connected up with some mechanical warning device.

I waited twenty minutes without moving until the moon had again gone behind the clouds, rose stiffly to my feet, crossed the wire and got down again. The land had now quite a definite dip to my right, towards the base of the mountain, and the railway track had been raised and banked on one side to meet the angle of the ground. It seemed like a good idea to crawl along beneath the raised edge of the embankment: I would be in shadow if the moon broke through again. Or I hoped I would be.

I was. After almost half-an-hour more of this elbow and knees caper, during which I saw nothing and heard nothing and thought with increasingly sympathetic admiration of the lower members of the animal kingdom who were doomed to spend their lives getting around in this fashion, the moon broke through again. And this time I really saw something.

Less than thirty hards ahead of me I saw a fence. I had seen such fences before and they weren't the kind that surround an English meadow. Where I'd seen them before had been in Korea, round prisoner of war cages. This one was a nine-stranded barbed-wire affair, over six feet high and curving outwards at the top: it emerged from the impenetrable darkness of the vertically-walled cleft in the mountain to my right and ran due south across the plain.

Perhaps ten yards beyond that there was another fence, a duplicate of the first, but what occupied my attention was not either of the fences but a group of three men I could see beyond the second fence. They were standing together, talking, I presumed, but so softly that I couldn't hear what they were saying, and one of them had just lit a cigarette. They were dressed in white ducks, round caps, gaiters and cartridge belts, and carried rifles slung over their shoulders. They were, without any doubt at all, seamen of the Royal Navy.

By this time my mind had given up. I was tired. I was exhausted. I couldn't think any more. Given time, I could maybe have thought up a couple of good reasons why I should suddenly on this remote Fijian island stumble across three seamen of the Royal Navy, but that seemed a daft sort of thing to do when all I had to do was stand up and ask them. I transferred the weight from my elbows to the palms of my hands and started to get to my feet.

Three yards ahead of me a bush moved. Shock froze me into involuntary and life-saving immobility, no relic dug out by the professor was ever half so petrified as I was at that moment. The bush leaned over gently towards another bush and murmured something in so low a voice that I couldn't have heard it another five feet away. But surely they must be hearing me. My heart was reverberating in my ears like a riveter's hammer. It was going about the same speed, too. And even if they couldn't hear me they must surely have felt the vibrations being transmitted through my body and ground, I was as near to them as that, a seismograph could have picked me up in Suva. But they heard nothing, they felt nothing. I lowered myself back to the ground like a gambler laying down the last card that's going to lose him his fortune. I made a mental note that all this stuff about oxygen being necessary for life was a tale invented by the doctors. I had completely stopped breathing. My right hand ached, in the moonlight I could see the knuckles of the fist clenched round the hilt of the knife gleaming like burnished ivory. It took a conscious effort of will to relax the grip even slightly, but even so I still clung on to the handle of that knife harder than I'd ever clung on to anything before.

Seven or eight aeons passed. By and by the three naval guards, who had that liberal interpretation of their duties possessed by naval guards the world over, disappeared. At least they seemed to disappear, until I realised that what I had taken for a dark patch in the ground behind them was really a hut. A minute passed, then I heard the metallic clacking and hissing of a primus stove being pumped into life. The bush in front of me moved again. I twisted the knife in my hand until the blade was pointing up, not down, but he didn't come my way. He crawled off silently, parallel to the wire, heading for another bush about thirty yards away, and I could see that other bush stir as he approached. The place was full of moving bushes that night. I changed my mind about asking the guards what they were doing there. Another night, perhaps. Tonight, the wise man went to bed and thought about things. If I could get to my bed without being chewed to pieces by dogs or knifed by one of Hewell's Chinese, I would think about things.

I made it back to the house in one piece. It took me ninety minutes altogether, half of it to cover the first fifty yards, but I made it.

It was coming on for five in the morning when I raised the corner of the seaward screen and slipped into the house. Marie was asleep, and there seemed to be no point in waking her, bad news could wait. I washed off the boot-black in a basin in the corner of the room, but I was too tired to do anything about rebandaging my arm. I was too tired even to think about things. I climbed into bed and have only the faintest recollection of my head touching the pillow. Even if I had had a dozen arms and each one throbbing with pain as was my left, I don't think they would have kept me awake that night.

CHAPTER SIX

Thursday Noon-Friday 1:30 A.M.

IT WAS after noon when I awoke. Only one wall screen had been pulled up, the one that gave on the lagoon. I could see the green shimmer of water, the white glare of sand, the washed out pastels of the coral and, beyond the lagoon, the darker line of the sea with a cloudless sky above. With three side-screens down there was no through draught and it was stiflingly hot under that thatched roof. But at least it made for privacy. My left arm throbbed savagely. But I was still alive. No hydrophobia.

Marie Hopeman was sitting on a chair by my bed. She was dressed in white shorts and blouse, her eyes were clear and rested, she had colour in her cheeks and altogether just looking at her made me feel terrible. She was smiling down at me and I could see that she had made up her mind not to be sore at me any more. She had a nice face, far nicer than the one she had worn in London. I said: "You look fine. How do you feel?" Original, that was me.

"Right as rain. Fever all gone. Sorry to wake you up like this, but there'll be lunch going in half an hour. The professor had one of his boys make those so that you could get over there." She pointed to where a pair of remarkably well-made crutches lay against a chair. "Or you can have it here. You must be hungry, but I didn't want to wake you up for breakfast."

"I didn't turn in till about six o'clock."

"That explains it." I took my hat off to her patience, to her ability to suppress her curiosity. "How do you feel?"

"I feel awful."

"You look it," she said candidly. "Just not tough at all."

"I'm falling to pieces. What have you been doing all morning?"

"Been squired around by the professor. I went swimming with him this morning—I think the professor likes going swimming with me—then after we'd had breakfast he took me round a bit and into the mine." She shivered, mock-earnest. "I don't care for the mine very much."

"Where's your boy-friend now?"

"Away looking for a dog. They can't find it anywhere. The professor's very upset. It seems that this was a particular pet and he was very attached to it."

"Ha! A pet? I've met the pet and he was very attached to me. The clinging type." I freed my left arm from the blanket and unwrapped the blood-stained strips of cloth. "You can see where he was clinging."

"My God!" Her eyes widened and the warm colour ebbed from her cheeks. "That—that looks ghastly."

I examined my arm with a kind of doleful pride and had to admit that she wasn't exaggerating any. From shoulder to elbow most of the arm was blue, purple and black, and swollen as much as fifty per cent above normal. There were four or five deep triangular tears in the flesh and the blood was still oozing slowly from three of them. The parts of my arm that didn't seem discoloured were probably just as bad as the rest, only they were hidden under a thick crust of dark dried-up blood. I had seen pleasanter sights.

"What happened to the dog?" she whispered.

"I killed him." I reached under the pillow and drew out the blood-stained knife. "With this."

"Where on earth did you get that? Where—I think you'd better tell me everything from the beginning."

So I told her, quickly and softly, while she cleaned up my arm and bandaged it again. She didn't like the job, but she did it well. When I'd finished speaking she said: "What lies on the other side of the island?"

"I don't know," I said truthfully. "But I'm beginning to make all sorts of guesses and I don't like any of them."

She said nothing to this, just finished tying up my arm and helping me into a long-sleeved shirt. After that she fixed up the splints and plaster again on my right ankle, went to the cupboard and brought back her handbag. I said sourly: "Going to powder your nose for the boy-friend?"

"I'm going to powder yours," she said. Before I was properly aware of what she was doing she had some kind of cream on my face, and rubbed it in and was dusting powder over it. After a bit she leaned back and surveyed her handi-work. "You look simply sweet," she murmured and handed me her pocket mirror.

I looked awful. One horrified glance at me would have had any life assurance salesman in the land jumping on his foun-tain pen with both feet. The drawn features, the bloodshot eyes with the blue under them were my own contributions: but the ghastly and highly convincing pallor of the rest of my face was entirely due to Marie.

"Wonderful," I agreed. "And what's going to happen when the professor gets a good whiff of this face powder?"

She drew a miniature scent-spray from her bag. "After I've sprayed a couple of ounces of Night of Mystery on myself he won't be able to smell anything else within twenty yards."

I wrinkled my nose and said: "I see your point." Night of Mystery *was* pretty powerful stuff, at least in the quantities she was using. "What happens if I start sweating? Won't all this cream and powder stuff start to streak?"

"It's guaranteed not to." She smiled. "If it does, we'll sue the makers."

"Sure," I said heavily. "That should be interesting. You know, 'The shades of the late J. Bentall and M. Hopeman herewith propose to raise an action—' "

"Stop it!" she said sharply. "Stop it, will you?"

I stopped it. She was a very touchy girl on some subjects. Or maybe I was just clumsy and careless. I said, "Don't you think the half-hour is just about up?"

She nodded. "Yes. We'd better go."

It took me until I had got down the steps and moved six paces into the sunshine to realise that Marie's careful preparation with the cream and powder was probably just so much wasted effort. The way I felt, nothing could have made me look worse. With only one foot in commission and the other shoeless foot swinging clear of the ground I was forced to throw much of my weight on the crutches and with every thud of the left-hand crutch on the hard-baked earth a violent jolt of pain stabbed clear through my arm, from the finger-tips all the way to the shoulder, then across my back to the very top of my head. I didn't see why an arm injury should give me a violent headache, but it did. This was something else to take up with the medical profession.

Old Witherspoon had either been watching or had heard the thud of my crutches for he opened the door and came hopping briskly down the steps to greet us. The broad beam of welcome changed to a look of distress as he caught sight of my face.

"God bless my soul! Bless my soul!" He came hurrying anxiously forward and took my arm. "You look—I mean, this has given you a terrible shake. Good God, my boy, the sweat's pouring down your face."

He wasn't exaggerating. It was pouring down my face. It

had started pouring at the precise instant that he had gripped me by the arm, the left arm, just above the elbow. He was screwing my arm off at the shoulder socket. He thought he was helping me.

"I'll be all right." I gave him my wan smile. "Just jarred my foot coming down our steps. Otherwise I hardly feel a thing."

"You shouldn't have come out," he scolded. "Foolish, terribly foolish. We would have sent lunch across. However, now that you're here ... Dear me, dear me, I feel so guilty about all this."

"It's not your fault," I reassured him. He'd shifted his grip higher to assist me up the steps and I noted with faint surprise that his house was swaying from side to side. "You weren't to know that the floor was unsafe."

"But I did, I did. That's what vexes me so much. Unforgivable, unforgivable." He ushered me into a chair in his living-room, fussing and clucking around like an old hen. "By jove, you do look ill. Brandy, eh, brandy?"

"Nothing I'd like better," I said honestly.

He did his usual testing to destruction act with the hand-bell, brandy was brought and the patient revived. He waited till I'd downed half my drink, then said: "Don't you think I should have another look at that ankle?"

"Thank you, but fortunately no need," I said easily. "Marie fixed it this morning. I had the good sense to marry a fully qualified nurse. I hear you've had a little trouble yourself. Did you find your dog?"

"No trace of him anywhere. Most vexing, most disturbing. A Doberman, you know—very devoted to him. Yes, very devoted. I can't think what has happened." He shook his head worriedly, poured some sherry for himself and Marie and sat beside her on the rattan couch. "I fear some misfortune has overtaken him."

"Misfortune?" Marie gazed at him, wide-eyed. "On this peaceful little island?"

"Snakes, I'm afraid. Highly poisonous vipers. They infest the southern part of the island and live in the rocks at the foot of the mountain. Carl—my dog—may have been bitten by one of those. Incidentally, I meant to warn you—on no account go near that part of the island. Extremely dangerous, extremely."

"Vipers!" Marie shuddered. "Do they—do they come near the houses here?"

"Oh, dear me, no." The professor patted her hand in absent-minded affection. "No need to worry, my dear. They

99

hate this phosphate dust. Just remind yourself to confine your walks to this part of the island."

"I certainly shall," Marie agreed. "But tell me, professor, if the vipers had got him wouldn't you—or someone—have found his body?"

"Not if he were in among the rocks at the foot of the mountain. Fearful jumble there. Of course, he may come back yet."

"Or he may have taken a swim," I suggested.

"A swim?" The professor frowned. "I don't follow you, my boy."

"Was he fond of water?"

"As a matter of fact, he was. By jove, I believe you've hit on it. Lagoon's full of tiger sharks. Monsters, some of them, up to eighteen feet—and I do know they move close in at night. That must have been it, that must have been it. Poor Carl! One of those monsters could have bitten him clear in two. What an end for a dog, what an end." Witherspoon shook his head mournfully and cleared his throat. "Dear me, I shall miss him. He was more than a dog, he was a friend. A faithful and a gentle friend."

We all sat around for a couple of minutes in silent sorrow, paying our last respects to this departed pillar of canine benevolence, and then we got on with the lunch.

It was still daylight, but the sun had sunk beyond the shoulder of the mountain when I woke up. I felt fresh and rested, and while my arm was still stiff and sore, the throbbing pain of the morning had gone: as long as I didn't have to move around, the discomfort was hardly worth mentioning.

Marie had not yet returned. She and the professor had gone out trolling for trevally—whatever trevally might be—with the two Fijian boys after lunch while I had returned to bed. The professor had invited me also, but it had obviously been only as a gesture of politeness, I hadn't the strength to pull in a sardine that afternoon. So they'd gone without me. Professor Witherspoon had expressed regrets and apologies and hoped I didn't mind his taking my wife with him. I'd told him not at all and hoped that they would enjoy themselves and he'd given me a funny look that I couldn't quite figure out, and I'd had the obscure uneasy feeling of having put a foot wrong somewhere. But whatever it was he hadn't let it puzzle him long. He was too interested in his trevally. Not to mention Marie.

I'd washed and shaved and managed to make myself look

more or less respectable by the time they returned. It appeared that the trevally hadn't been biting that day. Neither of them seemed very upset about it. The professor was in tremendous form at the table that evening, a genial thoughtful host with a fund of good stories. He really went out of his way to entertain us and it didn't require any great deductive powers to guess that the effort wasn't being made on my behalf or on the behalf of Hewell, who sat at the opposite end of the table from me, brooding and silent and remote. Marie laughed and smiled and talked almost as much as the professor. She seemed to find his charm and good humour infectious, but it didn't infect me any: I'd done a good solid hour of constructive thinking before I'd gone to sleep that afternoon and the thinking had led me to inevitable conclusions that I found very frightening indeed. I don't scare easy but I know when to be scared: and never a better time in my opinion than when you've made the discovery that you're under the sentence of death. And I was under the sentence of death. I had no doubt at all left in my mind about this.

Dinner over, I pulled myself to my feet, reached for the crutches, thanked the professor for the meal and said that we couldn't possibly trespass on his kindness and hospitality any more that night. We knew, I said, that he was a busy man. He protested, but not too violently, and asked if there were any books he could send across to our house. I said we would be pleased, but that I'd like to take a few steps down to the beach first and he clucked his tongue and wondered whether it would not be too much for me but when I said that he had only to look out of the window and see for himself how little I was exerting myself, he supposed doubtfully it would be all right. We said goodnight and left them.

I'd some difficulty in negotiating the steep bank overhanging the top of the beach, but after that it was easy. The sand was dry and hard-packed and the crutches scarcely sank in at all. We went about a couple of hundred yards down and along the beach, always keeping in line of sight of the professor's windows, till we came to the edge of the lagoon. There we sat down. The moon was as it had been the previous night, one moment there, the next vanished behind drifting cloud. I could hear the distant murmur of the surf breaking on the reef of the lagoon and the faint rustling whisper of the night wind in the nodding palms. There were no exotic tropical scents, I supposed that suffocating grey phosphate dust had crushed the life out of all but the trees and the toughest plants, all I could smell was the sea.

Marie touched my arm with gentle fingers. "How does it feel?"

"Improving. Enjoy your afternoon out?"

"No."

"I didn't think so. You were too happy by half. Learn anything that might be useful?"

"How could I?" she asked disgustedly. "He did nothing but babble and talk nonsense all afternoon."

"It's the Night of Mystery and those clothes you wear," I pointed out kindly. "You're driving the man out of his mind."

"I don't seem to be driving you out of your mind," she said tartly.

"No," I agreed, then, after a few seconds, added bitterly: "You can't drive me out of what I haven't got."

"What strange modesty is this?"

"Look at this beach," I said. "Has it ever occurred to you that four or five days ago in London, before we even took off, that someone *knew* that we would be sitting here tonight? My God, if ever I get out of this I'm going to devote the rest of my life to tiddley-winks. I'm out of my depth in this line. I knew I was right about Fleck, I knew I was. He was no killer."

"You're hopping about too much," Marie protested. "Sure, he wasn't going to kill us. Not nice Captain Fleck. He was just going to tap us on the head and push us over the side. The sharks would have done the dirty work for him."

"Remember when we were sitting on that upper deck? Remember I told you that I felt there was something wrong but that I couldn't put my finger on it? Remember?"

"Yes, I remember."

"Good old Bentall," I said savagely. "Never misses a thing. The ventilator—the ventilator we used as a hearing aid, the one facing the radio room. It *shouldn't* have been facing the radio shack, it should have been facing forward. Remember we got no air down there. No bloody wonder."

"There's no need to—"

"Sorry. But you see it all now, don't you? He knew that even a fool like me would discover that voices from the radio room could be heard down that pipe. Ten gets one he had a concealed mike down in that hold which let him know whenever Bentall, the Einstein of espionage, made such shattering discoveries. He knew there were rats there, and he knew that the rats would discourage us from sleeping on a low bunk, so Henry pushes back some battens which coincidentally happen to be at the very spot where we can start searching for tinned food and drink after we'd passed up that deliberately awful breakfast they gave us. More coincidences: behind the tinned food are battens with loose screws and behind them are lifebelts. Fleck didn't exactly hang up a sign saying 'Lifebelts in this box'—but he came pretty close to it. Then Fleck puts the wind up me good and proper, without in any way appearing to do so, and more or less lets us know that the decision to execute or not will be coming through at seven. So we latch ourselves on to that ventilator and when the word comes through we leave, complete with lifebelts. What do you bet that Fleck hadn't even loosened the screw on the hatch to make things easy—I could probably have forced it with my little finger."

"But—but we could still have drowned," Marie said slowly. "We might have missed the reef or lagoon."

"What—miss a six-mile wide target? You said old Fleck seemed to be changing course pretty often and you were right. He wanted to make good and sure that when we jumped we did so opposite the middle of the reef where we couldn't miss. He even slowed right down so that we couldn't hurt ourselves when we jumped overboard. Probably standing there killing himself laughing when Bentall and Hopeman, two stooges in search of a comedian, pussy-footed it down the stern. And those voices I heard on the reef that night? John and James out in their canoe, seeing that we didn't even put a foot wrong and sprain an ankle. God, how much of a sucker can you be?"

There was a long silence. I lit a couple of cigarettes and gave her one. The moon had gone behind a cloud and her face was only a pale blue in the darkness. Then she said: "Fleck and the professor—they must be working hand in hand."

"Can you see any other possibility?"

"What do they want with us?"

"I'm not sure yet." I was sure, but this was one thing I couldn't tell her.

"But—but why all the fake build-up? Why couldn't Fleck have sailed right in and handed us over to the professor?"

"There's an answer to that, too. Whoever is behind this is a very smart boy indeed. There's a reason for everything he does."

"You—do you think the professor—is he the man behind—"

"I don't know what he is. Don't forget the barbed wire. The Navy is there. They may have come to play skittles, but I don't think so. There's something big, very big, and something very secret going on on the other side of the island. Whoever is in charge there will be taking no chances. They know Witherspoon is there, and that fence doesn't mean a thing, that's just to discourage wandering employees, they'll have investigated him down to the last nail in his shoes. The Services have some very clever investigators indeed and if they're content to have him there that means he's got a clean bill of health. And he knows the Navy is there. Fleck and the professor in cahoots. The professor and the Navy in cahoots. What kind of sense do *you* make out of it?"

"You trust the professor, then? You're saying, in effect, that he is on the level?"

"I'm not saying anything. I'm just thinking out loud."

"No, you're not," she insisted. "If he's accepted by the Navy, he must be on the level. That's what you say. If he is, then why the Chinese crouching in the darkness down by the fence, why the trip-wire?"

"I'm just guessing. He may have warned his employees to keep clear of that place and they know of the dog and the wire. I'm not saying those were his Chinese employees I saw, I only assumed it. If there's something big and secret happening on the other side of the island, don't forget that secrets can be lost by people breaking out as well as by people breaking in. The Navy may well have some top men on *this* side, to see that no one breaks out. Maybe the professor knows all about it—I think he does. We've lost too many secrets to the communist world during the past decade through sheer bad security. The government may have learned its lesson."

"But where do we come in?" she said helplessly. "It's so—so terribly complicated. And how can you explain away the attempt to cripple you?"

"I can't. But the more I think of it the more convinced I am that I'm only a tiny pawn in this and that nearly always tiny pawns have to be sacrificed to win the chess game."

"But why?" she insisted. "Why? And what reason can a harmless old duffer like Professor Witherspoon have for—"

"If that harmless old duffer is Professor Witherspoon," I interrupted heavily, "then I'm the Queen of the May."

For almost a minute there was only the far-off murmur of the surf, the whisper of the night wind in the trees.

"I can't stand much more of this," she said at last, wearily. "You said yourself you've seen him on television and—"

"And a very reasonable facsimile he is, too," I agreed. "His name may even be Witherspoon but he's certainly no professor of archaeology. He's the only person I've ever met who knows less about archaeology than I do. Believe me, that's a feat."

"But he knows so much about it—"

"He knows nothing about it. He's boned up on a couple of books on archaeology and Polynesia and never got quarter of the way through either. He didn't get far enough to find out that there are neither vipers nor malaria in those parts, both of which he claims to exist. That's why he objected to your having his books. You might find out more than he knows. It wouldn't take long. He talks about recovering pottery and wooden implements from basalt—the lava would have crushed the one and incinerated the other. He talks about dating wooden relics by experience and knowledge and any schoolboy in physics will tell you that it can be done with a high degree of accuracy by measuring the extent of decay of radioactive carbon in those relics. He gave me to understand that those relics were the deepest ever found, at 120 feet, and I don't suppose there are more than ten million people who know that a ten million year old skeleton was dug out from the Tuscany hills about three years ago at a depth of 600 feet—in a coal-mine. As for the idea of using high explosive in archaeology instead of prying away gently with pick and shovel—well, don't mention it around the British Museum. You'll have the old boys keeling over like ninepins."

"But—but all those relics and curios they have around—"

"They may be genuine. Professor Witherspoon may have made a genuine strike, then the idea occurred to the Navy that here would be the perfect set-up for secrecy. They could have all access to the island forbidden for perfectly legitimate reasons and that would give them the ideal cover-up, nothing to excite the suspicions of countries who would be very excited indeed if they knew what the Navy was doing. Whatever that is. The strike may be finished long ago and Witherspoon kept under wraps with someone very like him to put up a front for accidental visitors. Or those relics may be fakes. Maybe there never was an archaeological find here. Maybe it's a brilliant idea dreamed up by the Navy. Again they would require Witherspoon's cooperation, but not necessarily himself, which accounts for the bogus prof. Maybe the story was fed to the newspapers and magazines. Maybe some newspaper and magazine proprietors were approached by the government and persuaded to help out in the fraud. It's been done before."

"But there were also American papers, American magazines."

"Maybe it's an Anglo-American project."

"I still don't understand why they should try to cripple you," she said doubtfully. "But maybe one or either of your suggestions goes some way towards an answer."

"Maybe. I really don't know. But I'll have the answer tonight. I'll find it inside that mine."

"Are you—are you really crazy?" she said quietly. "You're not fit to go anywhere."

"It's only a short walk. I'll manage. There's nothing wrong with my legs."

"I'm coming with you."

"You'll do nothing of the kind."

"Please, Johnny."

"No."

She spread out her hands. "I'm of no use to you at all?"

"Don't be silly. We've got to have someone to hold the fort, to see that no one comes snooping into our house to find two dummies. So long as they can hear even one person breathing and see another form beside him, they'll be happy. I'm going back for a couple of hours' sleep. Why don't you go and whoop it up with the old Professor? He can't keep his eyes off you and you may find out a great deal more in that way than I will in mine."

"I'm not quite sure that I understand what you mean."

"The old Mata-Hari act," I said impatiently. "Whisper sweet nothings in his silver beard. You'll have him ga-ga in no time. Who knows what tender secrets he might not whisper in return?"

"You think so?"

"Sure, why not. He's at the dangerous stage as far as women are concerned. Somewhere between eighteen and eighty."

"He might start getting ideas."

"Well, let him. What does it matter? Just so long as you get some information out of him. Duty before pleasure, you know."

"I see," she said softly. She rose to her feet and stretched out her hand. "Come on. Up."

I got to my feet. A couple of seconds later I was sitting on the sand again. It hadn't been so much the unexpectedness of the openhanded blow across the face as the sheer weight of it. I was still sitting there, feeling for the dislocation and marvelling at the weird antics of the female members of the race, when she scrambled over the high bank at the top of the beach and disappeared.

My jaw seemed all right. It hurt, but it was still a jaw. I

got to my feet, swung the crutches under my arms and started for the head of the beach. It was pretty dark now and I could have made it three times as fast without the crutches but I wouldn't have put it past the old boy to have night-glasses on me.

The bank at the top was only three feet high, but it was still too high for me. I finally solved it by sitting on the edge and pushing myself up with my crutches, but when I got to my feet, swung round and made to take off, the crutches broke through the soft soil and I fell backwards over on to the sand.

It knocked the breath out of me but it wasn't much of a fall as falls go, not enough to make me swear out loud, just enough to make me swear softly. I was trying to get enough breath to swear some more when I heard the quick light sound of approaching feet and someone slid over the edge of the bank. A glimpse of white, a whiff of Night of Mystery, she'd come back to finish me off. I braced my jaw again, then unbraced it. She was bent low down, peering at me, in no position at all to haul off at me again.

"I—I saw you fall." Her voice was husky. "Are you badly hurt?"

"I'm in agony. Hey, careful of my sore arm."

But she wasn't being careful. She was kissing me. She gave her kisses like she gave her slaps, without any holding back that I could notice. She wasn't crying, but her cheek was wet with tears. After a minute, maybe two, she murmured: "I'm so ashamed. I'm so sorry."

"So am I," I said. "I'm sorry, too." I'd no idea what either of us was talking about, but it didn't seem to matter very much at the moment. By and by she rose and helped me over the edge of the bank and I tip-tapped my way back to the house, her arm in mine. We passed by the professor's bungalow on the way, but I didn't make any further suggestions about her going in to see him.

It was just after ten o'clock when I slid out under a raised corner of the seawardfacing side-screen. I could still feel her kisses, but I could also feel my sore jaw, so I left in a pretty neutral frame of mind. As far as she was concerned, that is. As far as the others were concerned—the others being the professor and his men—I wasn't feeling neutral at all. I carried the torch in one hand and the knife in the other, and this time I didn't have any cloth wrapped round the knife. If there weren't more lethal things than dogs on the island of Vardu, I sadly missed my bet.

The moon was lost behind heavy cloud, but I took no chances. It was almost a quarter of a mile to where the mine shaft was sunk into the side of the mountain but I covered nearly all of it on hands and knees and it didn't do my sore arm any great deal of good. On the other hand, I got there safely.

I didn't know if the professor would have any good reason to have a guard at the entrance to the mine or not. Again it seemed like a good idea to err on the side of caution, so when I stood up slowly and stiffly in the black shadow of a rock where the moon wouldn't get me when and if it broke through, I just stayed there. I stood there for fifteen minutes and all I could hear was the far-off murmur of the Pacific on the distant reef and the slow thudding of my own heart. Any unsuspecting guard who could keep as still as that for fifteen minutes was asleep. I wasn't scared of men who were asleep. I went on into the mine.

My rubber-soled sandals heel-and-toed it along the lime-stone rock without the slightest whisper of sound. No one could have heard me coming and, after I was clear of the faint luminescence of the cave-mouth, no one could have seen me coming. My torch was off. If there was anyone inside that mine I'd meet them soon enough without letting them know I was on the way. In the dark all men are equal. With that knife in my hand, I was slightly more than equal.

There was plenty of room between the wall and the railway track in the middle to make it unnecessary for me to walk on the sleepers. I couldn't risk a sudden variation of length between a couple of ties. It was simple enough to guide myself by brushing the back of the fingers of my right hand against the tunnel wall from time to time. I took care that the haft of the knife did not strike solid rock.

Inside a minute, the tunnel wall fell away sharply to the right. I had reached the first hollowed-out cavern. I went straight across it to the tunnel opening directly opposite, guiding myself by touching the side of my left foot against the sleepers. It took me five minutes to cross the 70 yards' width of that cave. Nobody called out, nobody switched on a light, nobody jumped me. I was all alone. Or I was being left alone, which wasn't the same thing at all.

Thirty seconds after leaving the first cavern I'd reached the next one. This was the one where the professor had said the first archaeological discoveries had been made, the cavern with the two shored-up entrances to the left, the railway going straight ahead and, to the right, the tunnel where we'd found Hewell and his crew working. I'd no interest in the tunnel where we'd found Hewell working. The professor had given me to understand that that was the source of the explosions that had wakened me the previous afternoon, but all the amount of loose rock I'd seen lying there could have been brought down by a couple of good-sized fire-crackers. I followed the railway across the chamber straight into the opposite tunnel.

This led to a third chamber, and then a fourth. Neither of those had any exits to the north, into the side of the mountain, as I found by walking round a complete semi-circle to my right before regaining the railway track again: I completed the circle in both chambers and found two openings to the south in each. But I went straight on. After that there were no more caverns, just the tunnel that went on and on.

And on. I thought I would never come to the end of it. There had been no archaeological excavations made here, it was just a plain and straightforward tunnel quite unconcerned with what lay on either side of it. It was a tunnel that was going someplace. I was having to walk on the ties now, the diameter had narrowed to half of what it had been at first, and I noticed that the gradient was slightly upward all the time. I noticed, too, that the air in the tunnel, and this at least a mile and a half after I'd left the mine entrance, was still fresh, and I guess that that explained the upward slant of the tunnel—it was being kept deliberately near the rising slope of the mountain-side to facilitate the driving of vertical ventilation shafts. I must have been at least halfway across to the western side of the island by then and it wasn't very hard to guess that it wouldn't be long before the tunnel floor levelled out and started to descend.

It wasn't. The stretch of level floor, when I came to it, didn't extend more than a hundred yards, and then it began to dip. Just as the descent began my right hand failed to find the tunnel wall. I risked a quick snap of the torch and saw a thirty-foot deep cavern to my right, half full of rock and debris. For one moment I thought this must be the scene of yesterday's blasting, but a second look put that thought out of my mind. There were a couple of hundred tons of loose rock lying there, far too much for one day's work, and besides, there was no percentage in driving suddenly north, into the heart of the mountain. This was just a storage dump, one probably excavated some time ago to provide a convenient deposit for the rock blasted from the tunnel proper, when the need arose to do that quickly.

Less than three hundred yards further on I found the end of the tunnel. I rubbed my forehead, which had been the part of me that had done the finding, then switched on the tiny pencil-beam of light. There were two small boxes lying on the floor, both nearly empty, but still holding a few charges of blasting powder, detonators and fuses: this, beyond doubt, was the scene of yesterday's blasting. I played the torch beam over the end of the tunnel and that was all it was, just the end of a tunnel, a seven-foot high by four-foot wide solid face of rock. And then I saw that it wasn't all solid, not quite. Just below eye-level a roughly circular rock about a foot in diameter appeared to have been jammed into a hole in the wall. I eased out this lump of limestone and peered into the hole behind. It was maybe four feet long, tapering inwards to perhaps two inches and at the far end I could see something faintly twinkling, red and green and white. A star. I put the rock back in position and left.

It took me half an hour to get back to the first of the four caverns. I investigated the two openings leading off to the south, but they led only to two further caverns, neither of them with exits. I headed back along the railway till I came to the third of the caverns from the entrance, examined the two openings in this one and achieved nothing apart from getting myself lost in a maze for almost half an hour. And then I came to the second cavern.

Of the two tunnels leading off to the north, I passed up the one where Hewell had been working. I'd find nothing there. I found nothing in the neighbouring one either. And, of course, there would be nothing behind the timber baulks holding up the entrances to the two collapsed tunnels to the south. I made for the exit leading to the outer cavern when the thought occurred to me that the only reason I had for believing that those baulks of timber supported the entrances to a couple of caved-in tunnels was that Professor Witherspoon himself had told me they did and, apart from the fact that he knew nothing about archaeology, the only certain fact that I had so far established about the professor was that he was a fluent liar.

But he hadn't been lying about the first of these two tunnels. The heavy vertical three-by-six timbers that blocked the entrance were jammed immovably in place and when I pressed my torch against a half-inch gap between two of the timbers and switched it on I could clearly see the solid mass of stone and rubble that completely blocked the passage behind, all the way from the floor to the collapsed roof. Maybe I'd been doing the professor an injustice.

And then again maybe I hadn't. Two of the timber baulks

guarding the entrance to the second barricaded tunnel were loose.

No pickpocket ever lifted a wallet with half the delicate care and soundless stealth that I used to lift one of these baulks out of position and lean it against its neighbour. A brief pressure on the torch button showed no signs of a roof collapse anywhere, just a dingy grey smooth-floored tunnel stretching and dwindling away into the darkness. I lifted a second batten out of place and squeezed through the gap into the tunnel beyond.

It was then that I discovered that I couldn't replace the battens from the inside. One, yes, but even then only roughly in place, but it was impossible to manoeuvre the other through the six-inch gap that was left. There was nothing I could do about it. I left it as it was and went down the tunnel.

Thirty yards and the tunnel turned abruptly to the left. I was still guiding myself as I had done earlier on, by brushing the back of my right hand against the wall, and suddenly the wall fell away to the right. I reached in cautiously and touched something cold and metallic. A key, hanging on a hook. I reached beyond it and traced out the outlines of a low narrow wooden door hinged on a heavy vertical post of timber. I took down the key, located the keyhole, softly turned the lock and opened the door a fraction of an inch at a time. My nostrils twitched to the pungent combined smells of oil and sulphuric acid. I eased the door another two inches. The hinges creaked in sepulchral protest, I had the sudden vision of a gibbet and a swaying corpse turning in the night wind and the corpse was myself, then I snapped abruptly to my senses, realised that the time for pussyfooting was over, passed quickly round the door and closed it behind me as I switched on the torch.

There was no one there. One quick traverse of the torch beam round a cave no more than twenty feet in diameter was enough to show me that there was no one there: but there were signs that someone had been there, and very recently.

I moved forward, stubbed my toe heavily against something solid, looked down and saw a large lead-acid accumulator. Wires from this led to a switch on the wall. I pressed the switch and the cave was flooded with light.

Perhaps 'flooded' is the wrong word, it was just by comparison with the weak beam from my torch. A naked lamp, forty watts or thereabouts, suspended from the middle of the roof: but it gave all the illumination I wanted.

Stacked in the middle of the chamber were two piles of oiled yellow boxes. I was almost certain what they were before I crossed to examine them, and as soon as I saw the stencils on top I was certain. The last time I had seen those boxes with the legend 'Champion Spark Plugs' stencilled on them was in the hold of Fleck's schooner. Machine-gun ammunition and ammonal explosive. So perhaps I hadn't been imagining things after all when I thought I had seen lights that night we'd been marooned on the reef. I had seen lights. Captain Fleck unloading cargo.

By the right-hand wall were two wooden racks, holding twenty machine-pistols and automatic carbines of a type I had never seen before: they were heavily coated with grease against the drippingly damp atmosphere of the cave. Stacked beside the racks were three squarish metal boxes, for a certainty ammunition for the guns. I looked at the racked guns and the boxes and for the first time in my life I could understand how a gourmet felt when he sat down to an eight-course dinner prepared by a cordon-bleu chef. And then I opened the first box, the second and the third, and I knew exactly how the same gourmet would have felt if, while still adjusting his napkin, the maitre d'hotel had come along and told him that the shop was shut for the night.

The boxes contained not a single round of carbine or machine-pistol ammunition. One box contained black blasting powder, another beehive blocks of amatol explosive and a drum of .44 short-gun ammunition, the third primers, fulminate of mercury detonators, about a hundred yards R.D.X. fuses and a flat tin case of chemical igniters, most of it stuff, presumably, that Hewell used in his blasting operations. And that was all. My pipe dreams about a loaded machine-pistol and the radical difference it would make to the balance of power on the island were just that, pipe dreams and no more. Ammunition without guns to fire them, guns without ammunition to fit them. Useless, all useless.

I switched out the light and left. It would have taken me only five minutes to wreck the firing mechanisms on every carbine and machine pistol there. I was going to spend the rest of my days bitterly regretting the fact that the thought had never even occurred to me.

Twenty yards further on I came to a similar door on the right of the tunnel wall. No key to this one: it didn't need it for the door wasn't locked. I laid a gentle hand on the knob, turned it and eased the door open a couple of inches. The stench of foetid air that issued through the narrow crack was an almost physical blow in my face, a putrescent mephitis that wrinkled my nostrils in nauseated repugnance and lifted all the hairs on the back of my head. I felt suddenly very cold.

I opened the door further, passed inside and shut it behind me. The switch was in the same place as it had been in the previous cavern. I pressed it and looked round the cave.

But this was no cave. This was a tomb.

CHAPTER SEVEN

Friday 1:30 A.M.-3:30 A.M.

SOME freak in the atmosphere of the cave, possibly a combination of the moisture and the phosphate of lime, had maintained the bodies in a state of almost perfect preservation. Decomposition had set in, but to a negligible extent only, certainly not enough to mar any of the essential features of the nine corpses lying where they had been flung in a rough row at the far end of the cave. The dark stains on white and khaki shirt-fronts made it easy to see how they had died.

Again the ice-chill hand of fear touched the back of my neck. I looked quickly around as if expecting to see the old man with the scythe still waiting patiently in some dark corner of the cave. Waiting for Bentall. Only, there were no dark corners. Nothing, except the round smooth dank walls, the shabby stained bundles on the floor and the battery supplying feeble power to the dim yellow lamp, barely more than head high, that dangled from the centre of the low-vaulted roof.

With my hand to my nose and breathing through my mouth only, I switched on my torch to give extra illumination and scanned the dead faces.

Six of the dead men were complete strangers to me, labourers by the looks of their clothes and hands, and I knew I had never seen them before. But the seventh I recognised immediately. White hair, white moustache, white beard, here was the real Professor Witherspoon: even in death his resemblance to the impostor who had taken his place was startling in its closeness. Beside him lay a giant of a man, a man with red hair and a great red handle-bar moustache: this, beyond any doubt, would be the Dr. 'Red' Carstairs whose portrait I had been shown in a magazine. The ninth man, in a much better state of preservation than the others, I identified without a second glance: his presence there confirmed that the men who had advertised for a second fuel research specialist had indeed been in need of one: it was Dr. Charles Fairfield, my old chief in the Hepworth and Ordnance Fuel Research, one of the eight scientists who had been lured out to Australia.

Sweat was pouring down my face but I was shivering with cold. What was Dr. Fairfield doing there? Why had he been killed? Old Fairfield was the last man to stumble upon anything. A brilliant man in his own field, he was as shortsighted as a dodo and had a monumental incuriosity about everybody and everything except his own work and his consuming private passion for archaeology. And the archaeological tie-up between Fairfield and Witherspoon was so blindingly obvious that it just didn't make any sense at all. Whatever reason lay behind Dr. Fairfield's sudden disappearance from England, nothing was more certain than that it was entirely unconnected with whatever pick and shovel expertise he might show in abandoned mine-workings. But then what in the name of God was he doing here?

I felt as if I were in an ice-box, but the sweat was trickling more heavily than ever down the back of my neck. Still holding the torch in my right hand—the knife was in my left—I worked a handkerchief out of my right trouser pocket and mopped the back of my neck. To the left and front of me I caught a momentary flash of something glittering on the wall of the cave, something metallic, obviously, reflecting the beam of the still burning torch. But what? What metallic object was there? Apart from the dead men the only other objects in that cave were the light fitting and the light switch, and both were made of bakelite. I held the torch and handkerchief, both still over my shoulder, perfectly steady. The glimmer of light on the cave wall was still there. I stood like a statue, my eyes never leaving that gleam on the wall. The light moved.

My heart stopped. The medical profession can say what it likes, but my heart stopped. Then slowly, carefully, I brought down both torch and handkerchief, transferred the torch to my left hand as if to enable me to shove my handkerchief away with my right, then dropped the handkerchief, clutched the hilt of the knife in my right hand and whirled round all in one half second of time.

There were two of them, no more than four feet inside the cave, still fifteen feet distant from me. Two Chinese, already moving wide apart to encircle me, one in dungaree trousers and cotton shirt, the other in a pair of cotton shorts, both big muscular men, both in their bare feet. Their unwinking eyes, the oriental immobility of the yellow faces served only to emphasize, not mask, the cold implacability of the expressions. You didn't have to know your Emily Post to realise that they just weren't paying a social call. Nor would Emily have given them any medals for their calling cards, two of the most lethal-looking double-edged throwing knives I'd ever seen: the books on etiquette covered practically every possible situation in which strangers first made the other's acquaintance, but they'd missed out on this one.

It would be ridiculous to deny that I was frightened, so I won't. I was scared, and badly scared. Two fit men against one semi-invalid, four good arms against one, two undoubtedly skilled and cunning knife-fighters against a man who'd never even carved up a lump of cooked dead meat far less a live human being. And this wasn't the time to learn. But it was the time to do something, and do it very quickly indeed before one or other of them caught on to the idea that at five yards I was a target that could hardly be missed and changed over from a stabbing to a throwing grip on his knife.

I rushed at them, right hand and knife over my shoulder as if I were wielding a club, and both of them fell back an involuntary couple of paces, maybe because of the foolhardy recklessness of it, more likely because of the respectful fear which Orientals habitually show in the presence of madness. I brought the knife whistling forward over my shoulder and with the tinkling of glass from the smashed overhead light and the flick of my left thumb on the torch switch the cave became as pitch-black as the tomb it really was.

It was essential to move, and move as fast as possible before they realised that I had the double advantage of having a torch and being in the position to lash out indiscriminately with my knife in the hundred per cent certainty that I would be stabbing an enemy, whereas they had a fifty per cent chance of stabbing a friend. Reckless of the noise I made in that utterly silent chamber, I pulled away the occluding plaster on the face of the torch, slipped off my sandals, ran three heavy steps in the direction of the entrance, stopped abruptly and sent both sandals sliding along the ground to thud softly against the wooden door.

Had they been given another ten seconds to take stock of their position, to work out the possibilities, probably the last thing they would have done would have been to rush headlong to the source of the sudden noise. As it was, they had been given barely five seconds altogether in which to think, and the immediate and inevitable reaction must have been that I was trying to escape. I heard the quick patter of bare feet, the sound of a brief scuffle, a soft thud and an explosive gasp of agony that was lost in the clatter of something metallic falling to the floor.

Four swift soundless steps on my stockinged feet, a flick of the left thumb and they were pinned in the white glare of the torch, a tableau vivant but for their unnaturally petrified rigidity which gave them for all the world the appearance of a group sculpted from marble. They stood face to face, their chests almost but not quite touching. The man on my right had his left hand twisted in his companion's shirt front while his right hand was pressed against the other's body, just below waist level: the man on the left, his face averted from me, was arched over backwards like an overstrung bow, both hands locked over the right hand of his companion: the ridged and straining tendons turned the hands into waxen claws, the knuckles gleamed white like polished bone. I could see the blood-stained point of a knife sticking out two inches from the small of his back.

For two seconds, perhaps three—it seemed far longer than that—the man on the right stared unbelievingly into the face of the dying man, then the realisation of his lethal blunder and the awareness that death stood now at his own elbow broke the horror-numbed spell that had held him in thrall. He struggled frantically to withdraw his knife but the last agonies of his friend had locked right hand and knife fast in an iron-bound grip. He swung round desperately on me, his left arm flying upwards and outwards in a gesture that was half blow, half an attempt to shield himself from the beam I'd now directed into his shrinking eyes, and for a moment he had no guard left. The moment was enough and to spare. The blade of my knife was twelve inches long but for all that I jarred both wrist and knife as the hilt struck home against the breast-bone. He coughed once, a brief convulsive choked sound and drew his thin lips far back from the fast-clenched teeth into a hideous and blood-flecked grin: then the blade of my knife snapped and I was left with only the hilt and an inch of steel in my hand as the two men, still locked together, swayed over to my right and crashed heavily on to the limestone floor of the cave.

I shone the torch beam down on the faces at my feet, but it was a superfluous precaution, they would never trouble me again. I recovered my sandals, picked up the fallen knife and left, closing the door behind me. Once outside I leaned my weight against the tunnel wall, hands hanging by my side, and drew in great deep lungfuls of pure fresh air. I felt weak, but put it down to my damaged arm and the foul air inside that tomb, the brief and violent episode on the other side of that door had left me curiously unaffected, or so I thought until I felt the pain in my cheek muscles and jaw and realised that my lips were strained back in involuntary imitation of the death's head grin of the man I had just killed. It took a conscious effort of will to relax the overstrained muscles of my face.

It was then that I heard the singing. This was it, Bentall's tottering reason had gone at last, the shock of what I'd just seen and done had overstrained more than the facial muscles. Bentall unhinged, Bentall round the bend, Bentall hearing noises in his head. What would Colonel Raine have said if he knew his trusty servant had gone off his trolley? He would probably have smiled his little invisible smile and said in his dry dusty voice that to hear singing in an abandoned mine-working, even a mine under the control of murderous impostors and patrolled by equally murderous Chinese, was not necessarily evidence of insanity. To which his trusty servant would have replied, no, it wasn't, but to hear a choir of English women singing 'Greensleeves' most certainly was.

For that was what I was hearing. Women's voices and singing 'Greensleeves'. Not a recording, for one of the voices was slightly off-key and another trying to harmonise with what I could only regard as a very limited degree of success. English women, singing 'Greensleeves'. I shook my head violently but they still kept at it. I clasped my hands over my ears and the singing stopped. I took them away and the singing started again. Noises in the head don't stop when you put your hands over your ears. Maybe the fact that there were English women down in that mine was crazy, but at least I wasn't. Still like a man in a trance, but careful, for all that, to make not the slightest whisper of sound, I pushed myself off the door and went padding down the tunnel to investigate.

The sound of the singing swelled abruptly as I followed a ninety degree turning to the left. Twenty yards away I could see a faint backwash of light against the left side of the tunnel where it seemed to make another abrupt turning, this time to the right. I drifted up to this corner like a falling snowflake and poked my head around with all the dead slow caution of an old hedgehog taking his first wary squint at the world after a winter's hibernation.

Twenty feet away the full width of the tunnel was blocked by vertical iron bars, spaced about six inches apart, with an inset grille door. Ten feet beyond that were a similar set of bars, with a similar door. Halfway between the two doors,

117

suspended close to the roof, a naked bulb threw a harsh light over the small table directly beneath it and the two overalled men who sat one on either side of the table. Between them were a pile of curiously shaped wooden blocks and I assumed that they were playing a game, but it wasn't any game I'd ever seen. But whatever it was, it was obviously a game that called for concentration to judge by the irritated looks both men gave in the direction of the darkened space that lay behind the second set of bars. The singing showed no sign of stopping. Why people should be singing after midnight struck me as inexplicable until I remembered that to people imprisoned in a darkened cave day and night must have no meaning. Why they should be singing at all I couldn't even begin to imagine.

After maybe twenty seconds more of this, one of the men thumped his fist on the table, jumped to his feet, picked up one of two carbines that I could now see had been propped against a chair, crossed to the faraway set of bars and rattled the butt of the gun against the metal, at the same time shouting out something in an angry voice. I didn't understand the words but it didn't need a linguist to understand the meaning. He was asking for silence. He didn't get it. After a pause lasting maybe three seconds the singing came again, louder and more off-key than ever. Give them time and they'd start in on 'There'll Always Be an England'. The man with the carbine shook his head in disgust and disbelief and came wearily back to the table. The situation was beyond him.

It was beyond me too. Maybe if I hadn't been so tired, or maybe if I'd been someone else altogether, someone, say, about twice as smart as I was, I might have thought of a way to get past or even overpower the guards. But right then all I could think of was that I had one little knife and they had two big guns and that anyway I'd used up all my luck for that night.

I left.

Marie was sleeping peacefully when I finally got back to our hut and I didn't wake her at once. Let her sleep as long as she could, she wouldn't get any more sleep this night, maybe her dark fears of the future were justified after all, maybe she wasn't going to have any more sleep, ever.

Mentally, physically, emotionally, I was exhausted. Completely exhausted, let down as I'd never been before. On the way out from the mine I'd come to the conclusion that there was one thing and one thing only to do: I'd screwed what little was left of my nerve up to the sticking point to do it and when the doing had proved impossible the reaction had been correspondingly great. What I had planned to do had been to kill both Witherspoon—I still thought of him as that—and Hewell. Not kill them, murder them, murder them as they lay in their beds. Or maybe it was better to say execute them. Obviously, from the tunnel that went clear through to the other side of the island and the armoury in the mine, a full-scale attack was about to be launched on the naval establishment on the other side of the island. With Witherspoon and Hewell dead, it seemed unlikely that the leaderless Chinese would go through with it, and to me, at that moment, the prevention of the attack was the only thing that mattered. It mattered even more than the welfare of the girl asleep beside me, and I could no longer kid myself that my feelings towards her were the same as they'd been three short days ago: but she still came second.

But I hadn't killed them in their beds for the sufficient reason that neither of them had been in their beds: they'd both been across at the professor's house, drinking the chilled canned beer that the Chinese boy brought in from time to time, talking in soft voices as they pored over charts. The general and his A.D.C. preparing for D-Day. And D-Day was at hand.

The disappointment, the bitterness of what had seemed the ultimate defeat, had taken the last of the heart from me. I'd withdrawn from the window of the professor's house and just stood there dully, unthinkingly, careless of the risk of discovery, until after maybe five minutes a few of my brain cells started trudging around again. Then I'd walked heavily back up to the mine—it says much for my state of mind that the thought of repeating my earlier hands and knees crawl up there never entered my head—picked up some R.D.X. fuses and chemical igniters in the armoury, came out again, rummaged around the generating plant until I found a can of petrol and then returned.

Now I got pencil and paper, hooded the torch light and started writing a message in block capitals. It took me only three minutes and when I was finished I was far from satisfied with it, but it would have to do. I crossed the room and shook Marie by the shoulder.

She woke slowly, reluctantly, murmuring something in a drowsy voice, then sat up abruptly in bed. I could see the pale gleam of her shoulders in the dark, the movement as a hand came up to brush tousled hair away from her eyes.

"Johnny?" she whispered. "What is it? What—what did you find?"

"Too damn much. Just let me talk. We have very little time left. Know anything about radio?"

"Radio?" A brief pause. "I did the usual course. I can send morse, not fast, but—"

"Morse I can manage myself. Do you know what frequency ships' radio operators use for sending distress messages?"

"S.O.S.'s, you mean? I'm not sure. Low frequency, isn't it? Or long wave?"

"Same thing. You can't remember the wave-band?"

She thought for a few moments and I sensed rather than saw the shake of the head in the darkness. "I'm sorry, Johnny."

"It doesn't matter." It did matter, it mattered a very great deal, but I'd been crazy even to hope. "But you'll know old Raine's private code, though?"

"Of course."

"Well, code this message, will you?" I thrust the paper, pencil and torch into her hands. "As quickly as you can."

She didn't ask me the purpose of what must have struck her as an idiotic request: she just hooded the torch under the blanket and read the message in a low voice.

RIDEX COMBON LONDON STOP IMPRISONED VARDU ISLAND APPROX 150 MILES SOUTH VITI LEVU STOP DISCOVERED MURDERED BODIES DR CHARLES FAIRFIELD ARCHAEOLOGISTS PROFESSOR WITHERSPOON DR CARSTAIRS SIX OTHERS STOP BILEX WIVES MISSING SCIENTISTS HELD PRISONER HERE STOP MEN RESPONSIBLE PLANNING ALLOUT ASSAULT DAWN NAVAL INSTALLATION WEST SIDE VARDU STOP SITUATION GRAVE STOP IMPERATIVE AIRBORNE ASSISTANCE IMMEDIATELY BENTALL

The faint glow of the light died as the torch was switched off. For almost twenty seconds there was nothing to be heard but the far-off murmur of the surf on the reef, and when she finally spoke her voice was unsteady.

"You found all this out tonight, Johnny?"

"Yes. They've driven a tunnel clear through to the other side of the island. They've a well-stocked armoury hidden away in one of the caves, where they keep their blasting explosive. And I heard women's voices. Singing."

"Singing!"

"I know it sounds crazy. It must be the scientists' wives, who else could it be. Get busy on that code. I have to go out again."

"The code—how are you going to send this message?" she asked helplessly.

"Professor's radio."

"The professor's—but you're bound to wake him up."

"He isn't asleep. He and Hewell are still talking. I'll have to draw them off. I'd thought first of going up to the north for half a mile or so and setting some delayed action amatol blocks, but that wouldn't work. So I'm going to set the workers' hut on fire. I've got the petrol and fuses here."

"You're crazy." Her voice was still unsteady, but maybe she had something there. "The workers' hut is only a hundred yards from the professor's house. You could let off those amatol blocks a mile away, give yourself plenty of time and—" She broke off and then went on abruptly: "What's all the desperate hurry, anyway? What makes you so certain that they're going to attack at dawn?"

"It's the same answer to everything," I said wearily. "Letting off a few bombs to the north might draw them off all right, but as soon as they came back they'd start wondering where all the fireworks came from. It wouldn't take them any time at all to realise that they must have come from the armoury. The first thing they'll find up there is that a couple of their Chinese guards are missing. It won't take them long to find out where they are. Even if I don't set off bombs their absence is bound to be noticed by dawn at the latest, I imagine. Probably long before that. But we won't be here. If we are, they'll kill us. Me, at any rate."

"You said two guards were missing?" she said carefully.

"Dead."

"You killed them?" she whispered.

"More or less."

"Oh, God, must you try to be facetious?"

"I wasn't trying to be." I picked up the petrol can, fuse and igniters. "Please code that as quickly as possible."

"You're a strange person," she murmured. "I think you frighten me at times."

"I know," I said. "I should have stood there turning both cheeks at once and let our yellow friends carve me into little ribbons. I just haven't got it in me to be a Christian, that's all."

I dropped down under the back screen, lugging the can with me. Lights still burned in the professor's house. I skirted Hewell's hut and brought up at the back of the long house at the point where the steep-pitched thatch of the roof swept down to within four feet of the ground. I had little hopes of and no interest in burning the house down completely, the huge salt-water butts which stood to the rear of every house precluded any chance of that, but the thatch should make a
121

tidy enough blaze for all that. Slowly, painstakingly, careful to avoid even the faintest glug-glug from the neck of the can, I poured the petrol on a two foot wide strip of thatch over almost half the length of the roof, stretched out a length of R.D.X. fuse above this, one end going into the saturated thatch, the other into a chemical igniter. I placed the igniter on a small stone held in my hand, tapped it with the base of the knife, held the fuse long enough to feel the sudden warmth of the ignited powder train through its braided cover, then left at once. The empty petrol can I left under the floor of Hewell's house.

Marie was sitting at a table when I got back, a blanket draped over her and the table. From beneath the blanket came a dim yellow glow and even as I carefully lowered the side-screen facing the sea, the lamp went out. She emerged from the blanket and said softly: "Johnny?"

"Me. Finished?"

"Here it is." She handed me a slip of paper.

"Thanks." I folded it away in a breast pocket and went on: "The entertainment starts in about four minutes. When Hewell and Witherspoon come ankling by be at the doorway, wide-eyed, clutching your negligee or whatever and asking the usual daft questions appropriate to such occasions. Then you'll turn round and speak into the darkness, telling me to stay where I am, that I'm not fit to go anywhere. After that, get dressed quickly, slacks, socks, shirt or cardigan, everything as dark as you can, cover up as much as you can—, hardly the ideal bathing suit but in night waters you'll look a less appetising snack to the inshore tiger sharks the professor told us about than if you were wearing a bikini. Then take the shark-repellent canisters off the two spare lifebelts and fit them—"

"Swimming?" she interrupted. "We're going swimming? Why?"

"For our lives. Two canisters and one life belt apiece, we'll make better time that way."

"But—but your arm, Johnny? And the sharks?"

"My arm won't be much good to me if I'm dead," I said heavily, "and I'll take the sharks before Hewell any day. Two minutes. I must go."

"Johnny."

"What is it?" I said impatiently.

"Be careful, Johnny."

"I'm sorry." I touched her cheek in the darkness. "I'm pretty clumsy, aren't I?"
122

"Clumsy is no word for it." She reached up and pressed my hand against her cheek. "Just come back, that's all."

When I got round to the back window of the professor's house, he and Hewell were still pressing on with arrangements for the second front. The conference seemed to be going well. The professor was talking in a low emphatic voice, pointing towards a chart which seemed to be some section of the Pacific, while Hewell's gigantic features cracked into a cold little half-smile from time to time. They were busy, but not too busy to drink their beer. It didn't seem to have any effect on them but it did on me, it suddenly made me realise how dry and parched my throat was. I just stood there, waiting and wishing for two things, a beer and a gun, a beer to do away with my thirst and a gun to do away with Hewell and Witherspoon. Good old Bentall, I thought bitterly, nothing of the common touch about him, whenever he wishes for something it has to be really unattainable. Which once more just showed how wrong I could be: within thirty seconds one of those wishes was mine.

The Chinese boy had just entered the room with fresh supplies for the strategists when the black oblong of window behind Hewell's head became no longer black. A vivid yellow flash suddenly lit the darkness behind the hut of the Chinese—from the professor's house the rear of the hut was invisible—and within five seconds the yellow had given way to a bright orangey red as the flames leaped up fifteen, even twenty feet, overtopping the high ridge-pole of the hut. Petrol and thatch made a combustible combination of some note.

The Chinese boy and the professor saw it in the same instant. For a man who had consumed the amount of beer he seemed to have done I must say the professor didn't spend much time on double-takes. He passed some comment which bore no resemblance to his usual 'Dear me's' and 'God bless my souls', kicked over his chair and took off like a rocket. The Chinese boy had been even faster, but as it had cost him a second to lay his tray down on the nearest flat surface, which happened to be the blotter on the open roll-top desk, he arrived at the door at the same instant as Witherspoon. For a moment they jammed in the doorway, the professor made some other comment, not very learned in its nature, and then they were off, Hewell pounding along on their heels.

Five seconds later I was seated at the roll-top desk. I tore open the right-hand door, unhooked from its inside the ear-pieces and bakelite-bonded transmitting key, leads from both of which led to the back of the set, clapped the earphones to my head and set the key on the table. There were a knob and a switch placed close together on the set, it seemed logical to suppose that they might be the on-off power switch and the transmitting switch, I turned the one and pressed the other and I was right. At least I'd guessed right for the power switch, the earphones filled at once with a loud insistent crackling, so obviously it drew the receiving antenna into circuit.

Low frequency, Marie had said, she'd thought distress signals went out on low frequency. I stared at the five semi-circular calibrated tuning dials, the middle one of which was already illuminated, gazed at the names of East Asiatic towns marked in English and Chinese and wondered how the hell a man could find out which was long wave and which short.

Whether I could also hear my own transmissions on the earphones I didn't know. I tapped out a few experimental S.O.S.'s but heard nothing. I shifted the switch on the set back to the position I'd found it, tapped the transmitter again, but still nothing. It was then that I caught sight of the small push-pull switch just beyond the key on the bakelite transmitter. I pulled it towards me, made the signal again and this time I heard it come clearly through on the phone. Obviously I could either transmit and receive at the same time or transmit without receiving if I felt like it.

The tuning dials were calibrated in thin black lines to show wavebands but there were no figures to indicate which bands they were. That would have made no difference to an expert operator but it made a crippling difference to me. I peered even more closely, saw that the top two bands were marked KHZ at their outer ends, the lower three MHZ. For several seconds I failed to see their significance, my head was tired now and aching almost as much as my arm, and then, miraculously, I got it. K for kilocycles, M for megacycles. The topmost of the five bands would be the longest wavelength lowest-frequency of the lot. That's where I wanted to be, or at least I hoped it was where I wanted to be. I pushed the left hand knob of a group of what I took to be waveband selector buttons and the top dial came to life as the light behind the centre dial died away.

I turned the station selector dial knob as far left as it would go and started transmitting. I would send out a group of three S.O.S.'s, wait a second, repeat, listen for three or four seconds, move a fraction up the dial and start transmitting again. It was dull work but the beer helped me along.

Ten minutes passed, during which time I must have transmitted on at least thirty different frequencies. Nothing, no acknowledgment at all. Nothing. I glanced at the clock on the wall. One minute to three. I sent out another S.O.S. call. The same answer as all the others.

I was jumping by this time. I could still see the red glare of the fire reflected on the inside walls, but there was no guarantee that Hewell and the professor were going to stay there till the last dying ember turned to charcoal. They might be back any second, or anyone happening by either of the two windows or the open door would be bound to see me, but I didn't see that it mattered very much now, if I couldn't get through on this radio I was finished anyway. What really worried me was whether anyone had yet discovered the two dead men in the mine: that way I would be finished too, only an awful lot quicker. Was somebody already conducting a search because the guards had failed to report, was the professor checking to see if I really was in bed, had anyone found the petrol can under Hewell's house ... ? The questions were endless and the answers to all of them held so high a degree of possibility of so high a degree of unpleasantness that I put it all out of my mind. I drank some more beer and got on with the transmitting.

The phones crackled in my ears. I bent right forward, as if that would help to bring me into closer contact with the distant sender, and sent out the distress signal again. Once more the morse started buzzing my ears, I could make out the individual letters but not the words they spelled out. Akita Maru, Akita Maru, four times repeated. A Japanese ship. A Japanese radio operator. The Bentall luck was running true to form. I moved further across the waveband.

I wondered how Marie was getting on. She would be set to go by now and trying to figure out what on earth had happened to me, she would be looking at the time and knowing that the dawn was only three hours to go, that those three hours might be all the time we had left unless the dead men were discovered, in which case the time would be less. Maybe a great deal less. I kept on sending and composed a little speech I was going to make to Colonel Raine. When I got back. If I got back.

Fast fluent morse started stuttering through the earphones. First the acknowledgment signal followed by: "U.S. Frigate 'Novair County': position: name?"

A U.S. Frigate! Maybe only a hundred miles away. God, it would be the answer to everything! A frigate. Guns, machine-guns, armed men, everything. Then my elation ebbed a trifle. Position? Name? Of course, in a genuine S.O.S., position came first, always.

"150 miles south of Fiji," I tapped. "Vardu—"

"Lat. and long.?" the operator cut in. He was sending so fast that I could hardly pick it up.

"Uncertain."

"What ship?"

"No ship. Island. Island of Vardu—"

Again he overrode my transmission.

"Island?"

"Yes."

"Get off the air, you damn fool, and stay off it. This is a distress frequency." With that the transmission ended abruptly.

I could have kicked that damned transmitter all the way into the lagoon. I could have done the same with the duty operator on the 'Novair County'. I could have wept with frustration, but it was far too late for tears. Besides, I could hardly blame him. I sent again on the same frequency, but the operator on the 'Novair County'—it could have been no other—just leaned on his transmitting button and kept on leaning till I gave up. I twisted the selector dial again, but only a fraction. I'd learnt one invaluable thing: I was on the distress frequency. Keep burning, hut, I beseeched it silently, keep burning. For old Bentall's sake, please don't go out. Which was quite a lot to ask considering what I'd done to the hut.

It kept burning and I kept transmitting. Within twenty seconds I got another reply, the acknowledgment, then: "S.S. Annandale. Position?"

"Australian registry?" I sent.

"Yes. Position, repeat position." Getting testy and understandably so: when a man's shouting for help he shouldn't first of all enquire into the pedigree of his rescuer. I hesitated for a second before sending, I had to make an immediate impact on the operator or I'd likely get as short shrift as I'd had from the U.S. Navy. The distress frequency is sacrosanct to all nations.

"Special British Government investigator John Bentall requesting immediate relay coded message via Portishead radio to Admiralty Whitehall London. Desperately urgent."

"Are you sinking?"

I waited for a few assorted blood vessels to burst but when none did I sent: "Yes." In the circumstances it seemed that it might save a great deal of misunderstanding. "Please prepare receive message." I was almost certain that the glare outside was beginning to die down: there wouldn't be much of the hut left by this time.

There was a long pause. Someone was taking time to make up his mind. Then came the single word "Priority." It was a question.

"Telegraphic address carries over-riding priority all signals to London."

That got him.

"Proceed with message."

I proceeded, forcing myself to tap it out slowly and accurately. The red glow was fading on the inside of the walls of the room. The fierce roar of flames had died away to a lazy crackling and I thought I could hear voices. My neck was stiff from glancing back over my shoulder through the window nearest the fire, but I didn't need my eyes to transmit with and I got the message through. I finished: "Please dispatch immediately."

There was a pause of maybe thirty seconds then he came through again. "Master authorises immediate transmission. Are you in danger?"

"Vessel approaching," I sent. That would keep them quiet. "O.K." A sudden thought occurred to me. "What is your position?"

"Two hundred miles due east Newcastle."

For all the help that was they might as well have been orbiting the earth in a satellite, so I sent: "Thank you very much." And signed off.

I replaced the transmitting key and headphones, closed up the doors and went to the window, poking a cautious head round the corner. I'd been wrong about the value of these big salt-water butts, where the workers' hut had been there remained now only a five-foot high pile of glowing red embers and ashes. I'd get no Oscars for counter-espionage but as an arsonist I was neck and neck with the best. At least I wasn't a complete failure. Hewell and the professor were standing together, presumably talking, as the Chinese dumped buckets of water on the smouldering remains, and as there didn't seem to be much that they would be able to do at this late stage they'd likely be along any minute. Time to be gone. I went along the centre passage, turned right to pass through the still lit kitchen and then halted in a way that would have made an observer think that I had run into an invisible brick wall.

What had brought me up so short was the sight of a pile of canned beer empties lying in a wicker basket. My God, the beer. Good old Bentall, never missed a thing, not if you held it six inches from his nose and beat him over the head with a club to attract his attention. I'd drained two full beer glasses back in the living-room there, and just left the empties standing: even with all the excitement neither the professor nor Hewell struck me as a man who would be liable to forget that he had left a full glass behind him—certainly the Chinese house-boy wouldn't—and they wouldn't put it down to evaporation from the heat of the fire either. I picked up another couple of cans from the crate on the floor, opened them in four seconds flat with the steel opener lying on the sink unit, ran back to the desk in the living-room and filled up the two glasses again, holding them at a shallow angle so that a head too suspiciously high wouldn't be formed on the beer. Back in the kitchen again I dropped the cans among the other empties—in the pile that had been consumed that night another two were liable to go unnoticed—and then left the house. I wasn't any too soon, for I could see the house-boy making for the front door, but I got back to our house unobserved.

I entered under the seaward screen and saw the outline of Marie against the front doorway where she was still watching what was left of the fire. I whispered her name and she came to me.

"Johnny!" She seemed glad to see me in a way that no one I could ever remember had been glad to see me before. "I've died about a hundred times since you left here."

"Is that all?" I put my good arm around her and squeezed and said: "I got the message through, Marie."

"The message?" I was pretty well worn out that night, mentally as well as physically, but even so it took a pretty slow type to miss the fact that he'd just been paid the biggest compliment of his life. But I missed it. "You—you got it through? How wonderful, Johnny!"

"Luck. A sensible sparks on an Aussie ship. Halfway to London by this time. And then things will happen. What, I don't know. If there are any British, American or French naval craft near, they'll be nearer still in a few hours. Or detachments of soldiers by flying boat, maybe from Sydney. I don't know. But what I do know is that they won't be here in time—"

"Sshh," she touched my lips with her finger. "Someone coming."

I heard the two voices, one quick and sharp, the other like a cement truck grinding up a grade in low gear. Witherspoon and Hewell. Maybe ten yards away, maybe not even that: through the interstices in the screen wall I could see the
128

swinging of the lantern that one or other of them was carrying. I leapt for the bed, fumbled desperately for a pajama jacket, found one, shrugged into it and buttoned it up to the neck and dived under a blanket. I landed on the elbow of my injured arm and when I propped myself up on the other as a knock came and the two men entered without benefit of invitation, it was no difficulty at all to look sick and pale. Heaven knows I felt it.

"You must excuse us, Mrs. Bentall," the professor said with that nice mixture of smoothness, concern and undiluted unctuousness that would have made me sick if I hadn't been that way already. But I had to admire his terrific powers of dissimulation under any and all circumstances: in the light of what I had seen, heard and done it was difficult to remember that we were still playing games of make-believe. "We were naturally anxious to see if you were all right. Most distressing this, really most distressing." He patted Marie's shoulder in a paternal fashion that I would have ignored a couple of days ago, and brought his lantern closer to have a good look at me. "Merciful heavens, my boy, you don't look well at all! How do you feel?"

"It's only during the night that it gives me a little trouble," I said bravely. I had my head half-turned away ostensibly because the bright beam from the lantern was hurting my half-closed eyes but actually because, in the circumstances, it seemed hardly advisable to waft too many beer fumes in his direction. "I'll be fine tomorrow. That was a terrible fire, professor. I wish I'd been fit to give you a hand. How on earth could it have started?"

"Those damned Chinks," Hewell growled. He was looming massively just outside the direct radiance of the light and the deep-sunk eyes were quite lost under the craggy overhang of his great tufted brows. "Pipe-smokers and always making tea on little spirit stoves. I've warned them often enough."

"And against all regulations," the professor put in testily. "They know it very well. Still, we won't be here so much longer and they can sleep in the drying shed until then. Hope you haven't been too upset about this. We'll leave you now. Nothing we can do for you, my dear?"

I didn't think he was talking to me so I lowered myself down to the pillow with a stifled moan. Marie thanked him and said no.

"Good night, then. Incidentally, come across for breakfast when it suits you in the morning and my boy will be there to serve you. Hewell and I will be up betimes tomorrow." He chuckled ruefully. "This archaeology is like a mild poison in the blood—once it gets there it never lets you go."

He patted Marie's shoulder a bit more and took off. I waited till Marie reported that they'd reached the professor's house, then said: "As I was saying before the interruption, help will come but not in time to save our bacon. Not if we stay here. Got the lifebelts and shark-repellent ready?"

"They're a horrible pair, aren't they?" she murmured. "I wish that murderous old goat would keep his hands to himself. Yes, they're ready. Must we, Johnny?"

"Damn it all, can't you see that we must leave?"

"Yes, but—"

"We can't go by land. Sheer mountains on one side, a cliff on the other and a couple of barbed wire fences and assorted Chinese in between make that impossible. We could go through the tunnel, but though three or four fit men might pickaxe their way through the last few feet in an hour, I couldn't do it in a week the way I'm feeling."

"You could blast it down? You know where the supplies—"

"Heaven help us both," I said. "You're just as ignorant as I am. Tunnelling is a skilled occupation. If we didn't bring the roof down on top of us we'd certainly completely seal off the end of the tunnel and then our pals could come along and nab us at their leisure. And we can't go by boat, for the simple reason that both boatmen sleep in the boathouse and anyway it would be no good, if that simple method of approach was open to Witherspoon and Hewell and the doughty Captain Fleck available to them they wouldn't tunnel all that way through rock. If the Navy takes such precautions with fences and guards against imagined friends, what are they going to take against the sea where anybody may turn up? You can bet your life that they have two or three small interlocking radar positions capable of picking up a seagull swimming ashore, with a few quick-firing guns to back them up.

"The only thing I'm against is leaving the scientists and their wives here. But I don't see—"

"You never mentioned that the scientists were there," she said in quick surprise.

"No? Maybe I thought it was obvious. Maybe it's not. Maybe I'm wrong. But why else in the name of heaven should the wives be there? The Navy is working on some project of clearly considerable importance and this damned murdering white-haired old monster is just biding his time to pinch it. From his last remark, lying in his teeth to the end, I gather he's biding no more. He's going to get this thing, whatever it is, and use the wives as levers to make the back-room boys work on it and develop it further, for what purposes I can't even guess except that they're bound to be nefarious." I climbed stiffly out of the bed and pulled off the pajama jacket. "What other alternative occurs to you? Eight missing wives, ditto scientists. Witherspoon's bound to be using those wives as a lever, if they were of no use to him in that capacity he wouldn't even bother to feed them, he wouldn't waste anything on them except for a few ounces of lead, as he did for the genuine Witherspoon and others. The man is devoid of feeling to the point of insanity. Where the wives are, there the husbands are. You don't think Colonel Raine sent us out to the Fijis just to do the hula-hula dance, do you?"

"That's Hawaii," she murmured. "Not Fiji."

"My God!" I said. "Women!"

"I'm only teasing, you clown." She put her arms round my neck and came close to me: her hands were abnormally cold and she was trembling. "Don't you see I have to? I just can't go on talking about it. I thought I was quite good—in this business—and so did Colonel Raine, but I don't think so any longer. There's too much—there's too much calculated inhumanity, such an absolute indifference to good or evil or morality, just what's expedient, there's all those men murdered for no reason, there's us, and I think you're crazy to hope for us, there's all those poor women, especially those poor women . . ." She broke off, gave a long quivering sigh and whispered: "Tell me again about you and me and the lights of London."

So I told her, told her so that I half believed it myself, and I thought she did too, for by and by she grew still, but when I kissed her her lips were like ice and she turned away and buried her face in my neck. I held her so for all of a minute, then, on mutual impulse at the same moment, we parted and started to fasten on the lifebelts.

The remains of the workers' hut was now no more than an acrid-smelling dark red glow under the blackness of an overcast sky. The lights still burned in the professor's window. I would have taken odds that he had no intention of going to sleep that night: I was beginning to know enough of his nature to suspect that the exhaustion of a sleepless night would be small price to pay for the endless delights of savouring to the full the delightful anticipations of the pleasures of the day that was to come.

It started to rain as we left, the heavy drops sputtering to sibilant extinction in the dying fire. It couldn't have been better for us. Nobody saw us go, for nobody could have seen us unless they had been within ten feet. We walked almost a mile and a half to the south along the sea-shore and then as we approached the area where Hewell's Chinese might be loitering as they'd been the night before, we took to the sea. We went out about twenty-five yards, to waist level, half-walking, half-swimming along: but when we came to the spot where I could just barely discern through the rain the dark overhang of the cliff that marked the beginning of the barbed wire, we made for the deeper water until we were over two hundred yards out. It didn't seem likely, but the moon might just conceivably break through.

We inflated our lifebelts, very slowly, although I hardly thought the sound would carry to shore. The water was cool, but not cold. I swam in the lead and as I did I turned the operating screw of the shark-repellent canister and a darkish evil-smelling liquid—it would probably have been yellow in daylight—with extraordinary dissolving and spreading qualities spread over the surface of the sea. I don't know what the shark-repellent did to the sharks, but it certainly repelled me.

CHAPTER EIGHT

Friday 3:30 A.M.-6 A.M.

THE rain eased and finally stopped altogether, but the night stayed dark. And the sharks stayed away. We made slow time, because I couldn't use my left arm to help me along, but we made time and after almost an hour, when I calculated that we must be at least half a mile beyond the barbed wire fences, we started angling in slowly for shore.

Less than two hundred yards from land I discovered that our change in direction was premature, the high wall of cliff extended further round the south of the island than I had imagined it would. There was nothing for it but to trudge slowly on—by this time 'swimming' would have been a complete and flattering misnomer for our laboured and clumsy movements through the water—and hope that we wouldn't lose our sense of direction in the slight obscuring drizzle that had again begun to fall.

Luck stayed with us and so did our sense of direction, for when the drizzle finally lifted I could see that we were no more than a hundred and fifty yards from a thin ribbon of sand that marked the shore-line. It felt more like a hundred and fifty miles, at least it did to me. I had the vague impression that an undertow was pulling us out into the lagoon all the time, but I knew this couldn't be so, otherwise we would have been swept far out long ago. It was just sheer weakness. But my awareness was not of effort or exhaustion but almost wholly of frustration: the urgency so desperate, the progress so infuriatingly slow.

My feet touched bottom and I staggered upright in less than three feet of water: I swayed and would have fallen had not Marie caught my arm, she was in far better shape than I was. Side by side we waded slowly ashore and the way I felt no one ever looked less like Venus emerging from the deeps than I did right then. Together we stumbled on to the shore, then, two minds with but one thought, we sat down heavily on the damp sand.

"God, at last!" I gasped. The breath was wheezing in and out of my lungs like air through the sides of a moth-eaten bellows. "I thought we'd never make it."

"Neither did we," a clipped drawling voice agreed. We swung round only to be blinded by the bright white glare from a pair of torches. "You certainly took your time. Please don't try—Good Lord! A female!"

Although biologically accurate enough it struck me as a singularly inept term to describe Marie Hopeman, but I let it pass. Instead I scrambled painfully to my feet and said: "You saw us coming?"

"For the past twenty minutes," he drawled. "We have radar and infra-red that would pick up the head of a shrimp if it stuck itself above water. My word, a woman! What's your name? Are you armed?" The grasshopper mind, a clear cut case for Pelmanism.

"I have a knife," I said tiredly. "Right now I couldn't cut asparagus with it. You can have it if you want." The light was no longer directly in our eyes and I could make out the shape of three figures clad in white, two of them with the vague blurs of guns cradled in their arms. "My name is Bentall. You are a naval officer?"

"Anderson. Sub-Lieutenant Anderson. Where in all the world have you two come from. What is your reason—"

"Look," I interrupted. "Those things can wait. Please take me to your commanding officer, now. It's very important. At once."

"Now just a minute, my friend." The drawl was more pronounced than ever. "You don't seem to realise—"

"At once," I said. "Look, Anderson, you sound like a naval officer who might have a very promising career in front of him but I can promise you that a career stops today, violently, if you don't cooperate fast. Don't be a fool, man. Do you think I'd turn up like this unless there was something most desperately wrong? I'm a British Intelligence agent and so is Miss Hopeman here. How far to your C.O.'s place?"

Maybe he was no fool, or maybe it was the urgency in my voice because, after a moment's hesitation, he said: "The better part of a couple of miles. But there's a telephone at a radar post quarter a mile along that way." He pointed in the direction of the twin barbed wire fences. "If it's really urgent—"

"Send one of your men there, please. Tell your C.O.— what's his name by the way?"

"Captain Griffiths."

"Tell Captain Griffiths that an attempt will almost certainly be made to overpower you and seize your installation very shortly, perhaps in only an hour or two," I said quickly. "Professor Witherspoon and his assistants who worked on the archaeological excavations on the other side of the island have been murdered by criminals who have driven—"

"Murdered!" He came close to me. "Did you say murdered?"

"Let me finish. They've driven this tunnel clear through the island and need breach only a few more feet of limestone to emerge on this side of the island. Where, I don't know, probably about a hundred feet above sea-level. You'll need patrols, patrols to listen for their picks and shovels. They're unlikely to blast their way out."

"Good God."

"I know. How many men have you here?"

"Eighteen civilian, the rest Navy. About fifty all told."

"Armed?"

"Rifles, tommy-guns, about a dozen altogether. Look here, Mr.—ah—Bentall, are you absolutely sure about—I mean, how am I to know?"

"I'm sure. For heaven's sake, man, hurry up."

Another momentary hesitation, then he turned to one of the half-seen men by his side. "Did you get that, Johnston?"

"Yes, sir. Witherspoon and the others dead. Attack expected through tunnel, very soon. Patrols, listening. Yes, sir."

"Right. Off you go." Johnston disappeared at a dead run, and Anderson turned to me. "I suggest we go straight to the Captain. You will forgive me if Leading Seaman Allison walks behind us. You have made an illegal entry into an officially protected area and I can't take chances. Not till I have clear proof of your bona fides."

"Just so long as he keeps his safety catch on I don't care

what he does," I said wearily. "I haven't come all this length just to be shot in the back if your man trips over his own ankles."

We went off in single file, not talking, Anderson with a torch leading the way and Allison with another bringing up the rear. I was feeling dizzy and unwell. The first greyish streaks of dawn were beginning to finger their way upwards from the eastern horizon. After we had gone perhaps three hundred yards, following an ill-defined track that ran first through a scrubby belt of palms and then low bush, I heard an exclamation from the sailor behind me.

He came up close to my back, then called out "Sir!"

Anderson stopped, turned. "What is it Allison."

"This man's hurt, sir. Badly hurt, I should say. Look at his left arm."

We all looked at my left arm, no one with more interest than myself. Despite my attempts to favour it as we had been swimming, the exertion seemed to have opened up the major wounds again and my left hand was completely covered with blood that had dripped down my arm. The spreading effect of the intermingled salt water made it seem worse than it actually was, but even so it was more than enough to account for the way I felt.

Sub-Lieutenant Anderson went far up in my estimation. He spent no time on exclamations or sympathies, but said: "Mind if I rip this sleeve off?"

"Go ahead," I said. "But mind you don't rip off the arm at the same time. I don't think there's a great deal holding it in place."

They cut off the sleeve with the aid of Allison's knife and I could see the tightening of Anderson's thin brown intelligent face as he studied the wounds.

"Your friends across at the phosphate camp?"

"That's it. They had a dog."

"This is either infected or gangrenous or both. Either way it's pretty nasty. Lucky for you we have a naval surgeon here. Hold this, miss, will you?" He handed his torch to Marie, pulled off his shirt and tore it into several wide strips, using them to bandage my arm tightly. "Won't do the infection any good, but it should cut down the bleeding. The civilian quonset huts aren't any more than half a mile from here. Think you can make it?" The reserved tone in the voice had vanished. The sight of that left arm had been as good as a character reference from the First Sea Lord.

"I can make it. It's not all that bad."

Ten minutes later a long low building with a Nissen type

roof loomed up out of the greying dark. Anderson knocked at a door, walked in and touched a switch that lit up a couple of overhead lights.

It was a long bare barn-like structure of a place, with the first third of it given over to a kind of communal living venture while beyond that a narrow central passage bisected two rows of eight by eight cubicles, each with its own door, all of them open to the main roof. In the foreground, brown corticene on the floor, a couple of small tables with writing materials, seven or eight rattan and canvas chairs and that was it. No home from home, but good enough for something that would only be left there to rust and flake away when the Navy was finished with it.

Anderson nodded to a chair and I didn't need any second invitation. He crossed to a small alcove, picked up a phone I hadn't noticed and cranked a naval-type generator. He listened for a few minutes, then hung it back on its rest.

"Damn thing's gone dead," he said irritably. "Always when you need it most. Sorry, Allison, more walking for you. My apologies to Surgeon Lieutenant Brookman. Ask him to bring his kit. Tell him why. And tell the captain we'll be over as soon as possible."

Allison left. I looked at Marie, seated across the table from me, and I smiled back. The first impression of Anderson had been a wrong one, if only they were all as efficient as he was. The temptation to relax, to let go and close the eyes, was temptation indeed: but I'd only to think of those still prisoners in the hands of Witherspoon and Hewell and I didn't feel sleepy any more.

The door of the nearest cubicle on the left opened and a tall skinny youngish man, with prematurely grey hair and a pair of horn-rimmed glasses, clad only in a pair of undershorts, came out into the passage, glasses raised half way up his forehead as he rubbed the sleep out of myopic eyes. He caught sight of Anderson, opened his mouth to speak, caught sight of Marie, dropped his jaw in astonishment, gave a peculiar kind of yelp and hurriedly retreated.

He wasn't the only one who was astonished, compared to my own reactions he was a selling-plater in the jaw-dropping field. I rose slowly to my feet, propping myself up on the table, Bentall giving his incomparable impression of a man who has seen a ghost. I was still giving the impression when the man appeared a few minutes later, dressing-gown flapping about his lanky ankles, and this time the first person he saw was me. He stopped short, peered at me with his head outthrust at the end of a long thin neck, then walked slowly to where I was standing.

"Johnny Bentall?" He reached out to touch my right shoulder, maybe to make sure I was real. "Johnny Bentall!"

I got my jaw closed far enough to speak.

"No other. Bentall it is. I didn't exactly look to find you here, Dr. Hargreaves." The last time I'd seen him had been over a year previously, when he'd been the chief of hypersonics in the Hepworth Ordnance establishment.

"And the young lady?" Even in moments of stress Hargreaves had always been the most punctilious of men. "Your wife, Bentall?"

"Off and on," I said. "Marie Hopeman, ex-Mrs. Bentall. I'll explain later. What are you—"

"Your shoulder!" he said sharply. "Your arm. You've hurt it."

I refrained from telling him that I knew all about my arm.

"A dog bit me," I said patiently. It didn't sound right, somehow. "I'll tell you all you want, but, first, one or two things. Quickly, please. It's important. Are you working here, Dr. Hargreaves?"

"Of course I am." He answered the question as if he considered it mildly half-witted and from his point of view I suppose it was. He would be unlikely to be taking a holiday in a naval camp in the South Pacific.

"Doing what?"

"Doing what?" He paused and peered at me through his pebbles. "I'm not quite sure whether I—"

"Mr. Bentall says he is a Government Intelligence officer," Anderson put in quietly. "I believe him."

"Government? Intelligence?" Dr. Hargreaves was in a repetitive mood tonight. He looked at me suspiciously. "You must forgive me if I'm a bit confused, Bentall. What happened to that machine import-export business you inherited from your uncle a year or so ago?"

"Nothing. It never existed. There had to be some cover-up story to account for my departure. I'm betraying official secrets but not really doing any harm in telling you that I was seconded to a Government agency to investigate the leakage of information about the new solid fuels we were working on at the time."

"Um." He thought a bit, then made up his mind. "Solid fuel, eh? That's why we're out here. Testing the stuff. Very secret and all that, you know."

"A new type rocket?"

"Precisely."

"It had to be that. You don't have to take off to the middle of nowhere to carry out experiments on new stuff unless it's either explosives or rockets. And Heaven knows we've reached the limit in explosives without blowing ourselves into space."

By this time other cubicle doors had opened and a variety of sleepy men, in a variety of clothes and underclothes, were peering out to see what the matter was. Anderson went and spoke softly to them, knocked on a couple of other doors, then came back and smiled apologetically.

"Might as well have them all here, Mr. Bentall. If your facts are right it's time they were up anyway: and it'll save you having to tell the same story over again."

"Thanks, Lieutenant." I sat down again and closed grateful fingers over a large glass of whisky that had mysteriously appeared from nowhere. Two or three tentative sips and the room seemed to be floating around me: neither my thoughts nor my eyes were any too keen to be focussed on anything, but after another few sips my vision seemed to clear again and the pain in my arm began to recede. I supposed I was getting lightheaded.

"Well, come on, Bentall," Hargreaves said impatiently. "We're waiting."

I looked up. They were waiting. Seven of them altogether, not counting Anderson—and the late Dr. Fairfield was the missing eighth.

"I'm sorry," I said. "I'll keep it short. But, first, I wonder if any of you gentlemen have any spare clothes. Miss Hopeman here has just recovered from a rather bad chill and fever and I'm afraid—"

This gave me another minute's grace and time for the glass to be emptied and refilled by Anderson. The competition to supply Marie with clothes was brisk. When she'd given me a grateful and rather tired smile and disappeared into one of the cubicles, I told them the story in two minutes, quickly, concisely, missing out nothing but the fact that I'd heard women singing in the abandoned mine. When I'd finished, one of the scientists, a tall florid-faced old bird who looked like an elderly retired butcher and was, in fact, as I later discovered, the country's leading expert in inertial and infrared guidance systems, looked at me coldly and snapped:

"Fantastic, absolutely fantastic. Imminent danger of attack. Bah! I don't believe a word of it."

"What's your theory of what happened to Dr. Fairfield?" I asked.

"My theory?" the retired butcher snapped. "We all know

138

how poor old Fairfield met his dreadful end. No theory. We heard from Witherspoon—Fairfield used to visit him regularly, they were great friends—that they'd been out trolling for trevally—"

"And he'd fallen overboard and the sharks got him, I suppose? The more intelligent the mind the more easily it falls for any old rubbish. I'd sooner rely on the babes in the wood than a scientist outside the four walls of his lab." Dale Carnegie wouldn't have approved of any part of this. "I can prove it, gentlemen, but only by giving you bad news. Your wives are being held prisoner in the mine on the other side of the island."

They looked at me, then at each other, then back at me again.

"Have you gone mad, Bentall?" Hargreaves was staring at me through his pebble glasses, his mouth tight.

"It would be better for you if I had. No doubt you gentlemen imagine your wives are still in Sydney or Melbourne or wherever. No doubt you write to them regularly. No doubt you hear from them regularly. No doubt you keep their letters, or some of them. Or am I wrong, gentlemen?"

No one said I was wrong.

"So, if your wives are all writing from different homes, you would expect, by the law of averages, that most of them would use different paper, different pens, different inks, and that the different postmarks on the envelopes would not all be printed in the same colours. As scientists, you will all have respect for the law of averages. I suggest we compare your letters and envelopes. No one wants to read any private correspondence, just to make a superficial comparison of likenesses and differences. Would you like to cooperate? Or"—I glanced at the red-faced man—"are you scared to learn the truth?"

Five minutes later the red-faced man was no longer red-faced, and he had learned the truth. Of the seven envelopes produced, three had been of one brand, two of another and two of a third—enough not to make the incoming mail look suspiciously alike. The postmarks on the envelopes, so beautifully clear-cut as to suggest they had been stolen, not manufactured by unauthorised persons, were all in the same colour. Only two pens, a fountain and a ball-point, had been used for the seven letters and the last point was the final clincher—every letter but one had been written on exactly the same notepaper. They must have thought themselves safe enough there, middle-aged and elderly scientists don't usually show their letters around.

After I'd finished and given the letters back to their owners, they exchanged glances, dazed glances where the lack of understanding was matched only by the increasing fear. They believed me all right now.

"I thought my wife's tone was rather strange in recent letters," Hargreaves said slowly. "She's always been so full of humour and poking fun at scientists and now—"

"I've noticed the same," someone else murmured. "But I put it down to—"

"You can put it down to coercion," I said brutally. "It's not easy to be witty when a gun is pointing at your head. I don't pretend to know how the letters were introduced into your incoming mail, but it would be a simple matter to a mind as brilliant as that of the man who killed Witherspoon. For he is brilliant. Anyway, you can introduce mail into mailbags for a hundred years and no one will ever notice. It's only when you start taking it out that eyebrows begin to lift."

"Fairfield," the red-faced man said stupidly. "It wasn't sharks? We were told—"

"I don't have to draw a diagram to explain what happened to Fairfield, do I?" An ill-mannered interruption on my part and one that made little allowance for their state of shock, but I was feeling pretty low myself. "He knew Witherspoon well—all those archaeologists, amateurs included, know each other—and you say yourselves he visited him often. By boat, I assume. But Fairfield made one trip too many to see his friend, because by the time he made his last trip someone had killed Witherspoon and taken his place. Someone who could imitate Witherspoon well enough to deceive casual contacts. But he wouldn't have deceived Fairfield. So Fairfield had to die. Sharks made a convenient scapegoat— and they don't leave any traces. And so no need to produce a body."

"But—but what does it all mean?" Hargreaves' voice had a shake in it and his hands were clenching and unclenching in involuntary nervousness. "What will they—what are they going to do with our wives?"

"You must give me a minute," I said tiredly. "It's as big a shock for me to find you here as it is for you to find out where your wives are. I think you're safe enough now, and the rocket installation, but I believe your wives to be in deadly danger. There's no good blinking facts, expediency is all that matters to the men we're against and humanity not at all. If you move wrongly, you may never see them again. Let me think, please."

They wandered off reluctantly to complete dressing. I thought, but the first part of my thinking was far from constructive. I thought of that old fox Colonel Raine, and I thought of him with something less than affection. I supposed that after twenty-five years in the business it was impossible for him to let his right hand know what his left was doing. But, more than that, he had made an extraordinarily accurate assessment of the Bentall character. What there was of it.

I hadn't even bothered to ask the scientists whether they had been a party to those advertisements in the 'Telegraph'. Obviously, they must have been. The men for this job had been picked long before the advertisements had appeared and the adverts had merely been a device to have them removed from the country without raising any questions, and the fact that their wives had accompanied them had merely lent colour to the belief that they had gone abroad permanently. Obviously, too, as it had been a government project, Raine had known all about it, in fact he was probably the man who had made all the necessary undercover arrangements. I thought of how I had completely swallowed the old Colonel's story and I cursed him for his devious and twisted mind.

But, for Raine, it had been necessary, because, somehow or other—his contacts, his sources of information were legion—he had discovered or strongly suspected that the wives of the men who had gone to Vardu Island were no longer in their Australian homes. He would have come to the conclusion that they were being held captive or hostage. He would have worked out why and come to the same conclusion as I recently had.

But he would never have guessed that they were on Vardu, for it was almost certainly Colonel Raine himself who had worked out with the now murdered Witherspoon the scheme to have Vardu used as a protected area based on archaeological discovery: whether the discoveries were genuine or not was a matter of complete unimportance: old Witherspoon and his associates would have been screened with a toothcomb and the idea of associating any skullduggery with that part of the island would have been fantastic. Vardu would have been the last place Raine would have thought of to look for them: he had just no idea at all where they were.

So he had fed me this yarn about sending me out to find the missing scientists but what he had actually intended was that Marie should find the missing scientists' wives. She would find them, he reasoned, by being seized as they had been and for the same reasons, and all he could hope for was that she

141

or I or both could do something about it: but if he had let me think for a moment that that was what he had in mind he knew I would never have gone along with it. He knew what I thought about throwing women to the wolves. Instead of Marie coming along as local colour for me, I was going as local colour, little better than a stooge, for her. I remembered now what he had said about her being much more experienced than I was, that it might end up with her looking after me, not vice versa, and I felt about six inches tall. I wondered how much of all of this, if any, was known to Marie herself.

At this moment Marie made her appearance. She had dried and combed her hair and fitted into slacks and T-shirt that fitted only where they touched, but they touched in enough places to show that it wasn't the original owner who was inside them. She smiled at me and I smiled back but it was a pretty mechanical sort of effort on my part, the more I thought of it the more I suspected she must have known just how the land lay with Colonel Raine. Maybe neither she nor Raine regarded me as anything other than a lucky amateur, and in this business amateurs weren't trusted. Not even lucky ones. But what hurt was not the lack of trust but the fact that if I were right then she'd fooled me throughout. And if she could fool me about that, then she could fool me about many other things, too. I was tired and weak and the thought was acid in my mind. She was looking at me with the kind of expression on her face with which I'd always dreamed that someone just like Marie would look at me, and I knew it was impossible that I was being fooled. I knew it for all of two seconds, which was all the time it took me to remember that she had survived five years in one of the most hazardous professions in the world simply through an extremely highly-developed gift of fooling everyone all the time.

I was about to ask her some leading questions when Dr. Hargreaves came up to me. The others trailed behind him. They were now all dressed in their day clothes. They were worried stiff, all of them, and they looked it.

"We've been talking, and we've no doubt left in our minds that our wives are captive and in great danger," Hargreaves began without preamble. "Our—our wives are our sole concern at this moment. What do you suggest we do?" He was holding himself well in check, but the tight mouth, the straining tendons of his clasped hands gave him away.

"Damn it all, man!" The elderly butcher had the choler back in his face again. "We rescue them, that's what we do."

"Sure," I agreed. "We rescue them. How?"

142

"Well—"

"Look, friend, you don't begin to know the score. Let me explain. There are three things we can do. We can let the Chinese break through the tunnel into the open, then a few of us nip smartly in there, go through to the other end, release your wives and then what? Hewell's killers would be loose among the sailors here, and with all due respect to the Navy, it would be wolves among chickens. And after they'd gobbled up the chickens they'd find we were missing and come back to finish us off—and your wives as well: and they might take some time finishing off your wives. Or we can blockade the tunnel exit and prevent them from coming out. We can prevent them for about an hour which is all the time it will take for them to go back and collect your wives and by either using them as shields or putting a gun to their heads force us to lay down our arms."

I paused a moment to let this sink in, but one glance round the tense still faces let me see that it had already sunk. They were looking at me as if they didn't like me very much, but I suppose that it was what I was saying that they really didn't like.

"You said there was a third alternative," Hargreaves pressed me.

"Yes." I rose stiffly to my feet, glanced at Anderson. "Sorry, Lieutenant, can't wait any longer for your M.O. Time enough wasted. There is a third alternative, gentlemen. The only practicable one. As soon as they break through the mountain-side—or as soon as we hear them trying to break through—a party of us, three or four, with sledges and crowbars to force locks and armed in case guards have been left behind to look after your wives, will go round the south of the island by boat, land and hope to get your wives clear before Witherspoon and Hewell get the idea of sending back for your wives to use as hostages. In this day and age I assume the Navy no longer depends on oars and sails. A fast power boat should get us there in fifteen minutes."

"I've no doubt it would," Anderson said unhappily. There was an embarrassed silence, then he went on reluctantly: "The fact is, Mr. Bentall, we haven't got any boats."

"Say that again?"

"No boats. Not even a rowing boat. I'm sorry."

"Look," I said heavily. "I know there have been some pretty drastic cut-backs in naval estimates, but if you'll tell me how a Navy can function without—"

"We did have boats," Anderson interrupted. "Four of them, attached to the light cruiser *Neckar* which has been anchored in the lagoon off and on for the past three months. The *Neckar* left two days ago with Rear-Admiral Harrison, who is in overall charge, and Dr. Davies, who has been in charge of the development of the Black Shrike throughout. The work on it—"

"The Black Shrike?"

"The name of the rocket. Not quite in firing readiness yet, but we had an urgent cable from London forty-eight hours ago saying it was essential to complete the work at once and ordering the *Neckar* to the firing range immediately—about 1,000 miles south-west of here. That's why this particular island was chosen—all open water to the south-east if anything goes wrong with the rocket."

"Well, well," I said heavily. "What a lovely coincidence. A cable all the way from London. All the correct codes, hidden identification figures and telegraphic addresses, I'll bet. It wasn't the fault of your communication and coding boys that they fell for it."

"I'm afraid I don't understand—"

"And why should the *Neckar* leave if the rocket wasn't in complete readiness?" I interrupted.

"It wasn't much," Hargreaves put in. "Dr. Fairfield had all his part of the job finished before he—ah—disappeared. all that was required was that someone with a knowledge of solid fuels—I admit there aren't many—should complete the wiring up and fusing of the firing circuitry. The cable giving the sailing orders said that a solid fuel expert would arrive on the island today."

I refrained from introducing myself. That cable must have been sent off within hours of Witherspoon's being told that Bentall was spending a wet and uncomfortable night on a reef out in the lagoon. There was no question but that the man was a criminal: but there was equally no question but that he was a criminal genius. I was no criminal, but I was no genius either. We belonged in different leagues—the top and the bottom. I felt the way David would have felt if he had happened across Goliath and discovered that he had left his sling at home. I became vaguely aware that Anderson and the red-faced man, whom he addressed as Farley, were talking together, and then the vagueness vanished, I heard a couple of words that caught and transfixed my attention the way a tarantula in my soup would have done.

"Did I hear someone mention 'Captain Fleck'?" I asked carefully.

"Yes," Anderson nodded. "Fleck. Chap who runs a

schooner and transfers all our stores and mail from Kandavu to here. But he's not due again until this afternoon."

It was as well that I had risen to my feet, had I still been sitting in my chair I would probably have fallen out of it. I said stupidly: "Transfers your stores and mail, eh?"

"That's right." It was Farley speaking, his voice impatient. "Australian. Trader, mainly in Government surplus, but he's also on charter to us. Rigorously investigated, security clearance, of course."

"Of course, of course." My mind was occupied with visions of Fleck busily transferring mail from one end of the island to the other and then back again. "Does he know what's going on here?"

"Of course not," Anderson said. "All work on the rockets— there are two of them—are carried on under cover. Anyway, does it matter, Mr. Bentall?"

"It doesn't matter." Not any more, it didn't. "I think, Anderson, that we'd better go and consult with your Captain Griffiths. We have little time left. I'm afraid we may have no time left."

I turned to the door and halted as knuckles rapped on the outside of it. Anderson said "Come in" and the door opened. Leading Seaman Allison stood there, blinking in the sudden glare of light."

"The Surgeon-Lieutenant is here, sir."

"Ah, good, good! Come in, Brookman, we—" He broke off and said sharply: "Where's your gun, Allison?"

Allison grunted in agony as something struck him from behind with tremendous force and sent him staggering into the room to crash heavily into Farley. Both men were still reeling, falling together against one of the cubicle walls, when the massive form of Hewell appeared in the doorway. He loomed tall as Everest, the gaunt granitic face empty of all life, the black eyes far back and hidden under the tufted brows—he must have forced Allison to go first to give his own eyes time to become accustomed to the light—and in his huge fist was a gun, a gun fitted with a black cylindrical object screwed on to the barrel. A silencer.

Sub-Lieutenant Anderson made the last mistake of his life. He had a Navy Colt strapped to his waist and the mistake he made was trying to reach for it. I shouted out a warning, tried to reach him to knock his arm down, but he was on my left side and my crippled arm was far too slow.

I had a momentary glimpse of Hewell's face and I knew it was too late. His face was as still and as motionless and as empty of life as ever as he squeezed the trigger. A soft muffled thud, a look of faint surprise in Anderson's eyes as he put both hands to his chest and started toppling slowly backwards. I tried to catch him and break his fall, which was a foolish thing to do, it didn't help either of us, all it did was to wrench my left shoulder violently and there's not much point in hurting yourself trying to cushion the fall of a man who will never feel anything again.

CHAPTER NINE

HEWELL advanced into the room. He didn't even look at the dead man on the floor. He made a gesture with his left hand and two soft-footed Chinese, each with a machine-pistol in his hand, came in through the doorway behind him: they carried their guns as if they knew how to use them.

"Anybody here armed?" Hewell asked in his deep gravelly voice. "Anybody here with arms in this room? If so, tell me now. If I find arms on any man or in any man's room and he hasn't told me, I'll kill him. Any arms here?"

There were no arms there. If any of them had toothpicks and thought Hewell might have considered those as arms, they'd have rushed to get them. Hewell had that effect on people. Also, there was no doubt but that he meant what he said.

"Good." He advanced another step and looked down at me. "You fooled us, Bentall, didn't you? That makes you very clever. Nothing wrong with your foot, was there, Bentall? But your arm isn't so good, is it—I suppose the Doberman did that to you before you killed it? And you killed two of my best men, didn't you, Bentall? I'm afraid you will have to pay for that."

There was nothing sinister or menacing about the slow sepulchral voice, but then it didn't have to be, the man's looming presence, the craggy ruin of a face made any further menace completely superfluous. I didn't doubt that I would pay.

"But it will have to wait. Just a little. We can't have you dying on us yet, can we, Bentall?" He spoke a few quick words in a foreign language to the Chinese on his right, a tall sinewy intelligent looking man with a face as still as Hewell's own, then turned back to me. "I have to leave you for a moment—we have the guards by the boundary fence to attend to. The main compound and garrison are already in
146

our hands and all telephone lines to the guardposts cut. I am leaving Hang, here, to look after you. Don't any of you try anything clever with Hang. You might think one man, even with a Tommy-gun, can't hold nine men in a small room, and if any of you think that and try to act on it that's as good a way as any to find out why Hang was the sergeant-major of a machine-gun battalion in Korea." Hewell's thin lips cracked in a humourless smile. "No prizes for guessing what side he was on."

Seconds later he and the other Chinese were gone. I looked at Marie and she at me: but her face was tired and somehow sad and the small smile she gave me hadn't much behind it. Everybody else was looking at the Chinese guard. He didn't appear to be looking at anybody.

Farley cleared his throat and said conversationally: "I think we could rush him, Bentall. One from each side."

"You rush him," I said. "I'm staying where I am."

"Damn it all, man." His voice was low and desperate. "It may be our last chance."

"We've had our last chance. Your courage is admirable, Farley, which is more than can be said for your intelligence. Don't be a damned idiot."

"But—"

"You heard what Bentall said?" The guard spoke in faultless English, with a heavy American accent. "'Don't be a damned idiot.'"

Farley subsided in a moment, you could see the swift collapse of the stiffened sinews of his resolution, the draining of the insular arrogance which had led to the bland assumption that the guard could speak no language other than his own.

"You will all sit and cross your legs," the guard went on. "That will be safer—for yourselves. I don't want to kill anyone." He paused, then added as an after-thought: "Except Bentall. You killed two members of my tong, tonight, Bentall."

There didn't seem to be any suitable comment on that one, so I let it pass.

"You may smoke if you wish," he continued. "You may talk, but do not talk in whispers."

There was no hurry to take him up on his second offer. There are some situations which make it difficult to choose an agreeable topic of conversation and this seemed to be one of them. Besides, I didn't want to talk, I wanted to think, if I could do it without damaging myself. I tried to figure out how Hewell and company had got through so soon. It had been more or less a certainty, I'd known, that they were going to break through that morning, but it had come hours before I had expected it. Had they made a spot check to see if we were still in bed? Possible, but unlikely: they'd showed no signs of suspicion when we'd seen them after the fire. Or had they found the dead Chinese in the tomb? That was more likely, but even if true it was still damnably hard luck.

I suppose I ought to have been bent double under the weight of bitterness and chagrin but strangely enough it hardly crossed my mind. The game was lost and that was all that was to it: or the game up till now was lost, which seemed to be about the same thing. Or maybe it wasn't. It was as if Marie had read my mind.

"You're still figuring, aren't you, Johnny?" She gave me that smile again, the smile that I'd never seen her give anyone, not even Witherspoon, and my heart started capering around like a court jester in the middle ages until I reminded it that this was a girl who could fool anyone. "It's like the Colonel said. Sitting in the electric chair, the man's hand on the switch and you're still figuring."

"Sure, I'm figuring," I said sourly. "I'm figuring how long I've got to live."

I saw the quick hurt in her eyes and turned away. Hargreaves was regarding me thoughtfully. He was still scared, but he could still think. And Hargreaves had a good mind.

"You're hardly a goner yet, are you?" he asked. "From what I gather neither your friend Hewell nor this man here would hesitate to kill you. But they don't. Hewell said, 'We can't have you dying on us yet.' And you used to work in the same department as Dr. Fairfield. Could you be the fuel expert that we've been expecting?"

"I suppose I am." There was no point in saying anything else, I hadn't known the bogus Witherspoon half an hour altogether before I'd told him that. I wondered if, anywhere along the line there was a mistake I could have made and hadn't. Looking back, it seemed unlikely. "It's a long story. Some other time."

"Could you do it?"

"Do what?"

"Fuse up the rocket?"

"I wouldn't even know how to go about it," I said untruthfully.

"But you worked with Fairfield," Hargreaves persisted.

"Not on solid fuel."

"But—"

"I don't know a single thing about his latest solid fuel

development," I said harshly. And to think I'd thought he had a good mind. Would the damned fool never shut up? Didn't he know the guard was listening? What did he want to do—put a rope round my neck. I could see Marie staring at him, her lips compressed, her hazel eyes very far from friendly. "They've been too damned secret about all this," I finished. "They've sent out the wrong expert."

"Well, that's useful," Hargreaves muttered.

"Isn't it? I never even knew of the existence of this Black Shrike of yours. How about putting me in the picture about it? I'm one of those characters who believe that a man should go on learning till the day he dies: this looks like my last chance to collect some fresh information."

He hesitated, then said slowly: "I'm afraid—"

"You're afraid it's all very top secret," I said impatiently. "Sure it's very secret—but not to anyone on this island. Not any longer."

"I suppose not," Hargreaves said doubtfully. He thought for a moment and then smiled. "You will remember the late and bitterly lamented Blue Streak rocket?"

"Our one and only entrant in the inter-continental ballistic missiles stakes?" I nodded. "Sure I remember it. It could do everything a missile should do, except fly. Everyone felt this was very awkward. Considerable heart-burning when the Government dropped it. Much talk about selling out to the Americans, being absolutely dependent for nuclear defence on the Americans, Britain now a very second-rate power, if you could call her a power at all. I remember. The Government was vastly unpopular."

"Yes. And they didn't deserve any of it. They dropped the entire project because one or two of the better military and scientific minds in Britain—we have one or two—kindly pointed out to them that the Blue Streak was a hundred per-cent unsuitable for its purpose anyway. It was based on American type models, such as the Atlas I.C.B.M., which takes twenty minutes to count down and get under way from the moment of the first alarm, which is all very well for the Americans: with their DEW-lines and advanced radar stations, their infra-red detectors and spies-in-the-skies to detect exhaust trails of launched I.C.B.M.'s, they're counting on getting a half an hour when some maniac presses the wrong button. All the warning we can expect is four minutes." Hargreaves took off his spectacles, polished them carefully and blinked myopically. "Which means that if the Blue Streak had worked, and if the count-down had started the moment the warning had come through it would still have been wiped out of existence by a five megaton Russian ICBM sixteen minutes before it was due to take off."

"I can count," I said. "You don't have to spell it out for me."

"We had to spell it out for the Ministry of Defence," Hargreaves replied. "Took them three or four years to catch on, which is about par for the military mind. Look at the admirals and their battleships. The other great drawback of the Blue Streak, of course, is that it would have required a huge launching installation, all the ramps, gantries, and blockhouses, the enormous trailers of helium and liquid nitrogen to pump in the kerosene and liquid oxygen under pressure, and, finally, the vast size of the rocket itself. This meant a permanent and fixed installation, and with all those hordes of British and American planes flying over Russian territories, Russian planes flying over American and British territories—and for all I know, British and Americans flying over one another's territories—those locations have become so well known that practically every launching base in the U.S. and Russia has a corresponding ICBM from the other country zeroed in on it.

"What was wanted, then, was a rocket that could be fired instantaneously—and a rocket that was completely mobile, completely portable. This was impossible with any known missile fuel. Certainly not with the kerosene—kerosene, in this day and age!—which along with liquid oxygen still powers most of the American rockets. Certainly, either, not with the liquid hydrogen engines the Americans are working on today, the boiling point of -423°F. makes them ten times as tricky to handle as anything yet known. And they're far too big."

"They were working on cesium and ion fuels," I said.

"They'll be working on them for a long time to come. They've got a dozen separate firms working on those and you know the old saw about too many cooks. And so the mobile rocket ready for instant firing was impossible with any known propellant—until Hargreaves came up with a brilliantly simple idea for solid fuel, twenty times as powerful as used in the American Minuteman. It's so brilliantly simple," Hargreaves admitted, "that I don't know how it works."

Neither did I. But I'd learnt enough from Fairfield to learn how to make it work. But here and now I never would.

"You're sure it really does work?" I asked.

"We're sure, all right. On a small scale, that is. Dr. Fairfield fitted a twenty-eight pound charge to a specially constructed miniature rocket and fired it from an uninhabited island off the west coast of Scotland. It took off exactly as Fairfield had predicted, very slowly at first, far more slowly than conventional missiles." Hargreaves smiled reminiscently. "And then it started accelerating. We—the radar scanners— lost it about 60,000 feet. It was still accelerating and doing close on 16,000 miles an hour. Then more experiments, scaled down charges, till he got what he wanted. Then we multiplied the weight of the rocket, fuel, simulated warhead and brain by 400. And that's the Black Shrike."

"Maybe multiplying by 400 brings in some fresh factors."

"That's what we've got to find out. That's why we're here."

"The Americans know about this?"

"No." Hargreaves smiled dreamily. "But we hope they will one day. We hope to supply them with it in a year or two, that's why it's been designed far in excess of our own requirements, designed to carry a two-ton hydrogen bomb six thousand miles in fifteen minutes, reaching a maximum speed of 20,000 miles per hour. Sixteen tons compared to the 200 tons of their own ICBM's. 18 feet high compared to a hundred. Can be carried and fired from any merchant ship, coaster, submarine, train or heavy truck. All that and instant firing." He smiled again, and this time the dreaminess was suffused with a certain complacency. "The Yanks are just going to love the Black Shrike."

I looked at him.

"You're not seriously suggesting that Witherspoon and Hewell are working for the Americans, are you?"

"Working for the—" He pulled the spectacles down his nose and peered at me over the thick horn-rims, eyes wide in myopic astonishment. "What on earth do you mean?"

"I just mean that if they aren't I don't see how the Americans are going to have a chance to look at the Shrike, far less love it."

He looked at me, nodded, looked away and said nothing. It seemed a shame to destroy his scientific enthusiasm.

The dawn was in the sky now, even with the lamps still burning inside the quonset we could see the lightening grey patches where the windows lay. My arm felt as if the Doberman were still clinging to it. I remembered the half-finished glass of whisky on the table, reached up for it and said, "Cheers." No one said cheers back to me but I disregarded their unmannerly attitude and downed it all the same. It didn't do me any good that I could feel. Farley, the infra-red guidance expert, gradually recovered his colour, courage and indignation and carried on a long and bitter monologue, in which the two words 'damnable' and 'outrage' were the recurring theme. He didn't say anything about writing his M.P. Nobody else said anything at all. Nobody looked at the dead man on the floor. I wished that someone would give me some more whisky, or even that I knew where Anderson had found the bottle. It seemed all wrong that I should be thinking more about the bottle than the dead man who'd given me my first drink from it. But then everything was wrong that morning, and besides, the past was past, the future—what remained of it—was to come and, while the whisky might help, nothing was surer than that Anderson would never help anyone again.

Hewell returned at the dawn.

He returned at the dawn and he returned alone, and it didn't need the sight of his blood-stained left forearm to tell me why he had returned alone. The three guards by the wire must have been more watchful and more capable than he had imagined, but they hadn't been capable enough. If Hewell was worried by his wound, the death of yet another of his men or the murder of three seamen, he hid his worry well. I looked round the faces of the men in the quonset, faces grey and strained and afraid, and I knew I didn't need to spell out for them what had happened. In different circumstances—in very different circumstances—it would have been funny to watch the play of expression on their faces, the utter disbelief that this could be happening to them struggling with the frightening knowledge that it was indeed happening to them. But right there and then it wasn't any strain at all not to laugh.

Hewell wasn't in a word-wasting mood. He pulled out his gun, gestured to Hang to leave the hut, looked us over without expression and said the single word: "Out".

We went out. Apart from a sprinkling of palms down by the water's edge there weren't any more trees or vegetation on this side of the island than there had been on the other. The central mountain was much steeper on this side, and the great gash that bisected its southward side was well in sight, with one of the spurs running down from the north-east obscuring our view to the west and north.

Hewell didn't give us any time to admire the view. He formed us into a rough column of two, ordered us to clasp our hands above our heads—I paid no attention, I doubt whether I could have done it anyway and he didn't press the matter—and marched us off to the north-west, over the low spur of rock.

Three hundred yards on, just over the first spur—another

still lay ahead of us—I noticed about fifty yards away on my right a pile of broken rock, of very recent origin. From my lower elevation I couldn't see what was behind that pile but I didn't have to see to know: it was the exit of the tunnel where Witherspoon and Hewell had broken through in the early hours of the morning. I looked carefully all around me, plotting and remembering its position against every topographical feature I could see until I felt fairly certain that I could find it without trouble even on the darkest night. I marvelled at my incurable penchant for assimilating and storing away information of the most useless character.

Five minutes later we were over the low crest of the second spur and could see the whole of the plain on the west side of the island stretched out in front of us. It was still in the shadow of the mountain, but it was full daylight now and easy to make out every feature.

The plain was bigger than the one to the east, but not much, maybe a mile long from north to south and four hundred yards wide between the sea and the first slopes of the mountain. There wasn't a single tree to be seen. In the south-west corner of the plain a long wide pier stretched far out into the glittering lagoon: at our distance of four or five hundred yards this jetty seemed to be made of concrete but was more likely of coral blocks. At the far end of the pier, mounted on rails, with its supporting legs set very far apart, was a heavy crane of the type I'd seen in graving yards for ship repair work: the entire super-structure and jib—there was no counter-balance—were mounted on a ring of live rollers. This was the crane the phosphate company would have used to load its ships—and it was also the crane that must have formed one of the deciding factors in the Navy's decision to set up its rocket installation on the island. It wasn't often, I thought, that you would find ready-made unloading facilities with a pier and crane that looked as if it might be good for thirty tons in a deserted island in the South Pacific.

Two other much narrower sets of rails ran up the pier. A few years ago, I supposed, one of those would have brought loaded phosphate wagons down to the pierhead while the other took the empty ones away. Today, one could still see one of the original sets of lines as it left the pier curving away to the south, rusted and overgrown, towards the phosphate mine: but the other set had been removed and replaced by new lengths of fresh shining rail that led straight inland for a distance of perhaps two hundred yards. Halfway along its length it passed over a curious circular pad of

153

concrete about twenty-five yards in diameter, and finally ended in front of a hangar-shaped building, about thirty feet high, forty wide and a hundred in length. From where we stood almost directly behind the hangar it was impossible to see either its doors or where the rails ended, but it was a safe guess that the latter went all the way inside. The hangar itself was dazzling, it appeared to have been painted in pure white: but it was covered not in paint but in a painted white canvas, a measure, I supposed, designed to reflect the sun's rays and make work possible inside a building made of corrugated iron.

Some little distance north of this stood what were clearly the living-quarters, a group of haphazardly placed buildings, squat, ugly and obviously prefabricated. Further to the north again, at a distance of almost three-quarters of a mile from the hangar, was what seemed to be a solid square of concrete set into the ground. At that distance it was hard to tell, but it didn't look to be any more than two or three feet high. At least half a dozen tall steel poles rose from this concrete, each pole topped with a meshed scanner or radio antenna, all different in design.

Hang led us straight to the nearest and largest of the prefabricated huts. There were two men outside, Chinese, both with automatic carbines. One of them nodded, and Hang stood aside to let us pass through the open door.

The room beyond was obviously the rating's mess. Fifteen feet wide by forty long, it had three-tiered bunks arranged the full length of both walls, with walls and bunks liberally decorated with pin-ups in every shape and form. Between each pair of vertical trios of bunks was a three part locker. More art. Four mess tables, joined end to end to make one table and scrubbed as snowy white as the floor they stood on, ran the full length of the room. Set in the far wall of the room was a door. The sign above it read: 'P. O's Mess'.

On the benches round the two most distant tables sat about twenty men, petty officers and ratings. Some were fully dressed, others hardly dressed at all. One was slumped across the table, like a man asleep, his head pillowed on his bare forearms, and his forearms and the table below covered with clotted blood. None of the men looked shocked or scared or worried, they just sat there with tight and angry faces. They didn't look the type to scare easily, there were no kids among them, the Navy would have picked its best, its most experienced men for this operation, which probably explained why Hewell and his men, even with the elements of surprise and ambush on their side, had run into trouble.

Four men sat side by side on a bench by the top table. Like the men at the lower tables they had their hands clasped in front of them, resting on the wood. Each man had his epaulettes of rank on his shoulders. The big grey-haired man on the left ·with the puffed and bleeding mouth, the grey watchful eyes and the four gold bars would be Captain Griffiths. Beside him a thin balding hook-nosed man with three bars spaced by purple, an engineer commander. Next to him a blond young man with red between his two gold bars, that would be Surgeon-Lieutenant Brookman: and finally another lieutenant, a red-haired youngster with bitter eyes and a white compressed line where his mouth should have been.

Five Chinese guards were spaced round the walls of the room. Each carried an automatic carbine. By the head of the first table, smoking a cheroot, with a malacca cane—no gun—in his hand and looking more benign and scholastic than ever, was the man I had known as Professor Witherspoon. Or so I thought until he turned and looked directly at me and then I saw, even although there was no particular expression on his face, that I could be wrong about the benign part of it. For the first time ever I saw him without the tinted glasses, and I didn't like what I saw: eyes with the lightest pupils I had ever seen, but misted, eyes with the flat dull look of inferior coloured marbles. They were almost the eyes you sometimes see on men who are completely blind.

He glanced at Hewell and said: "Well?"

"Well," Hewell said. Every man in the room, except the red-haired lieutenant, was staring at him. I'd forgotten the impact that the first sight of this moving Neanderthalic mountain could make. "We got them. They were suspicious and waiting, but we got them. I lost one man."

"So." Witherspoon turned to the captain. "That accounts for everyone?"

"You murdering fiends," the grey-haired man whispered. "You fiends! Ten of my men killed."

Witherspoon gave a slight signal with his cane and one of his guards stepped forward and placed his carbine barrel against the back of the neck of the rating next to the one who lay with his head pillowed on his arms.

"That's all," Captain Griffiths said quickly. "I swear that is all."

Witherspoon gave another signal and the man stepped back. I could see the white mark where the gun had been pressing in the man's neck, the slow droop of the shoulders as

155

he exhaled in a long soundless breath. Hewell nodded at the dead man beside him.

"What happened?"

"I asked this young fool here"—Witherspoon pointed at the red-haired lieutenant—"where all the guns and ammunition were stored. The young fool wouldn't tell me. I had that man there shot. Next time I asked he told me."

Hewell nodded absently as if it were the most right and natural thing in the world to shoot a man if another withheld information, but I wasn't interested in Hewell, I was interested in Witherspoon. The absence of spectacles apart, he hadn't changed externally at all: but for all that the change was complete. The quick bird-like movements, the falsetto affected voice, the repetitive habit of speech had vanished: here now was a calm assured ruthless man, absolute master of himself and all around him, a man who never wasted an action or a word.

"Those the scientists?" Witherspoon went on.

Hewell nodded and Witherspoon waved his cane towards the far end of the room.

"They're in there."

Hewell and a guard started to shepherd the seven men towards the P. O's mess. As they passed by Witherspoon, Farley stopped and stood before him with clenched hands.

"You monster," he said thickly. "You damned—"

Witherspoon didn't seem even to look at him. His malacca cane whistled through the air and Farley screamed in agony and staggered back against the bunks, clutching his face with both hands. Hewell caught him by the collar and sent him staggering and stumbling the length of the room. Witherspoon never even looked at him. I had the vague idea that Witherspoon and I weren't going to get along very well in the near future.

The door at the far end opened, the men were bundled inside and then the door was closed again, but not before we all heard the high-pitched excited disbelieving voices of women.

"So you kept them under wraps while the Navy was doing your work for you," I said slowly to Witherspoon. "Now that you no longer need the Navy but do need the scientists—no doubt to supervise and develop the building of fresh rockets wherever you're going—well, you need the wives too. How else could you make their husbands work for you?"

He turned to face me, the long thin whippy cane swinging gently in his hand. "Who asked you to speak?"

"You hit me with that cane," I said, "and I'll choke out your life with it."

Everything was suddenly peculiarly still. Hewell, on his way back, halted in mid-stride. Everybody, for some reason best known to himself, had stopped breathing. The thunder of a feather falling on the floor would have had them all airborne. Ten seconds, each second about five minutes long, passed. Everyone was still holding his breath. Then Witherspoon laughed softly and turned to Captain Griffiths.

"I'm afraid Bentall here is of a rather different calibre from your men and our scientists," he said, as if in explanation. "Bentall is, for instance, an excellent actor: no other man has ever fooled me so long or so successfully. Bentall allows himself to be savaged by wild dogs and never shows a sign. Bentall, with one arm out of commission, meets up with two experienced knife-fighters in a darkened cave and kills them both. He is also, for good measure, highly skilled in burning down houses." He shrugged, almost apologetically. "But, then, of course, it requires a very special man to become a member of Britain's Secret Service."

Another peculiar silence, even more peculiar than the one that had gone before. Everybody was looking at their first Secret Service man, and they couldn't have been unduly impressed. With a drawn haggard face like that of a cadaver and a body that looked even more so, I wouldn't have done at all as a subject for a poster to attract fresh recruits to the service. Not, of course, that they used posters. I wondered how on earth Witherspoon had known. The Chinese guard, Hang, had heard us, of course, but he hadn't yet spoken to Witherspoon.

"You *are* a government agent, Bentall, aren't you?" Witherspoon asked softly.

"I'm a scientist," I said, just to see how it would go. "A fuel research technician. Liquid fuel," I added pointedly.

A sign that I didn't see and a guard advanced and pressed his gun-barrel against Captain Griffith's neck.

"Counter-espionage," I said.

"Thank you." The guard fell back. "Honest to goodness plain scientists aren't expert in codes, wireless telegraphy and morse. You appear to be well versed in all of them, don't you, Bentall?"

I looked at Lieutenant Brookman. "I wonder if you would be kind enough to fix up this arm of mine?"

Witherspoon took a long step towards me. His mouth was as white as the knuckles of the hand that held the malacca cane, but his voice was as unperturbed as ever.

"When I'm finished. It may interest you to know that within two minutes of my returning home tonight after the fire a message started coming through on our radio transmitter. From a vessel by the name of the *Pelican*, in which I have a considerable interest."

If it wasn't for the fact that my nervous system seemed to have completely stopped working, I'd probably have jumped a foot. If I'd the strength for any gymnastics like that, which I hadn't. As it was, I didn't move a muscle of my face. The *Pelican!* That had been the first name I'd seen on that list under the blotter, the copied list that now lay between my sock and the sole of my right foot.

"The *Pelican* was listening in on a certain frequency," he continued. "It had instructions to do so. You may imagine the radio operator's astonishment when an S.O.S. started coming through on that frequency, a frequency far removed from the distress channels."

I still didn't move any facial muscles, but it called for no will-power this time, the shock of realization was enough, the shock of appreciating the enormity of my blunder. But it wasn't really my fault. I had had no means of knowing that the 46 in the list I had picked up meant that the *Pelican* and the other ships—probably all the other names were ships' names too—were to begin listening in, to keep a radio watch at forty-six minutes past every hour. And, as nearly as I could remember, I had begun to transmit my first experimental S.O.S., when I was trying to line up the receiver and transmitter, at almost exactly that time and on the pre-set wave-length of Foochow, which just happened to be the transmitting wave-length they were using.

"He was a clever man, this operator," Witherspoon continued. "He lost you, and guessed it was because you had dropped down to the distress frequencies. He found you there and followed you. He heard the name Vardu mentioned twice, and knew something was far wrong. He copied down letter for letter your signal to the *Annandale*. And then he waited ten minutes and called back."

I was still giving my impression of one of the statues on Easter Island, carved from stone and badly battered. This wasn't the end, this wasn't necessarily the end. But it was the end, I knew it was.

" 'COMBO RIDEX LONDON'—the telegraphic address of the chief of your service, wasn't it, Bentall?" he asked. It seemed unlikely that I could convince him that all I had been doing was sending a birthday message to my Aunt Myrtle in Putney, so I nodded. "I guessed so. And I thought it might be rather useful if I sent a message myself. While Hewell—who had now discovered you were missing—and his men were already pickaxeing away what was left of the tunnel, I composed a second message. I had no idea, of course, what your coded message had been, but the one I sent to 'COMBO RIDEX LONDON' should meet the case. I sent: 'PLEASE DISRE-GARD PREVIOUS MESSAGE EVERYTHING UNDER CONTROL ESSEN-TIAL YOU DO NOT ATTEMPT TO CONTACT ME FORTY EIGHT HOURS NO TIME CODE', and took the liberty of adding your name. Do you think that will meet the case, Bentall?"

I said nothing. There was nothing I could say. I looked round the faces at the table, but no one was looking at me any more, they were almost all staring down at their hands. I glanced in Marie's direction, but even she wasn't looking at me. I'd been born in the wrong time and place, I should have been in Rome two thousand years ago and toppling slowly forward on to my sword. I thought of the nasty big hole a sword would make and then, by association of ideas, of the nasty big holes in my upper left arm, so I said to Wither-spoon: "Would you permit Surgeon-Lieutenant Brookman to fix up my arm now?"

He looked at me long and consideringly, then said quietly: "I could almost regret that life has placed us on opposite sides of the fence. I can well understand why your chief sent you on this mission: you are a highly dangerous man."

"I'm better than that," I said. "I'm a lucky man. I'll carry your coffin yet."

He looked at me for a brief moment, then turned to Brookman. "Fix this man's arm."

"Thank you, Professor Witherspoon," I said politely.

"LeClerc," he said indifferently. "Not Witherspoon. That babbling old idiot has served his purpose."

Brookman made a good job. He opened and cleaned the wounds with something that felt like a wire brush, stitched them up neatly, covered them all with aluminium foil and bandage, fed me a variety of pills then, for good measure, jabbed me a couple of times with a hypodermic syringe. Had I been alone I'd have put any dancing dervish to shame but I felt I'd done damage enough to future Secret Service recruit-ment so I kept reasonably still. By the time he was finished the room itself was beginning to go into a dancing dervish routine, so I thanked Brookman and without a by-your-leave made shakily for the table and sat down heavily opposite Captain Griffiths. Witherspoon—or LeClerc, as I had to think of him now—sat beside me.

"You feel better, Bentall?"

"I couldn't feel worse. If there's a hell for dogs I hope that damned hound of yours is roasting."

"Quite. Who is the senior scientist among those present, Captain Griffiths?"

"What damnable evil are you up to now?" the grey-haired man demanded.

"I won't repeat the question, Captain Griffiths," LeClerc said mildly. His misted white eyes flickered for a moment in the direction of the dead man collapsed on the table.

"Hargreaves," Griffiths said wearily. He glanced in the direction of the sound of the voices behind the closed doors of the P.O.'s mess. "Must you, LeClerc? He's only just met his wife for the first time in many months. He won't be fit to answer anything. There's not much going on that I don't know. I'm the man in overall charge, you understand, not Hargreaves."

LeClerc considered, then said: "Very well. In what state of readiness is the Black Shrike?"

"Is that all you want to know?"

"That's all."

"The Black Shrike is completely ready in every respect except for the wiring up and fusing of the firing circuitry."

"Why wasn't this done?"

"Because of the disappearance of Dr. Fairfield . . ." I tried to focus on Captain Griffith's face among the kaleidoscopic whirl of people and furniture and dimly realised that it was only now that Griffiths was beginning to understand why Fairfield had disappeared. He stared at LeClerc for long moments, then whispered huskily: "My God! Of course, of course."

"Yes, of course," LeClerc snapped. "But I didn't mean that. Why was the circuitry and fusing not finished earlier. I understand that the loading of the propellant charge was completed over a month ago."

"How—how in heaven's name do you know that?"

"Answer my question."

"Fairfield feared that the propellant mixture might show inherent instability in very hot weather and regarded that as sufficient risk in itself without the additional risk of fusing it." Griffiths rubbed a sun-tanned hand across his damp and bleeding face. "You should know that no projectile or missile, from a two-pounder to a hydrogen bomb, is ever fused until the last possible moment."

"How long did Fairfield say the fusing would take?"

"I once heard him mention a period of forty minutes."

LeClerc said softly: "You're lying, Captain. I know the

great virtue of the Shrike is that it can be fired instantaneously."

"That is so. In time of war or tension it would be permanently fused. But we are as yet not quite certain as to the inherent stability of the propellant."

"Forty minutes?"

"Forty minutes."

LeClerc turned to me. "You heard. Forty minutes."

"I heard bits of it," I mumbled. "I'm not hearing very well."

"You are feeling sick?"

"Sick?" I tried to stare at him in vast surprise, but I couldn't find his face anywhere. "Why should I be feeling sick?"

"You could fuse this, Bentall?"

"I'm a specialist in liquid fuel," I said with difficulty.

"I know differently." I could see his face now, because he'd stuck it within three inches of mine. "You were Fairfield's assistant at the Hepworth Ordnance Branch. You worked on solid fuel. I *know.*"

"You know an awful lot."

"Can you fuse this?" he persisted quietly.

"Whisky," I said. "I need a drink of whisky."

"Oh, my God!" He followed this up with some more language, most of which I fortunately couldn't catch, then called to one of his men. I suppose the Chinese must have gone to the officers' mess, for a few moments later someone was putting a glass in my hand. I gazed blearily at it, a hefty three fingers in a tumbler, and put it all away in a couple of gulps. When I'd stopped coughing and wiped the tears away from my eyes, I found I could see almost as good as ever.

LeClerc touched my arm.

"Well, what's the answer? Can you fuse up the Shrike?"

"I wouldn't even know how to start."

"You're ill," LeClerc said kindly. "You don't know what you're saying. What you need is some sleep."

CHAPTER TEN

Friday 10 A.M.-1 P.M.

I SLEPT for two hours. When I awoke the sun was high in the sky and Dr. Hargreaves, the hypersonics specialist, was shaking me gently by the shoulder. At least he thought he was shaking me gently, it was probably the fact that I had a blanket drawn over me that caused him to forget that he shouldn't have been shaking me by the left shoulder. I told him to be more careful, he looked hurt, maybe it was the way I said it, and then I pushed back the blanket and sat up. I felt stiff and sore practically everywhere, my shoulder and arm throbbed savagely, but much of the tiredness was gone and my head was clear again. Which, of course, was what LeClerc had wanted, you can't have a man fusing and wiring up the complicated circuitry on a propellant with the disruptive potential of a hundred tons of high explosive if he's peering, fumbling and staggering around with exhaustion like a drunken man. From time to time I have cherished my share of illusions but one which I didn't cherish was that LeClerc had finished with me.

Hargreaves looked pale and distressed and unhappy. I didn't wonder. His re-union with his wife couldn't have been a very happy one, the circumstances hadn't been very favourable and the immediate prospects even less so. I wondered what they had done with Marie, whether they had put her in with the other women, and when I asked him he said they had.

I looked around the tiny hut. It was no more than eight by eight, with racks along the walls and a tiny steel-meshed window above my head. I seemed to remember vaguely that someone had mentioned that it used to be the small arms and ammunition storage shed, but I couldn't be sure, I'd just dropped on to the canvas cot they'd brought in and gone to sleep instantly. I looked at Hargreaves again.

"What's been going on? Since this morning, I mean?"

"Questions," he said tiredly. "Questions all the time. They interviewed my colleagues, myself and the naval officers separately, then they split us up and separated us from our wives. We're all over the place now, two or three to a hut."

LeClerc's psychology was easy to understand. With the scientists and naval officers broken into tiny groups, agreement on a concerted plan of resistance or revolt would be impossible: and with the scientists separated from their wives and in a consequent and continuous state of fear and anxiety over their welfare, their cooperation with LeClerc would be absolute.

"What did he want to see you about?" I asked.

"Lots of things." He hesitated and looked away. "Mainly about the rocket, how much did any of us know about the fusing. At least that's what he asked me. I can't speak for the others."

"Do you—do any of them know anything about it?"

162

"Only the general principles. Each one of us knows the general principles of the various components. We have to. But that doesn't even begin to be enough when it comes to the complex particulars." He smiled wanly. "Any of us could probably blow the whole thing to kingdom come."

"There's a chance of that?"

"No one has ever given a guarantee on an experimental rocket."

"Hence the blockhouse—that sunken concrete shelter to the north?"

"The test firing was to have been carried out from there. Just a first-time precaution. It's also why they placed the scientists' quonset so far away from the hangar."

"The sailors are expendable, but not the scientists? Is that it?" He didn't answer, so I went on: "Have you any idea where they're intending to take this rocket, the scientists and their wives. The naval officers and ratings, of course, won't be taken anywhere."

"What do you mean?"

"You know damn well what I mean. They're of no further use to LeClerc and will be eliminated." He shook his head in what was more an involuntary shudder than a shake and buried his face in his hands. "Did LeClerc make no mention of his ultimate destination?"

He shook his head again and turned away. He seemed badly upset about something, unwilling to meet my eye, but I couldn't find it in my heart to blame him.

"Russia, perhaps?"

"Not Russia." He stared at the floor. "Wherever it is, it's not Russia. They wouldn't look at this old steam-engine affair."

"They wouldn't—" It was my turn to stare. "I thought this was the most advanced—"

"In the Western world, yes. But in the last few months it's been an open secret among our scientists, but one they're all frightened to talk about, that Russia has developed—or is developing—the ultimate rocket. The photon rocket. Hints dropped by Professor Stanyukovich, the leading Soviet expert on the dynamics of gases, don't leave much room for doubt, I'm afraid. Somehow or other they've discovered the secret of harnessing and storing anti-protons. We know about this anti-matter but have no conception of how to store it. But the Russians have. A couple of ounces of it would take the Black Shrike to the moon."

The implications of this were beyond me: but I agreed that it was unlikely that the Soviets would want the rocket.

163

Red China, Japan? The presence of Chinese workers and LeClerc's Sino-Japanese transmitting set seemed to point that way, but the possibility was that those pointers were far too obvious, there were other countries in Asia—and outside Asia—who would dearly love to lay hands on the Black Shrike. But even more important than the question of what nation could or would want such a rocket was the answer to the question how any nation in the world had known that we were building such a rocket. Far back in my mind the first beginnings of an answer were beginning to shape themselves towards an impossible solution ... I became gradually aware that Hargreaves was speaking again.

"I want to apologise for my stupidity this morning," he was saying hesitantly. "Damn silly of me to persist in saying you were a solid fuel expert. I might have been putting a rope round your neck. I'm afraid I was too upset to think at all, far less think clearly. But I don't think the guard noticed."

"It's all right. I don't think either that the guard noticed."

"You're not going to cooperate with LeClerc?" Hargreaves asked. His hands were clasping and unclasping all the time, his nerves were no match for his brains. "I know you could do it if you wanted."

"Sure I could. A couple of hours with Fairfield's notes, diagrams, coding symbols and examining the actual layout, and I think I could. But time is on our side, Hargreaves— God knows as it's the only thing on our side. As far as LeClerc is concerned, the fusing is the key. He won't leave till he gets the key. London knows I'm here, the 'Neckar' may get suspicious over the delay, anything can happen, and anything that can happen can only be to our advantage." I tried to think of anything that could be to our advantage but failed. "So I sit tight. LeClerc suspects I'm an expert on solid fuels: he cannot possibly know."

"Of course," Hargreaves muttered. "Of course. Time is on our side."

He sat down on an empty ammunition box and stared down silently at the floor. He seemed to have lost all inclination to talk. I didn't much feel like talking myself.

A key turned in the door and LeClerc and Hewell came in. LeClerc said: "Feeling better?"

"What do you want?"

"Just wondering whether you might have changed your mind about your alleged ignorance on the subject of solid fuel."

"I don't know what you're talking about."

"Of course not. Hewell?" The giant came forward and laid a squat leather-covered box on the floor—a tape recorder. "Perhaps you would care to hear the playback of a recent recording we made?"

I rose slowly to my feet and stared down at Hargreaves. His gaze was still fixed on the floor.

"Thank you, Hargreaves," I said. "Thank you very much indeed."

"I had to do it," he said dully. "LeClerc said he would shoot my wife through the back of the head."

"I'm sorry." I touched him on the shoulder. "It wasn't your fault. What now, LeClerc?"

"It's time you saw the Black Shrikes." He stood to one side to let me pass.

The doors of the hangar were wide open, the lights burning high up near the roof. The rails ran all the way to the back of the hangar.

They were there, all right, the Black Shrikes, stubby pencil-shaped cylinders with highly-polished steel sides and water-cooled porcelain noses above great scalloped air-scoops, the height of a two-storey house and perhaps four feet in diameter. They rested on flat eight-wheeled steel bogies, and on either side of each rocket was a gantry crane, almost as high as the rocket itself, each crane mounted on a four-wheeled bogie: from the top and bottom of the gantries protruding clamps reached out to hold the rockets firmly in position. Both rockets and all four gantries were resting on the same set of rails.

LeClerc wasted no time, no words. He led me straight to the nearest rocket and mounted an open-sided lift fitted to the inner side of the nearest gantry. Hewell jabbed me painfully in the spine with his gun: I got the idea and climbed up beside LeClerc. Hewell stayed where he was. LeClerc pressed a button, an electric motor whined and the lift slid easily upward for about five feet. LeClerc took a key from his pocket, slid it into a tiny hole in the side of the rocket, pulled out a flush-fitting handle and swung out a seven-foot high door in the casing of the Black Shrike: the door had been so meticulously machined, so beautifully fitted, that I hadn't even noticed its existence.

"Take a good look," LeClerc said. "That's all you're here for—to take a good look."

I took a good look. The outer hardened steel casing of the rocket was just that and no more—an outer case. Inside was another casing and the gap between the two was at least five inches.

Directly opposite me, welded on to the inner casing, were two flat steel boxes, about six inches apart and each six inches square. The one to the left, green-painted, bore the legend 'Propellant' and below that the words 'On-Off': the one to the right was a bright pillar-box red in colour, with the words 'Safe' and 'Armed' stencilled in white on the left and right side of the box respectively. On both boxes, just below the top, was a knob-handled switch.

From the foot of both boxes issued flexible armoured cables, with plastic sheathing below the armour—a measure almost certainly designed to protect the underlying electric cables from the tremendous heat which would be generated in flight. The cable to the left, coming from the box marked 'Propellant,' was almost an inch and a half in diameter: the other was half an inch in diameter. The former ran down the inner casing and, about three feet away from the box, split into seven separate cables, each one covered in the same plastic and armour: the latter crossed the gap to the outer casing and disappeared upwards out of sight.

There were two other cables. One, a small half-inch cable, joined the two boxes: the second, two inches in diameter, bridged the gap between the 'Propellant' box and a third box, larger than either of the other two, which was fitted to the inside of the outer wall. This third box had a hinged door facing me, secured by a couple of butterfly nuts: no other electric cables led either to or from it.

And that was all that was to be seen. I saw it all in ten seconds. LeClerc looked at me and said: "Got it?"

I nodded and said nothing.

"The photographic memory," he murmured cryptically. He closed the door, locked it, pressed the lift button and we hummed upwards again for about six feet. Once more the routine with the key, the opening of a door—much smaller this time, barely two feet in height, the invitation to inspect.

This time there was even less to see. A circular gap in the inner casing, a view beyond the gap of what appeared to be fifteen or twenty round pipes narrowing towards their tips and, in the centre of those pipes, the top of some cylindrical object, about six inches in diameter, which vanished down among the tubes. In the centre of the top of this cylinder was a small hole, less than half an inch across. Attached to the outer casing was an armoured cable of the same dimensions as the one which had issued from the box marked 'Safe' and 'Armed', and it seemed a pretty fair guess that it was the same cable. The end of this cable, which was tipped with a solid copper plug, bent right over and hung slackly downwards in the gap between the outer and inner casings. It seemed logical to suppose that this copper plug was intended to fit into the hole in the central cylinder but here, it would seem, logic would have been in error: the hole in the cylinder was at least four times the size of the narrow copper plug.

LeClerc closed the door, pressed the button, and the lift dropped down to the foot of the gantry. Another door, another key and this time a view of the very base of the rocket, a foot below where the last of the pipes in the inner casing ended. There was no impression of a confusion of pipes here as there had been at the top: everything was mathematically neat and completely symmetrical, nineteen cylinders all of which seemed to be sealed with a heavy plastic compound, each cylinder about seven inches in diameter, eighteen of them arranged in two concentric circles about an inner core. The cylinders, which completely filled the inner casing, were not entirely smoothsided: at various distances above their lower ends they were smoothly indented in their sides, and those indentations, it was no trick at all to guess, were for the purpose of introducing the leads which hung in an untidy bunch between the two casings. I counted the leads, nineteen in all, breaking out from the seven armoured cables leading from the 'Propellant' box above: a pair of leads from each of three cables, three leads from each of the other three cables and four leads from the remaining cable.

"You have it all, Bentall?" LeClerc asked.

"I have it all," I nodded. It seemed simple enough.

"Good." He closed the door, led the way towards the hangar entrance. "Now to have a look at Fairfield's notebooks, codes and references. At least we were able to save those."

I raised an eyebrow—it was one of the few muscular exercises I could perform without causing myself pain.

"There were some things you couldn't save?"

"The complete set of blue-prints for the rocket. I must confess we did not think that the British would have had the intelligence to take such precautions. They were in the lower half of a sealed metal box—a standard war-time device, much faster and more foolproof than burning—the top half of which was a glass tank of concentrated hydrochloric with a metal plunger. The plunger was depressed, the glass broken and the acid released before we realised what was happening."

167

I remembered the captain's bleeding and battered face.

"Good old Captain Griffiths. So now you're completely dependent on having a working model of the rocket, eh?"

"That's so." If LeClerc was worried, he didn't show it. "Don't forget we still have the scientists."

He led me to a hut just beyond the armoury, a hut rather primitively fitted out as an office, with filing cabinets, a typewriter and a plain wooden desk. LeClerc opened the cabinet, pulled out the top drawer and dumped a pile of papers on the table.

"I understand that those are Fairfield's papers, all of them. I'll come back in an hour."

"Two hours at least: probably more."

"I said an hour."

"All right." I rose from the chair where I'd just seated myself and pushed the papers to one side. "Get someone else to work the damn thing out."

He looked at me for a long moment, the slaty milky eyes without expression, then said evenly: "You take very many chances, Bentall."

"Don't talk rubbish." If I couldn't do anything else I could at least sneer at him. "When a man takes chances he can either win or lose. I can't possibly win anything now, and God knows I've nothing to lose."

"You're wrong, you know," he said pleasantly. "There is something you can lose. I can take your life away from you."

"Have it and welcome." I tried to ease the burning pain in my shoulder and arm. "The way I feel right now I'm just about finished with it anyway."

"You have a remarkable sense of humour," he said acidly. Then he was gone, banging the door shut behind him. He didn't forget to turn the key in the lock.

Half an hour passed before I even bothered looking at Fairfield's papers, I'd more important things to think about than those. It was not the most pleasant half-hour of my life. The evidence was all before me now, Bentall with the blinkers off—at last—and I knew the truth, also at last. Counter-espionage, I thought bitterly, they should never have let me out of the kindergarten, the wicked world and its wicked ways were far too much for Bentall, if he could put one foot in front of the other without breaking an ankle in the process that was all you could reasonably expect of him. On flat ground, of course. By the time I'd finished thinking, my morale and self-respect had shrunk so much you'd have required an electronic microscope to find them, so I reviewed all that had happened in the hope of discovering one instance where I had been right, but no, I'd a perfect and completely unmarred record, one hundred per cent wrong all along the line. It was a feat that not many people could have matched.

The one redeeming feature about being utterly wrong, of course, was that I'd also been wrong about Marie Hopeman. She had had no special instructions from Colonel Raine, she had never fooled me once. This was no mere hunch or opinion, it was a provable certainty. It was, I knew, rather late in the day to arrive at this knowledge, I couldn't see that it was going to alter anything now, but in different circumstances ... I gave myself up to the very pleasant contemplation of what things might have been like in different circumstances and was just finishing off the towers and battlements of a particularly enchanting dream castle in the air when a key turned in the lock. I'd barely time to open the folder and scatter a few papers around before LeClerc and a Chinese guard came in. He glanced down at the table, Malacca cane swinging idly in his hand.

"How is it coming, Bentall?"

"Very difficult and very complicated and continual interruptions by you don't help me any."

"Don't make it too difficult, Bentall. I want this test rocket wired and fused and ready to take off in two and a half hours."

"Your wants are a matter of complete indifference to me," I said nastily. "What's the hurry, anyway?"

"The Navy is waiting, Bentall. We mustn't keep the Navy waiting, must we?"

I thought this one over, then said: "Do you mean to tell me that you have the colossal effrontery to keep in radio touch with the *Neckar?*"

"Don't be so naive. Of course we're in touch. There's no one more interested than myself to have the Black Shrike land on time, on target. Apart from which, the one sure way to rouse their suspicions and send them steaming back at high speed to Vardu is *not* to keep in touch with them. So hurry it up."

"I'm doing my best," I said coldly.

When he left, I got down to working out the firing circuits. Apart from the fact that they were coded, the instructions for the wiring were such as could have been carried out by any reasonably competent electrician. What could not have been done by the electrician was the calculation of the settings on the time clock—part of the mechanism in the box attached to the inside of the outer casing—which regulated

169

the ignition of the nineteen propellant cylinders in their proper sequence.

From his notes it appeared that even Fairfield himself had been doubtful about the accuracy of his own recommendations as to firing sequences and times: they had been worked out on a purely theoretical basis, but theory and practise weren't the same things at all. The trouble lay in the nature of the solid fuel propellant itself. A completely stable mixture in limited quantities and at normal temperatures, it became highly unstable under extremes of heat and pressure and beyond a certain unknown critical mass: the trouble was that no one knew the precise limits of any of those factors, nor, even more worrying, did they know how they reacted upon one another. *What* was known was the highly lethal results of instability: when the safety limit was passed the fuel changed from a relatively slow burning propellant to an instantaneously explosive disruptive estimated, weight for weight, at five times the power of T.N.T.

It was to reduce the danger of mass that the propellant had been fitted in nineteen separate charges and it was to reduce the danger of too suddenly applied pressure that the charges had been arranged to ignite in seven consecutive stages: but, unfortunately, no one could do anything about the danger of heat. The propellant had its own inbuilt oxidising agent, but not nearly enough to ensure complete combustion: two high-speed turbine fans which started up two seconds before the ignition of the first four cylinders supplied air in quantity and under high pressure for the first fifteen seconds until the missile reached a high enough speed to supply itself with sufficient air through its giant air-scoops. But as the Black Shrike was absolutely dependent on its air supply, it meant that it had to leave the earth on a very flat trajectory indeed in order not to run out of atmosphere before the propellant burnt out: it was not until all the fuel was consumed that the missile's automatic brain lifted it sharply out of the atmosphere. But the need for even half a minute's supply of air meant a tremendous air resistance generating extremely high temperatures and while it was hoped that the water-cooled porcelain nose would cope with part of the heat, no one knew what temperature would be generated in the heart of the rocket. All in all, I thought, it looked like a very dicey deal indeed.

The two switch-boxes I'd seen attached to the inner casing had both to be set before firing—the 'On' switch closed the firing circuits, the 'Armed' switch closed the circuit for the suicide box: if anything went wrong with the rocket in flight, such as a deviation to land or shipping lanes, it could be electronically instructed to commit suicide. In normal missiles fuelled by lox and kerosene, the flight could be stopped simply by sending out a radio message that automatically cut off the fuel supply: but there was no way of shutting off a solid fuel already in combustion. The cylinder I had seen in the middle of the propellant at the top of the rocket had been a sixty pound charge of T.N.T., fitted with a primer, and the hole I had seen in the centre of the primer was to accommodate a 77 grain electrically fired fulminate of mercury detonator, which was connected to the cable I'd seen dangling in the vicinity. The circuit for this was triggered, as were all controls in the rocket, by radio, a certain signal on a certain wavelength activating an electrical circuit in the same box as the one that contained the timing mechanism for the firing circuits: this current passed through a coil which in turn activated a solenoid switch—a soft iron core in the centre of the coil—and this completed the circuit which fired the detonator in the T.N.T. charge. Again Fairfield had been very doubtful of the outcome: what was intended was that the explosion of the T.N.T. should disintegrate the rocket: but it was just as likely, he had thought, that the instantaneous change in heat and pressure would cause the whole rocket to blow up in sympathetic detonation.

If I was picked as the first man to go to the moon, I thought, I'd just as soon not travel on the Black Shrike. Let someone else go first while Bentall remained earthbound and watched for the explosion.

I reached for the typewriter, made a list of which coloured and numbered firing cables marked which fuel cylinders, worked out an average of Fairfield's suggested figures for the timing sequences and stuck the paper in my pocket. I'd just done this when Hewell appeared.

"No, I'm damned well not finished," I said before he could open his mouth. "Why don't you leave me alone to get on with it?"

"How much longer?" he asked in his rumbling gravelly voice. "We're getting impatient, Bentall."

"I'm worried stiff. Maybe fifteen minutes. Leave one of your men outside and I'll knock when I'm finished."

He nodded and left. I got to thinking some more, mainly about myself and my life expectancy and then I started thinking of the psychologists who speak of the tremendous power of the human mind, the power of positive thinking, and if you say to yourself a thousand times a day to be cheerful and optimistic and healthy, then you will end up that way: I tried it with a slight variation, I tried to see Bentall as a bent old man with silver hair but somehow the positive thinking didn't seem to work in my case, I couldn't see anything of the kind, all I could see was Bentall with a hole in the back of his head. Tonight, it would probably come tonight, but the one certain thing I knew was that it would come. The other scientists could live, but not me: I had to die, and I knew why. I got up and tore the cord from the window blind, but not with the idea of hanging myself before LeClerc and Hewell got round to torturing me to death or shooting me. I rolled the cord into a coil, stuck it in my hip pocket and knocked on the door. I heard the footsteps of the guard walking away.

A few minutes later the door opened again. This time both LeClerc and Hewell were there, accompanied by a couple of Chinese.

"Finished?" LeClerc asked abruptly.

"Finished."

"Right. Start wiring up right away." No thank-you's, no congratulations for Bentall's keen-witted intelligence in solving an abstruse problem. Just get started right away.

I shook my head.

"Not that easy, LeClerc. I must go to the blockhouse first."

"The blockhouse?" The blind-seeming eyes looked at me for a long moment. "Why?"

"You have the launch console there, that's why."

"The launch console?"

"The little box with all the knobs and buttons for remote radio control of the various circuits in the rocket," I explained patiently.

"I know it," he said coldly. "You don't have to examine that before fusing up the rocket."

"You're not the best judge of that," I said loftily.

He'd no option but to give in, which he might have done with better grace. He sent a guard to the captain's office for the keys while we walked in silence across the intervening half-mile, and not a very companionable silence either, but it didn't worry me. I didn't feel like talking, I felt like looking, looking at the white glitter of the sands, the shimmering green-blue of the lagoon, the cloudless blue of the sky above. I took a long long look at all of them, the look of a man who suspects that that look is going to have to last him for a long long time.

The blockhouse had all the strength and solidity of a medieval fortress with the notable difference that it was so deeply sunk in the ground that only the top two feet were visible. There were three radar scanners mounted on the top and three radio aerials and, what I hadn't seen before, the tops of four periscopes which could be tilted on a vertical axis and swung on a horizontal axis.

The entrance was at the back at the foot of a short flight of steps. The door was a massive steel affair mounted on equally massive hinges and must have weighed close on half a ton. It was designed to keep more than the flies out: the possibility of the shock of the equivalent of 100 tons of high explosive detonating just over 1,000 yards away was something that made such a door very essential indeed, even although it was at the back.

The Chinese arrived with two keys, heavy chromed flat-sided jobs like enormous Yale keys. He inserted one, turned it twice and shoved the door slowly open on smooth oiled hinges. He passed inside.

"My God!" I muttered. "What a dungeon."

It looked exactly like that. A ten by twenty room, concrete floor, concrete walls, concrete roof, the heavy door through which we'd just come and another only just less heavy door in the opposite wall. And that was all, except for wooden benches round the wall and the tiny glow-worm of a lamp near the ceiling.

Nobody took me up on my conversational gambit. The Chinese crossed the dungeon and opened the other door with the second key.

This part of the blockhouse was about the same size as the other, but brilliantly lit. One corner of the room, about five by five, was partitioned off with plywood, and it was an easy guess that the idea was to screen radar scopes from the bright light outside. In the other corner was a softly-humming petrol-powered generator with its exhaust pipe disappearing upwards through the roof. There were two tiny ventilators, one high up on either side. And in the middle, between the radar cabin and the generator, was the launch console. I crossed and looked down at it.

It wasn't much, just a sloping metallic box backed by a radio transmitter, with a number of labelled buttons set in a straight line, each button with a tell-tale lamp above it. The first button bore the legend 'Hydraulics' and the second 'Auxiliary'—those would be for the last-minute testing of the oil and electricity circuits: the third said 'Power-Disconnect', that would be for cutting off the battery-feeding external electricity sources: the fourth read 'Flight-Control', a radio signal to alert the guiding mechanism in the Shrike's electronic 'brain'. The fifth, with the legend 'Clamps' would, when pressed, show by lighting up the tell-tale that the gantry clamps supporting the missile were ready for instantaneous withdrawal when the missile took off. The sixth, 'Gantry-Ex', would move back the gantries leaving only the extension arms of the clamps in place: the seventh, the 'Commit' button, started up the power intake fans: two seconds after that, I knew, the revolving clock drum would trigger off the first four of the nineteen cylinders: ten seconds after that, another circuit would close and the suicide circuit would be ready and waiting, waiting only for the moment when something went wrong and the launch console operator pushed the eighth and last button.

The last button. It was set well away from the other seven. There was no possibility of mistaking it, for it was a square white push set in the middle of a six inch square patch of red and labelled EGADS in steel letters—Electronic Ground Automatic Destruct System: and there was no possibility of triggering it by mistake for it was covered by a heavy wire mesh that had to be unclipped at two sides, and even then the button had to be turned 180° on its axis before it could be depressed.

I gazed at this for some time, fiddled about with the radio behind, took out my notes and consulted them. Hewell loomed over me which would have made it very difficult for me to concentrate if I had had to, which fortunately I hadn't. LeClerc just stood there looking at me with those blind white eyes of his, until one of the guards murmured something to him and pointed in the direction of the back door.

LeClerc left and was back in thirty seconds.

"All right, Bentall," he said curtly. "Hurry it up, will you? The *Neckar* has just reported that she is running into gale conditions which will make observations of the test impossible when and if the weather deteriorates any further. Seen all you want to?"

"I've seen all I want to."

"You can do it?"

"Sure I can do it."

"How long?"

"Fifteen minutes. Twenty at the most."

"Fifteen?" He paused. "Dr. Fairfield said it would take forty minutes."

"I don't care what Dr. Fairfield said."

"Right. You can start now."

"Start what now?"

174

"Wiring up the firing circuits, you fool."

"There must be some mistake somewhere," I said. "I never said anything about wiring up those circuits. Can you recall my saying I would. I've no intention of touching the damned circuits."

The gentle swinging of his malacca cane stopped. LeClerc took a step nearer me.

"You won't do it?" His voice was harsh, blurred with anger. "Then what the devil was the idea of wasting the past two and a half hours pretending you were figuring out how to do it?"

"That's it," I said. "That's the whole point of it. Wasting time. You heard what I said to Hargreaves. Time is on our side. You made a recording of it."

I knew it was coming and I saw it coming, but I felt about ninety that day and my reactions were correspondingly slow and the vicious lash of that cane with all LeClerc's fury and weight behind it across my left cheek and eye was a razor-edged sword splitting my face in half. I choked in agony, staggered back a couple of paces, then flung myself at the blurred figure before me. I hadn't recovered a foot when Hewell's two great hands closed over my bad arm and tore it off at the shoulder—later inspection showed it was still there, he must have stuck it back on again—and I swung round lashing out with all the power of my good right arm, but I was blind with agony and missed him completely. Before I could regain my balance one of the guards had me by the right arm and the cane was whistling towards me again. I somehow sensed it was coming, ducked and took the full weight of the blow on the top of my head. The cane swung back for a third blow, but this time it didn't reach me: Hewell released my left arm, jumped forward and caught LeClerc's wrist as it started on its downward swing. LeClerc's arm stopped short as abruptly as if it had come to the limit of a chain attached to the roof. He struggled to free himself, throwing the whole weight of his body on Hewell's hand: neither Hewell nor his hand moved an inch.

"Damn you, Hewell, let me go!" LeClerc's voice was hardly more than a whisper, the trembling whisper of anger out of control. "Take your hand away, I tell you!"

"Stop it, boss." The deep authoritative boom brought normalcy, everyday sanity, back into the blockhouse. "Can't you see the guy's half-dead already. Do you want to kill him? Who's going to fuse up the rocket then?"

There was a few seconds' silence, then LeClerc, in a

completely changed tone, said: "Thank you, Hewell. You're quite right, of course. But I had provocation."

"Yeah," Hewell said in his gravelly voice. "You had at that. A clever-clever alec. I'd like to break his goddamned neck, myself."

I wasn't among friends, that was clear enough. But I wasn't worrying about them at that moment, I wasn't even thinking about them, I was too busy worrying and thinking about myself. My left arm and the left side of my face were engaged in a competition to see which could make me jump more and the competition was fierce, but after a while they gave it up and joined forces and the whole left side of my body seemed to merge into one vast agonising pain. I was staring down at the launch console and the various buttons were swimming into focus and out again, one moment gone, the next hopping around like a trayful of jumping beans. Hewell hadn't exaggerated any, if there was one thing that was certain it was that I couldn't take much more of this. I was just slowly coming to pieces. Or perhaps not so slowly.

I heard voices, but whether the voices were directed at me or not I didn't know. I stumbled against a stool and sat down heavily, clinging to the launch console to keep myself from falling.

The voices came again, and this time I could distinguish LeClerc's. He had advanced to within a couple of feet of me, the cane held in both hands, the backs of his thumbs gleaming white as if he were holding himself in check with an effort, as though he were trying to snap the cane in half.

"Do you hear me, Bentall," he said in a low cold voice that I liked even less than his hysterical outburst of a moment ago. "Do you understand what I'm saying to you?"

I stared down at the blood dripping to the concrete floor.

"I want the doctor," I mumbled. My jaws, my mouth were swelling, stiffening up already and I found speech difficult. "My wounds have opened up again."

"The hell with your wounds." The Good Samaritan to the life. "You're going to start on that rocket and you're going to start on it now."

"Ah!" I said. I forced myself to sit straight, and half-shut my eyes until I had him more or less in focus, like an image and six ghosts on a badly-adjusted TV screen. "How are you going to make me? Because you'll have to make me, you know. How? Torture? Bring out the old thumb screws and see if Bentall cares." I was half out of my mind with pain, I didn't know what I was saying. "One turn of the rack and Bentall is in a better world. Besides, I wouldn't feel it anyway. And a hand like mine, trembling like a leaf!" I held it up to let him see it trembling like a leaf. "How do you expect me to fuse a tricky—"

He gave me the back of his hand across my mouth, not lightly.

"Shut up," he said coldly. Florence Nightingale would have loved him, he'd exactly the right touch with sick men. "There are other ways. Remember when I asked that stupid young lieutenant a question and he refused to answer? Remember?"

"Yes." It seemed about a month ago but it had been only a few hours. "I remember. You shot a man through the back of the head. The next time the lieutenant did what you wanted."

"Just like you're going to. I'm having a sailor brought here and I'm going to ask you to fuse that rocket. If you won't, I'll have him shot." He snapped his fingers. "Like that!"

"You will, eh?"

He didn't answer, just summoned and spoke to one of the men. The Chinese nodded, turned away and hadn't gone five steps when I said to LeClerc: "Call him back."

"That's better," LeClerc nodded. "You're going to cooperate?"

"Tell him to bring all the other ratings with him. And all the officers. You can shoot the lot of them through the head. See if I care."

LeClerc stared at me.

"Are you quite mad, Bentall?" he demanded at last. "Don't you realise that I mean what I say?"

"And I mean what I say," I answered tiredly. "You forget what I am, LeClerc. I'm a counter-espionage agent and humanitarian principles don't matter a damn to me. You should know that better than anyone. Besides, I know damn well that you're going to murder them all before you leave here. If they shuffle off twenty-four hours ahead of schedule, then what the hell? Go ahead and waste your ammunition."

He looked at me in silence while the seconds passed, while my heart thudded heavily, painfully in my chest, while the palms of my hands grew moist, then turned away. He believed me all right, it was so exactly the way his own ruthless criminal mind would work. He spoke quietly to Hewell, who left with a guard, then turned back to me.

"Everybody has their Achilles' heel, Bentall," he said conversationally. "I believe you love your wife."

The heat inside that reinforced concrete blockhouse was sweltering, over-hot, but I felt myself turn as cold as if I had just stepped into an ice-box. For a moment all the fierceness

177

of the pain left me and all I could feel were goose-pimples running down my arms and back. My mouth was suddenly dry and I could feel deep in my stomach that hellish incapacitating nausea that can spring only from fear. And I was afraid, afraid with a fear I had not before known: I could feel this fear, I could feel it in my hands, I could taste it in my mouth and the taste was the taste of all the unpleasant things I had ever tasted: I could smell it in the air and the smell was an amalgam of all the evil odours I had ever known. God, I should have known this was coming, I thought of her face twisted in pain, the hazel eyes dark in agony, it was the most obvious thing in the world. Only Bentall could have missed it.

"You poor fool," I said contemptuously. It was hard to get the words past my dry mouth and swollen lips, far less inform them with the appropriately scornful tones, but I managed it. "She's not my wife. Her name is Marie Hopeman and I met her for the first time exactly six days ago."

"Not your wife, eh?" He didn't seem vastly surprised. "A fellow-employee of yours, one assumes?"

"One assumes correctly. Miss Hopeman is fully aware of the risks involved. She has been a professional government agent for many years. Don't threaten me with Miss Hopeman or she'll laugh in your face."

"Quite so, quite so. An agent, you say. The British Government is to be congratulated, the level of pulchritude among female agents is apt to be dismally low and Miss Hopeman does much to correct the balance. An astonishingly lovely young lady and one whom I, personally, find quite charming." He paused fractionally. "Since she is not your wife you will not mind so much if she accompanies the other ladies towards our destination?"

He was watching me closely to get my reaction, he didn't have to spell it out for me, but he didn't get the reaction. He had a pistol in his right hand now and what with that and the guard's automatic carbine pointing at my middle, there was nothing to be gained by reacting in the only way I felt like, so I said instead: "Destination? What destination would that be, LeClerc? Asia?"

"That should be obvious, I thought."

"And the rocket? Prototype for a few hundreds more?"

"Exactly." He seemed ready to talk, as all men are ready to talk about their obsessions. "Like many Asiatic nations my adopted country has a genius more, shall we say, for refined imitation than original invention. In six months we shall be turning them out in quantity. Rockets, Bentall, are today's bargaining counters at the table of world politics. We need lebensraum for what the papers of the world are pleased to call our teeming millions. The desert of Australia could be made to blossom like a rose. We should like to move in there, peacefully, if possible."

I stared at him. He'd gone off his rocker.

"Lebensraum? Australia? My God, you're mad. Australia! You couldn't catch up with the military potential of Russia or America in a lifetime."

"By which you mean?"

"Do you think either of those countries would stand by and let you run wild in the Pacific? You *are* mad."

"They wouldn't," LeClerc said calmly. "I quite agree. But we can deal with Russia and America. The Black Shrike will do it for us. Its great virtues, as you are well aware, are its complete mobility and the fact that it requires no special launching site. We fit out a dozen vessels—not our own, oh dear me no, but flags of convenience, ships from Panama or Liberia or Honduras—with two or three rockets apiece. Three dozen missiles will be enough, more than enough. We dispatch those vessels to the Baltic and the Kamchatka Peninsula, off the Russian coast, and off Alaska and the Eastern seaboard of the United States: those off the Russian coasts will have their rockets zeroed in on ICBM launching sites in America, those off the American coasts zeroed in on the corresponding sites in the USSR. Then they fire, more or less simultaneously. Hydrogen bombs rain down on America and Russia. The advanced radar stations, their long-range infrared scanners, their electronically relayed satellite photographs of intercontinental missile exhaust trails will show beyond dispute that those rocket-borne hydrogen bombs come from Russia and America. Any doubts left in their minds will be resolved by Moscow and Washington receiving radio messages apparently from each other, each calling upon the other to surrender. The two great world powers then proceed to devastate each other. Twenty-four hours later there will be nothing to prevent us from doing exactly as we wish in the world. Or do you see a serious flaw in my reasoning?"

"You're insane." My voice was strained and hoarse even in my own ears. "You're completely insane."

"If we were to do exactly as I have outlined, I would tend to agree with you, although it may come in the last resort. But it would be most foolish, most ill-advised. Apart from the cloud of radioactive dust that would make the northern hemisphere rather unpleasant for some time, we wish to trade with those two rich and powerful nations. No, no,

Bentall, the mere threat, the very possibility will be more than enough.

"Both American and Russian observers will be asked to attend highly convincing tests of the Shrike's—we shall probably rename it—power, pay-load, accuracy and range. Then we shall leak the information that those dozen vessels are strategically placed and also leak our intention of triggering off a war in which the two nations will devastate each other. Then we move on Australia.

"Note, then, the extremely interesting and delicate situation that will develop. One or other of the two great powers may move against us. Immediately it does, hydrogen bombs will fall on that country's territory. Say it was America that moved against us. Bombs devastate their ICBM launching sites, their Strategic Air Command airfields. But where do those bombs come from? Do they come from us, because America has moved against us? Or do they come from Russia, who sees in this the heaven-sent moment to destroy the United States without the possibility of immediate retaliation against it, knowing that the Americans have no proof that the hydrogen bombs came from Russia and assuming that the Americans will think that the bombs really did come from those strategically placed vessels of ours of which they have heard? But note this further: whether America really believed the hydrogen bombs came from us or not they would be forced to launch an all-out assault against the Soviet Union, for the bombs might just as possibly be coming from there and if they are and the Americans wait too long before launching their counter nuclear assault, the United States will be wiped out of existence. The same would happen, even more certainly, if we launched the missiles against Russia. What it comes to in effect, Bentall, is that both the great countries will know that if either of them moves against us, they will be forced to engage in a nuclear holocaust that may destroy them both. Neither of them will move an inch against us: instead they will combine to use their power to stop other countries like Britain or France moving against us. Or, once again, do you see a serious flaw in my reasoning?"

"You're insane," I repeated. "Completely, hopelessly insane." But they were only words, all conviction had left my voice. He didn't look like a man who was insane. He didn't talk like a man who was insane. It was only *what* he said that sounded insane, but it only sounded insane because it was so preposterous, and it was only preposterous because of the gigantic, the unprecedented scale of the blackmail and bluff involved, of the unparalleled deadliness of the threat that backed up the blackmail. But there was nothing insane about blackmail and bluffs and threats, and if a thing is not insane on a normal scale there is no necessary element of insanity introduced when the normal is multiplied to unimaginable proportions. Maybe he wasn't insane after all.

"We shall see, Bentall, we shall see." He turned as the outer door of the blockhouse opened and quickly switched off all the lights except a small bulb burning above the console.

Marie, with Hewell by her side, came into the semi-darkness. She caught sight of me standing there with my back to the light, smiled, took a step towards me then stopped abruptly as LeClerc lifted his cane to bar her passage.

"Sorry to bring you across, Mrs. Bentall," he said. "Or should it be Miss Hopeman? I understand you are not married."

Marie gave him the sort of look I hoped I'd never see coming my way and said nothing.

"Shy?" LeClerc asked. "Or just uncooperative? Like Bentall here. He's refusing to cooperate. He won't agree to fuse the Black Shrike."

"Good for him," Marie said.

"I wonder. He may be sorry. Would you like to persuade him, Miss Hopeman?"

"No."

"No? But we might persuade him *through* you, if not by you."

"You're wasting your time," she said contemptuously. "I'm afraid you don't know either of us. And we hardly know each other. I'm nothing to him nor is he anything to me."

"I see." He turned to me. "The stiff upper lip, the best traditions of the Secret Service. "What do you say, Bentall?"

"The same as Miss Hopeman. You're wasting your time."

"Very well." He shrugged, turned to Hewell. "Take her away."

Marie gave me another smile, clear enough proof that she couldn't see my battered face in the shadow, and left. Her head was high. LeClerc paced up and down, head bent like a man lost in thought, and after a time he gave some order to the guard and left.

Two minutes later the door opened and I saw Marie, with Hewell and LeClerc on either side of her. She had to have them there because she couldn't walk. Her feet trailed on the floor, her head lay far across her left shoulder, and she was

181

moaning softly, her eyes shut. The frightening thing was that she bore no mark of violence, not a hair of her head was out of place.

I tried to get to LeClerc, there were two carbines and Hewell's pistol on me, I never knew they were there, I tried to get to LeClerc to smash his face in, to lash out, to maim, to kill, to destroy, but I couldn't even do that right. On my second step one of the guards tripped me with his carbine and I crashed heavily and full-length on the stone floor. I lay there for some time, dazed.

The guards hauled me to my feet, waiting one on either side of me. Hewell and LeClerc stood as they had done. Marie's head had now fallen forward, so far forward that I could see where the fair hair parted on the nape of the neck. She was no longer moaning.

"Do you fuse the Shrike?" LeClerc asked softly.

"Someday I'll kill you, LeClerc," I said.

"Do you fuse the Shrike?"

"I fuse the Shrike," I nodded. "Then someday I'll kill you."

If I could carry out even half my promise, I thought bitterly, it would be a change for me.

CHAPTER ELEVEN

Friday 1 P.M.-6 P.M.

I'D SAID to LeClerc that I could close up the wiring circuitry and fuse the Black Shrike in fifteen minutes. In point of fact it took me exactly an hour. Bentall wrong as usual, but this time it wasn't Bentall's fault.

It wasn't my fault because my arm and face hurt so violently that it was impossible to concentrate on the job. It wasn't my fault that I was mad with anger, that my vision was so blurred and indistinct that I could scarcely decipher my own notes, that my right hand—I did practically everything with my right hand—was shaking so badly that I had great difficulty in adjusting the time clock, in feeding cables through their allotted grooves, in fitting the fuses into place in the bases of the solid fuel cylinders: it wasn't my fault that, when arming the sixty pound disruptive charge, my sweating hand dropped a fulminate of mercury detonator that went up with so white a flash and so loud an explosion that it was touch and go whether Hewell, who was supervising the operation, pressed the trigger of the pistol he had lined up on me.

And it wasn't my fault that LeClerc had insisted that I work on both rockets at once, or that I was hindered by the fact that he had appointed Hargreaves and another scientist by the name of Williams to check on every move and write it down in their notebooks. One on either side of me on the narrow gantry platforms, they got in my way with nearly every move I made.

I could see the logic of LeClerc's insistence on the simultaneous wiring. He'd certainly warned Hargreaves and Williams that if they as much as spoke to each other they would be shot and probably warned that the same thing would happen to their wives if their notes did not compare exactly at the end of the day. Thus, if the first firing of the Shrike was a success and the compared notes for the wiring up of both rockets were absolutely the same, then he would have a guarantee that the second rocket would also be perfectly wired.

The simultaneous wiring, of course, also served notice of sentence of death on me. Had he been intending to take me with him along with the others, he would hardly have had me wire up both rockets at once, especially in view of the urgency: the most recent message from the *Neckar* spoke of seas so high that there was a possibility of having to abandon the test. Not that I needed any notice of this sentence. I wondered when I was slated to die. Immediately after I had finished the wiring or later, along with Captain Griffiths and his men, after the scientists and their wives had been embarked? Later, I thought, even LeClerc wasn't likely to embark on a blood bath with so many witnesses watching. But I wouldn't have spent a penny to gamble on it.

A few minutes before two o'clock I said to Hewell: "Where are the keys for the destruct box?"

"Are you all ready to go?" he asked. The last move before the rockets were in final firing order was to make the switches in both the propellant and destruction systems, but the switch for the latter that completed the circuit to the 60 lb. T.N.T. charge couldn't be made without a key which operated a safety lock on the handle of the switch.

"Not quite. The switch in the suicide box is sticking. I want to have a look at it."

"Wait. I'll get LeClerc." He left, leaving a watchful Chinese in charge, and was back with LeClerc inside a minute.

"What's the hold-up now?" LeClerc demanded impatiently.

"Two minutes. Have you the key?"

He signalled for the lift to be lowered, told the two scientists with their note-books to get off, then climbed up beside me. When we regained working height he said suspiciously: "What's the trouble? Thinking of pulling the last minute fast one of a desperate man?"

"Try the switch yourself," I snapped. "It won't move across."

"It's not supposed to move more than halfway before the key is turned," he said angrily.

"It won't even move at all. Try it for yourself and see."

He tried it, moved it less than a quarter inch, nodded and handed me the key. I unlocked the switch, undid the four butterfly nuts that held the switch-cover in position and as I eased the switch-cover off over the switch I managed to dislodge with the tip of my screwdriver the copper core of a piece of flex which I'd forced in between switch and cover to make the former stick. The switch itself was of the common type with the spring-loaded rocker arm where, when the switch handle was pushed over to the right the two copper lugs jumped over from the two dead terminals on the right to the live terminals on the left. As quickly as my blurred vision and shaky right hand would permit I unscrewed the central rocker arm, lifted out the switch, pretended to straighten out the copper lugs and then screwed the switch back in place.

"Fault in design," I said briefly. "Probably the same in the other." LeClerc nodded, said nothing, just watched carefully as I replaced the cover and flicked the switch from side to side several times to demonstrate how easily it worked.

"All finished?" LeClerc asked.

"Not yet. I've got to set the timing clock on the other one."

"That can wait. I want this one on its way—now." He looked up to where Farley and an assistant were fussing around with the automatic guidance and target location systems. "What the hell's keeping him?"

"Nothing's keeping him," I said. Farley and I made a pair, both of us with great red and purple weals down the left hand sides of our faces: his was even more angry-looking and rainbow hued than mine, but that was only because it had had more time to develop: give me twenty-four hours and nobody would even notice his. Twenty-four hours. I wondered who would give me twenty-four hours. "He finished days ago," I went on. "He's just a last minute fusser, wondering if he turned all the taps off before he left home."

If I pushed LeClerc hard enough, I mused, he might break his neck on the concrete floor ten feet beneath: on the other hand he might not, and then I wouldn't have twenty-four seconds left me, far less twenty-four hours. Besides, Hewell had his cannon pointing at me.

"Good. Then we are ready to go." LeClerc turned the key in the switch cover, pushed the switch to the 'Armed' position, withdrew the key and closed and locked the door of the rocket. The lift sunk down to the ground and LeClerc beckoned to one of the guards. "Go tell the wireless operator to send a message. Firing in twenty minutes."

"So where now, LeClerc?" I asked. "The blockhouse?"

He looked at me coldly.

"So that you can hide there in safety while the rocket blows itself up because of some fix you made on it?"

"What are you talking about?"

"I'm talking about you, Bentall. I have no illusions. You are a highly dangerous man." Sure I was dangerous, but only to my friends and myself. "You have the ability to jinx the firing mechanism so that only you would know. Surely you were not so naive as to imagine that I would overlook the possibility? You, the scientists and naval men will remain out here in the open while the rocket is being fired. They are already assembled. We shall go to the blockhouse."

I swore at him, violently and viciously. He smiled.

"So you had overlooked the possibility that I would take precaution?"

"Leave men out in the open, you damned murderer. You can't do that, LeClerc!"

"Can't I now?" The slaty milky eyes stared into mine, as he went on softly: "Perhaps you *have* jinxed it, Bentall?"

"I've done damn all of the kind," I shouted. "It's just that this solid fuel is inherently unstable. Read Dr. Fairfield's notes and you'll see that. No one really knows what's going to happen. The fuel has never been tried before on this scale. Damn you to hell. LeClerc, if that thing goes up not a single man within half a mile has the ghost of a chance of survival."

"Exactly," he smiled. He smiled, but I became gradually aware that he wasn't feeling like smiling. His hands were out of sight in his pockets, but I could see they were knotted into fists: he had a nervous tic at the corner of his mouth and he was sweating more than the heat of the sun justified. This, for LeClerc, was the most crucial moment of all, the moment when all could be won or all could be lost. He didn't know just how ruthless I could be, he suspected I'd go to the limit and stick at nothing, that I'd even sacrifice innocent lives to stop him, after all I'd already told him that he could shoot every officer and seaman on the base as far as I was concerned. Maybe he thought I wouldn't be so willing to sacrifice my own life, but he wouldn't lay too much stress on that, he knew that I knew that I was going to die anyway. All his staggering plans, his hopes and his fears depended on the next few moments, would the Black Shrike take off or would it blow itself to bits and all his schemes and dreams along with it. He had no means of knowing. He had to gamble, he just had to gamble: but if he gambled and was wrong at least he wasn't going to let me know the satisfaction of winning.

We walked round the corner of the hangar. A hundred yards away, sitting in two ragged rows on the ground, were the naval and scientific personnel of the base. But no women, I couldn't see any women. Two Chinese were standing guard with automatic carbines at the ready.

I said: "How do the guards feel about having to stay there when the rocket is fired?"

"They don't: they come to the blockhouse."

"And do you seriously imagine we're just going to keep on sitting there like good little boys once the guards are gone?"

"You'll sit there," he said indifferently. "I have seven women in the blockhouse. If one of you stirs, they get it. I mean it."

The last three words were completely superfluous. He meant it all right. I said: "Seven women? Where is Miss Hopeman?"

"In the armoury."

I didn't ask why he hadn't shifted her also—I knew the bitter answer to that, she was probably either still unconscious or too unwell to be moved—and I didn't ask that she should be moved. If the Black Shrike exploded she would have no more chance than we had, the armoury was less than a hundred yards from the hangar, but better that way than to survive in the blockhouse.

I sat down at the end of one of the rows of men, Farley beside me. Nobody looked at me, everyone was staring fixedly at the doors of the hangar waiting for the Black Shrike to emerge.

They hadn't long to wait. Thirty seconds after LeClerc and Hewell had left us the two big gantry cranes with the Black Shrike between them rumbled slowly into view. Two of the technicians were at the controls of the gantries. The bogies of the gantries were spanned by two connecting bars that spanned the rocket bogie, so ensuring that the gantry clamps holding the Black Shrike remained in exactly the same relative positions. After about thirty seconds the bogies stopped, leaving the Black Shrike planted exactly in the centre of the concrete launching pad. The two technicians jumped down, removed the connecting bars and, at a gesture from one of the Chinese, came and sat beside us. Everything was now radio-controlled. The guards themselves left for the blockhouse at a dead run.

"Well," Farley said heavily. "A grandstand seat. The murderous devil."

"Where's your scientific spirit?" I asked. "Don't you want to see if the damn thing works?"

He glared at me and turned away. After a moment he said significantly: "My part of it will work, anyway. It's not that I'm worried about."

"Don't blame me if it blows up," I said. "I'm only the electrician around here."

"We can discuss it later on a higher plane," he said with heavy humour. "What are the chances, you think?"

"Dr. Fairfield thought it would work. That's good enough for me. I just hope you haven't crossed any wires and that it doesn't come down straight on top of us."

"It won't." He seemed glad to talk as everybody around seemed glad to talk, the strain of just sitting and waiting in silence was too much. "Worked before, often. Never a failure. Our latest infra-red guidance system is foolproof. Locks on a star and stays there."

"I can't see any stars. It's broad daylight."

"No," Farley said patiently. "But the infra-red cell can. Heat detection. Wait and see, Bentall, 1,000 miles and it will be bang on target to a yard. To a yard, I tell you."

"Yes? How's anybody going to pinpoint a yard in the South Pacific?"

"Well, eight foot by six," he conceded magnanimously. "A magnesium raft. When the rocket re-enters the atmosphere the stellar navigation unit is switched off and an infra-red homer in the nose takes over. The rocket is designed to home in on a heat source. A ship, of course, especially a ship's funnel, is also a heat source, so a magnesium raft, a source of tremendous heat, will be ignited by the *Neckar's* radio ninety seconds before the missile arrives. The rocket will make for the greater source of heat."

"I hope so for the *Neckar's* sake. Just too bad if they're ninety seconds late in igniting the raft."

"They won't be. A radio signal is sent from here when the

rocket leaves." He paused. "Well, if it leaves. The Shrike will take exactly three and a half minutes for the flight, so they ignite two minutes after receiving the signal."

But I was hardly listening to him any more. LeClerc, Hewell and the last of the guards had disappeared behind the blockhouse. I looked away, over the shining sands and the green gleam of the glass-smooth lagoon and stiffened abruptly as I saw a vessel about four miles out heading for a break in the reef. I didn't stay stiff long, this wasn't any knight-errant naval vessel coming to the rescue, it was that intrepid navigator Captain Fleck, coming to collect his wages. Hargreaves had mentioned that he was expected that afternoon. I thought about Captain Fleck, and I thought that if I were in his shoes I'd be steering my schooner in the diametrically opposite direction and putting as many sea-miles as possible between myself and LeClerc. But then Captain Fleck didn't know what I knew, or I was reasonably certain he didn't. Captain Fleck, I thought, a shock awaits you.

I twisted round as the rumble of bogie wheels came to my ears. The two gantry cranes, weirdly unmanned and controlled by radio, were moving slowly away in opposite directions, withdrawing their top clamps and leaving the Shrike supported only by the extensible clamps still gripping its base. Ten seconds to go, perhaps less. No one was talking any more, finding a suitable conversational topic when you've perhaps only eight seconds left to live isn't a thing that many people have had practice in.

The big high-speed turbine induction fans near the nose of the Shrike whined abruptly into life, two seconds to go, one, everybody rigid as stone and with eyes half-closed against the shattering shock they would never feel, the base clamps leapt apart, a single thunderclap of sound and a great seething ball of orange flame appeared at the foot of the Shrike, completely enveloping the bogie. Slowly, incredibly slowly, the Shrike lifted off the ground, the ball of orange flame riding up with it, and now the echoes of the thunderclap were replaced by a steady continuous roar, terrifying in its intensity, battering at our shrinking eardrums like the close-up thunder of giant jet engines, as a fifty-foot long brilliant red tongue of flame pierced the flaming sphere at the base of the rocket and lifted the Black Shrike on its way. Still it climbed slowly, unbelievably slowly, it seemed that it must topple over at any moment, then at 150 feet another violent explosion as the second set of fuel cylinders ignited, the Shrike doubled its rate of climb, a third explosion about 600 feet and then it began to accelerate at fantastic speed. At about five or six thousand feet it turned over abruptly and headed south-east on a trajectory that seemed almost to parallel the surface of the sea, and within eight seconds was completely lost to sight with nothing to show that it had ever been except the acrid stink of the burnt fuel, the flame-blackened bogie and the thick white trail of its exhaust which stretched bar-straight across the hot blue sky.

By this time my chest was hurting me, so I started breathing again.

"Well, it works!" Farley smacked a fist into a palm in grinning exultation. He gave a long tremulous sigh of satisfaction, he'd been without oxygen even longer than I had. "It works, Bentall, it works!"

"Of course it works. I never expected anything else." I rose stiffly to my feet, rubbing the wet palms of my hands against my drills, and crossed over to where Captain Griffiths sat with his officers. "Enjoy the show, Captain?"

He studied me coldly, not bothering to hide the dislike, the contempt in his eyes, and glanced at the left side of my face.

"LeClerc seems to like using his cane, doesn't he?" he asked.

"It's just an addiction he's got."

"And so you collaborated with him." He looked me up and down with all the enthusiasm of an art collector who's been promised a Cezanne and finds a comic coloured postcard in front of him. "I didn't think you would, Bentall."

"Sure, I collaborated with them," I agreed. "No moral fibre at all. But the court-martial can wait, Captain Griffiths." I sat down, pulled off shoe and sock, removed a paper from its plastic cover, smoothed out the creases and handed it to him. "What do you make of this? Quickly, please. I found it in LeClerc's office and I'm certain it's in some way connected with his plans for shipping the second Shrike to its destination. Nautical stuff isn't in my line."

He took the paper reluctantly as I said: "The Pelican's a ship, we know that, because LeClerc himself told us. I suspect the others are too."

"Pelican-Takishamaru 20007815" Captain Griffiths read. "Takishamaru is a Japanese ship name, no doubt about that. Linkiang-Hawetta 10346925. Probably all ships' names. All paired. Now, what would that be for. The numbers, always eight numbers." He was getting interested. "Times, could they be times? 2000 could be 8 p.m., none of the first four numbers go higher than twenty-four. But the second four do. References of some kind. Ships, eh? Now what kind of references—" His voice trailed off, I could see his lips moving, then he said slowly: "I think I have it. No, I know I have it."

"2000 is twenty point oh-oh. Latitude twenty degrees south. 7815 stands for 178.15 degrees east. Together they give a position less than fifty miles west of here." He studied the paper in silence for almost a minute while I looked over my shoulder to see if there was any sign of LeClerc approaching: there was none, he would be waiting to hear from the *Neckar* about the success of the firing.

"They're all lat. and long. positions," Griffiths said finally. "It's difficult to be sure without a chart but I could be fairly certain that if those positions were plotted they would represent a north-east curve from here to some position off the Chinese or Formosan coasts. I should imagine those ships—pairs of ships, rather—will be located on those positions. I should also imagine they would have the duty of escorting the vessel carrying the rocket, or keeping a lookout or seeing that the road is clear. LeClerc would have taken precautions, I imagine, against the premature discovery of the fact that the rocket had been stolen."

"They would be armed, those ships, you think?" I said slowly.

"Highly unlikely." He was an intelligent incisive old bird with a mind that matched his sharp speech. "It would have to be concealed arms, and no amount of concealed arms would be a match for any searching warship which would be the only thing they would have to fear."

"They might be radar-equipped vessels, searching the sea and air for fifty, a hundred miles round?"

"They might. They probably would be."

"But wouldn't this ship carrying the rocket be equipped with its own radar?"

Captain Griffiths handed me back the paper.

"It won't be," he said positively. "LeClerc is the kind of man who will always succeed because he takes precautions elaborate to the point almost of the ridiculous. Almost, I say. This paper is of no use to you, even if you could act on the information enclosed. Those vessels are almost certainly screen vessels which will travel some miles in advance and in the rear of the vessel carrying the rocket. At various points they will turn this vessel over to another pair, if air searchers saw the same two ships going in the same direction the same distance apart for days on end they'd start getting suspicious."

"But—wait a moment, Captain, my mind—it's just about stopped." I wasn't joking at that, the heat of the sun and the 'fact that my wounds hadn't been treated since I'd been knocked about in the blockhouse made my head reel dizzily. "Yes. But what happens if some warship or aircraft does come on the scene. You can detect them with radar but you can't shoot them down with radar. What does the vessel with the Black Shrike do then?"

"It submerges," Griffiths said simply. "It will be a submarine, it's bound to be a submarine. Enlarge the loading hatch and practically any submarine in service could carry the Shrike in its for'ard torpedo room. The screen vessels will enable it to travel on the surface at top speed. If anything happens it just submerges and proceeds at much lower speeds. But it'll get there. A hundred naval ships equipped with Asdic could search for a year and never locate just one solitary sub loose in the Pacific. I think you can take it for granted, Bentall, that if that rocket leaves the island we will never see it again."

"Thank you very much, Captain Griffiths." No question, he had the final truth of it. I pushed myself wearily to my feet, like an old old man making his final attempt to leave his death-bed, tore the paper into pieces and let them fall on the thin sun-browned grass. I looked in the direction of the blockhouse and could see several figures just appearing from the back. Out at sea Fleck was coming in through the gap in the reef.

"One more request, Captain Griffiths. When LeClerc returns ask him if you and your men can remain out in the open for the remainder of the day, in the fresh air instead of baking in those corrugated iron huts. It's likely they'll soon start encasing the other rocket"—I pointed to the two twenty-foot steel boxes with the built in cradles in the hangar—"ready for shipment, and point out the fact that it would then need only one guard to look after you instead of the four or five required to watch the doors and windows if you're locked up in the huts, so releasing more of his men for the work. Give him your word there will be no trouble. If the test went well, he'll be in a good mood and likely to grant your request."

"Why do you want this, Bentall?" The dislike was back in his voice.

"I don't want LeClerc to see me talking to you. If you want to live, do as I say." I wandered aimlessly off to inspect the extent of the damage caused by the rocket leaving the launching pad. Two minutes later, out of the corner of my eye, I saw LeClerc and Griffiths speaking to one another, and then LeClerc and Hewell came towards me. LeClerc was looking almost jovial, the way a man is apt to look when he sees his greatest dream coming true.

"So you didn't jinx it after all, did you, Bentall?" He obviously didn't want to embarrass me by showing too much gratitude for the job I'd done.

"No, I didn't jinx it." But I'll jinx the other one, Mr. LeClerc, oh, brother, how I'll jinx the other one. "Successful?"

"Completely. Absolutely on target—after a thousand miles. Right, Bentall, finish off the other one."

"I want to see Miss Hopeman first."

He stopped being jovial.

"I said finish it off. I mean finish it off."

"I want to see Miss Hopeman first. Five minutes. No more, I promise you. Either that or wire up your own damn rocket. See how long it takes you."

"Why do you want to see her?"

"Mind your own damned business."

He looked at Hewell, who gave an all but imperceptible nod.

"Very well. But five minutes. Five minutes only. You understand?" He handed a guard the key and gestured us on our way.

The guard unlocked the door of the armoury and let me in. I closed the door behind me, not worrying whether I was hurting his feelings.

The room was in near darkness, with its shutters drawn. Marie was lying in a cot in the corner, the same cot as I had slept in that morning. I crossed over and sunk to my knees by the side of the cot.

"Marie," I said softly. I shook her shoulder with a gentle hand. "Marie. It's me. Johnny."

She must have been in deep sleep and she took some time to come out of it. Finally she stirred and twisted round under the blanket. All I could see was the pale blur of the face, the sheen of the eyes.

"Who—who is it?"

"It's me, Marie—it's Johnny."

She didn't answer so I repeated my words, my face and mouth and jaws were so stiff and sore that perhaps she couldn't catch my thick mumble.

"I'm tired," she murmured. "I'm so very tired. Please leave me."

"I'm terribly sorry, Marie. Honest to God, I could shoot myself. I thought they were bluffing Marie, I really thought they were bluffing." Again no answer, so I went on: "What did they do to you, Marie? For God's sake tell me what they did to you?"

She murmured something, I couldn't catch it, then said in a low voice: "I'm all right. Please go away."

"Marie! Look at me!"

She gave no sign that she had heard.

"Marie! Look at me. Johnny Bentall on his knees." I tried to laugh, but it was only a froglike croak, a frog with bronchitis at that. "I love you, Marie. That's why I fused up their damned rocket, that's why I'd fuse up a hundred rockets, that's why I'd do anything in the world, anything that's right, anything that's wrong, just so no harm would ever come to you again. I love you, Marie. I've been so long in seeing it but you should know by now what to expect from a fool like me. I love you and if we ever come home again I want to marry you. Would you marry me, Marie? When we get home?"

There was a long silence, then she said softly: "Marry you? After you let them—please leave me, Johnny. Please leave me now. I'll marry someone who loves me, not someone—" She broke off and then finished huskily: "Please. Now."

I rose heavily to my feet and went to the door. I opened it and let the light flood into the room. A shaft of light from the westering sun illuminated the bed, the fair shining hair spread on the rolled-up coat that serves as a pillow, the great hazel eyes in the pale and exhausted face. I looked at her for a long long moment, I looked until I couldn't bear to look any longer, I'd never more shed tears for the martyrs who went to the stake, it was all too easy. I looked at the only person I'd ever loved and as I turned away, Bentall the tough guy to the end, not wanting even his Marie to see the tears in his eyes, I heard her shocked whisper: "Dear God, oh, dear God! Your face!"

"It'll do," I said. "It won't have to last me a great deal longer. I'm sorry, Marie. I'm sorry."

I closed the door behind me. The guard took me straight to the hangar and luck was with me and LeClerc, for I did not meet him on the way. Hewell was waiting for me, with Hargreaves and Williams, both with their notebooks at the ready. I got onto the lift without being told, the other two followed and we started work.

First I opened the junction box on the inside of the outer casing and adjusted the timing devices on the rotary clock, then, checking that the hand-operated switch on the destruct box was locked at 'Safe', I took a quick look at the second break in the suicide circuit, the solenoid switch directly above the timing device. The solenoid, normally activated when its enveloping coil was energised, was held back by a fairly stout spring which required, as a quick tug informed me, about a pound and a half of pressure to close. I left the box open, the lid hanging downwards and secured by a couple of butterfly nuts, then again turned my attention to the destruct box: when pretending to check the action of the switch I did the same as I had done on the first Shrike, forced a small piece of wire between switch and cover. Then I called down to Hewell.

"Have you the key for the destruct box? Switch stuck."

I needn't have bothered with the wire. He said: "Yeah, I have it. Boss said we might expect trouble with this one too. Here, catch."

I opened the cover, unscrewed the switch, pretended to adjust it, replaced it and screwed home the rocker arm. But before I'd replaced it I'd turned it through 180°, so that the brass lugs were in a reversed position. The switch was so small, my hands so completely covered it that neither Hargreaves nor Williams saw what I was doing: nor had they any reason to expect anything amiss, this was exactly, they thought, the same as they had seen me doing on the destruct box in the other rocket. I replaced the cover, shoved the lever to the safe position: and now the destruct box was armed and it only awaited the closing of the solenoid switch to complete the suicide circuit. Normally, the switch would be closed by radio signal, by pressing the EGADS button in the launch console. But it could also be done by hand . . .

I said to Hewell: "Right, here's the key."

"Not quite so fast," he growled. He signalled for the lift to be brought down for him, rode up to the open door and took the key from me. Then he tried the destruct box switch, checked that it was impossible to move it more than half-way towards 'Armed', let it spring back to the 'Safe' position, nodded, pocketed the key and said: "How much longer?"

"Couple of minutes. Final clock settings and buttoning up."

The lift whined downwards again, Hewell stepped off, and on the way up I murmured to Hargreaves and Williams: "Stop writing, both of you." The hum of the electric motor covered my words and it wasn't any trick to speak without moving my lips, the left hand side of my mouth was now so puffed and swollen that movement was almost impossible anyway.

I leaned inside the door, the cord I'd torn from the blind

concealed in my hand. To fasten one end of the cord to the solenoid should have taken maybe ten seconds but my hand was shaking so badly, my vision and coordination so poor that it took me almost two minutes. Then I straightened and started to close the door with my left hand while the cord ran out through the fingers of my right. When only a four-inch crack remained between the door and the outer casing of the rocket, I peered inside—the watching Hewell must have had the impression that I had one hand on either side of the door handle, trying to ease its stiffness. It took only three seconds for my right hand to drop a round turn and two half hitches round the inner handle, then the door was shut, the key turned and the job finished.

The first man to open that door more than four inches, with a pressure of more than a pound and a half, would trigger off the suicide charge and blow the rocket to pieces. If the solid fuel went up in sympathetic detonation, as Dr. Fairfield had suspected it would, he would also blow himself to pieces and everything within half a mile. In either case I hoped the man who would open it would be LeClerc himself.

The lift sank down and I climbed wearily to the ground. Through the open doors of the hangar I could see the scientists and some of the sailors sitting and lying about the shore, an armed guard walking up and down about fifty yards from them.

"Giving the condemned boys their last few hours of sunshine, eh?" I asked Hewell.

"Yeah. Everything buttoned up?"

"All fixed." I nodded towards the group. "Mind if I join them? I could do with some fresh air and sunshine myself."

"You wouldn't be thinking of starting something?"

"What the hell could I start?" I demanded wearily. "Do I look fit to start anything?"

"It's God's truth you don't," he admitted. "You can go. You two"—this to Hargreaves and Williams—"the boss wants to compare your notes."

I made my way down to the shore. Some of the Chinese were man-handling the metal casing for the rocket on to a couple of bogies, with about a dozen sailors helping them under gun-point. Fleck was just tying up at the end of the pier, his schooner looked even more filthy than I remembered it. On the sands, Captain Griffiths was sitting some little way apart from the others. I lay on the sand not six feet away from him, face down on the sand, my head pillowed on my right forearm. I felt awful.

Griffiths was the first to speak.

"Well, Bentall, I suppose you've just wired up the other rocket for them?" He wouldn't win many friends talking to people in that tone of voice.

"Yes, Captain Griffiths, I've wired it up. I've booby-trapped it so that the first man to open the door of the Black Shrike will blow the rocket out of existence. That's why I did so good a job on the other rocket, this is now the only one left. They were also going to shoot you and every other sailor on the base through the back of the head and torture Miss Hopeman. I was too late to stop them from getting at Miss Hopeman."

There was a long pause, I wondered if he had managed to understand my slurred speech, then he said quietly: "I'm so damnably sorry, my boy. I'll never forgive myself."

"Put a couple of your men on watch," I said. "Tell them to warn us if LeClerc or Hewell or any of the guards approach. Then you just sit there, staring out at sea. Speak to me as little as possible. No one will see me speaking in this position."

Five minutes later I'd finished telling Griffiths exactly what LeClerc had told me he planned to do after they had the Black Shrike in production. When I was finished he was quiet for almost a minute.

"Well?" I asked.

"Fantastic," he murmured. "It's utterly unbelievable!"

"Isn't it? It's fantastic. But is it feasible, Captain Griffiths?"

"It's feasible," he said heavily. "Dear God, it's feasible."

"That's what I thought. So you think booby-trapping this rocket—well, it's justifiable, you think?"

"How do you mean, Bentall?"

"When they get the Black Shrike to wherever it's going," I said, still talking into the sand, "they're not going to take it out to any remote launching field. They're going to take it to some factory, almost certainly in some heavily populated industrial area, to strip it down for examination. If this solid fuel goes up with the T.N.T. I don't like to think how many hundreds of people, mainly innocent people, will be killed."

"I don't like to think how many millions would be killed in a nuclear war," Griffiths said quietly. "The question of justification doesn't enter into it. The only question is—will the batteries powering the suicide circuit last?"

"Nickel cadmium nife cells. They're good for six months, maybe even a year. Look, Captain Griffiths, I'm not just telling you all this just to put you in the picture or to hear myself talking. It hurts me even to open my mouth. I'm telling you because I want you to tell it all to Captain Fleck. He should be coming ashore any minute now."

"Captain Fleck! That damned renegade?"

"Keep your voice down, for heaven's sake. Tell me, Captain, do you know what's going to happen to you and me and all your men when our friend LeClerc departs."

"I don't have to tell you."

"Fleck's our only hope."

"You're out of your mind, man!"

"Listen, carefully, captain. Fleck's a crook, a scoundrel and an accomplished rogue, but he's no megalomaniac monster. Fleck would do anything for money—except one thing. He wouldn't kill. He's not the type, he's told me so and I believe him. Fleck's our only hope."

I waited for comment, but there was none, so I went on: "He'll be coming ashore any moment now. Speak to him. Shout and wave your arms and curse him for the damned renegade you say he is, the way you would be expected to do, nobody will pay any attention except LeClerc and Hewell and all they'll do is laugh, they'll think it highly amusing. Tell him what I've told you. Tell him he hasn't long to live, that LeClerc will leave no one behind to talk. You'll find that LeClerc has spun him some cock-and-bull yarn about what he intended to do here, one thing you can be certain of, LeClerc never told him of the rocket or what he intended to do with the rocket, he would never have dared with Fleck and his crew calling so often at Suva and other Fijian harbours where one careless word in a bar would have ruined everything. Do *you* think LeClerc would have told him the truth, Captain?"

"He wouldn't. You're right, he couldn't have afforded to."

"Has Fleck ever seen the rockets before?"

"Of course not. Hangar doors were always closed when he called and he was allowed to speak only to the officers and the petty officer who supervised the unloading of the boat. He knew, of course, that it was something big, the *Neckar* was often anchored in the lagoon here."

"So. But he'll see the Black Shrike now, he can't help seeing it from where he's berthed at the end of the pier. He'll have every justification for asking LeClerc questions about it and I'm much mistaken if LeClerc will be reluctant to talk about it. It's the dream of his life and he knows that Fleck won't live to talk about it. Fleck might even then still have some doubts left as to what's in store for him, so just that he can understand exactly what kind of man he's dealing with, tell him to go—no, better tell him to send Henry, his mate, he himself better not be seen to be missing—to see what LeClerc really is capable of." I told Griffiths exactly how to find the spot where Hewell and his men had broken through the hillside, told him where to find the cave with all the dead men. "I wouldn't be surprised if there are two more dead men there now, Fijian boys. And ask him to find out if the radio in LeClerc's cabin is still there. After Henry comes back Fleck will have no more doubts."

Griffiths said nothing. I only hoped I'd convinced him: if I had I couldn't leave it in better hands, he was a wily old bird and sharp as they came. By and by I heard a movement as he got to his feet. I peered out of the corner of one eye and saw him walking slowly away. I twisted round till I saw the pier. Fleck and Henry, dressed in their best off-whites were just leaving the schooner. I closed my eyes. Incredibly, I went to sleep. Or perhaps not so incredibly. I was exhausted beyond belief, the aches in my head and face and shoulder and body merging into one vast gulf of pain. I slept.

When I woke up I'd yet another ache to add to my lists. Someone was kicking me in the lower ribs and he wasn't trying to tickle me, either. I twisted my head. LeClerc. Too late in the day for LeClerc to learn the more rudimentary rules of courtesy. Blinking against the sun, I turned round till I was propped up on my good elbow, then blinked again as something soft struck me in the face and fell on my chest. I looked down. A hank of cord—window cord—neatly rolled up and tied.

"We thought you might like to have it back, Bentall. We've no further use for it." No fury in that face, not the vindictive anger I would have expected, but something approaching satisfaction. He looked at me consideringly. "Tell me, Bentall, did you really think that I'd overlook so obvious a possibility—to me the certainty, rather—that you wouldn't hesitate to jinx the second Shrike when you knew there would be no further danger to yourself? You sadly under-rate me, which is why you find yourself where you are now."

"You weren't as smart as all that," I said slowly. I felt sick. "I don't think you did suspect. What I did overlook was the certainty that you would take Hargreaves and Williams apart and threaten to kill their wives if they didn't tell you *everything* that happened. Separate huts and the usual menaces if their stories didn't tally exactly. Maybe I do underestimate you. So now you take me away somewhere quietly and shoot me. I don't really think I'll mind."

"Nobody's going to shoot you, Bentall. Nobody's going to

shoot anybody. We're leaving tomorrow and I can promise that when we do we will leave you all alive."

"Of course," I sneered. "How many years practice does it take, LeClerc, to get that ring of conviction into your voice when you tell your damned lies?"

"You'll see tomorrow."

"Always tomorrow. And how do you propose to keep forty of us under control until then?" I hoped his mind worked as mine did, or I'd probably wasted my time in sending Griffiths to Fleck.

"You gave us the idea yourself, Bentall. The blockhouse. You said it would make a fine dungeon. Escape proof. Besides, I want all my men for the job of crating the Shrike tonight and I don't need guards for anyone inside the blockhouse." He looked at Hewell and smiled. "Incidentally, Bentall, I believe there is no love lost between yourself and Captain Griffiths. He was saying some pretty hard things about you for fusing up that first rocket."

I said nothing. I waited for it.

"You'll be pleased to hear he's met with a little trouble. Nothing serious. I gather he took it into his head to berate Captain Fleck—as one Englishman to another—for his treasonable activities. Fleck, one gathers, took exception to Griffiths taking exception. In age, height and weight the two master mariners were pretty evenly matched and if Captain Griffiths was a bit fitter Fleck knew more dirty tricks. It was a fight to see. Had to stop it eventually. Distracting my men."

"I hope they beat each other to death," I growled. LeClerc smiled, and walked away with Hewell. The world was going well for them.

It wasn't for me. The booby-trap sprung, Griffiths and Fleck at blows, the last hope gone, Marie finished with me, LeClerc winning all along the line and a bullet in the head for Bentall any hour now. I felt sick and weak and exhausted and beaten. Maybe it was time to give up. I rolled over on my face again, saw Griffiths approaching. He sat where he had been sitting before. His shirt was dirty and torn, his forehead grazed and a trickle of blood at the corner of his mouth.

"Congratulations," I said bitterly.

"They are in order," he said calmly. "Fleck believes me. It wasn't difficult to convince him. He was on the other side of the island this morning and found a dead man—or what was left of him—a Fijian, I think, floating out near the reef. He thought it was sharks. He doesn't now. His mate has gone to investigate."

"But—but the fight?"

"LeClerc came out of the hangar. He was watching us closely, much too closely. It was the only way to kill suspicion." I looked up and he was smiling. "We managed to exchange quite a bit of information as we were rolling around."

"Captain Griffiths," I said, "you deserve a battleship for this."

The sun sunk down towards the sea. Two Chinese brought us some food, mostly tinned, and beer. I saw another couple take some across to the blockhouse where the seven women were still held, probably as additional security against our making trouble. Lieutenant Brookman fixed my arm again and he didn't seem too happy with its condition. All afternoon the Chinese and about half the sailors, closely supervised by Hewell, were dismantling two gantries and setting them up one on either side of the railway track in preparation for lifting the Shrike into its metal crate, which was already in position on a pair of bogies. And all the time I wondered about Marie in her loneliness, whether she was asleep or awake, how she felt, whether she thought about me, whether her despair was half as deep as mine.

Shortly before sunset Fleck and Henry came strolling along the sands from the other side of the pier. They stopped directly opposite me, Fleck with his legs spread and arms akimbo. Griffiths shook his fist at him, there would be no doubt in any watcher's mind that another violent argument, verbal or otherwise, was about to begin. I rolled over on my right elbow, the most natural thing in the world if one heard two people arguing over one's head. Fleck's brown hard face was set and grim.

"Henry found them all right." His voice was husky with anger. "Eleven. Dead. The rotten lying murderous devil." He swore bitterly and went on: "God knows I play rough, but not that rough. He told me they were prisoners, that I was to find them by accident tomorrow and take them back to Fiji."

I said: "Do you think there's going to be any tomorrow for you, Fleck? Don't you see the armed sentry on the pier waiting to see you don't make a break for it with your ship? Don't you see you'll have to go the same way as the rest. He can't leave anyone behind who'll talk."

"I know. But I'm all right, tonight, anyway, I can sleep on my schooner tonight, a coaster from Fiji by the name of *Grasshopper* and manned by the most murderous crew of Asiatics in the Pacific is coming here at dawn. I've got to pilot them through the reefs." For all his anger, Fleck was playing his part well, gesticulating violently with every second word.

"What's the coaster for?" I asked.

"Surely it's obvious?" It was Griffiths who replied. "A big vessel couldn't approach the pier, there's only ten feet or so of water, and though they could load the rocket on to Fleck's after deck he hasn't anything in the crane line big enough to transship it to a submarine. I'll bet this coaster has a jumbo derrick, eh, Fleck?"

"Yes, it has. Submarine? What—"

"It can wait," I interrupted. "Did Henry find the radio?"

"No," Henry himself replied, lugubrious as ever. "They've blasted down the roof at the other end of the tunnel and sealed it off."

And tomorrow, I thought, they'll shove us all inside this end of the tunnel and seal that off. Maybe LeClerc hadn't been lying when he said he wouldn't shoot us, starvation wasn't as quick as shooting but it was just as effective.

"Well, Fleck," I said, "how do you like it. You've got a daughter in the University of California in Santa Barbara, right next to one of the biggest intercontinental ballistic missile bases in the world, the Vanderberry Air Force Base, a number one target for a hydrogen bomb. The Asiatics sweeping down on your adopted country of Australia. All those dead men—"

"For God's sake, shut up!" he snarled. His fists were tightly clenched and fear and desperation and anger fought in his face. "What do you want me to do?"

I told him what I wanted him to do.

The sun touched the rim of the sea, the guards came for us and we were marched away to the blockhouse. As we went in I looked back and saw the floodlight going up outside the hangar. LeClerc and his men would be working all through the night. Let them work. If Fleck came through, there was an even chance the Black Shrike would never reach its destination.

If Fleck came through.

CHAPTER TWELVE

Saturday 3 A.M.-8 A.M.

I AWOKE in the darkness of the night. I'd been asleep four hours, maybe six, I didn't know, all I knew was that I didn't feel any the better for it; the heat in that sealed ante-chamber of the blockhouse was oppressive, the air was stuffy and foul and the mattress-making companies had little to fear from the manufacturers of concrete.

I sat up stiffly and because the only thing I had left me were my few remaining shreds of pride I didn't shout out at the top of my voice when I inadvertently put some weight on my left hand. It was near as a toucher, though. I leaned my good shoulder against the wall and someone stirred beside me.

"You awake, Bentall?" It was Captain Griffiths.

"Uh-huh. What's the time?"

"Just after three o'clock in the morning."

"Three o'clock!" Captain Fleck had promised to make it by midnight at the latest. "Three o'clock. Why didn't you wake me, captain?"

"Why?"

Why indeed. Just so that I could go round the bend with worry, that was why. If there was one thing certain it was that there was nothing I or anyone else could do about getting out of that place. For thirty minutes after we'd been locked in Griffiths, Brookman and myself had searched with matches for one weak spot in either the walls or the door or that ante-chamber, a hopelessly optimistic undertaking when you consider that those walls had been built of reinforced concrete designed to withstand the sudden and violent impact of many tons of air pressure. But we had to do it. We had found what we expected, nothing.

"No sound, no movement outside?" I asked.

"Nothing. Just nothing at all."

"Well," I said bitterly, "it would have been a pity to spoil the fine record I've set up."

"What do you mean?"

"I mean that every damned thing I've touched on this damned job has gone completely wrong. When it comes to sheer consistency, Bentall's your man. Too much to hope for a change at this late hour." I shook my head in the dark. "Three hours overdue. At least three hours. He's either tried and been caught or they've locked him up as a precaution. Not that it matters now."

"I think there's still a chance," Griffiths said. "Every fifteen minutes or so one of my men has stood on another's shoulders and looked through the ventilation grill. Can't see anything of interest, of course, just the hill on one side and the sea on the other. The point is that there has been brilliant moonlight nearly all night. Make it impossible for Fleck to
202

get away unobserved from his ship. He might get the chance yet."

"Nearly all night, you said. Nearly?"

"Well, there was a dark patch, lasting maybe half an hour, round about one o'clock," he admitted reluctantly.

"He wouldn't want half an hour, fifteen minutes would be all he needed," I said heavily. "There's no future in kidding ourselves."

There was no future anyway. I'd expected far too much. To expect him to slip away unobserved from his ship, in clear moonlight, with a guard on the pier and a working party with brilliant floodlamps not a hundred yards away, was to expect a little bit too much: and to expect him afterwards to reach unseen the captain's hut where the keyboard was, not fifty yards from the hangar, steal the keys, free Marie from the armoury and then free us—well, it had been expecting far too much altogether. But it had been the only shadow of hope that we had had, and the clutch of a drowning man is pretty fierce.

The time dragged on, a night that could never end but, for all that, a night that would end all too soon. I don't think anyone slept, there would be time and to spare for rest later on. The scientists and their wives murmured away softly most of the time, it occurred to me with a sense of shock that I wouldn't have been able to identify any of those women had I met them again, I had never yet seen one in daylight. The air became more and more vitiated, breathing in that foul used-up atmosphere was becoming painful, the heat became steadily worse and sweat dripped from my face, ran down my arms and back. Every now and then a seaman would be hoisted up to look through the grill, and every time he had the same report: bright moonlight.

Every time, that was, until four o'clock. The seaman had no sooner reached eye-level to the grill than he called out: "The moon's gone. It's pitch dark outside. I can't see—"

But I never did hear what he couldn't see. There came from outside in quick succession the sounds of a quick rush of feet, a scuffle, a heavy blow and then a metallic scratching as someone fumbled for the keyhole. Then a solid click, the door swung open and the cool sweet night air flooded into the room.

"Fleck?" Griffiths said softly.

"Fleck it is. Sorry to be late but—"

"Miss Hopeman," I interrupted. "She there?"

"Afraid not. Armoury key wasn't on the board. I spoke to

her through the window bars, she told me to give you this."
He thrust a paper into my hand.

"Anyone with a match?" I asked. "I want—"

"It's not urgent," Fleck said. "She wrote it this afternoon.
Been waiting for a chance to—" he broke off. "Come on. No
time to waste. That damn moon isn't going to stay behind a
cloud all night."

"He's right, you know," Griffiths said. He called softly:
"Outside, all of you. No talking. Straight up the face of the
hill and then cut across. That's best, eh, Bentall?"

"That's best." I stuck the note into my shirt pocket, stood
to one side to let the others file quietly out. I peered at
Fleck. "What you got there?"

"A rifle." He turned and spoke softly, and two men came
round the corner of the blockhouse, dragging a third.
"LeClerc had a man on guard. Gun belongs to him. Everybody out? All right, Krishna, inside with him."

"Dead?"

"I don't think so." Fleck didn't sound worried one way or
the other. There came the sound of something heavy being
dumped unceremoniously on the concrete floor inside and the
two Indians came out. Fleck pulled the door quietly to and
locked it.

"Come on, come on," Griffiths whispered impatiently.
"Time we were off."

"You go off," I said. "I'm going to get Miss Hopeman out
of the armoury."

He was already ten feet away, but he stopped, turned and
came back to me.

"Are you mad?" he said. "Fleck said there's no key. That
moon comes out any minute now. You'll be bound to be
seen. You won't have a chance. Come on and don't be so
damned stupid."

"I'll take the chance. Leave me."

"You know you're almost certain to be seen," Griffiths said
softly. "If you're out they'll know we're all out. They will
know that there's only one place we could go. We have
women with us, it's a mile and a half to that cave entrance,
we would be bound to be intercepted and cut off. What it
amounts to, Bentall, is that you are prepared to risk the
almost certain loss of all our lives on the selfish one in a
thousand chance of doing something for Miss Hopeman. Is
that it, Bentall? Is that how selfish you are?"

"I'm selfish all right," I said at last. "But I'm not all that
bad, I just hadn't thought of it. I come with you to the point

where there is no further possibility of interception. Then I turn back. Don't make the mistake of trying to stop me."

"You're quite crazy, Bentall." There was anger and worry both in Griffith's voice. "All you'll do is lose your life, and lose it to no purpose."

"It's my life."

We moved straight towards the face of the hill, all in a closely bunched group. No one talked, not even in whispers, though LeClerc and his men were then well over half a mile away. After we'd gone about three hundred yards the hill started to rise steeply. We'd made as much offing as we could so now we turned south and began to skirt the base of the mountain. This was where things began to become dangerous, we had to pass by the hangar and the buildings to get to the cave entrance, and just behind the hangar a sharp spur of the mountain rose above the surrounding level and would force us to come within two hundred yards of where LeClerc and his men were working.

Things went well in the first ten minutes, the moon stayed behind the cloud longer than we had any right to hope, but it wasn't going to stay there all night, eighty per cent of the sky was quite free from cloud and in those latitudes even the starlight was a factor to be reckoned with. I touched Griffiths on the arm.

"Moon's coming out any second now. There's a slight fold in the mountain about a hundred yards further on. If we hurry we might make it."

We made it, just as the moon broke through, bathing the mountain and the plain below in a harsh white glare. But we were safe, for the moment at least, the ridge that blocked us off from the view of the hangar was only three feet high, but it was enough.

Fleck and his two Indians, I could now see, were dressed in clothes that were completely sodden. I looked at him and said: "Did you have to take a bath before you came?"

"Damn guard sat on the pier all night with a rifle in his hands," Fleck growled. "Checking us, checking to see we didn't go near the radio. We had to slip over the far side, about one o'clock when the moon went in, and swim for it, maybe a quarter mile along the beach. Henry and the boy, of course, went the other way." I had asked that Henry would make straight for the cave, hurry through the chamber that had served as an armoury and bring back amatol blocks, primers, RDX, chemical fuses, anything he could find. If they were still there, that was: there would certainly be neither arms nor ammunition left now, and though the explosives

205

would be a poor substitute for arms at least they would be better than nothing.

"Getting the keys was dicey," Fleck went on, "and there were only the two—the inner and outer blockhouse doors. Then we tried to force the door and window on the armoury to get Miss Hopeman out. It was hopeless." He paused. "I don't feel so good about that, Bentall. But we tried, honest to God, we tried. But we couldn't make a noise, you understand that."

"It's not your fault, Fleck. I know you tried."

"Well, anyway, we came to the blockhouse just as the moon came out. Lucky for us it did. LeClerc had left a guard. We had to hide there two solid hours waiting till it got dark so we could rush him. I've a pistol, so has Krishna here, but the water got through the wrappings. Couldn't have used them anyway."

"You did damn well, Captain Fleck. And we have a gun. Any good with it?"

"Haven't the eyes for it. Want it?"

"Hell no, I couldn't fire a pop-gun tonight." I turned and located Griffiths. "Any good shots among your men, Captain?"

"As it happens, I have. Chalmers here"—he gestured towards the red-haired lieutenant over whose refusal to answer a question a seaman had been shot—"is one of the best shots in the Royal Navy. Would you care to have a go at them, Chalmers, if the need arises?"

"Yes, sir," Chalmers said softly, "I would like that."

A cloud was approaching the moon. It wasn't much of a cloud as clouds go, it wasn't half as big as I would have liked it to be, but it was going to have to do, there wasn't another anywhere near the moon.

"Half a minute, Captain Griffiths," I said, "Then we're off."

"We'll have to hurry," he said worriedly. "Single file is best, I think. Fleck to lead the way, then the women and the scientists, so that they can make a break for the cave if anything happens. My men and I will bring up the rear."

"Chalmers and I will do that."

"So that you fade away and go down to the armoury when the moment comes, is that it, Bentall?"

"Come on," I said, "it's time to go."

We almost made it, but Bentall was around and nothing ever went right with Bentall around. We had safely passed the hangar where the two gantry cranes were slowly lowering the Black Shrike into its cradle, and were a good two hundred yards clear when one of the women gave a high-pitched cry of pain. We found later that she'd slipped and sprained a wrist. I glanced back, saw every man in the brightly illuminated space before the hangar stop what they had been doing and whirl round. Within three seconds as many men started running in our direction while others raced for their parked guns.

"Run for it," Griffiths shouted. "Go like hell."

"Not you, Chalmers," I said.

"Not me," he said softly. "No, not me." He sunk down on one knee, lifted, cocked and fired the rifle all in one smooth motion. I saw a puff of white jump up from the concrete two yards ahead of the nearest Chinese. Chalmers adjusted the sights with one quick turn.

"Shooting low," he said unhurriedly. "It won't be low the next time."

It wasn't. With his second shot the leading guard flung his rifle into the air, then pitched forward on his face. A second died, a third rolled over and over like a man in agony and then suddenly all the lights in the front of the hangar went out. Someone had just got on to the fact that they made a perfect target silhouetted against the flood-lit concrete.

"That's enough," Griffiths shouted. "Get back. They'll be fanning out, coming towards us. Get back!"

It was time to get back, nothing surer. A dozen guns, some of them automatic carbines, had opened up on us now. They couldn't see us, it was too dark for that, but they had us roughly located from Chalmers' gun-flashes, and bullets were beginning to smash into the solid rock all around us, half of them lifting in screaming ricochet. Griffiths and Chalmers turned and ran, and so did I, but in the opposite direction, back the way we'd come. I didn't see I'd any chance of getting back to the armoury, the moonlight was beginning to filter through the ragged edges of the cloud, but if I did get back the diversion made a perfect cover-up for smashing my way into the armoury. I took four steps then pitched my length on the rock as something smashed into my knee with tremendous force. Dazed, I pushed myself shakily to my feet, took one step and fell heavily again. I wasn't conscious of any great pain, it was just that my leg refused to support me.

"You bloody fool! Oh, you bloody fool!" Griffiths was by my side, Chalmers close behind him. "What's happened?"

"My leg. They got my leg." I wasn't thinking about my leg, I wasn't caring about my leg, all I was caring about was that my last chance to get to the armoury was gone. Marie was there, alone. She was in the armoury, waiting for me.

Marie would know I would come for her. She knew Johnny Bentall was every kind of fool there was, but she knew I wouldn't leave her to LeClerc. I was on my feet again, Griffiths supporting me, but it was no good, the leg was paralysed, completely without power.

"Are you deaf?" Griffiths shouted. "I'm asking if you can walk."

"No. I'm all right, leave me. I'm going down to the armoury." I didn't know what I was saying, I was too dazed to express the difference between a wish and an intention. "I'm really all right. You must hurry."

"Oh, God!" Griffiths took me by one arm, Chalmers by the other, and they half-hustled, half-dragged me along the flank of the mountain. The others were already out of sight, but after a minute Brookman and a seaman came hurrying back to see what had happened, and lent a hand with the job of dragging me along. I was a great help to everyone. Jonah Bentall. Come with me and you come a cropper. I wondered vaguely what I'd ever done to deserve luck like this.

We arrived at the cave almost three minutes after the last of the others were safely inside. I was told this, but I don't remember it, I don't remember anything about the last half mile. I was told later that we wouldn't have made it had the moon not broken through and Chalmers held up the Chinese by picking off two of them as they came over the last ridge. I was told, too, that I talked to myself all the way, and when they begged me to be quiet in case the pursuers caught us I kept saying: "Who? Me? But I wasn't talking," very hurt and indignant. Or so they told me. I don't remember anything.

What I do remember was coming to inside the cave, very close to the entrance. I was lying against the wall, and the first thing I saw was another man lying beside me, face down. One of the Chinese. He was dead. I lifted my eyes and saw Griffiths, Brookman, Fleck, Henry and some Petty Officer I didn't know, on the other side, pressed close against the wall. At least I thought it was them, it was still dark inside the tunnel. There was room enough for them to shelter. Although the tunnel had been four feet wide and seven high all the way to the end when I'd followed it, the last few feet where Hewell and his men had broken through was no more than three feet high and barely eighteen inches in width. I looked around to see where the others were, but I could see nothing. They would be a hundred yards back in the cavern Hewell had excavated for the temporary storage of the tunnelled-out limestone. I looked out again through the tiny opening of the tunnel. The dawn was in the sky.

"How long have I been lying here?" I asked suddenly. My voice sounded in my ears like the husky quivering of an old old man, but maybe it was just the echo inside the cave.

"About an hour." Funny, Griffith's voice didn't sound a bit like an old man's. "Brookman says you'll be all right. Chipped kneecap, that's all. You'll be walking again in a week."

"Did we—did we all get here all right?"

"Everyone made it." Sure everyone made it. Marie Hopeman didn't make it. Why should they care? What was all the world to me was only a name to them, Marie Hopeman was down there alone in the armoury and I would never see her again but she was only a name. It didn't really matter if you were only a name. And I would never see her again, never. Never was a long time. Even in this last thing, this most important thing I'd ever know, I'd failed. I'd failed Marie. And now it was never. Never was going to be for always.

"Bentall!" Griffith's voice was sharp. "Are you all right?"

"I'm all right."

"You're talking to yourself again."

"Am I?" I reached out and touched the dead man. "What happened?"

"LeClerc sent him in. I don't know whether he thought we'd retreated to the other end of the cave or whether it was a kind of suicide mission. Chalmers waited till he was all the way in. And then we had two guns."

"And what else. An hour is a long time."

"They tried firing into the cave after that. But they had to stand in front if they weren't going to do it blindly. They soon gave it up. Then they tried to blow up the entrance, to seal it off."

"They would try that," I said. "It wouldn't have made much difference, we could have got out. What they meant to do, if things had gone their way, would have been to blow in the tunnel roof for a hundred yards or so. That would really have finished us." I wondered vaguely why I was saying this, none of it mattered anymore.

"They set off one charge, above the entrance," Griffiths was continuing. "Nothing much happened. Then we heard them working just outside, using picks to make holes for more charges. We flung out a couple of fused amatol blocks. I think they lost some men. They didn't try anything like that again."

"The note," I said. "Didn't you tell them about the note."

"Of course," Griffiths said impatiently. I had told Fleck to leave a copy of a faked radio message on the wireless table,
209

saying: 'Message acknowledged: H.M.S. Kandahar proceeding high speed Suva-Vardu. Expect arrive 8:30 a.m.' The inference would be that Fleck had sent an S.O.S. by radio. "We told LeClerc a naval vessel was coming. He wouldn't believe us, saying it was impossible, the sentry had been there to prevent messages from being sent, but Fleck said he'd been asleep. Maybe the sentry was one of those killed, I don't know. We told him he'd find the message on the schooner. He sent someone to fetch it. LeClerc couldn't afford to ignore it, it might mean he had only three hours left. Less, for Fleck says the Captain of the *Grasshopper*, without him to pilot it in, wouldn't attempt the gap in the reef before daybreak."

"LeClerc would be pleased."

"He was mad. He was out there talking to us and we could hear his voice shaking with fury. He kept asking for you but we told him you were unconscious. He said he would shoot Miss Hopeman if you didn't come out, so I told him you were dying."

"That would cheer him up," I said drearily.

"It seemed to," Griffiths admitted. "Then he went away. Perhaps he took his men with him. We don't know."

"Yes," Fleck said heavily. "And the first man to stick his head out the entrance gets it blown off."

Time passed. The light at the mouth of the tunnel steadily brightened through all stages of dawn, until finally we could see a washed-out patch of blue. The sun was up.

"Griffiths." It was LeClerc's voice from outside and it had us all jumping. "Do you hear me?"

"I hear you."

"Is Bentall there?"

Griffiths waved a cautionary hand to silence me, but I ignored it.

"I'm here, LeClerc."

"I thought you were dying, Bentall?" His voice held a vicious overtone, the first time I'd heard anything of the kind from him.

"What do you want?"

"I want you, Bentall."

"I'm here. Come in and take me out."

"Listen, Bentall. Don't you want to save Miss Hopeman's life?"

This was it. I should have expected this last desperate move to force my hand. LeClerc wanted me badly, he wanted me very badly indeed.

"And then you've got us both, is that it, LeClerc?" I'd no doubt that was it.

"I give you my word. I'll send her in."

"Don't listen," Captain Griffiths warned me in an urgent whisper. "Once he's got you, he'll use you as bait to get someone like me out, and so on. Or he'll just kill you both."

I knew which it would be. He'd just kill us both. He wasn't interested in the others, but he had to kill us both. Me, at any rate. But it was a chance I had to take. Maybe he wouldn't dispose of us straight away, he might take us aboard the ship with him, it was one last chance, it wasn't a chance in a million, but it was a chance. That was all I asked, a chance. I might save us both yet and as the thought came I knew I never could. It wasn't even that million to one chance, but it was like what Marie had said, sitting in the electric chair, and the man pulling the switch, and still hoping. I said: "All right, LeClerc, I'm coming out."

I hadn't seen the signal. Fleck, Henry and Griffiths reached me in the same instant, pinning me to the ground. For a few seconds I struggled like a madman, but I hadn't the strength left to struggle any longer.

"Let me go," I whispered. "For God's sake let me go."

"We're not letting you go," Griffiths said. He raised his voice. "All right, LeClerc, you can leave. We've got Bentall, and we're keeping him. You know why."

"Then I shall have to kill Miss Hopeman," LeClerc said savagely. "I'm going to kill her, do you hear, Bentall? I'm going to kill her. But not today, not for some time yet. Or perhaps she'll kill herself first. Goodbye, Bentall. Thank you for the Black Shrike."

We heard the sound of departing footsteps and then there was only the silence ... The three men took their hands away and Fleck said: "I'm sorry, boy, I'm more sorry than I can say."

I didn't answer. I just sat there, wondering why the world didn't come to an end. By and by I heaved myself painfully on to my hands and one knee and said: "I'm going out."

"Don't be so damn stupid." I could see by the expression on Griffith's face that he was regaining his first impression of me, one that had been far from favourable. "They'll be waiting."

"He can't afford to wait any longer. It's what time, now?"

"Almost seven."

"He'll be on his way. He wouldn't risk the Black Shrike for a chance at my life. Don't try to stop me, please. I've something to do."

I crawled out through the narrow mouth of the tunnel and looked around. For a few seconds I couldn't see anything, the shooting stabs from my kneecap blurred my eyes and put everything out of focus. Then the focus came back. There was no one there. No living person, that was.

There were three dead men lying outside the entrance. Two Chinese and Hewell, of course it would have been Hewell who would have been supervising the placing of the charges to blow in the mouth of the tunnel, and the exploding blocks of amatol had torn half the giant's chest away, anything less than that would never have taken his life. I saw the metallic snout of a gun barrel sticking out from under his body. I bent and pulled it clear with difficulty. It was fully loaded.

"It's all right," I said, "they've gone."

Ten minutes later we were all making our way slowly down to the hangar. Brookman was right, I thought dully, it would be a week or more before I could walk properly again, but the navy boys took turns at helping me along, taking almost half my weight.

We came over the last ridge that separated us from the plain. The area round the hangar seemed deserted. A small coasting vessel was just clearing the reef. I heard Fleck curse bitterly, and then saw why: fifty yards out from the pier all you could see of his schooner was her masts and the top of her superstructure. LeClerc thought of everything.

Everyone was talking, talking and trying to joke and laughing, a nervous hysterical kind of laughter, but laughter all the same, you couldn't blame them, when you've been under the shadow of certain death and it suddenly lifts, it has that effect on nearly everybody. The strain of the long night, for the women the long weeks were over, the fear and the horror and the suspense lay behind, the world they'd thought was ended was just beginning again. I looked at the seven scientists and their wives, seeing the wives for the first time ever, and they were smiling and gazing into each other's eyes, each pair linked arm in arm. I couldn't look at them, I had to look away. No more gazing for me into Marie's eyes. But I'd walked arm in arm with her, though, once. Once for about two minutes. It hadn't been much. We might have been given more.

Only Fleck seemed depressed and heavy, only Fleck out of all of them. And I didn't think it was because of what had happened to his schooner, not primarily anyway. He had been the only one of them who had ever known Marie, and when he'd called her a nice girl I'd gratuitously insulted him.

And he had a daughter of about the same age. Fleck was sad, he was sad for Marie. Fleck was all right, he'd pay no price for his earlier activities, he'd cleared the slate over and over again.

We came to the hangar. I cocked the gun in my hands and prayed that LeClerc had left an ambush party—or himself—behind to get us when the disappearing vessel had tricked us into thinking they had all gone. But there was no one there. Nor was there in any of the other huts, nothing but every radio set and transmitter smashed beyond repair. We came to the armoury, and I walked in through the open door and looked at the empty cot. I felt the crumpled coat that had served as a pillow and it was still warm. Some instinct made me lift it and under there was a ring. A plain golden ring she'd worn on the fourth finger of her left hand. The wedding ring. I slipped it over my little finger and left.

Griffiths gave instructions for the burial of the dead and then he and Fleck and I made our way slowly to the blockhouse, Fleck half-carrying me. Two armed sailors followed us.

The coaster was beyond the reef now, steering due west. The Black Shrike and Marie. The Black Shrike, carrying with it the threat of millions of ruined lives, of scores of great cities lying in the dust, of more carnage and sorrow and heartbreak than the world had known since time began. The Black Shrike. And Marie. The Marie who had looked into the future and found nothing there. The Marie who had said that one day I would meet up with a situation where my self-belief would be no help to me at all. And the day had come.

Fleck turned the key in the blockhouse door, pushed the Chinese back at the point of his gun, then turned him over to the sailors. We passed inside the second door and switched on the lights. LeClerc had smashed every other transmitting mechanism on the base, but he hadn't smashed the launch console, because he hadn't been able to get at it. He wouldn't have wanted to smash it anyway: for LeClerc did not know that the suicide circuit in the Black Shrike was armed.

We crossed the room, I bent down to switch on the generator and as I did my shirt pocket fell open and I saw for the first time and remembered for the first time, the little note Fleck had given me. I picked it up and smoothed the creases.

There were only a few words altogether. It said: 'Please forgive me Johnny. I've changed my mind about not marrying you—someone has to or you'll be in trouble all your life.

P.S. Maybe I love you a little, too.' Then, at the foot: 'P.P.S. You and me and the lights of London.'

I folded the note and put it away. I adjusted the periscope above my head and could clearly see the *Grasshopper*, low down on the horizon, a plume of dark smoke trailing behind her, steaming steadily west. I removed the mesh cover over the EGADS destruct button, turned the white square knob 180 degrees then reached over and pushed the 'Commit' button. The light glowed green. The safety clock in the Black Shrike was running out.

Twelve seconds. Twelve seconds it took from the moment of pressing the button until the suicide circuit was fully armed. Twelve seconds. I stared down at my wrist-watch, seeing the sweep second hand jerking steadily forward, wondering vaguely whether the charge would only merely blow the Shrike apart or whether, as Fairfield had suspected, there would be a sympathetic detonation of the solid fuel and the Black Shrike blow itself out of existence. Not that it matered now. Two seconds. I stared blindly into the eyepiece of the periscope, all I could see was a misted blur, then leaned on the destruct button with all the weight of my arm.

The Black Shrike blew itself out of existence. Even at that distance the violence of the explosion was terrifying, a huge spouting volcano of seething boiling white water that drowned the shattered vessel in a moment of time, then a great fiery column of smoke-tipped flame that reached up a thousand feet into the blue of the morning, and vanished with the moment of seeing. The end of the Black Shrike. The end of everything.

I turned away, Fleck's arm round me, and stumbled out into the sparkling brightness of a new day, and as I did I heard the heavy rumble of the explosion rolling in from the sea and echoing back from the silent hill beyond.

Epilogue

A SMALL dusty man in a small dusty room. That's how I always thought of him, just a small dusty man in a small dusty room.

He'd jumped to his feet when I'd entered, and now he was hurrying round the desk, coming towards me, taking me by my good arm and helping me towards the chair in front of his desk. The royal treatment for the returned hero, I'd have taken long odds that he'd never done anything like this before, he hadn't even bothered to rise from his chair the first time I'd seen Marie Hopeman walk into that room.

"Sit down, sit down, my boy." The grey lined face was alive with concern, the steady watchful green eyes mirrored the worry that this man almost never showed. "My God, Bentall, you look awful."

There was a mirror behind his desk, small, fly-blown and covered with dust like everything else in that room, and he wasn't exaggerating any that I could see. Left arm in a black linen sling, right hand holding the heavy stick that helped me along, bloodshot eyes and pale sunken cheeks with the great livid weal that ran from temple to chin, if I could get into the market quick I could make a fortune hiring myself out to haunt houses.

"I look worse than I really am, sir. I'm just tired, that's all." God only knew how tired I was, I hadn't slept a couple of hours in the two days it had taken me to fly home from Suva.

"Have you had anything to eat, Bentall?" I wondered drily when this room had last seen such a display of solicitude, not since old Raine had taken over the chair behind that desk, I'd bet.

"No, sir. I came straight here after I'd phoned from the airport. I'm not hungry."

"I see." He crossed over to the window and stood there for a few moments, shoulders bent, thin fingers laced behind his back, gazing down at the blurred reflection of the lights on the wet glistening street below. Then he sighed, drew the curtains across the stained and dusty windows, went and sat down, hands lightly clasped on the desk before him. He said, without any preamble: "So Marie Hopeman is dead."

"Yes," I said. "She's dead."

"It's always the best who go," he murmured. "Always the best. Why couldn't an old useless man like myself have gone instead? But it's never that way, is it? If it had been my own daughter I couldn't—" He broke off and stared down at his hands. "We'll never see a Marie Hopeman again."

"No, sir. We won't see a Marie Hopeman again."

"How did she die, Bentall?"

"I killed her, sir. I had to."

"You killed her." He said it as if it were the most natural thing in the world. "I had your cable from the *Neckar*. I've had a rough outline from the Admiralty about what happened on Vardu Island. I know you have done a magnificent job, but I know nothing. Please tell me everything that happened."

I told him everything that had happened. It was a long story, but he heard me out without question or interruption. When I was finished he screwed the heels of his palms into his eyes, then pushed both hands slowly up and back across the high lined forehead, the sparse grey hair.

"Fantastic," he murmured. "I have heard some strange tales in this office, but—" He broke off, reached for his pipe and penknife and started up his excavations again. "A great job, a great job—but what a price. All the speeches, all the thanks in the world can never repay you for what you've done, my boy. And no medals in a job like ours, though I have already arranged that you shall have a very special— um—reward for what you have done, and have it very soon." A little tic at the corner of the mouth, I was supposed to guess from that that he was smiling. "You will, I think, find it positively—ah—staggering."

I said nothing, and he continued: "I have, of course, a hundred and one questions to ask you and you no doubt have one or two pointed questions for a small deception I was forced to practice. But that can all wait for the morning." He glanced at his watch. "Good heavens, it's half-past ten. I've kept you too long, far too long, you look almost dead."

"It's all right," I said.

"It's not all right." He laid down pipe and knife and gave me the up from under look with those iceberg eyes of his. "I have more than a vague idea of what you have suffered, not only physically, what you've been through. After all this, Bentall—do you still wish to continue in the service?"

"More than ever, sir." I tried to smile, but it wasn't worth

216

the pain it cost, so I gave it up. "Remember what you said about that chair of yours before I left—I'd still like to sit in it some day."

"And I'm determined you shall," he said quietly.

"So am I, sir." I put my right hand into the sling to ease my arm. "But that's not the only determination we share."

"No?" A millimetric lift of the grey eyebrows.

"No. We're both of us determined on something else. We're both of us determined that the other will never leave this room alive." I took my hand from the sling and showed him my gun. "That Luger under your seat. Leave it where it is."

He stared at me, his mouth slowly tightening.

"Have you taken leave of your senses, Bentall?"

"No, I just found them again, four days ago." I rose awkwardly to my feet and hobbled round to his side of the desk. My eye and my gun never left him. "Get out of that chair."

"You're overstrained," he said quietly. "You've been through too much—"

I struck him across the face with the barrel of my gun.

"Get out of that chair."

He wiped some blood from his cheek and rose slowly to his feet.

"Lay the chair on its side." He did as he was told. The Luger was there all right, held by a spring clip. "Lift it out with the forefinger and thumb of the left hand. By the point of the barrel. And lay it on the desk."

Once more he did as he was directed.

"Get back to the window and turn round."

"What in the name of God is—"

I took a step towards him, gun swinging. He moved quickly backward, four steps till he felt the curtains behind him, and turned round. I glanced down at the Luger. Heavy silencer, safety catch off, loading indicator registering full. I pocketed my own gun, picked up the Luger and told him to turn round. I hefted the Luger in my hand.

"The staggering reward I was to get very soon, eh?" I asked. "A slug in the middle of the guts from a 7.65 Luger would make anyone stagger. Only I wasn't quite as unsuspecting as the last poor devil you murdered when he was sitting in that chair, was I?"

He exhaled his breath in a long silent sigh, and shook his head, very slowly. "I suppose you know what you're talking about, Bentall?"

"Unfortunately for you, I do. Sit down." I waited till he

had straightened the chair and seated himself, then leaned against a corner of the desk. "How long have you been playing this double game, Raine?"

"Whatever on earth are you talking about?" he demanded wearily.

"I suppose you know I'm going to kill you," I said. "With this nice silenced Luger. Nobody will hear a thing. The building is deserted. No one saw me come in: and no one will see me go out. They'll find you in the morning, Raine. Dead. Suicide, they'll say. Your responsibilities were too heavy."

Raine licked his lips. He wasn't saying I was mad any more.

"I suppose you've been engaged in treason all your life, Raine. God knows how you got off with it for so long, I suppose you must be brilliant or they'd have caught on to you years ago. Do you want to tell me about it, Raine?"

The green eyes blazed into mine. I had never before seen such concentrated malignity in a human face. He said nothing.

"Very well," I said, "I'll tell you. I'll tell it as a little short story, a bed-time story before you go to sleep. Listen well, Raine, for it's the last story you'll ever hear before the last sleep you'll ever have.

"Twenty-five years you spent in the Far East, Raine, the last ten as chief of counter-espionage. Running with the hare and chasing with the hounds all the time, I suppose, God alone knows how much tragedy and suffering you caused out there, how many people died because of you. Then two years ago you came home.

"But before you came you were approached by one of the powers for whom you were working while you were supposed to be our counter-espionage chief. They told you they had heard rumours that English scientists were making preliminary investigations into solid fuel as a power source for missiles and rockets. They asked you to find out what you could. You agreed. I don't pretend to know what they promised you, power, money, heaven only knows.

"Nor do I pretend to know how exactly you set up your spying organisation. Contacts across Europe were easy for you to arrange, and the actual clearing-house was Istanbul, where my investigations finally took me. I suspect that the way you acquired your information was by introducing into the Hepworth Ordnance and Research Establishment, the place with the highest security rating in Britain, men whom

218

you yourself, in your official capacity, had thoroughly 'screened'.

"The months passed and information was gradually acquired, sent to Istanbul and re-transmitted to the Far East. But your predecessor got wind of what was happening, suspected a security leak and told the Government: they instructed him, I imagine, that the business of investigating this leakage was to be given the highest priority. He started getting too close to the truth and his plane crashed into the Irish Sea and was never traced. He was seen off on that flight, at London Airport. He was seen off by you. Some time-bomb in his luggage, I suspect—our luggage is immune from Customs examination. It was a pity that there were thirty others in that plane, but that wasn't really important, was it, Raine?

"You were then promoted. The obvious choice, a brilliant and devoted man who had given a lifetime to serving his country. You then found yourself in the fantastic position of having to send out agents to track down yourself. And, of course, you had to. One man you sent found out too much. He came back here and into this room with a gun in his hand to confront you with this evidence. He didn't know about the hidden Luger, did he, Raine? And then you spread this story about how he'd been subverted and ordered to kill you. How am I doing, Colonel Raine?"

He had no comment to make on how I was doing.

"Now the Government was getting really anxious. You persuaded them that the difficulty lay in the complex nature of the technical information that was being passed, that only a scientist could really understand it. Your own agents, the honest ones, were all right in their own way, but there was one great objection to them—they were too damn good at finding things out. So, having kidded the government, you shopped around until you found the most stupid scientist you could. The one least likely to succeed. You picked me. I can understand your reasons.

"And you picked Marie Hopeman. You tried to convince me that she was a first-class agent, tough, capable and highly-experienced. She was nothing of the sort. She was just a nice girl, with a beautiful face and figure, and a considerable capacity for acting which made her ideal for the passive and undemanding position of receiving and passing on information without arousing suspicions. But that was all she had. No great intelligence, no marked degree of inventiveness, certainly not the mental ruthlessness and physical toughness essential for success in this job.

219

"So you sent the two of us into Europe to find out what we could about this fuel leak. You must have been convinced that if there was any pair in the world who could never find anything it was Marie Hopeman and I.

"But you made a mistake, Colonel Raine. You checked up on my intelligence and inventiveness, and thought you'd nothing to fear on that score. But you forgot to check on other things. Toughness and ruthlessness. I am tough and I can be completely ruthless. You'll see that when I pull this trigger. I'll stop at nothing to finish something I've started. I began finding out things, far too many things. You panicked and called us back to London."

Colonel Raine showed no reaction to any of this. His green unblinking eyes never left my face. He was waiting, waiting for a chance. He knew I was a sick man, and very tired. One false move, one slow reaction and he'd be on to me like an express train, and the way I felt that night I couldn't have fought off a teddy bear.

"Because of my activities," I went on, "the fuel leak had practically stopped. Your eastern friends were getting worried. But you had another string to your bow, hadn't you, Colonel Raine? Some months before that the government had set up a testing station for the Black Shrike on Vardu. Security was essential and you, of course, were the man responsible for all the security arrangements. You arranged the set-up with Professor Witherspoon to have the island barred to visitors for a perfectly good and innocuous reason: you arranged for the scientists and their wives to go to Australia without arousing suspicion: you arranged for a security clearance for Captain Fleck—my God, who else but you could ever have given that rogue a clearance?—and then you told your eastern friends, under the leadership of LeClerc, to move in, eliminate and replace Witherspoon. Finally, probably by telling them that they were going to see their husbands and emphasising to all of them the need for complete secrecy, you arranged for the transport of the scientists' wives to Vardu. But they were landed on the wrong side of the island, weren't they, Raine?

"So now you had the two strings to your bow. If you couldn't give your friends every detail of the new fuel, you could give them the fuel itself. Only there was one snag. Dr. Fairfield got himself killed, and you had to have someone to arm the rocket.

"It was brilliant, I admit it. Two birds with one stone. I had already found out too much in Europe and you knew now I was the type who wouldn't stop till the answer was there. You told Marie Hopeman that I was the one man you could be afraid of and maybe for once you weren't lying. I knew too much and I had to be eliminated. So did Marie Hopeman. But before my elimination, a duty you'd arranged that your friend LeClerc would carry out, I had a job to do. I was to arm the Shrike.

"You could have sent me direct to the rocket installation, in a perfectly straight-forward fashion, while the Navy was still there. But you knew I'd be as suspicious as hell if I was pulled off a security job and put on a civilian job. I'd be doubly suspicious because there are more qualified men in the country than I am. And, of course, there would then be no reason for Marie Hopeman to accompany me. And you wanted her killed too. So you inserted this final and phoney advert in the 'Telegraph', showed it to me, spun us this cock-and-bull story and sent us off to the Pacific.

"There was only one potential snag, one vital matter on which everything else depended, and your psychological handling of this was perfect. The snag—and if you couldn't find an answer to it everything would have been lost—was how to get me to wire up the firing circuitry and fuses of the Black Shrike. The lamb you'd thought you'd caught had turned out to be a tiger. You knew by that time how stubborn and ruthless I could be. You guessed that threats of torture or torture itself wouldn't make me do it. You knew, if I thought it important enough, that I could stand by and watch others being tortured or threatened with death, as Captain Griffiths and his men were, and still not do it. But you knew a man in love will do anything to protect the one he loves. And so you arranged it that I fall in love with Marie Hopeman. You reckoned that no one could sit side by side in planes with Marie Hopeman for two days, spend a night in the same room, spend a night and a day in the hold of a ship, a night huddled together on a reef and two more days side by side in the same hut without falling in love with her. My God, even going to the length of having the bogus Witherspoon trying to make me jealous. Damn your black heart, Raine, you gave us the time, the situation and every opportunity to fall in love. And so we did. They tortured her, and let me see her. They threatened to do it again. And so, God help me, I armed the Black Shrike. And God help you, too, Colonel Raine, for it's because of Marie that you're going to die. Not because of all the deaths you've caused, the misery, the heartbreak, the suffering. But for Marie."

I pushed myself painfully off the table and limped round till I was within three feet of him.

"You can't prove any of this," Raine said hoarsely.

"That's why I have to kill you here," I agreed indifferently. "No court in the country would look at my case. No proof, but there were many things that pointed to your guilt, Raine, things that I didn't see till it was too late. How did Fleck know that Marie had a gun in the false bottom of her bag—scientists' wives don't usually carry guns. Why did LeClerc—Witherspoon, as I knew him then—say we weren't long married, we didn't behave that way? Later, why did he show no surprise when I told him we weren't married? He said I'd a photographic memory—how the hell did he know that unless *you* told him? Why did LeClerc and Hewell try to cripple me with a heavy safe—they *knew* I was an intelligence agent, *you* told them and they didn't want me snooping around? Who gave Fleck security clearance from London? How did they know the Shrike was about to be tested, if the word hadn't been relayed from London? Why was no attention paid to the S.O.S. cable I sent to London, no action taken? LeClerc spun a yarn about sending a second message cancelling the first, but you know every message to this office, coded or plain, must have my identification word 'Bilex' in the middle. Why were no enquiries made at the Grand Pacific Hotel after our disappearance: I checked on the way home and neither the government house nor the police had been asked to investigate? The observer who was supposed to accompany us on the plane never reported our disappearance—for there *was* no observer, was there Colonel Raine? Pointers, only, not proof: you're right, I couldn't prove a thing."

Raine smiled: the man seemed to have no nerves at all.

"How would you feel, Bentall, if you killed me and found out you were completely wrong?" He leaned forward and said softly: "How would you feel if I gave you absolute proof, here and now, that you're completely, terribly wrong?"

"You're wasting your time, Colonel Raine. Here it comes."

"But damn it, man, I've got the proof!" he shouted. "I've got it right here. My wallet—"

He lifted his left lapel with his left hand, reached for the inside pocket with his right, the small black automatic was clear of his coat and the finger tightening on the trigger when I shot him through the head at point-blank range. The automatic spun from his hand, he jerked back violently in his seat, then fell forward, head and shoulders striking heavily on the dusty desk.

I took out my handkerchief, pulling with it a piece of

paper that fluttered to the floor. I let it lie. Handkerchief in hand I picked up the fallen gun, replaced it in his inside pocket, wiped the Luger, pushed it in the dead man's hand, pressed his thumb and fingers against the butt and trigger, then let gun and hand fall loosely to the table. I then smeared doorknobs, armrests, wherever I had touched, and picked up the fallen paper.

It was the note from Marie. I opened it, held it by a corner above Raine's ashtray, struck a match and watched it slowly burn away, the tiny flame creeping inexorably down the paper until it reached the words at the foot, "You and me and the lights of London", until those, too, one by one, were burnt and blackened and gone. I crushed the ash in the tray and went.

I closed the door with a quiet hand and left him lying there, a small dusty man in a small dusty room.

A-10